ECHO IN AMETHYST

Young adult novels:
The Safe-Keeper's Secret
The Truth-Teller's Tale
The Dream-Maker's Magic
General Winston's Daughter
Gateway

Standalones, Collections, and Graphic Novels:
The Shape-Changer's Wife
Wrapt in Crystal
Heart of Gold
Summers at Castle Auburn
Jenna Starborn
Quatrain
Shattered Warrior

Echo in Amethyst

Sharon Shinn

Echo in Amethyst

Cover image by Dave Seeley; cover design by Andy Holbrook

ISBN: 978-1-68068-175-8

This book is published on behalf of the author by the Ethan Ellenberg Literary Agency.

This book was initially an Audible Original production.
    Performed by Emily Bauer
    Executive Producers: David Blum and Mike Charzuk
    Editorial Producer: Steve Feldberg
    Sound recording copyright 2019 by Audible Originals, LLC

Where to find Sharon Shinn:
Website: www.sharonshinn.net
Facebook: https://www.facebook.com/sharonshinnbooks/
Amazon: https://www.amazon.com/s?k=Sharon+Shinn&ref=dp_byline_sr_all_1

The Kingdom of the Seven Jewels

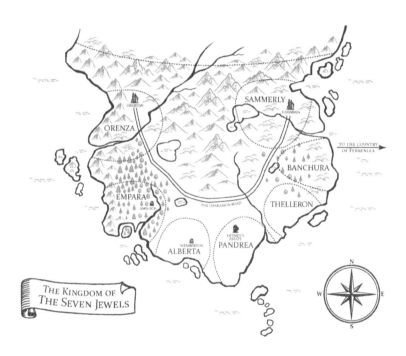

Cast of Characters

ROYALS
Harold: the king
Tabitha Devenetta: the queen, Harold's second wife, the mother of
    his daughter
Cormac: the king's oldest legitimate son and heir
Jordan: the king's second legitimate son
Annery: Harold and Tabitha's daughter
Jamison: Harold's bastard son

Edwin of Thelleron: the first king of the Seven Jewels (long dead)
Amanda: the first queen

NOBLES IN ALBERTA
Elyssa: a high noblewoman
Bentam: Elyssa's father
Hodia: Bentam's sister
Roland: a high noble who is courting Elyssa
Cali: a young noblewoman
Kendrick: a young nobleman
Velda: a young noblewoman
Vincent: governor of Alberta
Sorrell: his daughter
Clath: Sorrell's betrothed (from Thelleron)
Marietta: an older noblewoman
Fannon: an older nobleman

NOBLES FROM ELSEWHERE

Leonora, Letitia, and Lavinia: triplets from Banchura

Deryk: from Banchura

Norbert: Deryk's uncle, also from Banchura

Dezmen: from the province of Pandrea; a close friend to the princes

Darrily: Deznen's sister

Vivienne: from Thelleron

Marguerite Andolin: a noblewoman from Orenza

Garvin Andolin: her father; governor of Orenza

Renner Andolin: Marguerite's brother

PROFESSIONALS & WORKING CLASS FOLKS

Trima: Elyssa's maid

Gretta: another maid

Marco Ross: a young revolutionary allied with Lord Bentam

Lourdes: the head housekeeper at the royal palace

Malachi: the inquisitor of the royal city of Camarria

Bevvie: the daughter of a Camarrian innkeeper

The **abbess** of the temple of the triple goddess

CHAPTER ONE

The pain was so intense that there was nothing else in the world. It covered me, invaded me, defined me, created me. I couldn't see or think or move or scream, I could only be agony.

And then I opened my eyes.

It was as if I had never seen the world before, never noticed light or color or shape or shadow. For a moment, I was so bemused by the contours of walls and slants of light that I forgot to hurt. I just stared.

That color there. Just a few feet in front of me. I couldn't remember ever seeing it before, but I gaped at its silky opulence with a wash of wonder, and a word slipped unbidden into my mind. *Gold.* Then another word. *Curtain.*

I was staring at a gold curtain. It had been gracefully swathed over a tall, open space through which all that magnificent light was pouring in. *Window.*

I felt my mouth fall open with amazement. Without moving my head, I glanced around as much as I was able, greedy for other amazing sights. I seemed to be lying on a hard surface, so the only direction to look was up. But before I could get a sense of where I was, my whole field of vision was filled by one single image—a face, hovering just over mine, peering down at me.

"You're gazing around— Are you in there?" the face demanded. I couldn't say how I knew that the expression she was wearing was a smile or how I could be certain her name was Elyssa. But I could definitely name the emotion that spiked through me: terror.

Somehow I knew not to make any kind of sound in answer, not to look directly into her eyes, but I still formed a swift and comprehensive impression of her appearance. Her skin was a pale and flawless color—*White*, I thought—her black hair a mass of ringlets. Her gray eyes were so intense they seemed to gleam like silver. Somewhere in my head echoed the word *beautiful*. Then, as if someone had corrected me, I heard, *exquisite*. An entire phrase: *What an exquisite child*.

She was draped in more color, a rich but delicate hue that sparked a flurry of words in my mind: *lavender, violet, amethyst*. The one that stuck was *amethyst*.

"I hate you," she said fiercely as she stared down at me. "I wish you would die."

And then the pain came again.

The next time was longer. Pain woke me up again, but this time I could localize it more. It was in my arm and felt like a deep, welling gouge ringed with an edge of fire. I had a sense that some period of time had passed, though I didn't understand time or how I was moving through it. But I felt heavier, bigger, clumsier.

Elyssa's face had changed, too. The creamy skin was still flawless, the black curls were even longer and silkier, but her cheekbones had gained prominence and her gray eyes had accrued layers. But her expression hadn't changed at all. Still malevolent, still furious.

"Why won't you scream?" she burst out, her voice full of both dissatisfaction and loathing. "I've tried everything. You blink and your mouth moves, but you never cry out."

I didn't try to form words, didn't attempt to ask her what she had done and why she'd done it. I just fixed my eyes on a spot behind her and kept my expression blank.

She shrugged. "At least you seem to *feel* something. The other two never respond at all, no matter what I do to them. Only you. Why is that?"

I didn't know. I didn't know who *the other two* were.

I didn't know who *I* was.

She looked ready to say something else, but suddenly there was a noise behind her and Elyssa jumped to her feet as if afraid. I found myself gazing at the painted ceiling and an edge of decorative molding where it met the wall. I must have been sprawled on my back on the floor, as I had been last time. I didn't try to sit up and look around, but I did strain my senses to try to hear anything that might be said.

Elyssa's voice was filled with temper. "What are you doing just walking in here unannounced?"

The voice that replied belonged to a woman. She sounded older, confident, unimpressed by Elyssa's anger. "I've come to dress you for dinner. You don't want to be late."

"I don't want to be interrupted every five minutes, either!"

"I'm sorry, my lady, but I—" Her voice changed, and I had the distinct impression that she had just caught sight of me. "Sweet goddess, Elyssa, are you torturing the echoes again?"

Now Elyssa's voice was petulant, almost childish. "I was bored."

"Bored. When there's a whole houseful of guests about to arrive for dinner."

"Oh, yes. A couple of Empara lords who want to see if I might be a suitable bride for one of their sons."

"A fifteen-year-old girl is not too young to be thinking of marriage. It would please your father if you looked your best tonight."

Elyssa seemed to have lost all interest in me, so I carefully shifted my body and turned my head so I could try to get a better look at my surroundings. We were in a room that seemed very familiar, as if I had spent a lot of time there—a large chamber with many windows and pleasing proportions and elegant furniture. The colors were all muted versions of purple and oak and sage. I knew how to name each shade, though I didn't remember ever learning the words.

Elyssa and the other woman were standing near the door, arguing. The newcomer was dressed in a plain black gown and wore her brown hair pulled back in a bun. She had strong features, with a prominent nose and a firm chin. Something about her expression made me think she was no kinder than Elyssa.

Elyssa's voice was bitter. "My father only looks at me when he thinks I might bring him some advantage through a strategic marriage."

"I know it is your life's ambition to thwart him, but if I were you, I'd *want* to marry and get out of this house."

Elyssa's voice changed, becoming touched with anxiety. "Only if you come with me, Trima. I wouldn't trust a maid of my husband's choosing."

"Of course I'll come. I looked after your mother until she died, and I expect I'll look after you until *I* die."

"Well, that's a gruesome thought!"

"Just realistic," Trima said. She turned my way, and I saw her eyes glance at two spots behind me before they landed on me. "Speaking of gruesome! Please stop abusing the echoes."

"I don't like them."

Trima raised her eyebrows and brought her gaze back to Elyssa. "It's the echoes that mark you as noble enough to marry a high lord," she said. "So you'd better find a way to like them very much indeed. Now come over here and let's get you ready."

That was the third time she had said the word. *Echoes. What is an echo? Am I one? Are there others?*

Elyssa and Trima had moved off a few paces, still arguing, though the topic had turned to clothing. Moving very slowly, so I didn't attract attention, I shifted again, and then again, hoping to see what had caught Trima's notice behind me.

One more slight adjustment, one tilt of my head, and I could peek over my shoulder out of the corner of my eye. I could see two straight-backed chairs set against the wall, each one occupied by a young woman who sat stiff and unmoving, eyes unblinking, hands folded, expressions perfectly vacant.

Each one looked exactly like Elyssa.

Did that mean I looked exactly like her as well?

I squinted down the length of my body, straining to understand, but there was no time. The world stopped again, as completely as if I had shut my eyes and stuffed my ears. As if I had ceased to exist.

After that, there might have been a dozen bouts of awareness over the space of a couple of years. It was hard to gauge exactly, but I could tell that significant time had passed by the changes in Elyssa's face and by the different weight and balance in my own body. I struggled to understand where I had been just before my mind burst into consciousness, but it was such a gray and formless place. I could move, while in this place; I could, in some sense, see the world around me. But I couldn't comprehend it, and it made few lasting impressions on my memory.

Every period of wakefulness was preceded by a dire onslaught of pain—in my arm or my foot or my back. Each time I came to consciousness, the very first thing I did was bite back a scream of agony. Somehow I knew it was the only thing that Elyssa wanted from me, and that I didn't want to give it to her.

Each time, I stayed awake a little longer. But I managed to conceal that fact, maintaining the glassy stare that felt like my accustomed expression. I usually found myself slumped on some low piece of furniture, or curled on the floor where I had been driven by Elyssa's hot irons or sharp dagger points. Often I was naked. Usually I was bleeding.

I knew Elyssa hated me. I just didn't know why.

But every chance I got, I stayed in my beaten and crumpled position so I could look around stealthily and listen intensely. Trying to figure out who I was. Trying to understand the world.

We were always in the same room of lavender and sage and tall windows. The other two women who looked like Elyssa were always sitting off to one side, wearing blank expressions. Like me, they barely moved, though I watched them closely and occasionally saw them blink or breathe. They were alive then. Like me—but somehow not.

The maid, Trima, often came sweeping in to prepare Elyssa for some outing or another. Every time she saw me coiled up and bleeding, she would utter an exclamation of dismay. *Have you been mistreating the echoes again?* she would ask, in the same tone I had heard her use to say, *Have you gotten mud on your best shoes?* Maybe an echo had no more value than a shoe. Maybe it had less.

I was always glad to see Trima, though. Because in her conversations with Elyssa, I learned more and more about the world.

"Your father wants you to be especially nice to Chester tonight, even though he's only a low noble," Trima said one afternoon.

"Ugh. He's old and fat and his breath stinks."

"He's rich and he has powerful friends and he likes it when a pretty girl flirts with him."

"That's *all* my father wants me to do? Flirt with him?" Elyssa said in a voice heavy with sarcasm.

Trima gave her a stern look. "Don't talk like that."

"He'd send me to Chester's bed if he thought it wouldn't damage my marriage prospects."

"Lord Bentam wouldn't do that."

Elyssa laughed, not a pretty sound. "Of course he would! He'd have whored me out a dozen times since I turned sixteen if he thought it would have gotten him one more ally in his precious revolution."

"Don't say such things. Even your father—"

"Even my father," Elyssa repeated. "*Especially* my father. But he's still holding out for a grand alliance, so he has made sure his daughter is still a virgin."

"Well, I'm glad to hear that, at any rate," Trima said. "The way you flirt with inappropriate men—"

Elyssa laughed. "Oh, I've been good. *So* good, when I didn't want to be. But a little flirtation now and then is the only way I have to amuse myself. There's hardly anything else to do here."

"You could step up and take an interest in the manor, instead of leaving all the housekeeping decisions to your aunt Hodia. It would help your father immensely if you took on some of the duties of the lady of the manor."

Elyssa answered with another light laugh. "Darling Trima, why would you ever think I want to help my father in any way?"

It might have been only a few months after that conversation that the strangest thing happened.

I flickered to life one stormy afternoon when lashing rain turned the skies a dull pewter and made it impossible to see outside through the streaming windows. I was sitting on a pretty sofa, the other two echoes lined up on either side of me. All of us were staring in the general direction of the mirrored vanity, where Trima was arranging Elyssa's black hair in some complicated style. I could tell by Elyssa's reflection that Trima had already brushed delicate cosmetics on her face, for Elyssa'a bright eyes were brighter, her pale cheeks rosier, her pouting lips fuller. Whatever function she was attending this evening, she was looking forward to it because her face was brimming with excitement.

"I *do* think I'll be the prettiest girl there, and it will be so much fun to dance!" she was saying. "It's been so dreary—weeks and *weeks* of rain and no one coming to visit—"

"You know that's not true, Lady Marietta dropped by just two days ago."

"*Marietta*! She's more than a hundred years old!"

"She's not. She's barely your father's age."

"I bet she's never gone dancing in her life."

"You won't go dancing, either, if you don't sit still and let me finish your hair."

Elyssa subsided with a sigh, though she kept up a murmured commentary on who might be present at the ball and who might solicit her hand to dance.

I lost the thread of their conversation. In fact, I forgot to listen. I was too busy being stunned by a great revelation. I wasn't in any pain. Elyssa hadn't been cutting my arm or holding a burning coal to my foot. I had come to awareness randomly, independently, on my own.

I hadn't known I could do that. Might it happen again?

Might I hold on to consciousness longer?

Always?

I had barely had the thought when everything I knew about the world was suddenly reordered. Elyssa jumped to her feet—and at the exact same time, the echoes and I leapt up as well. She made a quarter turn, holding her arms above her head so Trima could slide her dress over her shoulders. The echoes and I turned with her, raised our arms, waited patiently. I heard a rustle behind me, but I couldn't turn my head so much as a fraction of an inch to see who else might be in the room. It was as if my bones, my muscles, my heartbeats were matched to Elyssa's—as if she powered us or controlled us by some unbreakable bond. A serving woman I had never seen before stepped into view, her arms loaded with crinkled purple fabric. In a few moments, the echoes and I were all wearing matching dresses.

"Done, my lady," the servant said, and Elyssa lowered her arms. The three of us lowered our arms as well.

Elyssa buried her hands in the folds of the skirt and twisted back and forth to feel the cloth swirl about her legs. Helpless to do anything else, I moved with her, mimicking her exactly, taking a quick sideways step as if practicing a dance move, then throwing back my head to laugh. No noise came from my throat, though, not the giddy, happy giggle that Elyssa offered—not the wrenching wail of horror that I would have produced if I had been able to make a sound.

I understood what an echo was now. I was a copy of Elyssa—a reflection, a shadow, a reverberation. I wasn't a separate being, like Trima and the other serving woman. I was part of Elyssa.

And she had absolute control over everything I could see or feel or do.

There followed a period of time—maybe months, maybe years, I simply couldn't judge—where my life was a patchwork of sleeping and waking, of unconsciousness and awareness, of being nothing and being something.

I still occasionally found myself coming to life because of some searing agony, and opening my eyes to find Elyssa laughing above me. But those days were increasingly rare; it seemed Elyssa the adult had many more distractions than Elyssa the girl, so she had less need to amuse herself with casual cruelty. More often now I would find myself suddenly and randomly becoming conscious, with no knowledge of where I was or how I had gotten there.

I might be riding with Elyssa and the other echoes in a carriage. Following Elyssa down a corridor. Sitting at a table in a massive dining hall, spooning up soup at exactly the same moment as Elyssa and the other echoes. Most of the time, my surroundings seemed comfortable and familiar, so I assumed we were in the house where Elyssa lived, though I had no real memories of the place. Other times, the environment seemed foreign and strange, and then I supposed we were visiting a place Elyssa barely knew. Gradually, as I had more and more episodes of consciousness, I began to build my bank of memories. *This is the dining room where we have eaten many times. This is the hall that leads to Elyssa's room. That man is her father.*

Now and then, I would find myself gaining awareness in the middle of some activity. Once I came to my senses to find myself on a crowded dance floor, caught in the embrace of an unfamiliar man with dark skin and a vague, abstracted expression. An echo, I realized. I had a moment's panic as I realized I didn't know how to dance, but that faded when I understood that I didn't have to know. I was bound to Elyssa, and *she* knew. My feet would follow her feet, my body would turn and sway precisely with hers.

As my fear subsided, my curiosity rose. I was unable to turn my head to look around, but soon enough the motion of the dance showed me more of the people nearby. There was Elyssa, simpering in the arms of a man who looked identical to the one who held me, except that his face was full of life and curiosity and his eyes were fixed intently on Elyssa. Nearby were her other two echoes, similarly held by blank-faced men who looked just like the one holding Elyssa.

Three echoes each, I thought. *Are there always three?*

I still didn't know who had echoes and who didn't—or why anyone would have echoes to begin with.

As we continued to twirl around the dance floor, I kept glancing around as much as I was able, trying to absorb information. It was quickly clear to me that any group of people wearing identical clothing included a man or a woman and that individual's echoes. I never saw anyone with more than three echoes, and most had only one or two. Some didn't have any echoes at all. Those people seemed to be mostly relegated to the sidelines, serving refreshments or clearing away dishes. They were dressed in dark, unadorned clothing—much like Trima's—and did nothing to draw attention to themselves. The word *servants* popped into my head.

So there were at least two classes of society, and only the glittering beautiful class had echoes. Which must mean echoes were symbols of status or wealth or power. I couldn't think of any practical reason for people to be followed around by creatures that looked exactly like them and copied their movements absolutely—but then, I wasn't used to thinking at all.

As I watched the dancers, I realized something. Even though four people might look exactly alike, it was easy to tell which ones were echoes and which one was not. The echoes all had unfocused eyes and blank faces; they smiled and laughed, but their expressions were rote and superficial, and they never spoke aloud. And there was something else odd about them, something indefinable and insubstantial, as if you might put out a hand to touch their shoulder and instead pass your arm right through.

Whereas the men and women they emulated were solid and hearty. Their faces showed emotion, their voices carried conviction, they were brimming with life. They were real, and the echoes were not.

I was an echo. Maybe I wasn't real.

But I was beginning to think I was.

Over the next few months, as I continued to fugue in and out of consciousness, I began to gather more bits of information about my life. I learned that Elyssa and her father and her aunt lived in a manor house in a province called Alberta, and Alberta was in the western half of a kingdom that contained six other provinces. Apparently, many of the people who lived in the three western provinces disliked their king, who lived in a far-off city called Camarria located in the province of Sammerly.

I also learned that society across the seven provinces was commonly divided into five classes—high nobles, low nobles, merchants and professionals, the working class, and the persistent poor—and only the high nobles were ever blessed with echoes. I learned that people with echoes were referred to as *originals*, and that they were envied by anyone who didn't have echoes of their own.

I listened closely, but I never heard anyone specify what category echoes might fall into. It was as if we didn't even exist. Or perhaps we were so much lower than the persistent poor that we didn't even deserve a class of our own.

None of those details interested me as much as gaining an understanding of the small, essential conventions that governed my day-to-day existence. I discovered that anytime we were someplace where other people could see us, Elyssa made sure all of her echoes were bound to her. If I woke up during a dinner or a ball or a stroll through the garden and there was even one other person nearby, I would always find myself walking in concert with Elyssa.

But if I opened my eyes and found myself in our familiar rooms, chances were good that the other echoes and I would be slumped on a sofa or even relegated to a darkened bedroom while Elyssa retired to some other part of her large suite, and we were no longer synchronized with her movements.

In fact, once I was awake for the last hour of a very long dinner and the short walk back to Elyssa's bedroom. Another woman strolled down the hallway with us, chatting with Elyssa and trailed by her own echoes, and all of us moved in lockstep. But the minute we had followed Elyssa into her own room and she had closed the door, I felt that binding compulsion snap. It wasn't just that she released us—she seemed to fling us away from her, as she might kick off a pair of shoes that pinched her feet and made every step unendurable.

I remembered something she had said to me the very first time she had brought me to consciousness. *I hate you. I wish you would die.*

Did everyone hate their echoes? And if so, why weren't all of us dead?

Something else I learned: Even once we were alone in our rooms and Elyssa released us, we echoes had very little volition. If she dumped us on a sofa or a set of chairs, we could shift around to achieve some level of comfort, but we never moved very much or very far. I had a chance to observe our nighttime ritual once when I happened to be awake for it. Trima and another serving girl came in and helped us wash our faces, comb our hair, and change into our nightgowns; during this time, all of our motions were flawlessly coordinated. Once the maids left, Elyssa instantly released us, barely waiting till the door closed to flick us away. She stalked toward the echoes' bedroom—a small, shadowy chamber with three hard beds—and pointed at the doorway. "Go to bed," she commanded, and we shuffled past her till we could flop down on our mattresses. Then she closed the door and left us in darkness.

I was awake for a long time after that, and I heard her moving around the big open room of sage and lavender for another hour. Eventually I heard another door shut, and I assumed she had closed herself into the last room of the suite, a much larger bedroom that held an ornate bed. To my memory, Elyssa had never allowed the echoes to follow her into that room.

There was a single, narrow, heavily curtained window in our bedroom and it admitted barely enough light for me to see my hand before my face. But I glanced around the room anyway, straining to see the other echoes lying on their own beds.

I supposed I had never been alone during the whole period of my existence; I had always had two replicas at my side and Elyssa before me, leading the way. But I truly thought I might be the most solitary creature in all the world.

CHAPTER TWO

Ijerked into consciousness to find myself in a man's close embrace. His arm was around my back, and he held me tightly to him as he pressed his mouth fervently against mine. His free hand roamed over my body until it closed over my breast and squeezed. I wanted to yelp and wrench back, but instead I found myself leaning in, wrapping my own arms around his waist, returning his kiss with a dizzying heat of my own.

Then, abruptly, I broke free and pulled back, staring up at the man holding me; around me, three other pairs of lovers did the same. I could hear four sets of kissing partners breathing heavily in the dark. We were in some kind of library or study that was unfamiliar to me, so I guessed we must be attending a party at the home of a nearby lord. Perhaps we had recently had dinner and now all the other guests were dancing, but Elyssa and her partner had snuck off to try to find a little privacy. This particular room clearly hadn't been set up to entertain visitors, as it offered no candlelight and the windows were swathed in heavy drapes.

"What must you think of me?" Elyssa asked breathlessly. "Behaving like a wanton."

The lord dropped a brief, hard kiss on her mouth, and all his echoes responded in kind. "I think you're everything that's wonderful," he said.

She laughed, pleased with the response. "You're so sweet to me."

"You're the sweetest girl in the whole Kingdom of the Seven Jewels."

This time her laugh was more rueful. "I'm not. Really, I'm not."

"You are, though."

She freed one hand to lift it up and skim her fingers gently across his face. I did the same, stroking my echo's cheek, though his expression did not melt into ecstasy the way the lord's did. "I know what people say about me," she said softly. "How I'm so unfriendly. So unlikable."

"They're jealous. The women especially. Because you're so much more beautiful than they are."

"I like to hear you say that."

"It's true! I have never seen a woman as stunning as you are."

Now she lifted both hands, rested them on his cheeks, then slid them down to curl around the back of his neck. "You're good for me, Roland," she whispered. "I wish I could always be with people who thought so highly of me."

"You could be—you could be with me always—"

She laughed again and shook her head. When he started to protest, she silenced him with another kiss, straining against him as if she was trying to meld her body perfectly with his. Against my will, I followed her lead, kissing Roland's echo as if I was trying to devour him. *This would be a good time to slip into insensibility again,* I thought, as his arms tightened around my waist in such a way that I could hardly breathe. I didn't have the faintest idea what came next, but I had a feeling I wouldn't like it, and there was no way I could stop it.

Fortunately, someone else could. There were voices in the hall, coming in through an imperfectly closed door. Elyssa and Roland leapt apart so quickly that Roland had to spin his arms to keep his balance. Elyssa and all her echoes pressed their hands to their mouths to hold back laughter.

"Are you sure they came this way? They might have gone to the garden instead," said someone who sounded like a young woman.

"Wherever they went, they shouldn't have slipped off like that! If her father finds out…" Another woman, this one older and more judgmental.

"Then don't tell him! I'm sure they've done nothing truly improper. But we do need to find them before the games start."

Their voices faded down the hall. There was just enough light for me to see the laughter on Elyssa's face as she gave Roland one last kiss. Then he crossed to the door, looked out, and motioned her to follow. In a few moments, they were strolling sedately down the hall, engaged in sober conversation, and rejoining all their friends in a large room set with many tables.

"There you are!" someone called out. "I sent Cali and Marietta to look for you. Come on. Let's play cards."

I was still in my conscious state that evening when we returned to Elyssa's home and Trima and the maid began undressing us for the night.

"Was young Lord Roland at the dinner this evening?" Trima asked as she pulled the dress over Elyssa's head.

My own dress was coming off and my face was buried in the clouds of satin, so I couldn't see Elyssa's expression. "He was," she said, her voice indifferent.

Trima made a sound of disapproval and my face was free again. I could see the maid was frowning. "I don't like that," she said.

Elyssa glanced quickly at the other serving girl, then back at Trima, and all of us shrugged infinitesimally. It was obvious Elyssa was conveying a message: *Let's not talk about this now.*

Trima pressed her lips together, then said, "And Lady Cali? She was present as well?"

Elyssa talked freely about the other guests until all of us had been dressed in bedclothes and the second maid had vanished out the door. Then she flung off her restraints on the echoes, pointed toward our room and commanded, "In you go." As soon as we were laid out on our beds, she shut the door behind us with a little unnecessary force. She usually did.

"So tell me about young Roland," Trima said in an even voice.

I had picked the bed nearest the door, and now I sat up, cocking my head in that direction so I could hear better.

Elyssa laughed, a wistful sound. I thought she might be pacing restlessly around the room. "Sweet goddess, he is the most delightful man! Naive and unworldly, of course, and I'm sure I'd get tired of him in a month if I was actually married to him, but he makes me feel so…" She couldn't seem to find the right word. "Adored," she finished at last.

"You want to be careful that you don't do anything that can't be undone," Trima said severely.

"I have been *most* proper."

"Somehow I doubt that. But as long as you have not been completely abandoned—"

Elyssa laughed again, and this time the sound had a cynical edge. "Dear Trima, don't you worry about that. I'm even more interested in preserving my marriage prospects than my father is. I'll be careful."

There was a short silence. "I would have thought he would have planned your marriage sometime before this," Trima said finally. "Your mother was eighteen at her wedding, and you're already twenty-four."

I heard a thumping sound that made me think Elyssa had flung herself onto some piece of furniture. When she was alone, she tended to move with a deliberate inelegance, as if to make up for all the perfectly polished mannerisms she had to maintain in public.

"Yes, but the fashion has changed for my generation," she drawled. "Or, at least, it has changed for all the high nobles who might have some remote chance of marrying into royalty. Prince Cormac has not yet taken a bride. Therefore, any high noblewoman with two or more echoes to her name wants to wait and see if he might choose *her*. And, of course, the noble*men* cannot marry if the women will not accept their proposals! I predict that the day after Cormac's wedding, every girl my age will have a husband. Or at least a fiancé."

"Then I hope he gets married soon," Trima said. "Now, come on. Up on your feet and into bed. You've had a long day."

It was another fifteen minutes before Elyssa was safely ensconced in her room and I heard the main door close behind Trima. I had had a long day, too, but I was filled with an unfamiliar, discordant restlessness, a sensation that ran under my skin like bubbles rising in a glass of champagne. I tried to lie back down, but I couldn't make myself relax under the coverlet, so I sat up again. I wished I could get up and stride around the room just to work off some of my unaccustomed energy.

Although—maybe I could.

Tentatively, I swung my legs over the side of the bed and rested my bare toes on the rug. I had never walked anywhere except at Elyssa's direction—never stood unless she was on her feet. I didn't know if my body would obey my own commands, didn't know if I could generate the sense of balance that would keep me from falling over. Slowly, keeping one hand braced on the mattress as long as I could, I transferred my weight to my legs and rose to a standing position.

I teetered precariously as I gazed over at the window. How could I make my body cross the room? What commands could I send to my feet that would cause them to step daintily in that direction? I knew *how* to walk, but I had never exercised my own will to attain a destination of my choosing.

I took a step.

I took another one.

I didn't fall, but it seemed that I might at any moment, so I remained close to the bed so I could collapse against it if my legs suddenly refused to move. My immediate goal was to make it to the wall so I could lean one hand against it for support. That objective achieved, I stood quietly for a moment, calming my jangled nerves and glancing round the room. Then I looked at the window again.

I only had to follow the wall for another ten yards, navigating around a chest of drawers and a couple of battered chairs, to reach it. I couldn't remember a time when the heavy curtain had ever been pulled back, and I was suddenly consumed with a desire to discover what I might see on the other side of the glass. Elyssa's rooms were set into a corner suite, and the windows in her sitting room looked out on a different view. But this view would be all mine.

I flattened my hand against the wall and moved forward with growing confidence. My body remembered all the mechanics of motion and seemed willing to follow my clear directives. I detoured carefully around the furniture and finally made it to my destination, where I peeled back the thick velvet fabric and peered outside.

It was a wonderland.

A full moon painted a silver patina over a landscape of hedges, lawns, and low buildings. I guessed that I was looking out toward the back of the manor, where I could see a small garden and a few buildings used to house tools or chickens, but the dramatic interplay of light and dark gave the view a magical, enchanted quality. And the sky! Remarkable! The moon was so low and heavy that it seemed unable to lift itself any higher overhead. Stars gathered in such bright clusters that I almost thought I could lift the sash and scoop them up in my bare hand. Nothing moved, not in the spangled heavens above, not in the brooding landscape below. Nothing in the entire vista was awake—was alive—except me, the echo standing at the window, staring out at the world as if it had just been created that very night, and just for her.

Elyssa did not, over the new few weeks, show any signs of losing interest in Lord Roland.

I was having fewer and fewer days when I was completely unaware, so I was beginning to get a better sense of time passing. And it was clear to me that she was taking every opportunity to spend time with the young nobleman.

They met, very properly, at the houses of friends for dinners or sedate parties. A few times he came calling at the house, and they sat demurely in her father's drawing room and ate light refreshments and talked of inconsequential things while her aunt sat nearby, reading a book as she chaperoned their conversation. On days when the weather was fine, they were able to escape outdoors for an unescorted walk through the gardens. On those occasions, as soon as they were out of sight of the house, Elyssa practically pounced on Roland, drawing him under the boughs of a convenient tree and covering his face with kisses. Naturally, all their echoes engaged in similar embraces.

"I've missed you so much!" he exclaimed on one of those afternoons.

She laughed up at him. "You saw me last night!"

"At Marietta's house! Across the table from you! We had only five minutes of private conversation."

She rested her cheek against his chest. "I know. It's so hard."

"Are you going to Kendrick's hunting party in two weeks?"

She lifted her head to gaze up at him again. "I hadn't planned to. I abhor hunting. And Kendrick isn't particularly fond of me."

"But you were invited, weren't you?"

"Of course."

He began playing with the fingers of her left hand. "I'll be there," he said in a coaxing voice. "And so will nine or ten others. For five nights. All of us sleeping under the same roof. Surely there will be opportunities for …" He glanced around. "Something a little more intimate than this."

As I stared up into the face of Roland's echo, I could feel my eyes narrow and my mouth purse—just slightly—as Elyssa thought over what he had said. Clearly she was trying to decide how much she was willing to risk for this impetuous young man. But I could tell that some part of his proposal pleased her, for my heart was racing and I felt a smile begin to shape my lips.

"Roland," she whispered. "You know I cannot give myself to you in a clandestine fashion."

He squeezed his hand tightly over her fingers. "No," he said quickly. "And I would not ask you to. But surely, at Kendrick's hunting lodge, we would have opportunities for something a little more secluded than this."

Now her lips were curving in a smile that was part mischief and part delight. "I'm sure we would," she repeated. "Let me dig out that invitation and tell Kendrick I am happy to attend his party after all."

Kendrick's property was a wearisome daylong carriage ride away through acres of open farmland where some low, scrubby crop was just beginning to grow heavy and green. Trima, who rode in the carriage with us, spent the entire journey lecturing Elyssa on the proper behavior expected of a young lady, and Elyssa spent the whole time looking out the window.

The house, when we arrived, proved to be small and dingy, at least in comparison to Lord Bentam's house and the homes of the rest of Elyssa's friends. It was a squarish shape built of dark, shaggy wood; it was two stories tall, though both levels appeared somewhat flattened. There was no welcoming courtyard and very little space for pulling up the carriage. Trima said, "I suppose this is what a hunting lodge looks like."

Elyssa was already gathering up her cloak and gloves and reaching for the door. "One doesn't come for the amenities, Trima, dear," she said with a smile. "One comes for the sport."

It was soon clear that the lodge was not only small, it was poorly staffed and badly managed. Our party was shown to a moderately sized bedroom clearly not designed for nobles with echoes—there was one decent bed taking up most of the space, and one large but lumpy pallet made up on the floor.

"Are all three of the echoes to sleep there?" Trima demanded, her voice scandalized.

Elyssa shrugged. "They won't even notice."

"I don't care about their comfort, I care about your consequence."

Elyssa was grinning with an edge of malice. "You might more profitably worry about your own consequence. I'm guessing you'll be crammed into a tiny room with three other maids, and probably sharing a bed with one of them."

Trima stiffened and her face took on a wintry look. "I've slept worse," she said, "but not since I joined your father's staff."

Elyssa was wandering around the room, touching chair backs and windowsills. "I don't think it's been dusted in days," she remarked. "Do you think the linens are clean?"

"It doesn't matter," Trima said. "I brought our own."

"Aren't you foresighted! It never would have occurred to me." Now Elyssa poked a toe into the cold hearth. "Do you suppose someone will come to build me a fire?"

"How many people are expected at this party?"

"I don't know—ten or twelve, I think."

"I saw one serving girl and one footman when we entered, and I have to suppose there's a cook and a housekeeper somewhere. If there are only four servants in the house—"

Elyssa couldn't hold back a laugh that sounded more appalled than amused. "Do you think we'll have to build our own fires? Carry our own bathwater?"

Trima surveyed her. "Do you *know* how to make a fire?"

"I was hoping you did."

Now Trima's glance dropped to the fireplace. "I can if there's coal."

"This grows more delightful by the minute!"

"We can always leave."

Elyssa turned to gaze out the window, and whatever she saw softened her expression. I wondered if Lord Roland had just ridden into view. "No, not yet," she said. "We may enjoy ourselves more than we expect."

CHAPTER THREE

It was hardly surprising that dinner at the hunting lodge was a scrambling affair. The dining room was set up sloppily and no one seemed sure where to sit. Normally, from what I'd observed, high nobles went to elaborate lengths to arrange dining rooms so that originals sat at elegant tables in the middle of the room and their echoes sat behind them at much less fancy boards.

But Kendrick, apparently, hadn't expected quite so many nobles, or echoes, to be in attendance. He and his eight guests crowded around a rectangular table meant to seat about half that many while the echoes took their places at a thrown-together collection of small tables, nightstands, and one scarred old desk. There weren't enough servants to make sure echoes received their food when the nobles did, and the nobles weren't inclined to wait, with the result that half the echoes were pantomiming the act of eating even though their hands were empty and no dishes sat before them. As a consequence, I was sure all the echoes would be half starved before the visit was over.

From the cramped dining hall, the whole party moved to an only slightly more spacious drawing room where, again, there was insufficient space for the echoes. Ignoring the difficulties, the nobles pulled chairs and sofas close together in the middle of the room and proceeded to engage in raucous conversation. The echoes squeezed themselves together on rustic benches, or tried to sit on top of each other in nearby chairs. One chaise lounge splintered under the combined weight of four echoes, who went crashing to the floor in a spray of wood and flying hair. The nobles laughed so hard that it seemed they might fall out of their own seats. The echoes all *appeared* to be laughing in their soundless way, but I wondered if any of them, like me, felt sadness and impotent anger.

Elyssa and Roland had managed to ensconce themselves on a love seat so narrow that their shoulders and thighs couldn't help but touch. Consequently, all six of their echoes were crammed together on a wooden bench made to hold four. Because we were out in public, Elyssa was synchronizing our actions to hers, so I had almost no independent control of my actions. What little volition I could muster I spent squirming to find a more comfortable position. It was a very long evening.

When we finally returned to Elyssa's room, it was clear it would be a very long night. Trima was already there and had obviously been busy: The bed was freshly made, there was a fire in the grate and water in assorted pitchers, and all our bedclothes were laid out. Including Trima's own.

"I'm sleeping in that chair tonight," the maid said when Elyssa expressed surprise.

"What, the servants' accommodations are more primitive than you can tolerate?"

Trima gave her a long, measuring look. "Exactly."

Elyssa laughed, genuinely amused. "No! You're afraid I'll sneak out in the middle of the night and head to Roland's room!"

"It's my duty to take care of you," was Trima's reply.

Elyssa laughed again and gestured toward the hallway. "Haven't you heard? Kendrick has overbooked his guests. Roland is sharing a room with Cali's brother. Even I am not so debauched that I would want to take a tumble with a man while his roommate snored in the next bed."

"Maybe not," Trima said. "But maybe *he* would be the one to go roaming."

"Maybe, but this place is so small someone would be bound to see him and ask what he's up to," Elyssa said. "I don't think a midnight assignation is in my future."

"Good," Trima said, but she did not offer to return to the room she had been assigned, wherever it was.

So the five of us slept together in the single chamber. It was the least restful night of my life—or whatever portion of my life I could recall. The pallet did nothing to disguise the hardness of the floor, and I was not used to having my fellow echoes lying so close to me that their limbs practically entangled with mine. Trima could not seem to get comfortable in the plush armchair; she sighed and tossed all night. By contrast, Elyssa fell asleep right away and woke in the morning appearing beautiful and pleased with herself.

"Look—sunshine," she said, even before she climbed out of bed. She stretched her arms over her head. "I'm certain this will be a lovely day."

Most of Kendrick's guests—and Kendrick himself—kept to their rooms until the noon hour, at which time they regrouped in the cramped dining hall to partake of a meal before turning their attention to the activity for which they had ostensibly gathered.

It turned out there was a fifth servant on the premises—a groom or groundskeeper or someone of that sort. As the guests finished eating, he showed up with a pack of dogs at his heels and asked how many planned to go on the hunt. It turned out that most of the men in the party had ridden there on their own horses, and the estate could offer four additional ones to those who had arrived in carriages.

"How silly of me not to bring my own mounts!" Elyssa exclaimed, as if just then realizing what an omission she'd made. "Because my echoes and I would take all of your horses." She gestured at two of the other female guests, each of whom could boast only one echo apiece. "*You* two go instead. I might take a carriage back to that charming little town we passed on the way in."

Roland turned to a chubby young lord who was wearing an expression dangerously close to a pout. I guessed that this particular nobleman had expected his host to provide horses and now realized that he was going to miss the outing. "I'll be happy to let you take my mounts for the day," Roland said. "Spent half the night coughing, and I'd rather head back to bed for a couple of hours. Maybe I'll be up for it tomorrow."

That neatly took care of everyone, I realized, since the only other woman in the party was the sporting type who announced that she had brought *six* of her own horses so she and her two echoes could have fresh mounts every other day. I supposed the stables must have been roomier than the house, and probably better run.

It took some time for the hunting party to organize itself, but it was rather an impressive sight: seven nobles and nearly a dozen echoes all on horseback, attended by a handful of grooms, and at least eight yapping dogs. Roland headed back to his room, but Elyssa stayed to watch them off, waving cheerfully and wishing them luck. Eventually they all moved off in one noisy, untidy clump. I found it hard to believe that they could be disciplined enough to flush out any game.

Once we stepped back into the suddenly quiet house, Elyssa seemed to be at a loss. She glanced at the stairwell leading to the second-story guest rooms, but seemed to decide it would be too bold to march upstairs and start knocking on doors. Instead, she explored the bottom level, flitting through the drawing room and down a narrow hallway that had a single door opening off to each side. One room was hardly bigger than a closet and held odds and ends—broken chairs, a tall mirror leaning against a wall, a narrow bookshelf empty of books. The other was a very small version of the library her father maintained back home. It was so musty and full of dust that I had to guess Kendrick had never set foot inside the room since the day he had acquired the property.

There was nothing else to see on the ground floor except the dining hall, the drawing room, the narrow foyer, and the door leading to the kitchens and the servants' quarters. Once Elyssa had completed her tour, she returned to the drawing room and simply stood there, lost in thought. I could hardly remember a time I'd seen her so still.

Her reverie lasted barely five minutes before we heard the sound of footsteps coming hesitantly down the stairwell. Through the open doorway, I could see Roland paused on the bottom step, craning his neck to look around. The echoes behind him mimicked his action.

"Have the hunters ridden off?" he asked in a loud whisper.

Elyssa smiled at him through the door. "They have! They all looked quite dashing, too, though I don't have high hopes of them catching any game."

Roland finished his descent and joined us in the drawing room. "No—no one ever does at these parties. Though, the meal was so sparse last night that I find myself hoping they chase down a deer just so we can add it to the menu."

Elyssa seemed amused. "I don't think any of us will starve in a few short days."

He smiled down at her, catching her hands in his. One of his echoes gave me the same besotted look—although it was far less convincing on the echo—and similarly took hold of me. "*I* could starve," Roland said. "If I don't get more time alone with you."

Elyssa drew their linked hands up to nestle against her heart—which, of course, meant they grazed the top of her bosom. I felt the echo's fingers working within mine, as if he was trying to brush the tips over the smooth expanse of bare skin. "Well, I think we quite cleverly managed to ensure ourselves a tiny bit of privacy," she said. "What do you think—a couple of hours before any of them come riding back? Unless someone falls off his horse, I suppose."

Now Roland lifted Elyssa's hands so he could kiss one set of her knuckles, then the other. I didn't know about Roland's mouth, but his echo's was slack and moist against my skin. Not a particularly enjoyable sensation.

"Surely there will be no untimely accidents," he said in a low voice. "Surely they're all splendid riders, and none of them will come to grief."

Now Elyssa's smile intensified. "So then—two hours? How shall we spend that time?"

Roland glanced back at the stairwell, silently suggesting they retire to one of their rooms.

Elyssa laughed. "No, no, too much of a risk, even with the house emptied! But I found a library at the end of the hallway—we wouldn't be disturbed there, I think, even by the servants."

Now Roland's grip shifted to her wrist and he started tugging her toward the hall. "Then by all means. Let's see what kinds of books Kendrick has assembled for the reading pleasure of his guests."

The minute we were back in the cramped and dusty room, Roland pulled Elyssa into his arms and began kissing her with a desperate hunger. Again, I was held in the echo's tight embrace; again, I felt his hands alternately hold me uncomfortably close or roam with distressing familiarity over my body. Both Roland and Elyssa were making small, sharp sounds that could have been pain but were probably pleasure, but the echoes all strained together in absolute silence.

Roland almost fell on his face when Elyssa abruptly pulled free. "No," she panted.

He reached for her. "What's wrong? What did I do?"

"Not you." She turned her head to gaze at the echoes, and the look on her face showed pure venom. "I want to be with *you*. Alone with *you*."

It was clear Roland didn't comprehend. "But we are alone. Just the two of us."

"And the six of *them*."

"But they're echoes," he said, still bewildered.

"I just don't— It feels like they're watching." She bit her lip, trying to explain. "I can't relax and be myself with you when they're in the room. I know that sounds odd." She shook her head.

Roland glanced around doubtfully. "I suppose we can put them out in the corridor. Though if someone sees them—"

"There's a closet across the hall," she said eagerly. "Can't they just wait there?"

Roland brushed his hand down the back of her silky hair and kissed her quickly on the cheek. "Why not? I don't know that I've ever been in a room without my echoes, but I'd rather be in a room with you."

"You're the sweetest man in the whole kingdom," she whispered. Almost the same words he'd said to her a few weeks ago. I thought they were truer now than then.

"Well, come on then. Let's move them," Roland said practically.

There was a very short parade along a very short route as the six of us followed our originals into the crowded closet. Naturally, the minute Roland and Elyssa stepped back into the hall, the echoes tried to exit behind them. Well—I didn't, and Elyssa's other two echoes seemed undecided; she had released us and we were no longer under a compulsion to behave exactly as she did. But Roland's echoes attempted to march out right behind him and couldn't understand why he closed the door in their faces. They tried several times to push it open, and if there hadn't been a lock that he was able to engage from the other side, I don't think they would have been willing to remain behind. Echoes can't speak, but all three of them pressed up against the door, making scrabbling motions with their hands and emitting strange, inarticulate cries.

"I'm right here," I heard him say through the door. "Right across the hall. Hardly any distance at all."

I might have believed Roland had terrible judgment when it came to love, but I liked him better when I saw that he was genuinely kind to his echoes.

I didn't have long to think about that because a second later I heard the door to the library close, and I was instantly in the arms of one of Roland's lookalikes. This time, neither Elyssa nor Roland held back; this time, the kisses were deep and passionate and full of purpose. The echo's hands worked more deftly than I would have expected to undo the buttons on the back of my dress. And when the bodice was loose enough, he pulled the gown down off my shoulders, tugging my chemise down after it. My chest was suddenly naked and exposed.

Now his hands ran greedily over my breasts, cupping them and squeezing them; now he bent and lay that slack mouth upon my nipples. I gasped and tried to back away, hampered by the loosened skirts that hung too low around my ankles and by the hopeless clutter of the room. I took another step back and knocked some household item crashing to the floor. The echo didn't even notice. Inches away from me on either side, the other pairs of echoes strove together, their breaths coming ragged and heavy.

I choked out a sound that was almost a word. *No.* Of course it wasn't a word. Of course he didn't hear me, or understand, or obey. *No,* I tried again.

The intensity between Elyssa and Roland increased. The echo's mouth returned to mine, but now his hand was traveling all across my bare skin, and his body moved against mine with a determined rhythm. He bent suddenly to lift my skirts to my waist, bunching them together to expose my thin silken underthings, and then began pressing his body against mine with renewed urgency. I could feel the crumpled fabric make a thick, uncomfortable roll between our stomachs, and I could feel a different kind of uncomfortable lump—part of his body—rubbing up against mine.

Then he reached down with one hand to undo his trousers, while his other hand pulled aside my thin undergarments. I was exposed to him, I was helpless, he was lunging for me—

I shoved him away with one hand and said, "*No!*" as loudly as I could.

He stumbled backward, clumsy and confused, but the instant he regained his balance, he came for me again. This time I pushed him even harder, and my voice was even louder. "No. No. *No!*"

On either side of me, the other echoes were joined in such an intimate manner that I couldn't tell where one body ended and the other began. There were strange sounds of grunting and panting and feet shifting and clothes rubbing together and chairs scraping across the floor as someone backed into them. The tiny room took on a faint but definite odor that was partly sweat and partly something else. I didn't understand exactly what was happening, but certainly it mirrored whatever was transpiring between Elyssa and Roland in the other room. I had the feeling that it was exactly the kind of behavior that Trima had warned Elyssa against.

The echo came toward me again, mindless and instinctual, but this time I was more sure of myself. "No," I said firmly, flattening my hand against his chest and locking my elbow. I had managed one word; might I be able to form others? Feeling my mouth work with the unaccustomed motion, I spoke clearly and deliberately, "Stay away from me."

And then—it was the oddest thing—his blank face became blanker, his strangely diffused focus on me evaporated. His body still moved in that rhythmic, sensual thrusting, tied to the actions of his original, but he no longer felt a compulsion to try to join himself with me. It was as if he no longer saw me, though I was standing inches away from him and still had my hand against his torso.

It was as if he no longer saw me as an *echo*.

Slowly, guardedly, in case I suddenly drew his attention again, I curled my fingers, I let my arm drop, I stepped away. Around me, the two paired sets of echoes continued to writhe and whisper, while the unmatched one attempted to copulate with empty air. But no one bothered me or touched me or looked at me or noticed me at all.

I did what I could to shrug myself back into my dress, though I couldn't reach all of the buttons behind me. There was no mirror in this small box of a space, so I smoothed down my hair as best I could and made sure the lace around my bodice fell demurely. Then I found a small, unoccupied corner where I could simply wait.

The second that I came to rest, that I had a moment to think, I was flooded with a complex and bewildering set of emotions. First was soaring elation. *Words! I spoke words!* No matter that the creature I had addressed couldn't hear or understand me—*I* had heard. *I* had understood. I had summoned thoughts and voiced them of my own volition. It was almost impossible to comprehend.

But hard on the heels of that stunning realization was a punch of fear. *Elyssa will destroy me.* She already suspected there was a sentient will buried deep within me, and she hated it. If she learned that I could walk and think and speak on my own, she would abuse me past endurance.

Then another thought, wholly new. *But how will she ever know?* Roland's echo certainly couldn't tell her—even if he understood what had happened, he couldn't say the words out loud, couldn't use gestures or facial expressions to convey the information. I was safe as long as no one ever realized that there was a functioning mind inside this slaved body.

I was safe as long as I didn't do anything stupid.

I was still mulling that over when, a few moments later, all the laboring echoes let out inarticulate cries and then leaned against each other, breathing heavily and clinging together. A moment only, then Elyssa's echoes smiled up at Roland's and pulled themselves free. All five of them went through much the same grooming process as I had, although the male echoes helped the women fasten their buttons in back. Not the echo I had been paired with—he simply plucked at the air as if dressing an invisible partner. Well, that wasn't very helpful. I struggled again to reach over my shoulder. I thought I only had one button still undone. Would Elyssa notice? Surely from that one small detail she wouldn't be able to deduce what had happened? I felt that wash of fear again.

There was a low murmur from the other room, the sound of a door opening, and then Roland unlocked our small prison. "There you are!" he said, unmistakable relief in his voice. "Quickly—into the library with all of you. Let's be certain everyone is presentable."

I made sure my eyes were unfocused and my gaze was averted as Elyssa and Roland drew us back into the library. In a few moments, they had fixed our clothing and wiped all smudges from our faces.

"Clean as if they'd just stepped from the hands of the valet," Roland pronounced, stepping back to appraise his efforts.

Elyssa was smirking. "Do you think so? I'm sure our expressions are so smug that everyone will merely take one look at us and know we've been up to something."

"I don't know how I'm going to sit across from you at dinner and not grin like an idiot the whole time," he admitted.

"I'll flirt with Kendrick all night, and that will set you to frowning instead."

"What? No, don't do that! I'm already jealous."

She laughed and patted his cheek. "We must make a *little* effort to be discreet, dear Roland. If I can bear to flirt with Kendrick, you can bear to watch."

He grumbled as he followed her down the hall and then headed up to his room when she insisted they had to separate. A few moments later, she had called for the carriage, and the four of us set off for the village. I was sitting across from her, terrified that something in the set of my shoulders or the comprehension in my eyes would draw her attention, but she seemed lost in her own thoughts and didn't even glance my way.

We strolled through the village for about an hour, though it was clear Elyssa was completely bored. Once we were back in the carriage, she was restless and on edge, but she cheered up when we arrived at the lodge to find some of the hunters had straggled back.

"How was the sport?" she asked as we alighted. "What did I miss?"

The rest of the day passed with the usual mix of talking, dining, and playing games. True to her promise, Elyssa spent much of the afternoon in close conversation with Kendrick, who seemed dazzled by her attention, while Roland glowered from the fringes. One of the other noblewomen took pity on him, sitting beside him and trying to draw him out, but he ignored her as if she were an echo. I didn't once see Elyssa glance his way.

Nothing else of note occurred until we returned to Elyssa's bedroom and Trima began undressing her for the night. She had hung up all our gowns and begun to strip away our underthings, when she froze with a handful of lacy drawers in her grip.

"What's this?" she demanded.

Elyssa was drawing on a robe and yawning. "What's what?"

"Your underclothes. What's this? Is it—is it *blood*?"

Elyssa took a seat on the bed and looked innocent. "I don't know, is it?"

Trima dropped the garment to the floor and frantically turned to the echoes to begin checking between our legs. "Yes—blood on this one, and this one—not this one, for some reason, but—" She swung around to stare at Elyssa. "Sweet merciful goddess, child, what have you *done?*"

Elyssa rolled her eyes and stretched herself out on the bed. "All right, I admit I went too far with Roland this afternoon, but it's nothing for you to worry about. I can handle him."

"Nothing for me to worry about!" Trima still stood there, staring, as if she couldn't force herself to believe what she had just heard. "If your father learns of this—"

"Well, how will he, unless you tell him? I certainly won't."

"Goddess have mercy on my soul. Don't you ever *think?* What if you get pregnant? Then your father won't be the only one who knows. The whole *world* will know."

Elyssa's expression drew into a sulky frown. "I won't get pregnant."

"How do you know that? Did you take any precautions?"

Now Elyssa's voice was as surly as her face. "No."

Trima threw her hands in the air. "Then your chances are very good! When did you last have your monthlies? If the weeks go by and they don't come when they should— Oh, this is a disaster!" She began pacing through the small room.

"If that happens, we'll deal with it then," Elyssa said in a voice that sounded calm, but I could tell she was making an effort. She was not used to making foolish mistakes, and she was beginning to realize just how badly she had erred this afternoon.

Trima was still pacing. "My sister lives in a small town on the other side of Alberta. We can go stay with her for a few months. Your father will come up with some reason. People will know—they always know—but maybe your reputation won't suffer too much for it. You're a high noble, after all, with *three* echoes. A lot can be overlooked."

Elyssa gestured toward the three of us. "What about them? Do they become pregnant, too?"

Trima threw her another glance of condemnation. "How can you be so ignorant? Of course they don't. If they did, we'd be overrun with echo babies by now."

"Good. Then there would be only one problem to deal with." She covered her mouth to hide a yawn, though I thought she faked it. "But I don't think the problem will arise."

Trima snorted and shook her head, and then turned to the task of preparing the echoes for bed—or rather, for our pallet on the floor. Soon enough, the lights were out and we all lay there in darkness. It seemed like a long time before anyone fell asleep.

Elyssa, I was sure, was reviewing the day's encounter, perhaps savoring it for its physical delights, but regretting it for the terrible price she might have to pay. She didn't toss and turn, like Trima, but she did shift around more than she ordinarily did, as if she couldn't quite find her accustomed ease in her body.

Trima kept sitting up and changing positions, making small muttering sounds under her breath. I wondered if she worried about her own future as well as Elyssa's. She was here as Elyssa's maid, true, but was she also in some sense a chaperone? If Elyssa became pregnant with Roland's child, would Lord Bentam blame Trima? Would she be out of a job?

I lay still on my hard bed, shifting as little as possible, scarcely breathing, but I was as wide awake as the other two. This day had been as momentous for me as it had been for Elyssa—I, too, had taken a path from which it seemed there was no turning back, chosen an action for which the consequences could prove enormous. Like Elyssa, I might have no control over what happened next, but that my future might be very different from my past—for good or ill—I was very certain.

Elyssa might be sorry. I thought she probably was. But for myself, I could only be grateful and amazed. And glad.

I had words.

I was a person.

CHAPTER FOUR

The weeks following our return from the hunting lodge were absolutely miserable. During the first five days, Elyssa was tense and moody, snapping at everyone, even Trima. A new housemaid gave her notice, and the girl who was hired to replace her quit after one day. Every other servant in the house avoided Elyssa, if at all possible, and no one—human or echo—was willing to meet her eyes.

She was filled with such bitter, restless anger that she revisited her favorite old pastime of torturing me. It was terrifying to kneel before her and feel the cool slice of the blade on my back between two ribs—a place no scar would ever be seen, except perhaps by the echo of her lover. Terrifying because I was awake, I was conscious, and I was in agony, but I had to endure the abuse with an echo's blind stoicism, no matter how long it lasted.

One afternoon, she shoved me facedown on the floor and knelt on my back, jerking my head up by clutching a handful of my hair. She had a knife in her right hand, and she buried the tip of it right under my left ear. I could feel a drop of blood trickle down my skin. I knew that with one casual swipe of the blade, she could cut my throat.

She leaned down so close to me, I could feel her breath against my cheek. "I swear by every face of the triple goddess," she whispered, "if I ever thought you were awake in there, I would kill you in an instant."

I didn't answer. I didn't squirm. I barely breathed. She could have been forgiven for thinking I was already dead. After a moment, with a cry of frustration, she scrambled to her feet. She flung the dagger aside and began kicking me in the ribs and the stomach, over and over, until her rage was exhausted. I never made a sound.

Roland came to call on the third day, but Elyssa refused to see him. I was standing near enough to the window to see him ride away, the slump of his shoulders showing his disappointment. As he and his echoes reached the end of the long, curving drive, they pulled up their horses and turned, all at once, to gaze back at the house in hope and despair.

Elyssa was close enough to the window to see him, too, if she wanted, but I couldn't be certain she looked.

At night, she dismissed Trima as quickly as possible, banished the echoes to our room, then spent hours pacing back and forth through the rest of her suite. I was not bound to her during these hours, but I was still connected to her in some profound fashion, and if I had wanted to, I could have replicated her every movement. So I knew that she spent much of her time, during every one of those hours, running her hand up and down her smooth, flat belly. Trying to detect any slight swelling, any evidence of disgrace. Often her fingers would clutch over the fabric of her nightgown, crushing the folds together. But she couldn't destroy something inside her that she couldn't reach.

I spent those same hours pacing, but much more cautiously than Elyssa. I was still learning exactly how to exercise control over my own limbs and muscles, still very aware of the effort it took to will myself forward on a course different from the one Elyssa set. True, I had walked under my own power whenever Elyssa released her echoes, but she always left us with some clear directive that we could feel setting us inexorably in motion. *Go to your room. Sit on the sofa. Turn toward the house.*

Now I had to summon my own intrinsic motivation. Now I had to discover what it meant to claim my body as my own.

I was awkward and uncertain at first, but every day the actions grew easier and more natural; every day I grew a little more sure of myself. Soon I was practicing other skills—picking up items and putting them back down again, buttoning and unbuttoning my clothes, braiding my hair. My fingers, clumsy at first, quickly grew deft. They had done these actions before, and my muscles remembered how; what was new was carrying them out under my own command.

At night, once Elyssa finally flung herself to bed and drifted off, exhausted from worry, I practiced my words. At first I would only whisper them, one at a time, naming the things I saw around me. *Bed. Chair. Window. Echo.* Once I was sure Elyssa was actually sleeping, I would say the words out loud, summoning the quietest possible voice that still produced a sound. And I began stringing the words together in sentences. *The echo is lying in bed. The chair is by the window.*

The rest of the world is sleeping, but I am awake.

We had been home two weeks when, one particularly sunny morning, Elyssa woke up and started laughing while she still lay in bed. I could hear the sound and feel her delight even from two rooms away. Not until I heard Trima enter the suite and step into Elyssa's room did I understand what had made her so happy.

"Good morning, my lady, it's time to—"

"Look, Trima! Blood! It's blood!"

Trima's voice quickened with excitement. "Your monthlies have come, then?"

"Yes! Oh, I'm so relieved I can hardly stand it!" And she laughed again.

"Well, it's excellent news, but we'll still have to change the bed linens," said Trima practically. "Come on, then. Up you go."

Elyssa was a completely changed person for the rest of the day: affectionate with Trima, civil to the servants, and kind to her aunt Hodia, with whom she played a few rounds of cards after the evening meal. She didn't even bother to scratch my arm or pull my hair when we were alone in the room; she seemed to have forgotten that she had ever hated me. I knew all too well that this new charity wouldn't last, but I was grateful for it while it held.

The next day her father called her into his study for a private meeting.

I had very few memories of interactions with Lord Bentam. I didn't think it was because my bouts of consciousness had been so infrequent until recently; I thought it was because he had never spent much time with his daughter. But now, as Elyssa and her echoes took seats across from him, I took the time to assess him.

His hair was as dark as Elyssa's, and his skin might once have been as fair, but age and hard living had darkened it to an unhealthy ruddy complexion. His eyes were black and bold, intelligent and fierce; my impression was that he missed very little. But there was an unpleasant aspect to his face—a sneering expression that seemed permanently engraved in his features. Under his fine coat, his shoulders were bulky; his hands were fleshy and powerful. He looked like a man who would be quick to anger and dangerous to cross. I had never heard Elyssa say anything that even hinted at affection for her father, and as I covertly watched him, I could understand why.

Behind him were his two echoes. They sat somewhat in the shadows that lay in the cramped space behind his massive desk, but I could still see the identical sneers across their faces. I wondered how common it was for a man with only two echoes to sire a child with three. Perhaps Elyssa's mother had had three echoes. Perhaps Bentam had, at one point, had three of his own, until one night in a fit of rage or boredom he had tortured one of them to death. I had absolutely no doubt that if he ever decided he wanted to abuse his echoes, he would be a lot more thorough about it than Elyssa.

Neither of them bothered with a greeting, they just watched each other over the desk, and Elyssa waited in silence for whatever he had to say. He glanced at a paper in his hand and said, "You can't marry that Roland fellow."

Her voice was perfectly level. "Did I say I wanted to?"

Bentam grunted. "You've spent enough time with him lately."

"I spend time with all the high nobles of Alberta. Isn't that what you want me to do?"

"I want you to speak to me respectfully, or do not speak at all!" he replied, raising his voice.

Elyssa was conspicuously silent.

"Well, no matter what *you're* thinking, young Roland seems to have marriage on his mind," Bentam said at a slightly lower volume. He waved the paper at her in an accusatory way. "He wants to come meet with me—" He consulted the letter to get the exact wording. "'At my earliest convenience.'" Now he tossed the paper aside with contempt. "There's only one thing he can mean by that."

"Perhaps he wants to buy one of your horses," Elyssa said in a dulcet voice.

"Not likely. A man who wants to buy your horse says so right there when he sees you on the road, or in the hunting field. He doesn't send delicate little missives asking for an audience."

"I suppose not," Elyssa said. "Anyway, Roland always buys sets of four matched horses. For himself and his three echoes, of course."

Even I could tell that was an insult. *And you only have two echoes, so you'd never have a set of four to sell him.* Bentam narrowed his eyes but chose not to respond directly. "He'll be by sometime this week, and I'm going to tell him no."

"Are you going to tell him why? Are you going to tell *me* why?" I couldn't deduce from her carefully controlled tone if she was angry or disappointed or relieved. "He's a high noble of some wealth. I thought you didn't care about anything except money and connections."

"And politics," he shot back.

"Oh, I forgot. The divine right of the western provinces to govern themselves without interference from the royal city."

He leaned back in his chair, his expression suddenly both closed and stormy. Something she'd said had made him angry—but had also touched on a topic he didn't want to discuss. "It's more complicated than that," he said in a quieter voice. "But I do think King Harold has had far too much influence in Alberta and Orenza and Empara for far too long."

Elyssa pretended to hold back a yawn. "I don't understand what this has to do with Roland. And why I can't marry him."

"Because you're going to marry Prince Jordan instead."

I felt the shock of that statement hit Elyssa with the force of a slap. She didn't even try to maintain her cool composure. "Because I'm *what?*"

"You're going to marry Jordan. A marriage between one of the princes and one of the western provinces is the best way to maintain peace in the realm."

"Does Harold happen to agree with you or have you just come up with this idea all on your own?"

Bentam smirked at her. "We've been in conversations for a few months now. Jordan has three echoes, you know, and there are hardly any marriageable young women in the western provinces who also have three echoes. He doesn't have much choice."

"How special that makes me feel," Elyssa murmured. "But I can hardly believe you even want such an alliance. You hate the king and you hate any interference from the crown."

Now Bentam's expression became crafty. "There are always negotiations when a member of the royal family chooses a partner. Alberta would profit considerably if Jordan took one of its daughters to be his wife. And once Alberta was pacified, Orenza and Empara would quickly fall in line."

"Even if that's true, I'm not sure your plan will work," Elyssa said. "I've known Jordan for years, and he's never shown the slightest interest in me. In fact, I rather think he dislikes me."

"Maybe he does," Bentam said, "but I'm sure he'll try to conceal that fact when he arrives in a few days."

Elyssa practically tumbled out of her chair, and all her echoes had to fling out their hands to keep their balance. "What? He's coming here? So *soon?*"

Bentam grinned, seeming pleased at her discomfort. "As I said. So my *earliest convenience* for speaking with young Roland will be tomorrow afternoon, because I don't want him skulking about when the prince comes to call."

Elyssa rose to her feet, not waiting to see if her father was done with the conversation. "There's so much to do! My clothes—my hair— I'll need at least one new gown, but there's hardly time—"

Bentam waved her toward the door and leaned back in his chair, finally showing a genuine smile. "Good. You go off and do everything you need to do in order to catch Jordan's attention. The whole realm is counting on you."

The next three days passed in a frenzy of fittings, since the echoes needed new outfits just as much as Elyssa did. Well, that wasn't strictly true. While our clothing always looked similar to Elyssa's, it was less ornate and stylish; we might wear the same purple dress to mirror three different gowns she had in her wardrobe. But to impress the prince, we all needed fashionable new attire that would rival anything he might see in the royal city. Hence, the parade of dressmakers and milliners and cobblers and perfumiers.

Four days after we learned that Jordan would be visiting, word spread through the manor that the prince's entourage would arrive late in the afternoon. Soon enough, the whole household was gathered in the parlor nearest the door, awaiting the prince's appearance. It seemed to take forever before there was a commotion outside the front entrance—the sound of many horses arriving all at once, wheels squeaking, carriages creaking, grooms calling out. Elyssa took a deep breath and practiced a smile.

Maybe I had seen Prince Jordan at some point in my life— before I was sentient, before I knew how to drink in all the details of the world—but I didn't remember him. Now, knowing Elyssa might marry him, and I might live in his household the rest of my life, I was consumed with curiosity. I managed to position myself behind and a little to one side of Elyssa, so I had a clear view over her shoulder. And, like everyone else in the foyer, I watched the great double doors with unwavering attention.

It was only a few moments before those doors opened and a phalanx of young men swept in. They traveled like a flock of migrating geese, one in the lead and the others spread out behind him in a roughly triangular formation. Scanning the crowd quickly, I determined that it was made up of four originals and an assortment of echoes.

SHARON SHINN

There could be no doubt that the man in the lead was Prince Jordan. He was tall and attractive, with an open and pleasant face, light brown hair, and brown eyes. Even in a room of wealthy people, it was clear he was expensively dressed. But it wasn't his clothes that gave him such a regal bearing, I thought. There was something about his expression, his posture, the very set of his shoulders. He looked like a man bred to responsibility and power.

But he didn't look as if arrogance was part of his makeup. I saw him nod his thanks to the servant who held the door open for him—a small gesture, but an unexpected one in a man of his position. His smile was warm and genuine, and he approached Lord Bentam with his hand already outstretched in greeting. The three echoes flanking him held their hands out as well; as Bentam had only two echoes, one of Jordan's was left to pump the empty air.

"Good afternoon," Jordan said. "How kind of you to welcome us to your house."

By contrast, I thought Lord Bentam's smile was calculating and cold, though his voice was smooth as cream. "Not at all. You honor us with your presence, my prince. How was your journey?"

"Surprisingly easy. The Charamon Road is well-maintained, and the hospitality throughout Alberta has been remarkable. We are a large party, but we were well cared for everywhere we stopped."

"I am glad to hear it, and the governor will be pleased as well."

"Do pass along my compliments to Lord Vincent."

Elyssa stepped forward just enough to catch the prince's attention before she dropped into a deep curtsey. Her echoes sank down beside her, our skirts spreading as wide as they would go, before we all rose and extended our hands to the new arrivals. "Jordan," she drawled. "How good to see you again."

It might have been my imagination that his smile dimmed noticeably when he turned to the daughter of the house, but he took her hand immediately in his. I was surprised by how warm his echo's hand was on mine; usually echoes had skin that was cool to the touch, and their limbs seemed almost weightless. "Elyssa," he said. "You're looking as beautiful as always."

42

"I'm glad you think so. I would hate to have all this effort go to waste." She followed this with her usual low laugh, and he responded with a somewhat perfunctory smile.

"The effort doesn't show, only the result," he replied.

"We are glad to have you here," she said.

Jordan gestured behind him, his echoes repeating the motion. "I'm not sure you've met all my companions. May I make introductions?"

One by one, the prince's friends stepped forward and made their bows to Bentam and Elyssa as Jordan reeled off their names. One was a lord from the nearby province of Pandrea, where all the inhabitants had dark skin and brown eyes; two others, both fair-complected and blue-eyed, informed us that they were from Banchura, a province on the far eastern coastline of the kingdom. Two had two echoes apiece and one only a single echo. For some reason, this made me think well of Jordan. He was not so full of his own consequence that he would only pick his friends from among the most elite. Of course, maybe he enjoyed being the only man in the room with three echoes, which would make him *more* arrogant, not less so. But somehow, that was not the impression I was left with.

"We're delighted to have you all," said Bentam. "Let us have you shown to your rooms. Are you hungry? We could have dinner served within the hour."

"Starving," said Jordan.

"The noon stop for lunch seems like hours ago," said the Pandrean lord.

Bentam motioned to one of the servants, who instantly slipped out of the room and headed toward the kitchen. "Then we will eat with all haste. Rejoin us here when you're settled in and we'll head straight to the dining hall."

It was another half hour before the whole group reassembled for what Bentam was calling "a simple family meal." By that I supposed he meant that no one was on hand except the three nobles who lived in the manor—Bentam, his sister, Hodia, and

Elyssa—and Jordan and his friends. Certainly, the food itself was hardly simple, consisting of a dozen courses of the most elaborately cooked dishes. I couldn't remember a time when the household had eaten so well.

"Naturally, we have more entertainment planned in the coming days," Bentam said as the servants laid out the first course. "Several of the young ladies from nearby manors are most interested in joining us for any activities—"

"And we are most interested in meeting them!" one of Jordan's friends replied, to general laughter.

"But as we were uncertain when you would arrive today, we made no special plans," Bentam finished up.

"I think our special plans will be to wash the travel grime from our faces and get a good night's sleep," Jordan said. "Tomorrow will be soon enough for us to go round meeting the neighbors."

Elyssa leaned forward and smiled charmingly at all the visitors at once. My guess was that she was enjoying being the only woman amongst so many men. Well, there was her aunt, of course, but Hodia was austere and unsmiling and unlikely to inspire any of the young men to flirt with her. "So tell me all the gossip from Camarria!" she invited. "I hear Queen Tabitha held a big spring gala that half the city attended!"

"It certainly seemed like half the city was there," Jordan agreed. "My father complained about the expense, but the event was so popular that it will probably become an annual event. I think she's already booking theatrical groups for next year's party."

Elyssa slanted a quick look at Lord Bentam. "I shall have to beg my father to send me to the royal city next spring," she said. Then she bestowed a bright smile on Jordan. "And beg *your* father to invite me, of course."

He gave her a courtly nod. "You are welcome anytime," he said politely. "I will make sure you are on the list of preferred guests."

"I would hope some of my special friends would be there, too," she pursued. "The triplets from Banchura—surely you would invite them?"

"Oh, they were on hand this year as well, *and* all their echoes," said one of the lords who was also from Banchura. "They are practically a party all on their own."

"And Vivienne of Thelleron," Elyssa added. "Was she present?"

I thought Jordan tensed up slightly. "She was."

Elyssa touched a napkin to her lips—just for show, I thought, as I repeated the gesture. I doubted she really needed to wipe any crumbs from her mouth. "We are all hoping for an interesting announcement very soon," she said. "Between Vivienne and the crown prince."

This time I did not imagine that there was a slightly awkward pause. "I'm not aware that my brother is about to make any such announcement," Jordan said.

"Really?" Bentam asked. "I thought it was long understood that Cormac and Vivienne were to marry."

"I'm not sure Cormac is eager to marry anyone," said the Pandrean lord. "He is enjoying being a handsome young prince for as long as he can."

His words elicited a light laugh from the others in his party, and even Hodia smiled. Elyssa was too clever to dwell on a topic that her guest clearly wanted to abandon, so she introduced a new subject. "What else has been happening in Camarria?" she asked. "I know better than to ask a pack of *men* about the latest fashions, but surely you can tell me what new color is all the rage? And don't say you don't know because I'm positive that your sister Annery has been wearing it all season."

"Oh, then, in that case it must be a very odd shade of yellow," Jordan answered. "I think my stepmother called it 'melted saffron.'"

"That's it," said one of his friends. "My sister is wearing it, too. I didn't think it was very flattering, but of course I didn't say so."

"But this is excellent news!" Elyssa exclaimed. "I have a new gown in that very color!"

Jordan saluted her with his glass of wine. "Then it appears you already have a dress in hand for next year's gala."

She laughed at him. "Silly man! By next spring, everyone will be wearing a different color entirely."

Bentam rolled his eyes and changed the subject with no pretense at subtlety. "Tell me, Highness, how goes the trade with Ferrenlea? I have been considering buying into a company that is shipping overseas, but I wasn't sure if the investment would pay off."

Jordan instantly grew serious. "I think it would. Recent talks have gone well, and my father plans to send another delegation to Ferrenlea's capital city. Trade is never a sure thing, of course, but the merchants I've talked to have been pleased at their returns."

"Do you have a sense of what items are proving most successful? I have a stake in a number of lavender farms—a product that's always found a market here in the Seven Jewels, but will it hold the same value overseas?"

Talk of commerce dominated the rest of the meal. It was not a topic that interested Elyssa; I could feel her growing restlessness, though she kept a pleasant expression on her face and didn't try to redirect the conversation. But her attention wandered, and within fifteen minutes she was offering a sly smile to the man sitting on her right. He was the fellow with only a single echo, and he hadn't said much since they arrived.

"Does your family engage in trade?" she asked him in a low voice.

"Not so far," he answered. "My parents seem to have all they can handle just to manage the manor farms."

"Oh, good," she said, smiling even more widely. "Then you and I can talk about something else."

CHAPTER FIVE

The rest of Prince Jordan's visit, which lasted three days, proceeded along the same lines. Everyone made an effort to be agreeable, though all conversations were a bit strained and no one ever entirely relaxed. I had the sense that Elyssa and her father were always delicately prying at the prince, trying to learn bits of privileged information, and that Jordan just as stubbornly was trying to refrain from saying anything interesting at all. But everyone was so polite that it was hard for me to be certain.

There was only one encounter that seemed both genuine and surprising, and it came late on the second night of the royal party's visit. Everyone had retired to their rooms, and Trima was brushing out Elyssa's hair while a new serving woman attended to the echoes. During the past three months, there had been four or five new maids brought in to assist Trima as she looked after Elyssa, but all of them had quit or been dismissed within a couple of weeks. I didn't think this one would stay much longer; she seemed terrified of Elyssa and not particularly fond of Trima. Tonight Elyssa dismissed her curtly the moment she had finished taking off our fancy dresses and combing out our hair.

As soon as she was gone, Elyssa took up a conversation with Trima. "I'm curious about Dezmen."

"Who?"

"The Pandrean lord. I've met him several times, but I can never remember who his family is. I don't think he's related to the governor, but if he *is*, then I need to be much nicer than I've been so far."

"Maybe you should just be nice to everyone."

Elyssa laughed. "No, I think I'll go down to the library and look him up. My father has a book with the lineages of all the high nobles across the seven provinces."

"What, now? It's after midnight."

"I'm not tired." She came to her feet, slipped on a dressing robe that was almost as ornate as a riding dress, and turned toward the door.

Trima spoke sharply. "Take the echoes."

Elyssa turned back, pouting in irritation. "I'm just running downstairs for a few minutes."

"If anyone sees you—the prince or any of his friends, even your father—they'll notice that the echoes aren't with you. They'll wonder."

Elyssa made a groaning noise. "Can't I be free of them for even five minutes?"

Trima watched her steadily. "Not if you want to marry the prince."

Elyssa strangled another groan and then snapped, "Fine. Find them robes so we can go mincing through the hall, where I assure you no one will see us."

Three minutes later, the echoes and I followed Elyssa out the door, through the halls, and to the lower level of the house. It did seem like everyone else in the whole place was already asleep because the only noises I heard were our soft cloth slippers shushing along the floors. The only wall sconces that were lit were widely spaced and inadequate for illuminating our way, but Elyssa marched through the shadows with the ease of perfect familiarity. When she pushed open the library door, just enough light from the hallway spilled in to show us the high shelves and bulky groupings of high-backed chairs.

Or—no—someone was there before us, and had brought a lamp with him. That was the light that fell on all our faces, showing us bewildered and at a loss.

Elyssa quickly regained her poise. "Prince Jordan! I'm so sorry to have interrupted you!"

The prince lay down the book he had been holding and offered her a small bow. His three echoes repeated the motion gracefully. "Not at all. It is your house, and I am the intruder."

She smiled at him. "Hardly an intruder. A most honored guest."

He smiled back, more to cover embarrassment than to show pleasure, I thought. "I couldn't sleep and thought perhaps if I read for an hour, I would become drowsy."

"I am here on much the same errand," she lied. "I find my father's history books so dull that they have me nodding off in minutes."

He rewarded that with another perfunctory smile. "Although history can prove instructive, so if you can manage to wade through a few volumes you might find yourself more interested than you expect."

"Oh, don't try to shame me into being smarter than I am! I assure you, my father has tried many stratagems designed to interest me in lessons, and none of them was ever successful."

"I find that hard to believe," Jordan said. "I have always thought you were quite clever."

She lifted an eyebrow at that. The echoes and I followed suit. My guess was that she was trying to decide if he had intended a compliment or an insult. "I know what I need to know, I suppose," she said softly. "We all do—learning what seems most crucial to our survival."

"Exactly," he said. "Though I think sometimes we're surprised to discover which odd pieces of knowledge come in handy."

She drew her robe closer around her shoulders and leaned against the back of an overstuffed sofa. The echoes and I copied her, and Jordan and his three shadows ranged before us. "Oh, now, you simply must tell me!" she exclaimed. "What stray bits of information have proved to be most valuable to you as you carried out your duties as prince of the realm?"

For the first time, his face relaxed into a grin that seemed authentic. "It's been quite shocking to me," he said. "I thought sword fighting and battle strategy would be the most important subjects I studied. Maybe even the recent history of international alliances. But no. The skills I draw on most often and most heavily are ballroom dancing and cravat tying. A prince with no social skills or fashion sense is a prince no one approves of. It is very disheartening."

Elyssa couldn't contain her laughter. I thought Jordan's reluctant smile looked immensely appealing on his pleasant face. "It is true—the high nobles are all obsessed with such trivial details as looks and courtesies," she said. "If you want to govern us, you must be as superficial as we are. But I am sorry it is such a hardship for you."

"Dancing, for instance," he said. "I imagine it would have been tricky to learn anyway, for although I am athletic enough, I am not naturally graceful. But to learn to dance with three echoes copying my every move—tripping over their feet when I did, bumping into the wall right next to me—it must have taken me three times as long as it would have if I was just an ordinary man."

She laughed again. "In that case, I would have thought sword fighting would be equally complex to learn."

"There was never a problem wielding a weapon," he said, shaking his head. "Perhaps because I was so interested in doing it! I had heard tales of echoes inadvertently slashing each other with a sharp blade, but I never experienced anything like that."

Now Elyssa leaned back on her hands and let her gaze wander deliberately from Jordan's face to that of each of his echoes. I did the same—noting, as I had before, how very alert Jordan's echoes appeared to be, how very close to human.

"But then, your echoes seem exceptionally well-developed," she said. "Most echoes seem like pale copies of their originals, but yours are so much more robust. I have noticed the same thing about your brother Cormac—yes, and your father and your stepmother as well."

His smile was back to being the stiff formal one that covered his real thoughts. "Ah, you'd find the explanation for that in those history books that you find so dull."

"So tell me," she invited.

He gave a slight shrug. "The theory goes that if someone ever tried to kill the king, his soul would simply flow into the body of one of his echoes. Supposedly that's what happened with King Edwin when his original body was killed in battle. So all the king's echoes have to be very well developed so that they can house the spirit of the king if they have to. Or the queen's echoes, of course. Same thing."

"I didn't know that!" Elyssa exclaimed.

"I don't know that it's ever actually happened, though. I mean, they tell stories about Edwin, but who knows if they're true? He lived hundreds of years ago."

"Is that why all the high nobles have echoes, too?"

Jordan grinned. "I don't *think* so. I believe *your* echoes came about because you were always warring amongst yourselves and there were so many betrayals and assassination attempts that the goddess created echoes as a form of protection. If a would-be murderer couldn't tell which of four people was the one he wanted to kill, he would be much less likely to attempt the act. So the high nobles developed echoes as a safety precaution."

Elyssa tilted her head to one side. "And they were bestowed upon us by the triple goddess?"

"So they say. She is one being in multiple incarnations, so she gave the same gift to the nobles." He shrugged. "They *also* say that whenever the kingdom is peaceful, very few nobles are born with echoes. But when there is unrest, the goddess generates more echoes to protect her people from violence."

Elyssa folded her arms across her chest. I could feel my own face copy her somewhat mutinous expression. "And does the goddess consider this a time of particular unrest?" she asked in a polite voice.

His own was cool in reply. "Apparently so. There are more nobles with echoes now than there have been in nearly a hundred years. More *adult* echoes with nobles," he amended.

"All of an age to go to war," she said.

"Precisely."

She stirred restlessly and came to her feet, once more drawing the robe tightly around her shoulders. "Well, let us hope the goddess has miscalculated—or misunderstood!" she said. "Let us hope there are no wars or assassination attempts or other assaults against the nobles."

"Or against the royal house."

"That goes without saying." She gave him a nod of clear dismissal. "Thank you for a most interesting conversation, my prince. Much more informative than a history book, I must say."

He summoned a smile. "But I fear I didn't put you to sleep."

"No, indeed, you've given me much to think over. I might lie awake all night instead."

"I apologize."

"No need. I often find sleep to be a waste of time."

He executed another shallow bow and held out his arm as if to formally escort her from the library. The small courtesy made her smile again, and she slipped her hand around his elbow. As her echoes linked their arms with his echoes, she paused to once again glance from one face to the next.

"It *is* remarkable, though," she murmured. "How very lifelike your echoes are. I do think it is possible that if I encountered one of them on its own, alone in some hallway, I might almost mistake it for you."

"Would you?" he answered, his voice slightly edged. "I don't think I would ever mistake anyone for you, Lady Elyssa—not even one of your echoes. You are entirely unique."

As she laughed, he underscored his point by briefly staring at each of her echoes in turn. I was the last one he looked at, and I gazed back in frank curiosity, scanning for the details that would set him apart from his shadows. Despite what Elyssa had said, to me the differences were obvious. There was a firmness, a certainty, an intelligence to Jordan's expression that no echo could emulate; it was as if his echoes were portraits painted by the most gifted artist, but Jordan was the living model. Jordan was the undisputable prince.

And the prince was staring at me with outright astonishment. My heart bounded with a primal terror. An echo never made eye contact! An echo never wore anything but a vague and indifferent expression! I quickly let my eyes lose focus, trained my gaze on his right ear, and let all the muscles in my face go lax. For a moment it seemed like no one in the whole room was breathing.

"Well?" Elyssa said impatiently, swinging her head around to frown at him. "What are we waiting for?"

The prince cast me one last troubled look, then shook his head and urged her toward the door. "Nothing. Nothing at all. It's high past time we bid each other goodnight."

The last full day of the prince's visit was slightly alarming for me, and it was my own fault. If only I had not looked at him so openly the night before! But my inquiring expression had caught his attention, and he seemed like a man of some curiosity.

That entire day, anytime he could do so without being too obvious about it, Jordan scanned the faces of Elyssa's echoes, looking for some sign of sentience. At the breakfast table, when Elyssa sat across from him but was engaged in conversation with someone else. In the early afternoon, as an undisciplined group of young lords and ladies gathered in the garden for a high-spirited stroll. In the evening, as nobles from nearby manors joined us for a fine meal and some informal dancing. Anytime Jordan could reasonably be expected to look in Elyssa's direction, he looked in *mine* instead.

But I didn't repeat that careless mistake. I made sure my features were slack, my eyes fixed on the floor or the wall or some distant horizon. I was fairly certain he couldn't tell the three of us apart; his gaze didn't rest on me more often or linger a bit longer than it did on the other two echoes. I hoped he would soon come to think he had just imagined that brief exchange of glances.

I must confess, I was even more fascinated by him than he could have been by me; out of the corner of my eye I watched him constantly, even when Elyssa was concentrating on someone else. I saw nothing to make me change my initial impression of

an openhearted man with a good soul. All the nobles smiled and
flirted and *pretended* to be nice people; perhaps Jordan was just better at pretense than the rest, but I didn't think so.

For instance, when the dancing began, he naturally solicited
Elyssa as his first partner. She was his hostess—and, perhaps, the
woman he was going to marry—so she deserved that courtesy. But
the second woman he asked was a shy young noble with only one
echo. Although Elyssa and her friends had been polite enough to
the girl's face, I had heard them mocking her when there was a
good chance she might be able to overhear. She was clearly as close
to being a nobody as anyone with an echo could be. And yet Jordan
extended her a signal honor just because he could. I had to think
he did it on purpose.

I also noticed that he continued to thank anyone who did him
even the slightest service. The footman who brought his dinner
plate. The butler who poured his wine. The housemaid who ran
after him with a coin that had fallen from his pocket. He'd laughed
and handed it back to her. "You keep it," he said. I hadn't seen the
denomination, but the color was gold. No doubt his father had vaults
full of gold in Camarria, but it was still a kind thing for him to do.

I formed an equally high opinion of the Pandrean man, Lord
Dezmen, who also extended an effortless courtesy to everyone he
came in contact with. I had ample opportunity to observe him
because Elyssa had decided he was worth cultivating. She spent
much of that day maneuvering to sit next to him in the dining
hall or to walk beside him in the garden. Because he had only two
echoes, I was left unpaired while we made our way through the
garden's flower beds and follies. I enjoyed the brief moments of
comparative solitude so much I had to be careful to keep a smile
off my face for fear the prince might notice it. But I wasn't worried
about Lord Dezmen seeing my expression. He seemed like a thoroughly nice man, but I didn't think he was the sort of person who
would pay any attention to an echo.

The following morning, Jordan and all his friends departed.
The whole household turned out to see them off, fanning out in the

courtyard to say farewell. Jordan thanked Hodia for her hospitality, bowed politely over Elyssa's hand, lifted his eyes to do one more quick scan of Elyssa's echoes, then turned to Bentam to make his final goodbyes.

"I'll tell my father what an agreeable time I passed in your house," Jordan said.

"And tell him I'll be happy to come to Camarria anytime he wants to discuss business of any kind," Bentam replied.

Jordan's mouth tightened slightly, but he said, "My father is always glad to do friendly business with any of the western provinces." He glanced at the three carriages arrayed on the flagstone, all of them large enough to accommodate nobles and their echoes, then back at his companions. "Are we ready?"

"Eager to get on the road," said Dezmen. "The trip will be a long one."

"Then let's be on our way."

It took a few more moments of mild turmoil for the visitors to find their assigned places in the vehicles, and there was a certain amount of good-natured banter among the prince and his friends as they complained about who might have the most uncomfortable seat. I could feel Elyssa's impatience to be done with this part of the visit, but Bentam and Hodia stood fast, obviously prepared to wait until the last carriage was out of sight, so Elyssa kept her spot, too, though her smile grew increasingly strained.

Finally, they were all inside the carriages and the doors were closed; a few of the travelers were peering out the windows to offer a last goodbye. Jordan was one of them.

"Thank you again!" he called as his carriage, the first in line, began to pull away.

Elyssa and all her echoes lifted their hands in one final wave. I saw Jordan respond in kind—and then I saw the expression on his face change to bewilderment and speculation. Glancing around quickly, I realized that Elyssa had already dropped her arm and pivoted toward the door. I had been so busy registering my last farewell to the prince that I hadn't even noticed when she turned away.

CHAPTER SIX

If Bentam and the king were in conversations about a possible marriage between their children, none of that information was shared with Elyssa. Weeks passed, and a chilly spring melted into an indolent summer, and still there was no word from the royal palace. Jordan did not return to visit, which was a severe disappointment to me; neither did Roland, which I thought was a great relief to Elyssa. I had the distinct impression that her passion for him had waned almost the minute she consummated it.

Plenty of other people made their way to Lord Bentam's estate during that period of time, however.

All during the late spring and early summer, Bentam entertained a stream of assorted visitors. Some arrived in fine carriages, attended by obsequious servants and silent echoes, wearing expensive clothing and dripping in amethysts, emeralds, and bits of onyx. I already knew that amethysts were the traditional gems worn by the high nobles of Alberta; now I learned that those from Empara decked themselves in emeralds, and those from Orenza favored jewelry made with onyx in white, red, and black.

Other visitors rode in on sturdy horses outfitted with the plainest tack and bridles. They wore nondescript dark clothing and could scarcely boast even a simple gold pin among the lot of them. They often trotted up to the house at nightfall but didn't join the family for meals; sometimes the only indication that strangers were in the house was the murmur of low voices coming from Bentam's study. While nearly half of the noble visitors were women, all of the furtive arrivals were men.

Elyssa had developed the habit of lurking in the library before going to bed, just so she could step casually into the hall whenever she heard the voices of newcomers. She never spoke to the late-night guests or acknowledged them in any way, but I could sense her excitement and curiosity whenever any of them were in the house.

All of that changed late one night when muffled sounds from the corridor indicated that the servants had admitted some mysterious new visitor. Elyssa lifted her head as if to listen better, then put aside the book she had been pretending to read and headed for the door. The echoes followed.

When she stepped into the hallway, she stopped so abruptly that all three of us bumped into her before we could stop ourselves. She didn't bother to berate us; she didn't even seem to notice. She was staring at the slim, silent man who stood in the shadows, staring back at her.

He was dressed all in black, and his hair was black, and he wore black gloves on his hands, so all that was visible was his face. His skin was nearly as pale as Elyssa's but his features were much stronger, including deep-sunk eyes, a prominent nose, and a square jawline just now stubbled with whiskers. It must have been raining outside, for the darkness that wrapped all around him glittered with wet. He seemed almost like a spirit summoned from some otherworldly place and still trailing bits of cloud and vapor.

"*Oh,*" Elyssa said.

There was a long moment of silence while they continued to regard each other, both of them absolutely unmoving. Finally, the man took a single step forward. His eyes were still fixed on Elyssa and he seemed webbed with mist and intrigue. "I didn't realize you would be awake at this hour," he said, his voice low and serious. "Have you been sitting in on your father's councils?"

Elyssa shook her head, seeming to have an uncharacteristically difficult time finding her voice. "No, he— I have not been invited."

A swift smile lit his somber features. "A mistake," he said. "I am sure you would have much to contribute."

Now Elyssa was the one to step forward, the echoes following daintily in her wake. "I didn't know—my father never mentioned—I didn't realize that you were still…" She didn't seem to know how to end that sentence, but finally just added, "Involved."

This might have been the first time I had laid eyes on the man—or, at least, the first time I had been conscious enough to see him—but it clearly was not the first time for Elyssa.

He shrugged. "I have never lost my passion for the cause. But politics change, and alliances rearrange, and the high nobles of the western provinces have in recent years seemed more interested in reconciliation than secession. But now the sentiment seems to be growing again. We'll see. I am here to learn what new developments might be unfolding."

She summoned a smile, although, judging by the one I felt on my own lips, it was shaky and uncertain. "I'm sure those developments are very exciting."

His eyebrows lifted. "I've heard about *one*," he said. "That you are to be sacrificed on the royal altar."

"*Oh,*" she said again, in a faint voice, and then, more vigorously, "You mean that I am to marry Jordan?"

"That's what I hear."

"It's not a settled thing yet."

"But the prince was here visiting just a few weeks ago."

Her voice recovered some of its usual mocking lilt. "I imagine the prince often rides around the countryside, visiting the high nobles on behalf of his father. His brother, too."

"Maybe," the man replied. "But he could hardly expect to go anywhere else in the kingdom and find another woman so beautiful—and so eligible—and so strategic."

She laughed, half pleased and half disgruntled. "So you would rate those charms of mine all equally?" she inquired.

He immediately dropped into an elegant bow so low that his dark hair brushed the floor before he quickly straightened. "I think a prince might be forced to consider eligibility and strategy when he goes looking for a bride," he said softly. "We poor, unfortunate ordinary men notice only beauty, and it often blinds us."

Down the hall, in the direction of her father's study, there was the sound of a door opening and someone speaking in a low voice. Lord Bentam, no doubt, instructing a footman to bring the visitor to see him. Elyssa glanced that way, then spoke in a quick and urgent voice.

"How long do you stay? Overnight, surely?"

He hesitated. "I had planned to stop at an inn nearby and not trouble your household by asking for a room."

"But it's storming!"

He smiled. "I am not afraid of a little rain."

At that moment, the footman stepped into view. I thought he showed surprise at finding Elyssa in conversation with this midnight visitor, but he managed an impassive tone as he said, "My lord will see you now."

Elyssa assumed her haughtiest pose and coolest voice. "Have a room prepared for our guest. Marco Ross. He will be spending the night with us."

"Yes, my lady. This way, please."

Under the servant's watchful eye, Elyssa offered Marco Ross a brief, uninterested nod, then turned toward the stairwell. She had too much pride to peer over her shoulder to watch saunter him down the hall, so naturally her echoes could not do so, either.

I scarcely noticed. I was puzzling over a piece of information that she might have inadvertently let fall. She had told the footman to prepare a room for "our guest," but surely if the man had a title, she would have called him "my lord"? Was it possible that he wasn't a high noble—wasn't even a low noble—came from the merchant category or even the working class?

I couldn't believe it to be true. Clearly, Elyssa had some history with the man, and it was obvious he was fascinated by her. But I couldn't imagine that she could ever be romantically interested in someone who was not every bit her equal in rank and wealth.

Particularly if she had a chance to marry someone like Jordan instead.

Elyssa was habitually a late riser, but the following morning she was up practically at dawn, joined by the bewildered and yawning echoes. She poked her head out the door to demand a passing servant girl to send her new maid up *right now*. I thought it was interesting that she didn't request Trima's presence. That had to mean that Trima already had some acquaintance with this handsome fellow and greatly disapproved of him.

We were all quickly attired in our plainest frocks and had our hair pulled back in the simplest style; the object appeared to be for us to get out the door as soon as possible. But Elyssa did not hurry down the main stairwell the minute the maid left. Instead, she stood for a moment just outside her door, listening to the sounds of the household, then headed the opposite way, toward the back stairs that were generally only used by the servants.

Moving with the imperfect stealth that is the best that four people can manage, we exited the house through one of the rear doors and headed straight for the garden. Last night's storm had left the air brisk and damp, but the morning sun seemed determined to bake the air to its accustomed summer temperature. Elyssa hurried down the winding path to a gazebo at the far edge of the garden. It was painted a bright, cheerful white, but was so covered with climbing roses that it seemed to be a small enchanted cottage of green vines and red blossoms. The roses were so thick along the trellised walls that, from five yards away, you could not see if anyone was already within.

We stepped inside and found that, yes, someone was before us.

The slender, dark-haired man turned to greet us as Elyssa offered a light, false laugh. "Oh! You're up early! I hadn't expected—"

He crossed the small space in three steps and captured her hands. "You *did* expect," he said, his voice low and rough. "You knew I would be here waiting."

As if she could not bear the intensity in his eyes, she turned her head sideways and down. "I thought perhaps you would," she said softly.

"Your father thinks I set out at sunrise," he said with a flash of humor. "I even rode off this morning—in case anyone was watching—went two miles down the road, and left my horse tied up by some trees before creeping back here. I hope no one steals the beast before I get back."

"That would be dreadful," she agreed. "And all my fault!"

He freed one hand so he could lift her chin. All of us tilted our heads at the phantom touch. "Such a loss! How will you make it up to me?"

Now her voice was sad. "Marco—"

He flattened his hand against her cheek. "I don't ask much payment," he said. "A kiss would do."

She didn't answer, unless her steady, yearning regard was an answer. Marco bent down and pressed his lips to hers—chastely enough, at first. Then he suddenly shifted his hands and wrapped his arms about her waist, drawing her so close I heard her slight cry of pleasure or pain. I felt certain that, if I had been in the arms of his echo, I would be struggling to breathe.

The kiss lasted a long, tense moment, then Elyssa gasped and broke free. "I mustn't—you can't—it's too dangerous," she said.

He stood motionless, his hands clenched at his sides, his face stormy; he looked like he was exerting all his will not to sweep her back into his arms. Elyssa half turned away from him, her hands against her cheeks. My own skin was cool against my palms.

"Then maybe it's best if I just leave," he ground out.

"No—stay—just a while. Just to talk for a bit," she said, a little desperately. "Tell me—what you've been doing—and what you'll be doing next. And things like that."

He held his coiled pose another moment, then exhaled on a sharp, short breath. "Very well. We can sit here on this bench and pretend to be mere acquaintances, and I will see if I can come up with a few tales to amuse you."

She turned back to him with a painful smile. "I'd like that."

We all pressed toward the bench, but Elyssa made a sound of deep annoyance. "Echoes—out! There's a bench right outside. Go sit."

She dropped her control over us so abruptly that for a moment I swayed on my feet, seeking my balance; I saw the copies on either side of me similarly lose their footing. As soon as we had adjusted, we pivoted smartly and filed out the opening of the gazebo. There was a stone bench practically backed up to the rose-covered trellis, and we wordlessly took our seats.

The view before us was pleasant but unremarkable, showing a few branching pathways of the well-tended garden, lined with sprays of lavender and blooming hedges, and overseen by a bronze statue of some grim, disapproving forebear. More interesting to me was the fact that, from our position, I could overhear every word spoken inside the gazebo.

"So you still don't like having echoes," Marco said, sounding amused.

"I can't abide them," she said. "If there was some way to dispense with them altogether without shocking everyone I know, they would be gone by now."

"They could meet with some unfortunate accident."

She laughed. "Believe me, I've thought about it! Shoving them all off some bridge in Camarria. Or hiring someone to kidnap them and hold them for ransom before—most regrettably, of course—slitting their throats."

"An excellent notion," he said. "And then, think of the additional benefits to you! Everyone would feel so sorry for you that they would treat you with exceptional kindness."

"That's actually what stops me," she said. "I hate being pitied."

"Well, if you ever change your mind," he replied, "let me know."

"You think you know someone I could trust to carry out the job and never betray me?"

There was a moment's silence. By the whisper of sensation across my skin, I could tell Marco had picked up Elyssa's hand and kissed it. "I would do it myself if it would make you happy."

There was another long moment of silence. "I will keep that in mind," she said.

He laughed, but there was a dangerous edge to it. "You're supposed to say that you would do anything to make *me* happy."

She laughed in response. "Oh, I know better than to make such a rash promise!" she exclaimed. Her voice changed, became tentative, a little sweeter. "Though I do wish— I hope you *are* happy, Marco? What have you been doing these past three years?"

"Happy enough," he said, the verbal equivalent of a shrug in his voice. "Plotting revolution, mostly."

She sighed. "From what I can tell, the high nobles of the western provinces cannot agree on what action to take, if any. My father shares very little with me, so I'm not even sure *what* is being plotted."

"It's all very disorganized," Marco agreed. "Five years ago, all the talk in Alberta and Orenza and Empara was about secession or outright civil war. Then Harold made some commercial deals that placated all the lords, so the talk died away. The common people didn't benefit much from the new deals, but that's the way it always goes. Then Harold reneged on an agreement with Orenza, and suddenly the governor started talking war again."

"Do you think it will come to that?"

Marco made a sound of uncertainty. "Hard to say. What I really think is that the western provinces need to do *something* to prove to the king that they are serious in their bid for independence. Maybe they start an uprising. Or maybe they grab the king's attention with a single, shocking act of violence."

"What kind of violence?"

"An assassination."

"Of the *king*?"

"More likely, one of his sons."

"Marco!"

My hands felt suddenly warm and tight; I thought he had grabbed hers in a reassuring hold. "It sounds dreadful, I know. But think about it! One man dead so that the whole kingdom escapes war. It would be worth the price, don't you think?"

"I don't know. If I was the king and someone murdered my son, I'd be *more* likely to go to war, not less."

"That's because you think with your heart. A king must think with his head, making cold calculations of value and cost. He will say, 'Ah, these rebels are willing to shed blood at the highest levels. How many more lives can I save by giving in to their demands?' But, I admit, it is drastic."

"Would it be Jordan who is sacrificed?"

"I thought you didn't care for him."

"I don't! But it is very peculiar to think that someone you know, someone you've *danced with*, someone you might *marry*, is about to be murdered."

"It would probably be Cormac," Marco answered. "He's the crown prince. His death would be impossible to overlook."

"And are there any plans to—to carry out the act?"

Now Marco expelled his breath on a long, angry sigh. "I thought there were, but suddenly Orenza is backing off again."

"Why? What's happened?"

"The governor has told the king that he will keep Orenza in check and promote peace throughout the western provinces if Cormac marries the governor's daughter."

"Marries— Oh, that explains it!"

"Explains what?"

"When Jordan was here, I asked about Cormac's wedding plans, because for *years* everyone thought he would marry Vivienne of Thelleron. But Jordan said there was no announcement in the offing. *That's* why! Harold will risk the anger of Thelleron to keep peace with Orenza."

Marco made a scoffing sound. "Thelleron will never rebel. Not even if the prince ruptures his engagement. It is a smart move, if you're Harold. Marry Cormac to Orenza, marry Jordan to Alberta. Harold himself is already married to a woman from Empara. He could hope to generate goodwill for generations."

Elyssa took a deep breath. "So you think it's settled? You think that's what will happen? Marriages—and peace?"

Another indeterminate sound from Marco. "Maybe. Hard to tell. I think it will go one way or another. Weddings and peace—or assassination and war."

Elyssa was silent a moment. "It feels strange," she said at last, "knowing that I might play such a big part. I'm not sure I like it."

I thought he kissed her hand again. "No one I know is more qualified to play such a part with grace."

"But that girl from Orenza—the governor's daughter. *She* has an even bigger part, I suppose," said Elyssa.

"Do you know her?"

"I don't think I've ever met her. Orenza is a little provincial for my tastes, and she's never been to Camarria anytime I was there. She has three echoes, though, I know that. And her name is—is—Marguerite. I can't believe I remembered it."

"You'll remember it well enough if she gets engaged to Cormac."

"It's all very exciting," she answered. "And a little unnerving."

"A lot of changes are about to come our way," Marco agreed. "It will take bold souls to withstand them all—and to capitalize on the opportunities."

"You should do well, then. You're the boldest man I know."

"And you, Elyssa?" he said, dropping his voice to a caress. "Are you bold enough reap the harvest of revolution?"

Her voice huffed out in a sound that was half a laugh, half a gasp. I thought maybe he had placed his hands on her waist, drawing her closer. I felt invisible fingers on my own body, digging in just below my ribs. "I think I can match you," she said a little breathlessly.

After that, they did not speak for a long time. I was glad that the man had no echoes, glad that Elyssa had released the three of us, so that I did not know exactly what transpired between them for the next twenty minutes. As it was, I felt strange, unwelcome pressures on my mouth, my hips, my body, as their embrace intensified. Then suddenly all sense of contact ceased as Elyssa gasped and jumped to her feet with such urgency that the other echoes and I did the same thing. My breath came short and fast, and I put my hands to my cheeks, though neither of the echoes copied me. We were still only partly connected to Elyssa—but there was no way to mistake her passion and unease.

"No—I can't—not here and now, at all events," she said in a ragged voice.

I thought I heard Marco come to his feet. "Should I apologize, or should I promise to keep trying to earn your love?" he asked, his own voice uneven, though he tried to infuse it with sarcasm. "We've been at this brink many times before, and it's always ended this way."

A small susurrating sound; maybe she kissed him. "Someday it will end differently, but for now we both have our parts to play, and neither of us can afford a distraction."

His laugh sounded bitter. "If you think you are just a distraction—"

"I think your heart lies with the revolution, not with me."

"I think the revolution might deliver my heart to you," he countered.

"What do you mean by that?"

"I'm a merchant's son. No high noblewoman would ever consider me a candidate for her hand. But if I serve well in an action against the crown, I could end up with wealth and property of my own. Everything changes if we win this war. The stakes are more personal for me than you realize."

She was silent a long moment, seeming to ponder his words. "If that's the truth—"

"It is."

There was second long silence, but this time I thought it passed in another kiss. Finally she whispered, "Then I am ready for the revolution to begin."

CHAPTER SEVEN

E lyssa spent the next two weeks alternately moping around the house, lashing out at the servants for the slightest infraction, and displaying an almost feverish gaiety anytime she had occasion to join some social event. Lord Roland happened to be at one of those dinner parties, and he spent the first hour staring at her woefully across the room. She never once looked in his direction, but laughed and flirted so determinedly with every other man in the room that I saw him abruptly spin on his heel and stalk out. I assumed he left the house, since he didn't make another appearance that night.

In her own household, perhaps only her father remained unaffected by her moods. Her aunt Hodia developed the habit of leaving the breakfast room before Elyssa came down in the mornings, and calling for dinner in her room whenever there weren't other guests at the table. The servants went to great lengths to avoid interacting with Elyssa, except for Trima, who told her flatly that she would give her notice if her mistress didn't start treating her with more courtesy.

"You wouldn't leave me after all these years," Elyssa scoffed.

"Maybe not," Trima said, jerking a comb through the black curls with such force that Elyssa actually yelped. "But I might accidentally fry your hair with a curling tong or sew one sleeve of your gown too short. You watch how you speak to me."

That made Elyssa laugh with genuine amusement for the first time in ten days, but after that she did speak civilly, at least to Trima.

When, at the end of that second week, her father called her into his study for a private conversation, I wondered if he was about to deliver a stern reprimand of his own. But Lord Bentam was so wrapped up in his own concerns it was highly possible he hadn't even noticed Elyssa's temper.

"Don't bother to sit," he said as the four of us filed in through the door. "But I thought you'd want to know the news."

"What is it?"

He waved a heavy cream envelope in front of his face with such satisfaction it might have been perfumed with his favorite scent in the whole kingdom. "It appears that Prince Cormac is making a tour of the western provinces and he intends to make a stop in Alberta. While he is here, he has asked if he can stay at our house. Naturally I have told him yes."

My first thought was concern for the crown prince, who might be riding toward his death, if assassination was still being plotted. I thought Elyssa might be having the same thoughts, though plainly she couldn't say so without revealing her secret meeting with Marco. She leaned casually against the wall, crossing her arms, and her echoes copied her.

"Brave prince!" she said lightly. "All this talk of revolution, and yet he still feels safe sleeping overnight in manors throughout the western provinces."

Bentam grunted. "He would hardly come to grief under some lord's roof. It would be too obvious who had done him in! Harold's not above having a high noble executed for treason right there in the public square if he thought anyone had tried to harm one of his children. No, Cormac's safe enough as long as everyone knows where he is."

"Then he's not so brave after all," Elyssa said. "When do you expect him?"

"In three weeks. Best start preparing now."

The excitement in the household upon learning of Prince Jordan's visit was nothing to the uproar that descended when we heard that Prince Cormac would be passing through. Even though he and his companions would only be staying one night, the housekeeper insisted that every room be aired and scrubbed, every servant be outfitted with new clothing, and the entire countryside scoured for the plumpest pigs, chickens, and cows to be slaughtered for the feast.

"Such a fuss for a man no one in the entire province even *likes*," Elyssa muttered one day over breakfast when the tea urn was unavailable because it was in the kitchen being polished.

Hodia frowned at her. "He honors us by staying in our household, so we honor him by offering him our best," she said.

While Elyssa pretended to be annoyed by all the turmoil, my guess was that she was secretly thrilled Cormac would be visiting. From listening to conversations she'd had with Trima, I'd gathered that she'd met the crown prince many times during visits to the royal city of Camarria.

"He doesn't like me any more than Jordan does, but he's always polite," she said as Trima styled her hair in elaborate braids and loops. The new maid was moving as quickly as she could between the three echoes, trying to produce a simplified version of Elyssa's grand coiffure. An outrider had arrived around noon to say the prince expected to be on our doorstep in time for dinner, so the frenzy in the household had reached a fever pitch.

"It's probably just your father he doesn't like," Trima said with a sniff. "He knows Lord Bentam is not a supporter of the crown."

Elyssa laughed. "No, it's me. I can always tell."

"I don't know how any man could dislike a girl as beautiful as you," Trima answered.

I was sitting close enough to see Elyssa lift her eyes to seek Trima's in the mirror. "Don't you?" she said quietly. Trima met her gaze steadily and didn't answer.

That was the only time I ever witnessed anything pass between them indicating Elyssa was a monster and they both knew it.

We dressed in delightful confections of gold silk and blond lace, colors that made Elyssa's dark hair look black as coal. Elyssa wore so many amethysts I gave up trying to count them. Her most striking piece of jewelry was a necklace that she often wore on grand occasions. It consisted of three interlocking gold rings, each about two inches in diameter; the somewhat triangular space where they intersected was set with a large, smooth amethyst of wine-dark purple. The echoes and I were more modestly bedecked with a few strategic jewels that people would only notice if they looked at us. Which, of course, they wouldn't.

As soon as every curl had been patted in place, every gem secured, Elyssa gathered the echoes to her and we made our way downstairs to await the prince's arrival. Her father and Hodia were already in the formal drawing room. Bentam only grunted in approval when he saw Elyssa, but Hodia came over to give her a close inspection.

"You look very good," she approved. "It helps that you're such a beautiful girl."

"Trima said much the same thing," Elyssa said in a mocking voice. "Where would I be without my good looks?"

"You mean if you had to rely on your sweet nature?" Hodia said dryly. "I can't think."

Elyssa actually laughed at that. She didn't bother to reply because just then one of the footmen came running in, excited and out of breath. "The prince has been spotted! He will be here in ten minutes!"

"Excellent," Hodia said. "We are ready."

The impression I formed of Cormac was not quite as favorable as the one I had formed of Jordan, though I had less time to observe him and he was certainly an appealing man. He was handsomer than his brother, with coloring almost as dramatic as Elyssa's and hair just as dark. He held himself with a regal self-assurance that was both attractive and a bit off-putting, as if he would always reserve some part of himself that you could never get to know. He smiled less easily than Jordan, and although he was perfectly polite to everyone, from the nobles to the servants, he didn't seem as kind as I'd decided Jordan was. Perhaps the weight of expectations sat heavily on him. He knew he was next in line to rule the Kingdom of the Seven Jewels, and he never for an instant forgot his responsibilities.

Like Jordan, he had three echoes. Like Jordan's, his echoes were so present and alert that you could almost believe they were as real, as human, as the prince. When one of them took my arm to lead me into dinner, his skin was so warm and his clasp was so firm that I had to sneak a quick sideways glance to make sure he wasn't Cormac. The instant I did so, I felt a spurt of panic. He was looking down at me with an intent expression, as if listening closely for an answer I was about to give to an important question he had asked. His eyes met mine and I could have believed he was taking in every passing emotion on my face.

Then I heard Elyssa laugh and make a light reply, though I was so flustered I didn't catch the words. Cormac was gazing at Elyssa, so his echo was gazing at me. Nothing more sinister than that. But I would need to be careful during this blessedly brief visit. It did not seem beyond the bounds of possibility that Cormac's echoes were as alive as I was, possibly even gathering information that they could, in some fashion, share with their original. I would have to behave like an ordinary echo, even if *they* didn't, to avoid rousing suspicions.

The meal was sumptuous and absolutely endless. When I wasn't concentrating on my food, I was surreptitiously glancing around the dining hall, trying to determine who was present. The room was about as full as it could be: The prince had brought a handful of his own friends, some with echoes and some without, and Lord Bentam had invited a few of the nearest neighbors. All of the local guests were high nobles, but only a couple of them had echoes. I was sure that was deliberate. Bentam wanted to make it very clear who the most important people in the room were.

While Cormac was the clear focus of attention, another man in the party kept drawing my eyes. He was big and burly, with hair and a beard in a brightly burnished shade of reddish gold. He drank heavily and laughed loudly and seemed to make the young woman next to him very uncomfortable. She was a neighbor's daughter, a shy girl named Velda, with a mousy appearance and no echoes. It seemed to me that, as the evening progressed, she edged her chair farther and farther from the laughing lord and studiously refrained from looking in his direction. As far as I could tell, the only person in the room who noticed her distress was her brother, who was seated too far away to intervene.

Well. Perhaps Elyssa noticed her. More than once, emulating Elyssa as she turned her head, I sent a quick glance in Velda's direction. Then a small, malicious smile curled my lips and was instantly banished.

The meal was halfway over when the lord made some intemperate gesture that sent his wineglass toppling to the table. Fortunately, he had drained it so completely that there was hardly a drop left to soil the tablecloth, but it landed against a crystal bowl with enough of a clatter that everyone finally looked his way.

"Jamison, behave yourself," Cormac said sternly.

"I haven't done anything wrong!" Jamison protested. "You behave *yourself.*"

Cormac made a half-bow in Lord Bentam's direction. "Forgive my brother," he said. "We have been on the road for weeks, and he tends to get rambunctious."

Bentam gestured for the footman to pour Jamison more wine and spoke in an indulgent voice. "As all young men do," he said. "I'm sure he'll be happy to be back in Camarria."

"I believe we all will be," said Cormac. "This is our final stop before we head home."

"So what else have you seen on your travels? Who have you visited?"

Cormac launched into a travelogue while I sat there puzzling over his words. *My brother,* he had said. Then this must be King Harold's illegitimate son, born before he married his first wife. The few times his name had been mentioned in my hearing, he had been spoken of with impatience and contempt. Apparently, his behavior tonight was typical. I wondered why Cormac allowed him to act so badly. I wondered what kindhearted Prince Jordan thought of his half brother's antics. I wondered if Elyssa had deliberately seated

Velda next to the bastard prince because she didn't like Velda. I doubted I would ever know the answer to any of my questions.

The meal finally ended, all the diners so replete that I found it difficult to believe they could rise to their feet and shuffle to the drawing room for more wine and some light musical entertainment. Yet they all did. There was a great deal of maneuvering and shifting as the various guests tried to position themselves to catch Cormac's eye, or at least find themselves in a group of congenial conversational partners. After about an hour of this, a moment came when Elyssa, Lord Bentam, and Prince Cormac—and the eight echoes they had between them—found themselves in a small circle with no one else near enough to overhear a quiet exchange of words.

"Excellent," said Cormac in a low voice. "I did not want to make a general announcement over dinner, but I am sponsoring a small get-together in Camarria in a couple of weeks, and I am hoping Lady Elyssa can attend."

"Of course she can," Bentam replied instantly.

I thought Cormac tried to hide his smile at the lord's eagerness. "I have been inviting young men and women from all over the kingdom and hope to entertain them for a month. It will be a small party—twelve women and as many men, if you count myself and my brother Jordan—and all of them from the noblest houses."

Even I could interpret that. *All of them with multiple echoes.*

Bentam was nodding sagely. "A very select group."

"Naturally, you would not want to describe such an event in front of Velda, if she is not to come," Elyssa said.

Cormac gave her an unreadable look. "Precisely," he said. "Besides, I am not sure she would be eager to visit the royal city after tonight."

Elyssa's surprise seemed sincere. "Why not? Who wouldn't want to go to Camarria?"

Cormac gestured toward the far end of the room, where Jamison stood sulking by himself. "Apparently my brother spoke to her offensively over the meal and *her* brother had words with him in the hallway," Cormac said. "I have told Jamison he must stay a day or two and make amends, but I fear Lady Velda would just as soon avoid any city where my brother happens to be in residence."

"Well, *I* am looking forward to the visit," Elyssa said. "Who else are you inviting? Will I know them?"

"Probably, or at least you will know *of* them," he replied. "They include the

triplets from Banchura, Dezmen and his sister Darrily from Pandrea, Marguerite Andolin of Orenza—"

"Marguerite," Elyssa interposed. "I have wanted to meet her for so long! Is this her first visit to Camarria?"

Cormac's expression did not change in the slightest; if he had plans to marry the noblewoman, you wouldn't have known it by his face. "I believe so, yes."

"Do you know her? What's she like?"

"I just came from Oberton, in fact. She impressed me as thoughtful and intelligent, but a little reserved. My guess is that she is not an easy woman to get to know."

Elyssa made a graceful gesture. "But then, all women know how to be mysterious. It is how we enthrall men!"

The prince laughed. "Yes, that has been my experience."

"So who else will be there?" Elyssa asked with apparent artlessness. "Vivienne of Thelleron?"

This time his self-control cracked, just for an instant. I thought I saw something on his face that might have been pain and might have been anger. "She has been invited," was all he said.

Elyssa put her hands together. "It sounds absolutely marvelous!" she said. "I will run up to my room tonight and begin packing!"

Cormac managed a smile. "I am glad you will be able to join us. I'm sure my brother is looking forward to renewing his acquaintance with you."

Elyssa was smiling widely. "I am sure it will be the event of the year."

Preparations for Elyssa's trip to the royal city consumed the manor house for the next week. If anyone—from the head housekeeper to the youngest footman—had any other occupation, it was invisible to me. Parades of tradesman trooped through the halls, bringing fabrics, shoes, jewels, headpieces, scarves, cosmetics, and anything else that Elyssa might need for her appearance at the royal court. An entire team of seamstresses took up temporary residence in a few of the guest bedrooms so they could work day and night on a new wardrobe.

Two days before we were due to set out for Camarria, a small tragedy struck. Trima was carrying a pile of freshly washed underthings up the back stairwell when her foot slipped and she fell backward, landing badly on one leg. One of the housemaids found her twenty minutes later, nearly unconscious from the pain, the filmy drawers and chemises settled over her body like drifts of lacy snow. The housekeeper and the head groom, old hands at dealing with injuries, set her leg and dosed her with concoctions meant to ease the pain, but they made it clear she would be bedbound or at least housebound for the foreseeable future.

"What—You mean she can't come with me to Camarria?" Elyssa demanded, when Hodia told her the news. "But I *need* her."

"The new maid, Gretta, will travel with you. And you can take one of the other serving girls if you think you need two. Though I myself have always made do with one maid, and I think you can manage for the duration of your visit."

"I don't like Gretta."

"Well, then you can dress yourself," Hodia said coldly.

Elyssa was so angry she stalked from the room, ran up the stairs, and flung herself into her suite, slamming the door the instant the last echo had crossed the threshold. As was her habit, she released us the second the door was shut, but apparently we didn't march to our own bedroom quickly enough, for she turned on us with an ungovernable fury. Slapping our faces, tearing at our hair, punching one of the echoes so hard in the stomach that she doubled over, gasping and retching. "Go—go—*go!*" Elyssa shrieked, pointing at our bedroom door, and we hurried as fast as we could, limping a little, holding our hands to our clawed cheeks. I was the last one through, and I shut the door between us. She was so busy pacing up and down in the sitting room that she didn't even seem to notice.

Elyssa was furious that Trima wouldn't be with us to cosset her and cajole her and care for her no matter how badly she behaved. *I* was terrified that Trima wouldn't be with us to keep Elyssa somewhat in check. Without the presence of the one person in the household who had the slightest influence over this wild and selfish girl, what might Elyssa do while we were in the royal palace?

Chapter Eight

We arrived in Camarria on a warm, close afternoon after a tedious but uneventful six-day journey. I had dreaded the prospect of being cooped up in a carriage with Elyssa for such a long time—but not, apparently, as much as *she* had dreaded the thought. About an hour into the first day of the trip, she ordered the coachman to pull into a small country innyard, and the four of us disembarked. Grooms came running over to offer assistance, but she ignored them, merely awaiting the arrival of the second, much less fancy coach that was carrying the maid and the bulk of our luggage.

As soon as the second vehicle stopped and Gretta stepped down, an inquiring look on her face, Elyssa pointed. "Echoes—go sit in the other coach." And she released us from our usual thrall.

Gretta, a practical and hardworking woman of middle age, couldn't hide her surprise. She had been with the household long enough to realize that Elyssa could set us free but not long enough to learn how much Elyssa hated us. "But, my lady," she said. "Can they be so far from you? Won't that feel odd?"

"It will feel wonderful," Elyssa replied. Without another word, she climbed back into the lead carriage and pulled the door tightly shut.

Gretta glanced doubtfully at the three of us, clearly not sure if we were now her responsibility, and if we were, how she should manage us. But our instincts were still to emulate Elyssa, so the three of us needed no instructions from her to climb into the second coach and take our seats. The maid climbed in beside us, still wearing that uncertain expression, and soon we were in motion.

I couldn't tell if our presence made Gretta uncomfortable or curious. Several times during the next hour, I saw her gaze sweep through the interior of the vehicle as she glanced at the echoes one by one. Once or twice I saw her open her mouth, then close it again and shake her head, but finally she couldn't resist the urge to speak.

"Everyone says that echoes can't utter a word," she remarked. "So if *I* talk to *you*, is it better or worse than talking to myself? Don't suppose it matters because I don't suppose I can stop myself."

Indeed, for the rest of the trip, she kept up a random series of observations about the weather, the quality of the roads, and the attractions of the countryside we were passing through. She was entranced by the endless fields of lavender that lined the route through most of our first two days of travel, marveling at their soft, misty color and their sharp, sweet scent.

"That's where your father gets all his money, you know," she said. "Owns so many lavender farms he could make a sachet for every woman in Alberta and still have bushels left over. I suppose you'll inherit all this land once he's dead." She glanced at the echoes sitting expressionlessly on the facing bench, and she grimaced. "Well, I don't suppose you *echoes* will inherit," she corrected herself. "But you know what I mean."

At moments like this, I amused myself by wondering how she would react if I cast off my vacant expression, straightened on my seat, and offered an observation in reply. My guess was that she would shriek in terror and fling herself from the coach, scrabbling to get away. She would most assuredly betray me to Elyssa.

So of course I never said a word. Because Elyssa could never know.

It was a relief to all of us to arrive in the royal city. Gretta practically hung out the left-hand window, gaping at the sights, so I felt like I could lean over just enough to peer out the right-hand window and get a glimpse of marvels. I knew that Elyssa had been there before, so I must have as well, but I had no memories of the wide, clean streets and varied storefronts and soaring buildings that were ten and twelve stories high.

"I see a bridge—Oh, and there's another one!" Gretta exclaimed. Over the past six days she had gotten in the habit of talking to us in the careless, familiar way she might speak to a cat or a baby. "They say there are so many bridges in Camarria even Harold can't count them all, and most of them don't lead anywhere at all. Just for show! Can you imagine?"

From my vantage point, I had spotted a few bridges as well, built of every material from weathered wood to smooth marble. But I was more interested in the people. They were everywhere! On foot, on horseback, in carriages, stepping out of shop doors, poking their heads out of high windows to call to friends below. Did all of them lead free, independent lives? What could that possibly be like?

I could have spent an entire day driving through the city streets and admiring the views, but soon enough we arrived at the palace, an enormous structure of terra-cotta brick, green tile roof, and black wooden accents. The instant the vehicles came to a halt, I felt a powerful jerk across my entire body as Elyssa bound us to her again and all semblance of volition was lost. The other two echoes and I turned in concert toward the door, causing Gretta to yelp and lean back as we scrambled to exit our coach exactly when Elyssa exited hers.

Servants were already clustered around the vehicles, waiting to help us alight. I managed one quick look around the courtyard, a huge open space crammed with people and noisy with activity. Then a large, majestic, confident woman strode up to Elyssa and said, "Welcome to Camarria. I am Lourdes, the housekeeper, and I will have you shown to your room."

Nothing about the palace accommodations pleased Elyssa. "I can't believe this!" she exclaimed the minute the footman left us alone in our quarters. "They've just given me one large room with all these beds, and I have to hear the echoes breathing all night. And the walls are an ugly color, don't you think? That shade of blue makes my skin look gray."

"Well, I don't suppose anyone but me will see you standing here against those walls, so it doesn't matter," Gretta said.

"It matters because it bothers *me*," Elyssa said in a dangerous voice. "And when I feel ugly, I act ugly."

After that, Gretta prudently kept her mouth shut.

I was just as dismayed as Elyssa that the four of us would be sleeping in four beds lined up in a row, though the echoes' accommodations were much plainer than the plush, well-padded bed that was clearly designed for a noble guest. I had grown accustomed to my stolen moments of mobility and freedom whenever Elyssa banished us to our own room. It would be difficult to lie still and pretend to be sleeping when Elyssa was so near and so watchful. I was going to have to be very careful while we stayed in the royal city.

But even that couldn't entirely dampen my excitement at being here.

I wondered how soon we would be seeing Prince Jordan again.

The answer was: that very night.

It turned out that Elyssa was one of the first five guests to arrive, and they were all invited to partake of what was described as "a casual meal in the small dining hall." Still, five nobles, two princes, and twenty echoes made for a large and unwieldy group, and it took some orchestrating to get us seated at various tables so we could partake of a meal.

Once everyone was in place, I furtively looked around to see who I could identify. There was the self-possessed Prince Cormac, offering his reserved smile impartially to everyone in the room. There was the Pandrean lord named Dezmen who had visited Lord Bentam's house in the spring. There was an overwhelming and undifferentiated sea of young women in matching blue dresses—a group that I finally figured out consisted of triplets and their nine echoes. While I heard others toss out their names in conversation—Leonora, Lavinia, and Letitia—I couldn't imagine that anyone tried very hard to tell them apart.

And there was Prince Jordan.

I was most fortunately placed at a table behind Elyssa and a little to one side; if I looked over her shoulder, I could see Jordan sitting across from her. Here in this opulent setting, in contrast to his intense brother and the distinctive Pandrean lord, Jordan looked more like an ordinary man. Handsome but not intimidating, friendly but not fawning, regal but not unapproachable. The ideal man, really.

Elyssa did not appear to share my sentiment. She was perfectly charming to Jordan, but in a way that seemed insincere, even rote. She was seated too far from Cormac to engage in anything but light banter across the table, so she devoted most of her attention to Dezmen, asking him questions about his journey and his family. I hardly knew him well enough to be certain, of course, but I thought his politeness to her was just as insincere as hers to Jordan.

But Jordan, I thought, was genuinely enjoying his interactions with two of the triplets in blue. Listening very hard, I was able to catch scraps of their conversation, enough to determine that the young women were from the far eastern province of Banchura and that they seemed to be frequent visitors to the palace. At any rate, they talked to Jordan with the ease of long friendship, exchanging stories about absent friends and fond memories of past encounters. The sisters seemed to find each other endlessly amusing, for they were constantly breaking into laughter. Jordan smiled more often than he laughed, but he smiled most of the night.

I wondered if he would rather marry one of those sunny-tempered girls than the sullen, scheming Elyssa. Did he have a preference for one of the sisters over the other? From my vantage point, it was hard to tell, though I watched as closely as I could. It was depressing to think that he might already be in love with someone but forced to marry another woman simply because his father insisted. Well, actually, it was depressing to think he might be in love. Though I couldn't imagine why I would care.

As the meal drew to a close, Cormac came to his feet and everyone followed suit. "I'm afraid I don't have much entertainment planned for you early arrivals," he said. "There will be dinners and excursions and balls once the party is complete, but that won't be for another day or two. We can go sit in one of the drawing rooms and talk some more, but I won't be offended if anyone just wants to go back up to their rooms and recover from travel."

"That sounds good," one of the triplets said, smothering a yawn. "We left at sunrise this morning and I swear I feel every mile we traveled as if I had walked it myself."

"I'd play cards if you have nothing better to do," Dezmen said.

"Elyssa?" Cormac said courteously, glancing her way. "If you're brave enough to be the only woman in a room full of men, we'd be happy to have you join us."

Her laugh was even more false than it had been most of the evening. "And damage my reputation on my very first night?" she exclaimed with manufactured horror. "Even I am not quite so rebellious as that. No, I'll be happy to seek an early bed so I am rested for tomorrow."

Cormac offered a general bow to the ladies as they converged on the door. "Then we'll see you in the morning."

It appeared that all the women had rooms on the same floor, so we climbed the stairs together in a great froth of blue accented by Elyssa's black and gold. After gaily spoken goodnights, all the nobles disappeared into their own rooms, followed by their echoes, and I heard three doors shut down the hall.

Elyssa closed her door with a certain amount of care, perhaps to keep from slamming it, then stood before it in an attitude of silent, hysterical shrieking. Her bunched fists hovered around her cheeks; her face was contorted into an expression of fury, her eyes closed and her full lips drawn back from her clenched teeth. I could only guess that she was furious to be sent back to her room with no entertainment and no occupation, unable to pursue her primary goal of snaring a prince. Something she wasn't even sure she wanted to do in the first place.

She had released us the second we stepped in from the hall, before she had even shut the door, but I at least was frozen in place. I didn't want to make the slightest move that might catch her angry attention.

But it scarcely mattered. Elyssa shook her head, opened her eyes, and spun around as if to fling herself toward her bed. Except her echoes stood directly in her path.

"And *you!*" she hissed, the words just as venomous as if she had screamed them aloud. "Trapped in here all night with *you!* With all of *you!*"

And she slapped the nearest echo so hard she sent the creature tumbling to the floor. Whirling around, Elyssa began throwing wild punches at the other echo, then at me, the blows raining down, erratic and hard. None of us made a sound, though it took all my self-control to keep from gasping in pain. When a heavy hit sent the second echo careening to the floor, Elyssa turned on me with a deliberate shove and pushed me right down beside the other two. Then she came to an abrupt stop and caught her breath on a shuddering sob. "What am I going to *do?*" she cried.

In three steps, she had thrown herself onto her bed and began weeping into the pillow. She kicked her legs and punched the mattress and wailed aloud, trying to muffle the sounds by stuffing the edge of the comforter into her mouth. Sometimes it seemed like she was saying words—*I don't know* or *It's not fair*—and sometimes it seemed like she was just howling out uncontainable rage. The tantrum lasted a good half hour, and that whole time, the other echoes and I kept our safe positions on the floor.

I didn't know how long Elyssa could have kept up that display of wretchedness and self-pity, but finally there was a knock and the door opened a couple of inches. "My lady?" Gretta called inside. "The other maids said all the ladies were making an early night of it, but you haven't rung for me. Do you need me to get you ready for bed?"

When Elyssa made no answer, Gretta pushed the door open wider. "My lady? Do you— Now, what's all this?"

Obviously, she had looked in just enough to see the echoes curled up on the floor. I heard her gasp, felt her hesitate and wish she could run back down the hall, but then heard her take a deep breath as she realized she was the one who had to deal with the situation. She came inside, shut the door firmly, and stepped around the three of us as if we weren't even there.

Elyssa had stopped her wailing and now lay facedown on the bed, panting, still dressed in her finery and jewels. Gretta approached slowly, making a slight tsking sound, and looking like she wished she could be anywhere else in the kingdom.

"Well. Let's get that dress off of you so you can wash your face and get comfortable," Gretta said. "Can you stand up? There you go—I'll help you. That's good. I'll be as fast as I can."

In an admirably short period of time, Gretta had Elyssa undressed, in a nightshirt, and under the covers. I could sense Elyssa's exhaustion, and I guessed it wouldn't be too long before she was asleep. Gretta had drawn the same conclusion.

"I'll undress the echoes, then I'll put out the lights and you can just fall right to sleep, doesn't that sound good?" the maid asked, turning toward the three of us. By this time we had pushed ourselves to sitting positions, though we hadn't had the courage to stand.

Elyssa stirred restlessly on the bed. "No," she said. Then, more forcefully, *"No."*

Gretta looked back at her uncertainly. "No what?"

"I don't *want* them. In here. With me."

Gretta looked helplessly between Elyssa and us. "But they— Where else can they go?"

"Put them in the hall."

"My lady, you can't—they can't—someone will see them there—"

"Nobody will. Everyone's in *bed,*" she said with much bitterness.

"But one of the footmen, checking the house to make sure all is secure—or a maid, in the morning, coming around to build the fires—"

"I don't care what some stupid housemaid thinks!"

"One of the young noblewomen staying down the hall, then. If one of them gets up in the middle of the night for some reason! What would she think? What would she say—to Prince Cormac, perhaps?"

Elyssa started crying again, a quieter, more helpless kind of weeping this time. "I don't care," she said. "I don't want them here with me! Staring at me at all night!"

"My lady, I don't think—"

"*Put* them somewhere!"

Gretta glanced around the room, looking for inspiration. Although it was not nearly as large as Elyssa's suite back home, it was spacious enough and nicely laid out. The four beds were against one wall; a cluster of chairs and tables made a small sitting nook in front of the windows; and two armoires, a vanity, and a large chest of drawers created a dressing room of sorts.

"Well, let's see. I could move some furniture around and make a little corral, maybe. Would that work?" Gretta asked, seeming to think out loud. "I could turn these two tables on their sides—and then open one of the armoire doors and drape a sheet over the back of a chair...and if we just put blankets on the floor for the echoes to lie on— Why, I don't think you'd see them at all!"

Sniffling and swiping at the tears on her cheeks, Elyssa flounced over in bed, staring at the wall. "Do it! Do something! I can't stand to look at them."

Gretta shook her head and gave the echoes a sharp look. "I don't suppose you could help me organize your pallets for the night, could you?" she asked, sighing when none of us responded. "No, and what the maid will think in the morning I have no idea. I'll just have to be the first one here so I can put everything back in place. No sleeping in for you, Gretta, that's for sure!"

She was efficient, though, and created a cramped, private sleeping area for the echoes within a surprisingly short period of time. With equal efficiency, she undressed us for the night and herded us onto our pallets on the floor.

"I don't suppose you'll be very comfortable—but I don't suppose echoes even feel discomfort, do they? Still, I'll see if I can think of something better in the morning."

Within a few moments, she was gone, leaving the room in darkness and near-perfect silence. The only sound I could hear was

Elyssa's ragged breathing, which quickly smoothed out enough to convince me she was sleeping. Beside me, the echoes were so quiet that I had to suspend my own breathing to be sure they were still alive.

It was a perilous start to our adventure in the royal palace, and I couldn't help but wonder what other disasters might accrue. No Hodia, no Trima, no one to make sure Elyssa behaved, and Elyssa unhappy already for so many reasons. It did not seem like a good time to be wholly at her mercy.

CHAPTER NINE

Our second day in Camarria was much better than the first. Although Elyssa was sulky and silent when she first woke, she responded positively to Gretta's good cheer when the maid arrived in the morning to get us ready for the day. Gretta worked with her usual quick competence, and it wasn't long before the four of us were out the door, heading downstairs in search of breakfast.

The first few hours unfolded much as the previous day had, with various nobles gathering in dining halls and sitting rooms to talk and flirt and pass the time. The only difference was that, every few hours, we were joined by some new arrival and his or her attendant echoes. By dinnertime, I thought there were perhaps twenty originals in the room and somewhere around fifty echoes. We had been moved to a very large dining hall, where the servants engaged in an elaborate choreography of serving all the echoes at the exact same time they served the nobles. It was an impressive feat.

As Cormac announced that he would lead the group to yet another sitting room for the evening, Elyssa was approached by a footman dressed in palace livery.

"My lady," he said. "The queen has requested a moment of your time."

By the way my own mouth smiled in response, I could tell Elyssa was delighted at the invitation. "The queen," she repeated, loudly enough to be overhead by one of the Banchura triplets sitting nearby. "Let's not keep her waiting."

We followed the servant through the wide, airy halls of the palace. I knew absolutely nothing about art or decor, but I admired the paintings, the statuary, the woven tapestries gracing the walls and alcoves as we passed. There was simply so much wealth and artistry on display.

We found the queen in a small sitting room filled with delicate chairs and small settees and spindly tables that looked like they wouldn't hold anything weightier than a teacup. She did not glance up when we first arrived, but kept her attention on a piece of linen she was embroidering within a square wooden frame. About half of it appeared to be already completed, showing a scene of cottages and roses along a country lane. Behind her in three identical seats, her echoes held identical poses, their fingers just as deftly plying their needles. But whereas the queen was working in red thread on a half-finished image, the needles of the echoes were empty and their scraps of linen completely blank.

The footman had spoken Elyssa's name, backed out of the room, and closed the door before Queen Tabitha finally knotted her thread and looked up. Elyssa, not known for her patience, stood all that time in respectful silence. They took a moment to survey each other.

The queen had deep auburn hair, braided back with wide green ribbon in a style meant to look both casual and elegant. Her features were clear-cut and fine, her skin a pale rose, but her expression was so cold and composed that I wouldn't have called her pretty. The word was too soft for her. There didn't appear to be anything soft about this woman at all.

"Elyssa," she said, inclining her head.

Elyssa dropped into a curtsey so low that her chin almost touched her knees. We had practiced this many times, or I thought I might have fallen over. "Majesty," she said as we all rose with creditable grace.

Tabitha gestured. "Sit down for a few moments and we'll talk."

Elyssa sank into the nearest of those delicate chairs, and the echoes and I arranged ourselves behind her. We moved in absolute synchronization; this was obviously not the time for Elyssa to be unconventional. "It is good to see you again," Elyssa said.

"How was your journey? My husband insists that some goodly portion of the annual taxes go to the upkeep of the Charamon Road, so I hope you found it in excellent repair."

"Yes, the whole trip was trouble-free."

"Harold will be glad to hear it."

There was a short silence as the queen measured out a length of green thread, cut it, and expertly inserted it through the eye of the needle. Then she spoke again, "I understand that my stepson visited you a couple of weeks ago, and there was some unpleasantness."

Elyssa's voice was amused. "Cormac? Unpleasant? I don't think I've ever seen that side of him."

"No, Cormac knows very well how to appear most agreeable," Tabitha replied, slightly stressing the word *appear*. "I was referring to Jamison. Harold's oldest son."

"Oh! Yes, there was a minor incident. A local woman joined us for dinner one night, and apparently Jamison made her uncomfortable. I'm sure he didn't mean to."

Tabitha carefully wound the thread around the needle to create some kind of complicated knot. "I'm sure he did. Jamison has long indulged himself in behaviors that his father and his brothers regrettably make no effort to check." She glanced up, briefly meeting Elyssa's eyes. Her own eyes were a deep and complex green. Her voice was expressionless when she added, "We love him anyway, of course."

"Of course," Elyssa repeated. "I believe Cormac insisted he stay behind a day or two to make reparations. So his behavior did not go entirely unremarked."

"I am glad to hear it," the queen said. "And Jordan? I understand he, too, has recently made his way to Alberta."

"Yes, we have been honored to have been shown so much favor by the royal family."

Tabitha set a few more stitches. "Of course, you realize there is talk of much greater honor that might be shown your father's house."

"I hear rumors," Elyssa said, her voice as calm as Tabitha's. "Naturally, I am ready to do anything that would benefit the kingdom. But I have no particular expectations."

"I have found that, when it comes to Harold's sons, it is wise to have no expectations," Tabitha agreed. "They are stubborn and contrary when it suits them, and Harold indulges them entirely too much. Cormac can generally be made to see reason, but none of them is biddable. Not like my daughter, who has always allowed herself to be guided by me."

"Princess Annery is lucky to have always had you in her life," Elyssa said. "My own mother died when I was young, and I have always felt that loss."

"The princes, sadly, were not interested in any mothering I could provide, and they rarely seek my advice," Tabitha said. "But in this instance, my husband and I are in agreement. It would be in the best interests of the kingdom if Camarria were to align with Alberta. You are the most eligible young woman in Alberta. The circumstances seem unambiguous—and yet neither my husband nor Jordan is ready to make any kind of formal overture. Thus you are left in a somewhat unenviable position."

Elyssa's breath was coming a little faster. Tabitha's words made it clear that a royal wedding could be in Elyssa's future—and yet it wasn't. Not yet. But her voice was still composed as she answered, "What do you mean?"

Tabitha snipped off the green thread and began searching through the embroidery silks for another color, settling on gold. "You must behave like a woman affianced to a prince without actually having that prince paying court to you," she said. "You must dance and flirt like any unattached woman, and yet never raise the hopes of the other men in your circle. In other words, your behavior must be irreproachable—fit for a princess—even though you have no guarantee of ever holding that position. I admit, it can be difficult."

I thought Elyssa's smile was a little strained, but her voice was perfectly smooth. "But, Majesty, I flatter myself that my behavior has always been beyond reproach."

Tabitha knotted her new piece of thread and inserted the needle through the back of the linen. "I am certain that is the case,"

90

she replied, in a voice that made it clear she was anything but certain. "But as a woman who grew up in the countryside—much like you, in fact—I know how easy it is to spend a few unsupervised hours on the grounds of a large rural manor surrounded by fields and gardens. In a city such as Camarria, you will find that there is always someone watching you. Your most innocent excursion—or your most clandestine one—is sure to be witnessed by a maid or a shopkeeper or a low noble or a friend. All of them, you will find, are willing to carry tales if they believe there will be the smallest benefit to them to do so." Tabitha briefly raised her green eyes from her canvas to give Elyssa a single unreadable look. "Even if their only benefit is to see you suffer the slightest discomfort merely because they do not like you."

Every muscle in my own body was rigid with anger, so I knew Elyssa was seething. But when she answered, her voice was still light and unconcerned. "Your Majesty sounds as if you speak from bitter experience."

Tabitha did not seem offended. "I learned very quickly that Camarria is not Empara," she said. "I thought you might appreciate gaining the knowledge without having to undergo the lesson."

"Indeed," said Elyssa. "I treasure any advice Your Majesty can offer."

There was a soft knock, but Tabitha did not immediately bid the visitor to enter. "I realize you have been to Camarria many times, yet parts of it might still remain unfamiliar to you," she pursued. "It might be useful for you to know whom you might count on if you have questions about the city, so I thought you should meet Harold's head inquisitor. There is nothing that happens in the royal city that he does not instantly learn about. He has proved to be an invaluable resource to me."

"I understand," Elyssa said, in a tone that made it clear she did. Tabitha had essentially said, *You must behave with absolute circumspection, and if you don't, here is the man who will catch you in your misdeeds.* Even the insensate echoes had probably caught the queen's blunt implication.

"Good," said Tabitha, and then raised her voice to call, "Come in!"

The man who entered should have been wholly unremarkable. He was of medium height, stockily built, bald, and possessed no physical characteristics that would set him apart in a crowd. And yet something about his bearing was filled with such latent menace that had I been sitting somewhere by myself when he walked by, I would have recoiled in alarm. I thought it was no wonder that Elyssa's whole body corded with stress, though she managed to retain a serene expression, as did all her echoes. We gave him only the slightest nod of acknowledgment, as if he were a tradesman who was about to perform a useful service.

"Malachi, this is Lady Elyssa, the noblewoman from Alberta you have heard my husband and me talking about. We consider her quite precious and would like you to take special care to keep her safe while she is visiting. Elyssa, this is Malachi Burken, head inquisitor for Camarria. He has been in royal service for more than twenty years, and has done an exemplary job."

Malachi bowed, not quite as low as I would have expected, and trained his dark eyes on Elyssa. "I will guard her most assiduously, my queen." It was clearly a threat as much as a promise.

"I always appreciate extra attention," Elyssa drawled.

"Malachi is an Empara man," the queen went on with a touch of pride. "And wholly to be trusted."

"Thank you, Majesty," he said quietly. A moment longer his gaze held on Elyssa's face, and then he shifted his eyes to look at each of her echoes in turn. Who notices echoes? The head inquisitor of Camarria, apparently. But we were all copying Elyssa so exactly that he found nothing of interest in our faces, so he turned back to the queen. "Is there anything else you need from me?" he asked.

She waved a negligent hand. "I don't think so. Thank you for your prompt attention."

He bowed again and let himself out. The queen was sorting through her packets of embroidery thread again. "I believe we've covered everything I wanted to discuss with you," she said in a tone that was obviously a dismissal. "I do hope you enjoy the rest of your time in Camarria."

Elyssa rose gracefully to her feet and repeated her deep curtsey. "Majesty," she said, "it becomes more interesting by the hour."

Elyssa's interview with the queen had left her so ruffled that I was apprehensive about how she might treat her echoes once we returned to her room. Fortunately, a few of the prince's guests had gathered in one of the many sitting rooms, and someone called out to Elyssa as we stalked by. She had to force a smile as she stepped into the room, but during the next hour, between the wine and the banter, her mood lifted and her natural confidence returned.

I felt my dread flood back as we finally made our way upstairs to our bedroom, but I found that Gretta had been busy all day on Elyssa's behalf.

She greeted us as soon as we crossed the threshold, saying, "Look, my lady, I've procured a nice folding screen to create a sort of dividing wall. I told the housekeeper that you can't sleep without something to block out every breeze and bit of light, and she had this sent right up. I've arranged it around the echoes' beds to make a tiny little room for them."

Elyssa approached the screen to run her hand down its smooth panels. It was made of dark wood, very plain, with no embossing or decoration, and it was quite sizable. Each of its five panels was probably six feet high and four feet wide. You could practically hide an army of echoes behind it.

"Thank you, Gretta," she said, smiling in satisfaction. I wondered if it was the first time I had ever heard her thank someone and mean it. "That was clever of you. Now I won't have to look at them at all."

I wondered how astonished Elyssa would be to realize that we—or at least I—would be as relieved as she was to have the screen between us.

The bedtime ritual was accomplished with much less drama this night, but both Elyssa and I lay awake for a long time after

Gretta left. I didn't know what Elyssa was thinking, but I was wishing I was back in my old room where I had freedom to move around under cover of darkness. I was wondering if, after a month of close supervision in the city, I would lose some of my independence of thought and motion. I was thinking that, if Elyssa really did marry Jordan, I would be in the palace for the rest of my life, always under the watchful eye of the unnerving royal inquisitor.

I was thinking, while the echoes slept dreamlessly on either side of me, how much simpler life might be if I was as untroubled, insensate, and unaware as they were.

Over breakfast the following morning, the noblewomen from Banchura insisted that Cormac arrange for an expedition to Amanda Plaza. "Whenever we are in Camarria, we *always* go to Amanda Plaza to toss coins at the feet of the goddess, and we are going today," one of them said firmly. "So you can provide carriages and come with us, or you can stay behind, but we are going."

"I'm sorry, but my father requires my attendance this morning," Cormac said. "But my brother would be happy to accompany you, wouldn't you, Jordan?"

"Yes, and anyone else who would like to come," Jordan replied. "Dez? Nigel? Cali? We'd best go now, before the day gets too hot."

It turned out that everyone *except* Cormac wanted to join the expedition, which meant a whole caravan of coaches had to be pressed into service. I could tell Elyssa wasn't thrilled with the outing, but she wasn't about to be left behind, so she joined all the others in the courtyard as the vehicles lumbered up.

I assumed it was due to some deft maneuvering on her part that we ended up in the carriage along with Jordan, two other nobles, and all of their combined echoes. The vehicle was enormous, holding room for twenty people on several rows of benches and being pulled by a team of six strong horses. There were so many people who had to climb in and find seats that, in the chaos, originals and echoes were mixed together on the benches. One of Jordan's echoes was placed between Dezmen's two, and a noblewoman was seated in the very back row.

I was sitting next to Jordan.

I had not been so close to him since that night at Lord Bentam's manor when he and Elyssa had had that midnight conversation in the library. I had met his eyes, and he had *noticed* me, and I had not been able to forget him ever since.

But surely *he* had forgotten *me*. It was indisputably best for my continued health and safety that I never catch his attention again.

I had been very careful since we arrived at the palace two days ago. I had never looked at him directly—had never looked at *anyone* directly, keeping always that placid, blank expression on my face, focusing my eyes on some point in the middle distance. He had not had many conversations with Elyssa since we had arrived, and those few encounters had been light and brief; I had never caught his eyes scanning the faces of her echoes, wondering if he had imagined that one quick exchange of glances. He had forgotten. He must have.

But now I was seated next to him, the folds of my dress drifting against the fabric of his breeches, my shoulder so close to his I could feel the heat coming off his body. I wondered what it would be like to lay my hand over his, to feel that warmth seep into my bones and muscles.

Impossible to do it. Disastrous to speculate. I sat there, my motions completely in thrall to Elyssa's for this very public outing, but felt my breath grow more uneven, my heart beat faster. I wanted to clench my hands to keep myself from reaching out to him, but I could not make my fingers respond to my will.

Beside me, Jordan seemed completely oblivious to my presence. "The carriage ride is only about ten minutes," he said. "It might have been faster and easier to walk the whole group over."

"Walk! You must be joking," said the woman in the back of the carriage. "I find it fatiguing to walk from my bedroom all the way down to the breakfast room!"

Elyssa answered, her voice light and careless but the buried barb surely intentional. "But fortunately for you, Cali, there is so much food waiting at the end of the forced march that you are able to restore yourself after the journey," she said.

If Cali was offended, she hid it with a laugh. "I do love the dining rooms at the palace," she said. "Your cooks are magnificent, Jordan."

"No credit to me," he said amiably. "But I will tell the queen you approve of her staff."

Jordan was right—the trip was short, and I could not be certain if I was sharply relieved or deeply disappointed when the carriage jostled to a halt a few minutes later. Once we had disembarked from our fleet of vehicles, we did have a bit of a walk ahead of us, since it turned out that the roads leading to the plaza were too narrow to admit the great lumbering carriages. Cali grumbled good-naturedly about the exercise, but Jordan said, "Here, let me ease your way," and offered her his arm. That made her smile and stop complaining. Elyssa stared straight ahead of her and fought to keep her lips from twisting in a bitter smile.

As for myself, I could only be grateful that I was still mimicking Elyssa so closely, otherwise I would have given myself away by gaping in delight at Amanda Plaza. As it was, I cut my eyes back and forth to take in as many details as I could. Amanda Plaza was a wide open space floored with intricate brickwork and dotted with things to admire—two different groupings of statues, a large ornamental tree, and a high arching bridge made of a warm golden stone. The place was thronged with people pausing before the statues or racing across the bridge or merely passing through on their way to some urgent appointment. It was clear that the square was a meeting place for friends, a destination for visitors, and a touchstone for the residents of Camarria, all at once. My guess was that people could be found here night and day, making this place the beating heart of the royal city.

Our carriage had been the last to arrive and the others in our party were already making their way across the brickwork to the central feature of the plaza—three bronze statues that I assumed were meant to represent the triple goddess who watched over the kingdom. The statues stood with their backs toward each other, their faces turned out to the crowd. One held her arms above her head, one stretched her hands out to either side, and one reached down toward the ground. Lord Bentam's house had never been an overly religious one, so I knew nothing about the goddess or what her poses signified. Still, there was something about the stillness and serenity of each face that I found appealing.

The blond women from Banchura began laughing and calling out to each other. "Take the poses! Remember? Pretend to be the goddess!" And with a swirl of blue fabric they spun around till their shoulders touched and their bodies made a small triangle behind their backs. One lifted her arms over her head and cried, "I'm joy!" Another spread her hands out as if seeking to find balance and answered, "I'm justice." The third one lowered her palms toward the brick and said, "Then I guess I'm mercy. Why don't I ever get to be joy?" Around them, like endless replicas of the goddess's incarnations, their echoes reached and stretched and bent over the herringboned brick.

"Very nice," Jordan said. "Should we also toss coins at your feet? Will you grant our prayers if we do?"

The triplet pretending to be joy started laughing and couldn't hold the pose any longer, and instantly the whole tableau dissolved. "You can certainly throw money at me!" she exclaimed. "I'd be happy to go shopping as soon as we leave the plaza."

"Money collected by the goddess is supposed to go to the temple so it can be distributed to the poor," Jordan said, mock stern.

"Well, that's not nearly as much fun," one of the other sisters said. "But I still wouldn't mind going shopping."

Cali stepped up and ran a reverential hand along the smooth metal arm of the goddess who represented mercy. "I didn't bring any coins," she said regretfully. "It didn't occur to me."

Jordan gestured to a footman who had accompanied us to the plaza. The man jogged forward and handed over a leather satchel that made a muted jingle. "I brought enough for everyone," Jordan said.

Cali turned to smile at him. "It doesn't seem right that you should have to fund our supplications to the goddess."

He returned the smile. "The palace supports the temple in many ways. A few coins won't materially affect our arrangement."

She held her hand out and the echoes beside her did the same. Jordan dropped disks into every open palm. "Then I will happily turn your largesse into my prayers."

She and her echoes turned back toward the statues and I saw them all close their eyes and curl their hands into fists. Cali's lips moved slightly, so perhaps she was indeed speaking a prayer. Then they all opened their eyes and, in perfect unison, lobbed their coins between two of the statues. That was when I realized that there was a small grate at the center of the three statues, set into the brickwork at their heels. The coins all dropped smoothly past the grill.

"It will be interesting to see if that wish comes true," Cali observed. She paused a moment longer, bringing her fingertips briefly to her forehead, down to her heart, and back up to her lips, before stepping away to make room for the next petitioner.

Jordan, meanwhile, was parceling out money to everyone in the group who came forward, which included all of the women and some of the men. Then, one by one, the nobles tossed their coins into the grate before touching their foreheads, their chests, and their mouths. I thought that must be some ritualistic act that honored the three incarnations of the goddess, but no one bothered to explain it.

Elyssa hung back, still displeased with this whole outing, but once he had doled out coins to everyone else, Jordan turned to her with his pleasant smile. "Elyssa?" he asked. "Surely you have some favor you would sue for?"

Her own smile was edged. "So many I could hardly narrow it down to one," she said, but she extended her hand anyway. The echoes and I were right beside her. "But I'm happy to throw down money for your beggars."

I held my breath as Jordan dropped a coin in my palm. I felt the barest brush of his fingertips against my skin, and my face flushed with sudden heat. Surely the color wouldn't be noticeable in the bright sunlight.

"Gold," Elyssa said. "That's generous."

"As I said," Jordan replied, his voice determinedly polite, "the palace supports the temple with many types of funding."

She didn't answer, just turned away from him and stepped closer to the statues. The echoes and I spread out just enough so that the four of us made a ring around the three goddesses. Elyssa brought her clenched hand to her heart and stared meditatively at the nearest statue.

What was she wishing for? I wondered. Did she hope that the marriage with Jordan would go forward—or that it would somehow be averted? Did she pray that some assassin would slip into the city and take Cormac's life, igniting revolution? Or did she wish for something simpler, more primal, such as happiness or security?

I briefly closed my eyes and squeezed the coin as tightly as my bones would allow. I was practically face-to-face with the goddess offering mercy, and I knew what I would ask for if she would listen to the pleas of an echo. *Freedom,* I thought, and opened my eyes.

Elyssa gracefully swung her hand forward and pitched her coin into the grate. She had grown a little careless as the afternoon progressed and her mood deteriorated, so she had not maintained perfect control of her echoes, and our movements were not entirely synchronized with hers. However, the difference was so slight I couldn't imagine that anyone would notice. She also didn't bother indulging in the ritual benediction afterward, but simply turned back to rejoin the group. I thought that, if I was going to hope the goddess would grant my prayer, I should show her more honor than that. I had just enough willpower to lift my arm and touch my fingertips to my forehead, my heart, and my lips. Then I turned to follow Elyssa as she strolled across the plaza behind the others, heading toward that impressive golden bridge.

And found Jordan staring at me with so much astonishment he might have just seen one of the statues come to life.

I was so careful for the next few hours. So careful. I focused so intently on Elyssa that even though she was keeping us on a loose rein, I mimicked her precisely enough that I might have been her reflection in a mirror. I followed her up the gentle grade of that long, golden bridge and rested my elbows on the stone balustrade, just as she did, and looked out at the lively view below. I paraded behind her as we returned to ground level and toured the rest of the plaza, only half listening to the explanations that Jordan provided to the first-time visitors. *These statues represent Queen Amanda and her echoes. She was married to King Edwin, the first man to unite the warring provinces and create the Kingdom of the Seven Jewels... This tree was a gift from the country of Ferrenlea... We don't need to linger here by this wall, it is where traitors are executed...*

It seemed to me that he made an effort to stick close to Elyssa while he showed us around, for he was never more than a few steps away and often had a hand out to help her over some slight obstacle. I could tell she was pleased by the attention, for her attitude improved and her smile grew more genuine, but I wasn't fooled. His gaze kept slipping from her face to skim over the faces of her echoes, hoping to catch them in an unguarded moment of alertness. It was a comfort to me that he would glance from one of us to the next to the next, clearly unable to distinguish us from each other.

And I gave him no clues. My expression was absolutely blank, even when my lips curved in Elyssa's smile. I made sure that I was always in the middle of our small group, that there was always a body between us, so he couldn't accidentally brush up against me and feel my involuntary start of pleasure. I made sure I was not distinctive in any way.

He would think he was imagining things again. As he had imagined them that night in Lord Bentam's house. He certainly wouldn't address the matter with Elyssa, would he? *Is it possible that one of your echoes misbehaves? I'm certain that I saw her act in an independent manner, almost as if she had volition of her own.*

Surely, he wouldn't say such a thing, even if he had noticed.

Surely, even if he had noticed, he didn't care.

CHAPTER TEN

That night as the noble guests gathered before the meal, there was a new arrival who drew all eyes. She was a striking woman with dark skin and dark hair, wearing a dress of antique lace and displaying opals on her hands, at her throat, and braided into her midnight hair. I heard someone mention that she was Dezmen's sister Darrily. She seemed to be well-known at court because both Jordan and Cormac stood by her for some time, talking with the ease of old friends. Jordan even took her arm to escort her into dinner.

Elyssa stared after them with swelling indignation. I couldn't entirely blame her. After Jordan had been so solicitous all afternoon, she had put extra effort into dressing for the meal, with the expectation that his attentions would continue. But Darrily's arrival had made him forget Elyssa completely.

Or, well, forget *me*. But it would be even worse if she knew why he had followed her so closely all afternoon before abandoning her now.

"Well, *he* doesn't look like a man who's ready to announce an engagement any time soon," murmured a man's voice at her ear. Elyssa spun around in a small fury.

But as soon as she recognized the speaker, most of her anger fled. "Deryk," she said, leaning forward so he could kiss her on the cheek. Her echoes bent forward as well, each of us receiving our own chaste salutations. The man and his three echoes all had a rakish, piratical air, enhanced by a deep scar running through one eyebrow. However, none of his shadows matched his air of malice and mischief, instead appearing to be as placid and dull as an echo should.

"Did you just arrive?" Elyssa asked. "I looked for you earlier but you were nowhere in sight."

"We pulled up not more than an hour ago," he answered, tucking her hand under his arm and strolling toward the short hallway that led to the dining room. They moved slowly, absorbed in their private conversation, and all the others preceded them down the corridor. My own hand rested on an echo's arm, but it was like clinging to a piece of driftwood, hollow and light. Deryk went on, "I thought I would be the last to arrive, and be met with much acclaim, but I see that Darrily has upstaged me. As always, Camarria fawns over Pandrea."

"So much so that I can't imagine why the king hasn't announced Jordan's marriage to Darrily any time these past ten years," Elyssa said, her voice spiteful.

"Oh, no! Pandrea is so loyal there is no need to offer crowns and husbands," Deryk said. "It is only rebellious little provinces like *yours* that need to be placated and wooed." He squeezed her hand playfully.

She gave a short laugh. "There hasn't been much wooing since I've been here. Just politeness and rumors. Oh! And that *bitch!*" Elyssa didn't trouble to name the queen, but it was clear Deryk knew who she meant. "She summoned me into a private room merely to tell me I had to behave like a royal fiancée, or I'd never win a proposal."

Deryk crowed with laughter. "Did you claw her eyes out?"

"No, but I wanted to."

"So I haven't had a chance to look over all the guests," said Deryk. "Which one is the girl from Orenza—the one who might marry Cormac?"

"She's not here yet, but they seem to expect her tomorrow. Oh, and you know who *else* isn't here yet?"

"I haven't a clue."

"Vivienne."

Deryk came to a standstill just outside the door to the dining hall. He appeared delighted. "No—she's actually been *invited*? So she can watch Cormac pay court to another woman? I thought *I* was coldhearted, but even I wouldn't have been so cruel!"

"Maybe she won't come. She'll send some excuse."

"That would make her even more pathetic," Deryk said callously. "She'll be here. You'll see."

"Well, I don't care about any of the rest of them," Elyssa said as they finally stepped across the threshold into the crowded dining hall. "As long as *you're* here."

"Oh, yes, do flirt with me outrageously for the whole visit," Deryk said. "That will make Jordan so jealous he'll propose within a week."

She laughed, seemingly genuinely amused. "And if he doesn't, at least I will have been greatly entertained."

But she was neither amused nor entertained as the evening wore on and Jordan essentially ignored her. It wasn't just the Pandrean noblewoman who diverted his attention; he engaged in a long conversation with Cali that started over the dinner table and continued when the group withdrew to a parlor after the meal. I had only the vaguest memories of meeting Cali in the past, but I was certain she was from Alberta because she was decked out in the signature amethyst jewelry. She was not especially tall, not exactly slender, and not particularly beautiful; compared to Elyssa's dramatic looks, her curly brown hair and rosy cheeks seemed ordinary, though her expression was open and cheerful. She only had two echoes, but even they had pleasant looks on their faces.

Late in the evening, Deryk brought Elyssa a glass of wine and whispered, "Bad enough to be supplanted by a Pandrean, but by a girl from your own province? My dear, how can you bear the insult?"

His echoes had brought glasses for the three of us as well, and I was dismayed when Elyssa consumed the contents with a few swallows. It was not the first measure of wine she'd downed that night, and I was beginning to feel my head swim. "If you were a true friend to me, you'd flirt with Cali yourself," she informed him, but she was clearly furious.

"Ugh. Virginal and kind. Not my type at *all*."

"Type doesn't matter in this particular game," she replied.

"It does if no one is forcing you to pick your partner."

She gave him one hard, level look. "Tonight would not be the time for you to tell me I'm *not* the woman you'd choose if you could choose from the whole kingdom."

He smiled down at her. "We'd kill each other inside a week."

"I might kill you right now," she agreed.

"But for that week I'd like you better than anyone else in the room."

"Well, that's something," she said. "Maybe we would make it a month instead."

He turned slightly, as if to block her view of the room; his echoes made a wall around us and I couldn't see over their shoulders. "Don't look that way, but the Banchura girls are whispering together," he said. "I think they disapprove of us having a private conversation."

"Oh, that's right, I'm supposed to behave like a royal princess, even though I might never be one," Elyssa said. "I think I need another glass of wine."

Deryk followed her as she wended her way through the room, and both of them paused from time to time to speak to some of the other guests. I could tell she was still raging inside, but she managed to keep her voice light and her expression amiable as she bantered with nobles from Thelleron and Sammerly. She did drink two more glasses of wine, but fortunately no one bothered to hand goblets to any of her echoes.

Neither Cormac nor Jordan spoke to her for the rest of the evening.

Darrily was the first one to make her excuses and head off to bed, claiming that she was tired from a full day of travel. Elyssa lingered just long enough to not seem to be in a rush, and then she, too, said graceful goodbyes and led the three of us toward the door. The Banchura triplets were right behind us, so engrossed in their own conversation that they didn't seem to notice that we were only a few feet ahead of them as we climbed the stairs and headed down the wide corridors.

104

We stepped inside our room and Elyssa closed the door as carefully as if she was setting down a sleeping baby. She turned the lock and kept her fingers on the key, as if checking to make certain that she had done it right. Then she stood there motionless for the longest moment of my life. Filled with silent dread, I stood with the other echoes in a semicircle around her, trying to avoid making any movement that would catch her attention. I could see the tension stringing across her shoulders, noted the way her ribs moved as she took in short, sharp breaths on a rising wave of rage.

When, without warning, she whirled around, I held fast, my gaze fixed on the floor. But one of the other echoes took a reflexive step backward. That was all it took. With a choked cry of fury, Elyssa dove for her, closing her hands around the echo's throat and kicking hard at her legs. The echo's face contracted with fear and pain, but she made no sound and did not seem to have the volition to try to free herself. The lack of response just made Elyssa angrier, and she shook the creature so hard her head wobbled and bobbed and her eyes became wide and glassy.

She's going to strangle the echo—kill it! I thought wildly. Could I stop her? Did I have the physical strength to break Elyssa's grip? Would I be able to withstand her fury once it was turned on me?

I had taken a step toward them when, with a choked cry of loathing, Elyssa opened her hands and flung the echo away from her. The creature fell to the floor, boneless, gasping for air, but otherwise still silent, still offering no resistance. Something about the echo's empty expression reignited Elyssa's rage, and she rushed forward in a feral leap, landing on the echo's ankle with both feet. The echo spasmed and lay still.

For a moment, Elyssa stood there panting, staring down at the twisted body. I wondered if, even in her haze of fury, she realized she had just made a grave mistake. The poor creature might be too injured to leave the room for the next few days; surely someone would notice her absence, even if Prince Jordan no longer felt curious about Elyssa's echoes. How would she explain this away?

But she seemed, at the moment, so filled with wild emotion that she still couldn't think clearly. "Get out of my sight," she grunted, then lunged across the room and bolted out the door. I imagined her standing in the hallway, still breathing heavily, her hands balled into fists and her face showing every nuance of her enflamed temper. If one of the other noblewomen were to step out of her doorway and see Elyssa in such a state...

I couldn't think about it. I couldn't do anything about it, one way or the other. I merely bent over the injured echo, pulled her up, and led her as gently as possible across the floor toward our small alcove behind the screen. I lifted her onto the bed, stripped off her dress and pulled a nightgown over her head; then, as best I could, I cleaned and bound her ankle. She lay there the whole time, simply staring.

The third echo had followed silently behind me. I helped that one into a nightshirt as well, then changed my own clothes. All three of us were lying quietly on our beds, staring up at the ceiling, when we finally heard the door open again. I tensed with alarm, listening for any sound that would indicate Elyssa's mood. Any sound that would indicate she was still furious enough to come for one of us again.

But there was only the noise of the lock reengaging, and Elyssa's footsteps crossing the floor. She didn't bother to peer behind the screen to see what had become of the injured echo, or even to check that any of us were still in the room. She just continued on to the bed and dropped heavily on the mattress and began a low, steady weeping.

I lay there and listened for hours.

In the morning, Gretta tended to the four of us in absolute silence. She had come by once during the night, but Elyssa had refused to let her in. So the maid must have been somewhat apprehensive the following day when Elyssa unlocked the door upon her knock. I supposed that one look at Elyssa's face had warned Gretta to keep her thoughts to herself because she merely said, "My lady," and set about the task of getting Elyssa dressed for breakfast.

After about an hour of quiet activity, Elyssa said in a casual voice, "The echoes will need some help." That could hardly be a surprise, since Gretta commonly dressed us, but it was no doubt a warning that things might be a little different this morning.

Gretta came around the edge of the screen a bit hesitantly. I wasn't looking directly at her face, but even so, I could see the way she blanched at the sight of the injured echo lying on the bed, her face and arms bruised, her wrapped ankle swollen under my hasty bandage. Gretta's mouth opened as if she would demand what had happened, but snapped shut when she realized what the only possible answer could be.

She tended to the hurt echo first, cleaning her face thoroughly and changing the bandage with competence. I also saw her discreetly press her hands over the echo's stomach and hips—checking for hidden damage, I thought. But nothing made the echo wince in pain, so it seemed her only real injuries were the visible ones. A small comfort.

Then Gretta dressed the other echo and me in dark blue gowns edged with white piping, and pulled our hair back in a simple style. Once she was done with us, we lingered behind the screen while Gretta went out to tell Elyssa we were ready.

"I only dressed two of them," she added. "The third one must have twisted her ankle. She won't be walking anywhere for some time. I'll go down to the kitchen and bring up some food for her, shall I?"

"Yes, excellent," Elyssa said coolly. She didn't even bother trying to construct an explanation for what had happened. "Make sure the purple gowns are ready for tonight. All the other guests are supposed to have arrived by dinnertime, and it will be the first formal meal the prince is hosting."

"Certainly, my lady. Anything else?"

"No." And on the word, she tightened that mental leash, and the other ambulatory echo and I jumped to our feet, bound once again to Elyssa's will. We came around the screen with our heads bowed and our eyes down, as if we were truly mindless shadows.

As we headed to the breakfast parlor, I found myself wondering what the other noble guests would say to Elyssa when they realized one of her echoes was missing. Who would notice first? Sharp-eyed, sharp-tongued Deryk? Self-assured Cali, an Alberta woman who wouldn't have to think hard to remember how many echoes Elyssa was *supposed* to have?

Prince Jordan, who had been paying more attention to her echoes than she knew?

I fantasized that he would demand to know what had happened, race to her room to check on the echo's well-being, then proclaim, "You have no right to the ancient tradition of echoes. I hereby free them from your control." *Could* he do such a thing? Could the king? Could anyone?

It didn't matter if he could because he didn't notice. No one noticed. The nobles circled through the breakfast room and filled their plates and sat by their favorites and talked and laughed and filled their plates again, and not one of them knew or cared that Elyssa was missing an echo or that she had done her best to practically murder that echo in a fit of rage. There was no succor. There were no champions. The echoes might as well not even exist.

It was my darkest day since I had achieved any kind of sustained sentience. It was also the first day in all these months that I moved and functioned almost completely as an echo—blind, listless, wholly without volition. If Prince Jordan had looked my way even once this day, he would have been convinced that he had never seen a spark of awareness on my face.

My attention did sharpen again that night, but only slightly, as the nobles gathered to socialize ahead of the evening meal. Elyssa made a point of introducing herself to the newest arrival, Lady Marguerite of Orenza, and I was roused to enough curiosity to make an effort to look her over. If she thought she was here to win Prince Cormac's favor, she didn't show it; her face was composed, even guarded, and her manner was reserved. She was pretty enough, with fair hair and a heart-shaped countenance, but she didn't have Elyssa's striking looks or Darrily's arresting style. I let my attention stray to her echoes; I was always curious to see if one of them might look back at me with a consciousness like my own. But it was hard to even see their faces through the fine mesh veils they all wore. Some kind of fashion trend from the city of Oberton, I supposed. At any rate, none of them looked like a kindred spirit.

The meal was long, the post-dinner gathering even longer, and I had to think Elyssa was exhausted by the end of the endless day. I certainly was, and the echo beside me would have drooped to the floor by now if it hadn't been slaved to Elyssa's inflexible will. None of us had slept much the night before. I could only hope Elyssa was too tired to throw another tantrum when we retired to our room.

My attention was caught by only one of the night's conversations, and that came very late in the evening, as Elyssa was making her way toward the door to go upstairs. Deryk fell in step beside her, ready to gossip.

"Have you heard?" he said. "No one knows where Jamison is."

She seemed only mildly interested. "Where is he supposed to be?"

"Well, last time anyone saw him, he was in *your* father's house, apparently insulting one of the noble neighbors."

That actually made her laugh. "Oh, that's right. Poor little Velda. She shrank away whenever the bastard prince so much as looked in her direction."

"And apparently he offended the girl's brother so much that Cormac ordered him to stay behind a day and make amends," Deryk went on with relish.

"I did hear something to that effect." Elyssa yawned. "Not that I would ever expect one of Jamison's apologies to be sincere."

"Or to take very long," Deryk added. "He should have been back a week ago, but no one's heard from him. The king is worried, they say, and so is Cormac."

Elyssa laughed again. "If there's anyone in the entire kingdom who can take care of himself, it's Jamison. He's probably found some other pretty girl to seduce—one who *doesn't* have a righteous brother to interfere."

Deryk snorted. "My thought exactly. Still, it's delicious to think someone might have slipped a knife between his ribs."

Elyssa gave him a warning look. "Careful who you say that to. He's abominable, but his father and his brothers are fond of him. And with the royal inquisitor lurking about, this is not the place to make jokes about murder."

Deryk smirked. "Only to you, dear one, because your heart is just as evil as my own."

She smiled back. "Surely not. You flatter me."

They had reached the stairwell, and he bowed as if he had escorted her as far as he planned to go. "I flatter myself," he corrected her. "You outdo us all."

CHAPTER ELEVEN

Now that the full complement of guests had arrived at the palace, Prince Cormac apparently had events planned daily. At least that was the case the next day, when we learned there would be shopping in the morning and a formal dinner at night, followed by presentations to the king and queen. In the following weeks, there would be more daytime excursions, more evening activities such as card parties and balls. The men seemed most interested in the card games, the women in the balls.

Today's shopping trip involved the deployment of a dozen or more coaches and the splintering off of groups once we had arrived at our destination. It was a charming section of town, three or four blocks square, where quaint stone storefronts offered wares that varied from fabrics to jewels to shoes. Elyssa strolled along idly beside the Banchura triplets, but when they squealed over a selection of gloves displayed in a store window, and slipped inside to try them on, she continued walking along, alone except for her two echoes. I had already lost track of Jordan, and most of the women had disappeared inside jewelry stores the minute we arrived. It didn't seem impossible that Elyssa would wander so far off from the others that she would be left behind when they climbed back in the carriages to return to the palace. She didn't seem particularly interested in buying anything, or interested in this excursion at all. I thought she had only come along because she was determined not to be left out of anything. Marguerite had stayed behind, which intrigued all the other women, and Elyssa did not want to be the subject of gossip.

We came to a perfumier's place and she paused before the window, looking in at the displays of fantastically shaped and colored bottles. The air drifting out from the half-open door was full of tantalizing smells, some floral and delicate, some heavy and cloying, some elusive and strange. I sniffed the air appreciatively and wondered what scent I would choose if I could have my way.

There were light footsteps behind us and then a man's shape materialized beside Elyssa. Taken by surprise, she stiffened and drew back, drawing breath to call for help. But a second later she recognized him, and her emotion transmogrified from alarm to delight.

"Marco!" she exclaimed in a low voice. "I didn't know you were in Camarria!"

"Longer than you," he retorted. "I saw your carriage pull up the day you arrived."

"You should have sent me word."

"So far I don't have any spies set up in the royal palace, so I couldn't find a safe way to send you a message," he replied. "I have to assume that every communication that comes through the door is read by an inquisitor or two."

His words seemed to strike a memory, and she edged a few inches away. "Yes, and inquisitors are sneaking around outside the palace, too," she answered bitterly. "The queen made a point of telling me that I would be closely watched and I had best behave."

He sounded amused. "Really? Had you done anything to draw her censure?"

"No! I have been most demure. But because of my possible connection to Jordan, she says—"

"Oh, yes! Your royal romance! How is that progressing?"

She shrugged. "Some days he is attentive and some days he is not, and I think he would prefer any other bride to me. So some days I try to charm him and other days I ignore him. I don't think anyone is sure of what will happen next."

"Poor Elyssa," he said lightly.

"We all know why *I* am in Camarria," she said. "Why are *you* here?"

"Merely investigating possibilities," he said.

She frowned at the vague answer. "Planning for the revolution, I suppose."

He smiled. "It is not certain there will be a revolution."

She spoke slowly, trying to work it out. "I suppose there must be some nobles here in the province of Sammerly who dislike Harold and would be willing to join an uprising if there was one."

"That is not how they talk," he said. "They express concern that the king's attention is divided—that he puts so much effort into placating the western provinces that he does not have the attention to devote to concerns of the wider realm. In particular, they wish he would spend more time developing foreign trade with countries like Ferrenlea. Some are even willing to let the western provinces secede if it means the king would focus on building a stronger eastern kingdom."

From behind us came the sound of women talking together as they approached the perfumier's shop. Elyssa made a slight gesture, and she and Marco began strolling forward at a slow pace. Her echoes fell in place behind them.

"It makes no sense to me," she said. "Why *wouldn't* the king let the western provinces break away and rule themselves?"

Marco shrugged. "Many people believe a larger kingdom is a stronger kingdom—it brings in more tax dollars, which enables the crown to maintain a larger army and better roads. An enemy nation would think twice about invading a country the size of the Seven Jewels, but it might be willing to attack a country only half that big. And there are plenty of nobles in the western provinces who are against secession. Thus the king has allies as well as enemies in Alberta and elsewhere."

"And he thinks to buy more allies with strategic marriages," Elyssa said. They had come to a halt before a shop that advertised potions to ease any ailment. The scents drifting out through this doorway were even more varied and complex than the ones at the perfumier, but generally sharper and more bitter. If the draughts tasted the way they smelled, I thought it would be difficult to convince people to ingest them.

"The governor of Orenza—Lord Garvin—he would certainly give up plans for rebellion if he saw his daughter wed to Cormac," Marco agreed. He slanted her a sideways look. "I am not so sure about your father."

"No, my father likes to keep all his options open," she agreed, and her voice had an edge to it. "He would have me marry Jordan and enjoy all the advantages of that union while still plotting an uprising to bring down the palace and everyone inside it."

"Except you, of course."

Elyssa made a sound of uncertainty. "I don't think my father would worry overmuch about my safety if he thought he had a chance to overthrow the crown."

There was a short silence. I saw Marco's hands bunch into fists before he carefully relaxed them. "Well, *I* would worry about your safety," he said quietly. "It is intolerable enough to think of you married off to that insipid man, but to imagine you in danger on top of it? Unendurable."

My lips curved into a smile, mimicking Elyssa's genuine expression of pleasure. "Then I shall count on you to rescue me if the palace ever falls under siege," she said.

"I will make sure you are safe before any attack occurs."

We were so far from the others in our party that Elyssa seemed to feel it was safe to face Marco directly. "Do you really expect such an attack?" she asked bluntly.

"Like your father, I believe any option is worth considering," he answered. His voice held a burr of anger when he added, "You look shocked. Is it possible the prince has won you over? Or are you just so enamored of the idea of marrying into royalty that you would sacrifice the dreams of all your countrymen to attain your own high position?"

"Don't you dare accuse me of selfishness," she shot back. "I have tried to play the part my father has pushed me into. If I am shocked, it is because I am not used to seeing the people around me murdered. I admit I have an unkind heart, but not, so far, a bloody one."

He took her arm in a hard hold; I felt a ghostly grip against my own skin. "And if I *did* warn you that an assault was coming?" he demanded. "Would you warn the king or your princely lover?"

She shook off his hand, glancing around to see if anyone had witnessed this exchange. "He is not my lover," she hissed. "And I would tell no one. You insult me on both counts."

"It is just that you seem so at ease with royalty," he muttered. "It is hard to know what you truly want."

"What I truly want?" she said, and now her voice was mocking. "Are my only two choices violent rebellion or a loveless marriage? How could any woman pick between such attractive alternatives?"

"That's no answer."

She shrugged, glanced over her shoulder, and then turned to head back toward the center of the shopping district, where most of the other royal visitors were already congregating.

"What I want is some chance at a life that is not completely miserable, whether that is in Camarria as Jordan's wife or in Alberta with the rebel factions," she told him. "I do not plan to betray my father and his allies. But you cannot blame me if, no matter where I end up, I seek a little happiness. You can call that selfish, if you like. But you had better remember that if you expect my cooperation."

They walked on a few steps in silence. I guessed Marco was trying to parse the meaning behind her words. Had she just threatened to expose the rebel network if Marco or her father didn't take her wishes into account? My own hunch was that Elyssa couldn't have verbalized exactly what she wanted, whether it was the pomp of being a princess or the excitement of being a rebel. All she knew was that she was bitter, manipulated, and wretched now, and she wanted to be free and joyful.

The irony wasn't lost on me. Maybe her cruelty could, in some measure, be forgiven because it sprang from such a hopeless place. Or maybe she would have been cruel no matter what.

"You have to leave me now," Elyssa said in a completely changed voice. "People will see us together."

"All right—but—we have more to discuss," Marco said. "Can we meet again? Where and when?"

"It isn't safe."

"I suppose you don't want me walking up to the palace doors in search of you."

That made her laugh; they both knew he wouldn't take that risk, but she liked the idea that he might be so impetuous. "Tell me a place I would be likely to find you on some fine morning," she suggested. "If I happened to go out walking."

He thought a moment. "There is a botanical garden in the heart of the city. I

will endeavor to be there most mornings in case you want to look for me."

"I'll do what I can."

And with that bare, insufficient promise, she stepped away from him, decisively and without once looking back. I turned my head a few inches, just enough to see him staring after her, his eyes narrowed, his expression unsure. He desired her and he distrusted her, I thought. And she desired him but despaired of him. Both combinations seemed dangerously volatile.

We had not gone twenty paces when Lady Cali fell in step beside us. "And who was that attractive rogue?" she asked in a friendly way. She either didn't realize that Elyssa didn't like her, or she was too self-confident to care.

Elyssa offered a careless laugh. "Someone my father sent to check on my well-being," she said. "Do you think he's handsome? I believe he's some low noble's bastard son, so I've never paid him much attention, but I'd be happy to introduce you if you think you could weather the scandal."

Cali smiled. "Well, some scandals are worth the trouble," she said. "He might be one of them."

"I'll let him know you think so," Elyssa said. "So tell me! Did you buy anything? I never even stepped inside a store."

Cali happily displayed a few ribbons and gloves, and talk turned to shopping and the prospect of lunch. But I was interested to note that Elyssa wasn't entirely able to discipline her heart. Once the Banchura triplets had joined them to show off their own purchases, Elyssa glanced behind her, to the spot where she had left Marco standing alone. He was no longer anywhere to be seen. Elyssa did not allow herself to sigh. She merely turned back to admire a pair of embroidered slippers that Lady Letitia was showing off as if nothing else in the world was more important.

The evening was full of tension and excitement as the king and queen joined the visitors for dinner and held an audience afterward, where they spoke a few words with all of the guests who were newcomers to the palace. More frequent visitors—like Elyssa, Dezmen, and the women from Banchura—joined the others in the great, drafty throne room, but didn't take a turn being presented to the royal couple.

We hadn't been standing there very long when the triplets descended in a swirl of blue silk and endless echoes. "Elyssa!" one of them exclaimed. "I only just now noticed, but you're missing an echo! What happened?"

Elyssa shrugged. "The silly thing tripped and fell over a shoe that had been left in the middle of the room. Twisted her ankle and now she can't walk."

"She fell? But you didn't?" one of the other triplets said. "I've never heard of such a thing."

"No, I've seen *my* echoes fall when *I* was the one who tripped over something, even when there was absolutely nothing in their way," the third sister said. "But never the other way around."

"Perhaps my shadows are just clumsier than yours," Elyssa said. "I did speak sharply to my maid about allowing clutter in the room."

"But the poor thing! She must be miserable to be left alone! I think my echoes would be so desperate to be with me, they would come after me even if they had to crawl on their hands and knees."

"And poor *you*," one of the other women added. "Don't you miss her at your back? Do you find yourself turning around a hundred times a day, looking for her, just *aching* from her absence?"

There was a touch of derision in Elyssa's voice. "Aren't you the most romantic girls! Swooning over the magical bond between echoes and originals."

The third sister was frowning. "You mean you *don't* feel that way?"

"It's actually been something of a relief not to have three of them dragging behind me," Elyssa said. "I feel twenty pounds lighter."

All three of the triplets stared at her, struck dumb. Elyssa burst into laughter. "Of all the things I've ever said and done, *that's* the one that's shocked you?" she demanded.

Before any of them could answer, Deryk glided up to join the group, standing so close to Elyssa that I could feel his echo's breath against my cheek when he turned his head my way. "Elyssa's saying shocking things?" he said. "Someone fill me in."

Their conversation went on, somewhat strained, but I had stopped listening. I had spotted Prince Jordan and I found myself far more interested in him than anyone else in the room. He had been standing in casual conversation with Dezmen and Darrily, but I saw his eyes track someone across the room. In a moment, he excused himself and went to speak to the dark-haired woman who had caught his attention.

She was standing near the group that needed no introduction to the king and queen, but apart from the others, as if she had no friends in their midst. She was finely dressed and clearly noble, but there was something vulnerable about her wan complexion and tense shoulders. She looked like she wished she could be anywhere else in the entire kingdom. I couldn't remember Elyssa speaking to her during the past few days, and she had not been introduced to anyone in my hearing, so I wondered who she was and why nobody liked her.

Well, Jordan seemed to like her or, at any rate, to feel sympathy for her. He approached her with an easy smile and said something that made her face light with gratitude. She made a small, graceful gesture, and the two echoes behind her repeated the motion. I thought they looked as sad as she did.

But Jordan kept up the conversation, perhaps complimenting the color of her dress, or telling her an amusing story, trying to cajole her into a smile. He wasn't successful, but it seemed—from my view halfway across the room—that he made her feel a little less desolate.

Elyssa had taken a few steps back to begin whispering with Deryk, but I was still standing near enough to the Banchura women to overhear their conversation. One of them demanded, "Who's Jordan talking to?"

"I can't tell," said another one. "Is that— Goddess have mercy on my soul, it's Vivienne!"

"I didn't realize she was here! She must have arrived this afternoon."

"The poor, brave dear. And Cormac entirely ignoring her, of course."

"It's not his fault! If his father is going to make him marry Marguerite—"

"That doesn't mean he should act as if Vivienne is *invisible*."

"Well, I imagine this is hard on him, too. He's been in love with her for ages."

"But look at Jordan. Just smiling and talking and trying to ease her through the evening. Exactly what I'd expect of him."

One of the triplets produced an inelegant snort. "Since he doesn't want to talk to his *own* affianced bride."

Another one sighed. "Sweet goddess, if he really does marry Elyssa, I swear I will never come back to Camarria."

"Shhh! She's right behind you."

"Well, it's true. I don't care if she hears me."

"I'm going to go talk to Vivienne. She needs to know she still has friends among the high nobility."

"Yes, let's go talk with Vivienne." And just like that, the whole crowd of them swirled off to the other side of the room.

So that was the young woman who had been spurned so Harold could sew up an alliance between Orenza and the crown. I agreed with the triplets—it was brave of her to be here.

And I was moved, once again, by Jordan's casual kindness. I didn't dislike Cormac, what little I'd seen of him, but I thought Vivienne would really have reason to mourn if *Jordan* was the prince she had lost to the king's machinations. *He* was the finest man in the room tonight—perhaps in the entire kingdom.

What a terrible fate if he were forced to marry someone as awful as Elyssa.

The entertainment the prince had put together on the following day involved another caravan of carriages making slow progress around the city and stopping at several historic sites. The last place we visited was a temple that Cormac informed us was the oldest one in Camarria. To reach it, we had to exit from the carriages and cross a slim wooden bridge that spanned a brook that completely encircled the land where the temple stood. In fact, I realized, there were three bridges, painted three different colors—red, white, and black.

"Naturally, the colors correspond to the different manifestations of the goddess," Cormac was explaining to Lady Cali when I happened to be close enough to overhear. "Red for joy, white for mercy, black for justice. You see how the temple is made up of three circular buildings all joined together in the center? Each of the towers also represents one of the goddess's incarnations, and there is a different door for each one. You choose your door by your state of mind on any particular day."

"Oh, let's go in the entrance for joy," Cali said.

"Indeed, let's do that," purred Elyssa. "Since we're all so happy."

I couldn't help wondering which door she would have selected if she'd been left to her own devices. She was rarely joyful, she was never merciful, and I had never seen any indication that she believed in justice. Then again, I had never seen much indication that she believed in the goddess, either.

Nonetheless, she followed Cormac and Cali and all their echoes through the red door and into the cool interior, which was lit only by a couple dozen votive candles and what sunlight could make it through a few narrow windows. I couldn't say that I immediately felt joyful, but I did find a sense of peace stealing over me as we made our way slowly around the quiet space. At the front of the room was a low dais holding a single statue—the goddess with her arms lifted toward the high ceiling—and it was before this statue that all the candles had been placed. Facing the dais and filling the central portion of the room were a series of wooden pews, though there were hardly any people sitting in them on this warm afternoon. I spotted two women dressed in formal robes moving from pew to pew as if offering counsel to the people who were visiting. Priestesses, perhaps? They looked like they belonged here, at any rate.

"Is this where you come on Counting Day?" Cali asked, speaking in a low voice suitable for the venue.

"Ever since I was born," said Cormac. "They say that, since this is the biggest temple in the kingdom, more nobles can be found here on Counting Day than anywhere else."

I searched my memory, but I had no conscious recollection of what Counting Day might be. That left me slightly uneasy; I had the sense it was important. Fortunately, Deryk chose that moment to sidle up beside Elyssa, and the two of them dropped back to enjoy their own conversation.

"Counting Day," she repeated, her voice full of contempt. "When all the nobles in the kingdom have to show up at a temple because otherwise the goddess will take away their echoes. It's such a stupid superstition."

"Have you ever been brave enough not to do it, though?" Deryk asked. "I admit, no one I know has been willing to risk it. So I have no idea if it's even true."

"Oh, no. I go every year—but only because my father makes me. He can't bear the idea that we'd lose all our prestige if the goddess took away our echoes. Otherwise, I'd be happy to stay home."

"But what if it *is* true?" Deryk argued. "And your echoes just vanished? You'd be sorry then."

"Not as much as you'd think," she muttered.

"I don't believe you," he said. He gestured in my direction. "It has to bother you to be missing just one of them right now."

She lifted her eyes to give him a long, level look. "Not as much as you'd think," she repeated.

He raised his eyebrows and I thought even he might be taken aback at her callousness. But he smoothly moved on. "Well, you know who *is* in agony to be missing an echo?" he said in his usual gossipy tone.

"I didn't know anyone else was."

"Yes! Vivienne! Apparently her carriage practically overturned on her journey here, and one of the echoes was paralyzed or something—at any rate, injured so badly she had to be sent back to Thelleron. Vivienne's been weeping all over the palace ever since she got here. I'm surprised you haven't noticed."

"I've never paid too much attention to sad little Vivienne," Elyssa said, causing Deryk to muffle a laugh. "And now that she's out of favor, I don't think I've even bothered to *look* in her direction."

"No, it's hard to care about her too much these days," Deryk agreed. "But you know who I think we *should* be befriending?"

"Who?"

"The Orenza girl. Marguerite."

"Is she interesting enough to befriend?"

"If she marries Cormac, she'll be plenty interesting. And if you marry Jordan—"

"Gorsey," she said in a mocking tone. I had recently discovered that *gorsey* was a word people used when they didn't feel like producing all the syllables in *goddess have mercy on my soul*. People like Elyssa only used the word in a joking manner, but I'd heard servants say it as if it were an actual prayer. "She'll be my sister-in-law. Maybe my closest friend."

"Well, it wouldn't hurt you to do something nice for her, if you get the chance," he said. "I know that's not your usual style, but who knows? It could pay off."

By this time, we had completed our slow circle around the first chamber, and we moved past a massive central column to step into a second round room. I glanced at the statue on the dais to find her holding her arms out to either side. Apparently we were now in the portion of the sanctuary dedicated to justice. There were many more people sitting in these benches, praying, staring fiercely at the statue, or speaking earnestly with one of the priestesses. I supposed the world held far more injustice than joy, so more people had congregated here to seek the goddess's intervention.

"Well, I won't go out of my way to do her a service, but I suppose if an opportunity arises, it couldn't hurt," Elyssa said with a shrug.

"And you *know* Jordan will appreciate any evidence of your good heart," Deryk added provocatively.

Elyssa laughed loudly enough to cause a few petitioners to glare at her with disfavor. "Come on, let's go outside and wait," Elyssa said, heading for the nearest door. "I have had enough piety for the day."

"Possibly for the year," Deryk agreed, and followed her out into the light.

CHAPTER TWELVE

The evening's entertainment was a card game that commenced directly after the meal. Tables for four were set up in a strict formation—those for the originals running down the center of the room, those for their echoes fanning out behind them. We quickly learned that the women would keep their same seats all night long, while the men would move from table to table after every few hands.

"So every woman gets a chance to flirt with Prince Cormac, and every man gets a chance to look over the women who aren't good enough for Cormac and consider them for their own brides," Elyssa murmured to Deryk as they took their places together at one of the tables. She was wearing a gold satin dress that made her hair look black and glossy, and he had already complimented her on her appearance. "Was anything ever so romantic?"

Deryk signaled to one of the servants circling through the room carrying trays of wineglasses. "I need a drink," he said. "I imagine I'll need many before the night is through."

I was located at the echoes' table nearest to Elyssa, in a seat that afforded me a good view of the originals. I could see the back of Elyssa's head, the profiles of the men sitting with her, and occasionally the face of the Banchura triplet who was seated at her table— Lavinia, if Deryk's greeting was accurate. Elyssa was in a careless mood, so she wasn't binding her echoes to her very tightly, which gave me an opportunity to glance around the room whenever I didn't have to pretend to pay attention to my cards.

And "pretend" was the right word. I had to shuffle and deal and discard in concert with Elyssa, but other than that, no effort was

124

required from me at all. The cards the echoes used were all blank rectangles—unlike the ones the nobles held, which appeared to be covered with pictures and numbers. I wondered if the game was interesting when the players could see those pictures and numbers; it certainly was dull without them. Watching the others in the room was far more entertaining.

Deryk made good his promise and began drinking as soon as the first hand was dealt. Elyssa matched him for his first two glasses, but then slowed her intake considerably; she would never let herself get tipsy in such a public place. The servants were providing drinks to the echoes as well as the originals, but they weren't paying close attention to how well our levels of consumption matched. Since I barely touched my lips to my wine whenever I lifted my glass, I never needed it to be refilled.

After about a half hour of play, the men stood up and rotated to the next table. The new echoes who sat down with me belonged to nobles I couldn't remember meeting before, but I could feel the smile tugging at Elyssa's face as she flirted with them over the next few hands. Judging by the answering smiles on the faces of the echoes, they were responding to her enthusiastically. These must be men who didn't know Elyssa well enough to hate her. Lavinia's echo tried to keep her expression noncommittal, but I saw disapproval and impatience shape her face several times in the next thirty minutes. I had the impression that Lavinia held a low opinion of any man who would find Elyssa enchanting. It made me like the Banchura women even more.

We had been at the game close to two hours when the rotation of players brought Jordan and his echoes to our tables. I found myself sitting straighter in my chair and smiling even more widely than Elyssa. I didn't even bother watching Jordan's echo, sitting on my left and seeming almost as solid as a real man; I kept all my attention on the prince.

He smiled impartially at the three other players but addressed Lavinia first. "Is this the longest stretch of time that you've been separated from your sisters by more than five inches?"

She laughed. "No, indeed, we are perfectly capable of being in entirely different rooms, and once Letitia even spent a whole week at our cousin's house while Leonora and I stayed home. But I admit she was only five miles away. I'm not sure we've ever been farther apart than that."

"I'm afraid to ask what will happen if any of you ever decide to marry," Jordan said.

"Oh, that's easy!" she responded cheerfully. "We'll just pick meek and amiable men who are willing to move into our father's house so we can all live together."

Elyssa tossed down a discard. "And yet you are all still unwed!" she marveled. "Impossible to believe that no men have been convinced to join such an enticing arrangement!"

Jordan's echo gave me a reproving look, but Lavinia's echo just laughed silently. "I do wonder if we will ever find the right kinds of husbands," she said. "I must say, it doesn't concern me overmuch. Scheming and plotting to catch the eye of some noble or some royal— What a dreary way to live."

So the Banchura women could joust with the best of them. I felt the whiplash of Elyssa's anger, but she was still smiling. "And yet here you are," she said. "Scheming and plotting."

Lavinia opened her blue eyes as wide as they could go and stared soulfully at the prince. "Oh, no! Jordan! Have I seemed to be throwing myself at you? You'll have to forgive me. I didn't *mean* to show myself so desperate for your attention."

The other lord at our table gathered up all the cards and sighed mournfully. "Why is no one scheming to catch *my* attention? That's what I want to know," he said, obviously trying to lighten the mood. "I'm not a prince, but I have a manor! And extensive lands! And three echoes! Am I not worth a little flirtation?"

Elyssa's grin seemed a little more genuine as she turned in his direction. "But you live in *Thelleron*," she said. She might as well have said, *But you live in a barnyard.*

He did not seem particularly offended. "I cannot recall that you have ever set foot within the borders," he replied. "I don't know that you are particularly well-suited to judge."

Jordan seemed eager to change the subject. "Oh, Thelleron's a fine place," he said. "And don't forget, it's the birthplace of Edwin, the first king of the Seven Jewels."

"Yes, you can hardly find a town square in any hamlet of more than thirty people that doesn't have a statue of Edwin right in the middle," the other noble said.

Lavinia's attention had drifted to one of the other tables; I saw her echo follow her gaze and frown slightly. "Look at that," Lavinia said in a dismayed voice. "Deryk is causing a scene."

Everyone twisted around to get a better look. Deryk was sitting at the table with the reserved Lady Marguerite and two other nobles I couldn't name. He was kissing her hand in a very apologetic way, so I supposed we had just missed him saying or doing something outrageous.

Jordan looked concerned. "I wonder if I should have a word with him. Marguerite seems uncomfortable."

"Oh, he's harmless," Elyssa said. "Annoying, maybe, but just high-spirited."

"He's just drunk," Lavinia said flatly. "He had three glasses of wine before he left this table, and I'm sure he's had another bottle's worth since he moved on."

"But it's such good wine," Elyssa said provocatively. "Nothing but the best in the royal cellars."

Jordan sat back slightly in his chair. "He seems to have settled down for the moment. But I'll watch him."

Elyssa shuffled and dealt the cards. My hands followed her movements as closely as possible, but she was barely paying attention to her echoes, so it was hard to keep up. She said, "I hope I don't seem like I'm *flirting* with you, Jordan, when I ask how you've been enjoying all your visitors? Everyone else is having a grand time, but you and your brother have seemed preoccupied."

He gave her one quick look, as if surprised that she'd been so observant, but he answered readily enough. "I'm sorry if we've appeared that way! It's just that we've begun to worry about Jamison. He should have been back at court before any of you arrived, but we've heard no word from him for days."

"The little time I've spent with Jamison has convinced me he can take care of himself," Elyssa said.

Jordan smiled. "That's true, of course. Still, when it's your brother..." He shrugged and didn't finish his sentence.

"You don't have sisters *or* brothers, do you, Elyssa?" Lavinia asked. "I don't."

"I can't imagine what that's like," Lavinia went on. "The world would seem so *empty*."

Elyssa was sorting her cards. "I have always found the world over full of people as it is," she said. "I suspect having siblings would have made it seem even more crowded."

"Well, I always thought—" Lavinia began, but before she could go on, there was a small commotion on the other side of the room. We heard the sounds of a glass falling over, a woman gasping, and a chair scraping back. We all automatically looked in that direction, to find one of Marguerite's echoes on her feet, holding her skirts away from the wine spilling out of a glass that had been overturned by Deryk's echo.

Then we all froze, staring in wordless astonishment. The *echo* was standing, but Marguerite was not.

The echo had reacted when her original had held fast. The echo was... the echo was... *The echo was independent.*

I felt my breath moving so rapidly in my chest that my vision started to blur. Could there be other creatures like me in the world, shadows that were not quite shadows, echoes that could move and think and act and dream? Was I not entirely alone? And did calm, reserved Marguerite know of her echo's sentience—did she allow the creature some leeway, some chances to make its own choices, or did she try to crush its wild spirit and force it into the mold of her own making?

Or was this the first time the echo had ever moved on her own initiative, and was Marguerite as shocked as the rest of us?

While we stared, still mute and amazed, one of Marguerite's other echoes came to her feet. After a moment, the third. They each took slightly different stances—deliberately, I thought—so it was clear all three of them could move under their own volition. The last one to stand was Marguerite herself.

Still staring, the woman at her table exclaimed, "Your echoes. They have minds of their own?"

"Hardly that," Marguerite answered. "They are capable of some individual motion, but only when I choose to release them. Mostly I control them—" She snapped her fingers, and the three echoes instantly assumed Marguerite's exact pose and expression.

"I've never heard of such a thing!" someone exclaimed.

I felt a sense of bitter letdown. Now that they were slaved to Marguerite again, the three echoes looked every bit as vacant and mindless as any shadow. I gazed more closely at the third one, the one who had jumped up first, but there was nothing extraordinary to be seen on her face. These echoes were just like Elyssa's—they could be freed, but they could not think or feel. They were nothing like me at all.

I might have been crushed at the turn of events, but it was clear that the lords and ladies who had witnessed this byplay were feeling unnerved and suspicious. It was if Marguerite had suddenly revealed she was an imposter or a spy—not truly a high noble after all. I wondered how Cormac would react to this revelation. Would a prince want to marry a woman who couldn't even control her own echoes?

There was a rustle from the table nearby. "Then you've been living in some unsophisticated backwater," Elyssa said, rising gracefully to her feet. She smiled at the assembled nobles but directed a silent command to my fellow echo and me, and both of us kept to our seats, our hands folded before us. "It's a common enough thing among people who have particularly fine command of their thoughts."

A second later, she made a slight twist of her wrist and gathered us tightly to her again, and we both instantly jumped up and assumed her precise pose. "But, generally speaking, I find life less tedious when I don't have to wonder if my echoes are behaving themselves." She laughed. "So I usually don't give them freedom."

The others in the room began glancing at each other, and whispering back and forth, seeming just as shocked but much less suspicious. *That's why she did it,* I thought. *Deryk told her to befriend Marguerite if she could, and this was an easy way for her to do it.* I wondered if Marguerite would be grateful, if she had even noticed that sudden, yawning chasm of doubt that had briefly opened before her. I wondered if Elyssa had paused long enough to reflect on how that doubt might now extend to her.

I cut my eyes over just enough to give Elyssa a considering look. She appeared completely unruffled, even bored, as she sank back to her seat and drew both of us down with her. Maybe she hadn't interfered as a kindness to Marguerite. Maybe she simply was trying to draw attention to herself in some dramatic fashion; this opportunity had presented itself, and she took it. Maybe she thought Prince Jordan would be intrigued by the idea of a woman with unconventional echoes.

On that thought, I shifted my gaze to Jordan to see if I could read his reaction. He was staring at me, his brows drawn down, his eyes narrowed. Caught unaware, I stared back, meeting his eyes with a frankness no echo should ever show. He nodded once, short and sharp, as if confirming something to himself, but did not look away.

"Jordan!" Lavinia exclaimed. "Are you going to deal the cards or not?"

His voice was perfectly normal, perfectly light, as he turned his gaze from me and smiled at his tablemates. "My apologies! Of course I'm going to deal. I'm at a sad deficit in this game and I must make up my losses."

It was clear Jordan wasn't going to make any observations about the scene that had just played out, but the irrepressible Lavinia could only contain her curiosity for as long as it took him to parcel out the cards. "So, Elyssa, tell us all about having echoes who think for themselves! How odd that would be! As if they are separate people! It would make me very uncomfortable."

"Oh, they don't think for themselves," she said. "You have just witnessed the extent of their abilities. I usually only release them at night so that I can send them to bed while I enjoy an hour or two of complete solitude. I find it so freeing to be able to comb my hair or turn the pages of a book without having them copy my every move."

"*Do* you?" Lavinia asked in wonderment. "I would find it so ... strange. Like my body wasn't properly weighted, or something."

"Dezmen can't free his echoes, not the way you can," Jordan said. "But he says he can send them to a sort of trance, where they just sit unmoving for a little while. I've never seen him do it, though."

"We will have to compare stories sometime, Dezmen and I," Elyssa said.

"I'm sure he would enjoy that," was Jordan's polite response.

Lavinia threw down a discard, then glanced over at Jordan. "Though if anyone was going to have freethinking echoes, I'd expect it to be you or your brother," she said.

"Oh? And why is that?"

She gestured. "Well, look at them! They're so—so *vigorous*. Not like mine and Elyssa's and everyone else's, which are so obviously copies. Yours look real enough to step forward and have a conversation."

"They never have, though."

"Just as well," said the Thelleron lord in a firm voice. "Nobles should be nobles and echoes should be echoes. That's the way the world works."

I was not quick enough to glance away before Jordan cast another look in my direction. "Well," he said, "the world will often surprise you."

Elyssa was in a good mood that night as Gretta got her ready for bed. "And the ball is tomorrow night, so I need to look my very best. I shall wear the lavender gown. And all my amethysts."

"Very good, my lady."

Behind the screen, under cover of her chatter, I tended to the hurt echo, unwrapping her bandaged leg and rubbing on some ointment that Gretta had brought. The bruising was still purple and dark, but the swelling had gone down. I had originally feared the ankle might be broken, but now I thought it was only sprained. The echo didn't exhibit too much pain when I pressed carefully on the discolored flesh. Good. Maybe she would be well enough to walk again in a few days.

Maybe we would draw less attention from Prince Jordan if there were three of us. If we all behaved as we were supposed to. Maybe he wouldn't glance over so often with that puzzled and assessing gaze. I told myself that was what I hoped for—that Prince Jordan wouldn't notice me, wonder at me, look at me.

I wasn't even remotely convinced.

The only activity that occupied any of the women on the following day was getting through the hours until the ball that night. It was all they could think of and all they could talk about.

"So do you plan to spend half the night dancing with Nigel and Dezmen?" Cali asked Elyssa over lunch. "I think that's probably what I'll be doing, too. Oh, and that fellow from Orenza who's been so quiet."

Elyssa looked both annoyed and puzzled. "Of course not," she snapped. "Why would you think so?"

Cali's round face was guileless, but I sensed a certain deliberate malice behind her warm voice. "Oh, you know, because when you only have two echoes, it's easier to dance with someone else who only has two echoes, and you're down to two at the moment—"

"You don't have to worry about that," interposed one of the Banchura triplets in a breezy way. "Cormac will have hired extra men and women to fill in whenever the number of echoes don't match up. It makes the whole evening go more smoothly."

"That's how they do it in all the finest houses," Elyssa said, getting in her own dig. "I suppose you didn't know that."

Cali just offered her usual friendly smile. "What a relief! Though I suppose it will be odd to have 'extra women' following us around all night."

The Banchura sister smothered a grin and said firmly, "Nothing will be odd. It will be a marvelous evening."

The whole day seemed to stretch out as long as three ordinary days combined, but finally it was time to dress for the evening's festivities. Gretta took inordinate care styling Elyssa's lustrous black hair, lacing her into the lavender silk gown, and decking her with amethysts. The scoop necklace of her dress seemed designed expressly to show off her favorite piece of jewelry, the gold necklace with the three interlocking circles that curved around the large central gem.

"I can't imagine anyone will be lovelier than you tonight," Gretta said when she was done.

Elyssa studied her reflection in the mirror. "Then let's hope that loveliness is enough," she said and headed for the door. The other echo and I fell in step behind her.

After dinner, all the nobles and echoes made their way through the wide corridors of the palace in a rustling, murmuring, bejeweled river of excitement. They poured themselves into the ballroom, which was a large, well-lit space full of graceful architectural accents. Musicians sat on a low stage in one corner, playing lively music. Most of the women positioned themselves near the doorway, trying to look casual and artless, but clearly awaiting the arrival of Cormac and Jordan, who had fallen to the back of the parade.

The minute the princes entered the room, the musicians segued into a rousing waltz. I couldn't tell how Cormac and Jordan chose their partners—by prearrangement, by proximity, or by preference—but Cormac did not solicit Marguerite's hand and Jordan did not ask for Elyssa's. The Thelleron lord appeared at Elyssa's side and she turned smoothly into his embrace. I felt his echo's cool hands close over my fingers as he pulled me onto the floor behind them. Out of the corner of my eye, I saw a plain-faced woman in a black gown step forward to partner with the man's third echo. She was so unobtrusive that I thought she must have acted in this capacity hundreds of times.

I quickly lost interest in her and put all my attention into performing the dance, which I enjoyed immensely. During my periods of wakefulness in the past couple of years, there had been many social events, but only a few balls. Once I'd realized that Elyssa was an excellent dancer—which meant I was, too—I'd found myself enjoying this activity above all others. Tonight was no exception, and I quickly found myself skimming over the floor with delicious abandon. My bones were light as willow branches, my feet were dainty as flower petals, and the music produced a more urgent beat than my own heart. Around me flashed bright swirling colors of garnet and amber and emerald. It was the first time I could ever remember experiencing the word that I had heard others describe as *delight*.

Too soon the dance ended, and as we came to a halt, my body felt heavy and leaden, unaccustomed to stillness. But it was only a few moments before the music started up again, and another lord bowed to Elyssa, and she and her echoes and her shadowy extra woman all curtseyed in return. Back to dancing. Back to revelry. Back to something akin to flying.

The evening continued like this for the next couple of hours, as couples traded partners, the pace of the music slowed, the type of dancing shifted from one style to the next. There was a short pause while refreshments were served and all the participants fanned themselves and pretended they were fatigued. But the minute the musicians started tuning their instruments again, the nobles set down their plates and goblets and looked around for partners.

Elyssa was gazing to her left, where Deryk was chatting with one of the Banchura sisters, so the voice on her right came as a surprise.

"Are you enjoying yourself this evening?" Jordan asked.

She turned to him with a smile. "I am! I find there are few pleasures purer than dancing."

He cocked his head. "'Purer,'" he repeated. "An interesting word choice."

She laughed and explained. "Oh, every conversation has an edge to it—you are trying to create an impression or uncover a secret. Every meal brings with it a series of calculations. If I try this unfamiliar dish, will I hate the taste and want to spit it out? If I have another glass of wine, will it dull my senses and lead me to say something regrettable? But a dance is just a dance. There is no requirement beyond pleasure."

He was smiling. "Well, some would say there is a requirement to be graceful," he said. "A standard many do not meet."

"Not something you have ever needed to worry about, I think."

"Ah, but I distinctly remember telling you that dancing was not a skill that came naturally to me. The echoes made me clumsy at first—but I flatter myself that all four of us are now as nimble as men might be on the dance floor."

Elyssa glanced from Jordan to his echoes, who seemed so much more substantial than those of the other nobles. This night, their clothing mirrored Jordan's so exactly that they might have been his living brothers, not his hollow shadows. "I have often wondered if dancing with an echo would be the same as dancing with a man," she remarked. "Particularly with your echoes, who seem so present and alive."

"I have wondered the same thing!" he exclaimed, just as the musicians completed their discordant warmups and produced the first measures of another waltz. "Let us try it, just for this dance. I will partner with one of your echoes and you with one of mine."

Her face was a quick study in surprise and dismay. "I don't think—" But he had already turned away and reached out his arms to one of her echoes.

Reached out his arms to *me*.

Even as I stood there, ossified with shock, I marveled at the heat of his hands as one wrapped around my fingers and one settled at my waist.

I sensed Elyssa's fury and helplessness, checked somewhat by her reluctance to make a scene, as she allowed one of Jordan's echoes to pull her into a similar embrace. I felt Jordan's hands tug me into motion, felt my feet unglue themselves from the floor, felt myself gliding into the first dip and turn of the waltz. It was coincidence, surely, that Jordan held me so that his back was to Elyssa—and so that his echo, copying Jordan meticulously, held Elyssa in a way that prevented her from turning to see my face.

All this time, I was staring at Jordan and he was staring intently back at me. He kept his eyes on mine as he spoke under cover of the music and asked, "Can you speak?"

CHAPTER THIRTEEN

I was too astonished to reply, and so we trod out a few measures in silence. Jordan watched me with unabated curiosity.

"She cannot see you," he said in a reassuring voice. "So you may nod or shake your head and she will not know. Unless this is one of those moments when she has you in perfect thrall, and you cannot deviate from her actions in the slightest?"

I had been enjoying the other dances so much I hadn't paid much attention to how closely Elyssa was maintaining her bond, but I tested it now, cautiously, and found the connection loose. I slowly shook my head.

Excitement blazed in Jordan's eyes. "So you *can* communicate," he breathed. "But you can't speak aloud?"

I had to try three times before I could get my mouth to cooperate. "I can," I said, my voice barely above a whisper. "But I have not often done so."

His hands tightened on my body and his expression grew even more intense. "You *are* in there," he said, triumphant. "I thought I could not have imagined it."

"Don't tell her," I begged.

His eyebrows arched; I couldn't read his expression. "You mean she doesn't know?"

"I—" I could not imagine how to explain and I was well aware that we had only the length of the dance for me to do so. In the end, all I said was, "She has no idea how truly conscious I am."

He absorbed this for a moment as he continued to move me around the dance floor. Normally, the waltzers would spin in circles and make grand sweeps around the whole room, but Jordan was determinedly keeping us in a position that would prevent Elyssa from seeing my face. I supposed his echo had such strength of will that she would not be able to swing him around and gain a different view. Of course, she could always wrench herself free and stalk off the dance floor, but I didn't think she would do that. She was probably hoping that, if she didn't draw attention to her situation, no one would realize who her partner really was.

"So you live a secret life," Jordan said at last. "Not quite human and not quite—whatever echoes are. Supernatural creatures, I suppose. You can think for yourself and act for yourself, and yet your every move is governed by the desires and whims of someone else— Someone who, I must guess, is not the easiest person to live with at close quarters."

"No," I said, "she is not."

He grimaced but did not enquire for details. Just as well, perhaps. I could not believe this conversation was actually occurring, and I was filled both with eagerness to talk and terror that every word I said was ensuring my doom. Between the disbelief, the elation, and the despair, I could hardly gauge how much I was willing to share—but I had a feeling I would tell Jordan anything he asked.

"How does it work?" he asked. "Do you always possess some degree of freedom? Can you break your connection with her whenever you wish?"

"She decides," I said. "Whenever she is with company, she generally keeps all of us closely tied to her. Sometimes she is a little sloppy about it—"

"As when I saw you in Amanda Plaza, making the sign of the benediction before the goddess statues."

I nodded. "Yes. We were attuned to her, but I could muster some independence." The longer we talked, the easier I was finding it to speak complete and complex sentences. "Other times, it's like she has complete power over me, over all my bones and muscles. I can't even blink unless she blinks. I can't breathe unless she does. And she can invoke that connection whenever she wants."

"You said she keeps you tied to her when you are in the presence of others," he said. "What happens when you're alone?"

"Usually the minute we step into a private room, she cuts the connection—practically flings us away from her. At home, she sends us to our own bedroom. Here, the maid has set up a folding screen so she doesn't have to look at us."

He was frowning. "She dislikes her echoes that much? I realized she found them cumbersome, but she actually despises them?"

I found I did not want to tell him the entire truth. "That has been my conclusion," I said.

"Are the other two as aware as you are?"

I shook my head. "No. They can take a few independent steps, they can sit on the bed or turn over in the night without Elyssa's permission, but I have never seen them display more sentience than that."

He studied me a moment. "So then. At night when you have been released. In your separate bedroom where Elyssa cannot see you. Is that the only time you are truly free?"

"Yes," I whispered.

"What do you do?"

I just looked at him, shaking my head slightly and lifting my shoulders. How to describe it? "I walk around the room. I look out the window. I whisper words to myself. I just exist."

"Then in the morning, she wakes and calls you back to her side."

"Yes."

His warm brown eyes were narrowed in concern. "How do you bear it?" he demanded.

"It has not been easy," I acknowledged.

"Has it always been this way? Since you were born?"

"No. For a long time, my awareness came only in bursts and flashes. A few moments on one day. A few moments on a later day. Only gradually did those moments stretch out into days and weeks. Only during the past six months have I been in a sustained state of consciousness—what I might call truly alive."

He shook his head. "I have never heard of such a thing."

"But you said— You told Elyssa a tale about King Edwin—"

His eyes lit at the memory. "That's right! We were in the library at her father's house, and I saw your face and I realized you were listening! You were, weren't you?"

"I was. And you said that King Edwin took over the bodies of his echoes."

"Yes, but only when someone killed off his original," he pointed out. "His echo didn't just suddenly come to life and start thinking its own thoughts." We executed a few steps in silence while he mulled that over. Then he said, "I'll have to ask my father what he thinks."

"No!"

"Why not?"

"Because she— Because Elyssa will not like it," I floundered.

He studied me as we passed another measure or two in silence. "Is she cruel to her echoes?" he asked at last.

Oh, I so much did not want to go into the details of that. "Sometimes."

"The echo that is missing tonight—the one Elyssa says tripped and fell—what really happened to her?"

I didn't know how to answer, so I just shook my head.

"I see," he said. I could hear the anger in his voice, although his tone remained polite. "So Elyssa takes out her grievances on the most helpless creatures in the kingdom, and there is nothing you can do about it. And you're afraid that if she knows you are— aware—that she will do something abominable to you."

"Yes," I whispered.

"That's why I want to talk to my father," he said. "There might be some precedent I'm unaware of. Sometime in the past when an echo came to life and was granted a legal status of personhood."

"I'm too afraid," I said in an urgent voice. "She would be so angry."

He nodded. "I will make inquiries, but discreetly. And when I learn something I will let you know directly—" He paused and a ludicrous expression came over his face.

I couldn't help a sad smile. "It is not like we will be able to find many opportunities to converse," I pointed out. "This might be the only time."

"We will find ways to communicate," he said. "If nothing else, I can tell Elyssa things that I want you to know."

Now my smile was almost a laugh. "I am having difficulty imagining that conversation," I said. "'By the way, Elyssa, did you know that if one of your echoes attains consciousness, you are by law required to set it free?' She will think you have gone mad."

A smile tugged at his own mouth. "I can be more subtle than that, I think. But I would want to be sure you were actually aware and listening before I tried to drop bits of information. We should agree on a signal of some kind."

"I can't be sure that I will have enough freedom to be able to nod or gesture," I said. "But I always seem to be able to control where I turn my gaze. I can simply meet your eyes. No other echo looks at you so boldly, do they?"

"No! It was most unnerving the first time you stared me straight in the face." He looked down at me a moment. "What a wondrous creature you are," he said at last. "You seem both wise and innocent, like a child just discovering the world."

"That's how I feel sometimes," I admitted. "Like I am learning so much every day—or *remembering* things that I learned long ago, before I was aware. It's confusing and frightening and exhilarating all at once."

"So you don't retain conscious knowledge of all those years you were just Elyssa's shadow?"

"Bits and pieces. People don't look familiar to me, but sometimes a room or a building does. And sometimes scraps of knowledge just snap into place, and suddenly I *know* something that I didn't know before."

"Maybe someday all those memories will come rushing back."

"Maybe," I said. "I'm not sure I want all those memories."

He winced slightly. "That was thoughtless of me. It's just that your situation is so impossibly strange."

"That it is."

His hands tightened briefly on my fingers, on the curve of my waist. I was once again flooded with awareness of how warm his skin was, how reassuringly solid his body seemed compared with that of an echo. Only Elyssa and Gretta had ever been this close to me, and neither of them had such mass and heat and presence. "I know this song, and it is about to end," he said, frustration in his voice. "And there is so much left that I want to ask you!"

"I am just stunned and grateful for the chance to speak at all," I said. "I never expected to have any conversation with any other human being for the whole of my existence."

"You will have more," he promised. "I don't know how or when, but you will."

"I will look forward to that."

"But one thing I have to know," he said, speaking in a rush. Even I could tell that the musicians were producing a lively swirl of notes that signaled the conclusion of the piece. We were lucky it had lasted so long. "Do you have a name?"

I stared at him. It had never occurred to me that I might need one. "No," I said blankly.

"I thought of one that might suit you. It just came to me."

"What is it?"

Before he could answer, the musicians crashed out three final chords and abruptly stopped. There was a moment of absolute silence in the ballroom. No one could speak a word without everyone in the whole place overhearing.

Then a few people laughed and a few applauded, and nobles murmured compliments as they offered their partners final bows and curtseys. Jordan kept his eyes on mine as he bowed over my hand and whispered, "Hope."

The prince had barely released me when Elyssa descended upon us, a bright smile pasted on her face to cover her mortification. "What an interesting experiment that was!" she said lightly. "I cannot decide if your echo was the worst conversationalist I have ever met or the best one. On the one hand, he didn't offer a single observation, which made him very dull. On the other hand, he allowed me to prattle on about myself without interruption, which made him the perfect companion!"

Jordan turned his attention to her so completely I was momentarily disoriented. He had been focused on me so intently that I had forgotten there was anything to look at but his face. "Yes, I had much the same experience with your echo," he replied. "I don't know what I was expecting, but it wasn't that."

"I saw your echo's lips moving, so I thought you must be speaking to mine," Elyssa said.

"I couldn't seem to help myself," he said. "She looked so much like you. And yet she was nothing like you at all."

"Let's keep this a secret between us, shall we?" Elyssa said, still lightly, but I was certain she desperately wanted Jordan to agree. Everyone would think Jordan had intended some insult by choosing her echo over her, and there was no way he could counter with the truth.

"I have no intention of telling anybody," he replied solemnly— as much to reassure me, I thought, as Elyssa. "We have a pact."

Servants began circulating through the crowd, bearing trays of refreshments, so it seemed as if the dancers and musicians would be taking another break. I could use one, I thought faintly, to mull over everything that had just happened, but I didn't think the ballroom was the place for quiet musing. I would need a long night of solitude and silence to fully absorb what it might mean to have caught Prince Jordan's attention—perhaps to have gained him as a friend.

Jordan flagged down a servant distributing glasses of wine, and the seven of us nearly emptied the tray. Dezmen and his two echoes approached, carrying wineglasses of their own, and the three originals engaged in a few moments of light banter. Then Jordan asked, "Are either of you hungry? They're setting up tables of food under the balcony."

"I'd love something sweet," Elyssa said.

"That sounds good," Dezman responded, but he seemed distracted. He nodded toward the main doorway. "I wonder if something's wrong. The inquisitor just showed up, and the look on his face says he has bad news."

Jordan swiveled around to get a look. Sure enough, the unsettling man we had met in the queen's chambers was hovering on the threshold, glancing around as if trying to locate someone. I saw Cormac already working his way over to him, cutting a dark wake through the colorful sea of dancers. Many of the other revelers had already noticed the inquisitor's appearance and watched apprehensively as Cormac reached Malachi's side and said something in a low voice.

"I don't know," Jordan said in a grim voice. "But Malachi tends to stay invisible. If he's come here so openly tonight— Here, take my wine." He handed his glass to Dezmen, made a brief bow to Elyssa, and met my eyes for a fleeting moment. "I'll go see what's happened."

He strode off, his echoes moving purposefully behind him. He was only halfway across the dance floor when we saw Cormac reel back in shock and then turn to look urgently through the crowd, probably searching for his brother. A moment later, Jordan joined him at the door and heard whatever terrible news Malachi had brought. The three of them exchanged a few more sentences, then disappeared into the hallway without a word of explanation.

"Well!" Elyssa exclaimed. "What do you suppose *that* was all about?"

"I don't know, but nothing good," Dezmen answered, frowning.

Most of the other dancers began to cluster in the middle of the room as

people gathered to share surprise and speculation. Dezmen sketched a bow and went to join the others, while Elyssa looked around for her best source of information. It was already wending its way in her direction—Lord Deryk, the most inveterate gossip in the Seven Jewels.

"What do you know?" Elyssa demanded.

He leaned down to whisper his answer, although the only ones close enough to overhear were the echoes. "Lord Jamison has been found dead."

"Dead! How?"

"Drowned. In a lake near some backwater town off the Charamon Road."

"What happened?"

"No one knows yet. The inquisitor is going to organize an investigation."

"I can't pretend anyone will miss Jamison, but how inconvenient that he should die just now!" Elyssa exclaimed. "Cormac can hardly go on as if nothing has happened."

"Perhaps he will disband his little party," Deryk said. "Bad news for you and sweet Marguerite, still standing around hoping for royal proposals."

She swatted him on the arm, though she didn't seem too offended. I often thought that she liked Deryk precisely because he said the most atrocious things—things she herself was probably already thinking. "It will be most awkward," she said. "Well, I suppose there's nothing we can do about it tonight."

"No, I very much fear the evening's entertainment is over," Deryk agreed.

Sure enough, women began streaming for the doors, though some of the men remained behind to discuss the matter at greater length. Elyssa opted to leave early, since there was no point in staying, and we found Gretta waiting in our room.

"My lady!" the maid exclaimed. "Have you heard the news?"

"About Jamison, you mean? Yes," said Elyssa, reaching up to pull off her earrings. "What are they saying down in the servants' hall?"

Gretta moved behind her to begin undoing the many buttons of the lavender gown. I sat on a divan beside the injured echo, and the second echo sank down beside me, all of us awaiting our turn to be undressed. Normally we would have taken refuge behind our screen, but I didn't want to miss a word, and the other two echoes seemed content to follow my lead. Elyssa, surprisingly, didn't seem to notice us at all.

"No one knows anything yet," Gretta said. "But the footman's brother is one of the inquisitor's assistants. He says he'll know everything in a few days."

"Well, let me know anything you find out," Elyssa said. "Servants *always* learn what's going on in a house long before the guests do."

Gretta smirked at her in the mirror. "Yes, my lady, I wouldn't be surprised."

After that, there was almost no conversation. Elyssa was quickly in her nightclothes, and then Gretta turned to the echoes and me. She was out the door barely a half hour after we had arrived.

The four of us lay on our beds in the darkened room, thinking our very different thoughts. Even though Elyssa had released us, I retained enough connection with her to realize that she was uncertain and a little anxious; she moved restlessly under her covers and lay awake a long time. Something about Jamison's death had disturbed her, though I couldn't guess what. Maybe just the fact that his passing would change the tenor of this whole visit and definitely turn Jordan's attention away from her.

Like Elyssa, I had much on my mind and found it even harder to fall asleep. What a night this had been! I had spoken to another living soul—to *Jordan,* of all the people in the Seven Kingdoms—he had seen me and heard me and recognized me as a separate, functioning, independent human being. It was almost unfathomable. I felt as if his notice had entirely transformed me. As if, because Jordan acknowledged me, I was *real* in some way I had not been when I was the only one who knew I existed.

I didn't put much credence in his notion that other echoes might have come to consciousness before and won their way to freedom. I couldn't imagine such a fate might lie in store for me—and, truthfully, I couldn't bear to wish for such an outcome and then spend the next fifty years of my life chained to Elyssa's side. It was better to accept my circumstances than to allow myself the terrible betrayal of hope.

Hope.

It was the last word Jordan had said to me, the name he had offered me, and now I had to decide if I would lean into that benediction. Hope.

I couldn't afford it. I knew that. It would leave me famished when it was snatched away from me; it would crush me under the weight of its unfulfilled expectations. Hope.

I had never had it. I had only ever had pain and awareness and a small growing sense that what I thought and felt and did was mine and mine alone. I had only had this shadowed, guarded, silent space inside my own head that no one else, not even Elyssa, could touch.

Could I possibly allow myself to believe that there might be a world outside that fragile garden?

Could I possibly turn down any gift of Jordan's making?

I could give myself another name. I could create one for myself, put together a string of syllables that I found pleasing, as I had created my very self out of thoughts and reactions and memories. I could, in the privacy of my mind, call myself whatever I wanted.

But if Jordan called me Hope, I knew I would answer to that name.

I wrapped my arms around my body and hugged to myself the memory of his intent eyes, his warm hands, his insistent questions. Perhaps no one else would ever look into my face and see the person behind the deliberately blank eyes—but Jordan had seen me, once, and that was enough.

I smothered a sigh and turned to my side, amused to note that the other two echoes turned when I did. It didn't take much thought to realize that—however intrigued Jordan had been by our conversation tonight—in the coming days he was not going to have a minute to spare to think about a strange sentient echo and any half-promises he might have made to her. His brother had been found dead, and he and his family would be shocked and full of grief. All his attention would be taken up by this crisis; there would be none left to spare for me.

But I had had an evening. I had had one conversation. One dance. I thought those things would last me a lifetime.

CHAPTER FOURTEEN

The mood in the breakfast room the next day was a strange mix of excitement, uncertainty, and gloom as everyone continued to discuss the news of the previous night.

"I simply do not know what to do," said one of the noblewomen with a heavy sigh. "It seems callous to pack up and go home, but it seems intolerable to stay here and expect to be entertained."

"I think we must all stay a few days, showing faces of earnest concern, and then graciously excuse ourselves," said a lord named Nigel. "At the very least, we must stay long enough to offer our condolences directly to the king and his sons—which means we must wait until our hosts make an appearance again."

"In the meantime," said one of the Banchura women, "I suppose we must find ways to amuse ourselves."

"Well, it's a big city," Elyssa drawled. "Surely there must be things we can do."

Indeed, about half of the visiting nobles arranged to go on a shopping expedition later in the day, but from what I could tell, no one bought anything and no one enjoyed the outing. Dinner was subdued, and most of the guests disbanded as soon as it was over. Gretta, whom we found awaiting us in Elyssa's room, was the most animated person we'd encountered all day.

"There's been news," she said self-importantly as she began undressing Elyssa.

"I can't wait to hear it."

"The footman says his brother says that the inquisitor says the bastard prince was murdered."

Elyssa was so astonished that she jerked around to stare at Gretta, causing the maid to murmur that she'd almost ripped out a button. "Murdered! Why would he think that?"

Gretta was wide-eyed. "I don't know, but he heard Malachi say it."

Elyssa slowly faced forward again and Gretta continued her work. "Well, plenty of people disliked Jamison," Elyssa said thoughtfully. "Half the brothers and fathers in the Seven Jewels probably would have liked to drown him! But I wonder—" She fell silent.

Gretta lifted the gown over her head. "Wonder what, my lady?"

"Nothing. Never mind. Let's just finish up here and then—I want you to lay out a simple morning dress for me to wear tomorrow. I have an errand I need to run."

Gretta's face was alive with curiosity. Elyssa never ran errands. Never did anything that wasn't either pleasurable or guaranteed to bring her some kind of personal return. "Yes, my lady," she said. "Shall I come with you?"

"Oh, no. This is something I need to do by myself."

The following morning, Elyssa, the uninjured echo, and I were all downstairs and crossing the wide, polished floor of the foyer before any of the other nobles appeared to be stirring. The vigilant housekeeper, Lourdes, intercepted us at the front door and offered to send a footman with us. Elyssa merely said, "I know my way," and brushed past her without a backward look.

She moved at a brisk pace through the city, clearly focused on heading directly to her destination, but I glanced around eagerly, trying to take in the sights. I was impressed by the tall buildings, the wide streets, the orderly traffic, and the jumbled clatter of horses, humans, and carriages. The day was warm but the air was not oppressively humid, making the energetic walk more enjoyable than it might be at a later hour.

Not until we arrived at our destination did I have any clue where Elyssa was headed. But as we approached a huge, open gate set at the entrance to an extensive parkland, I suddenly remembered the conversation Elyssa had had with the mysterious Marco a few days ago. Marco had told Elyssa to meet him at the botanical garden if she ever needed to get in touch. She had agreed without much enthusiasm—but I could only assume that the death of the bastard prince had made her eager to learn whatever Marco knew.

She paid a fee at the gate and we were all admitted onto the lush property. I admired the well-tended flower beds, the sculpted bushes, the trees of every height and shape, but Elyssa didn't seem interested in our surroundings. She continued at the same rapid pace until we reached what I had to think was the center of the garden, where a pretty reflecting pool was watched over by a larger-than-life bronze statue. The figure wore a crown and flowing metal robes, so I assumed he was some past king of the Seven Jewels.

A pair of lovers stood at one end of the pool, murmuring secrets in each other's ears, but no one else was around. Elyssa frowned and glanced down nearby paths, but they were also empty. With a small sound of annoyance, she made her way to a convenient bench and flounced down on one end. The echo and I perched on the other end, settling in for a wait.

We might have been sitting there only ten minutes, watching the lovers kiss and the early-morning risers hike along the paths, before we spotted a figure hurrying in our direction. Elyssa straightened up as she recognized Marco, and a few moments later he dropped down on the seat beside her.

"I have been here every day this week, hoping you might come looking for me," he said. "But you only show up when you think I might have news. You don't care about *me*, you only care about what I might know."

"Of course I care about you," she said sharply. "But I must be careful about meeting strange men in public venues."

"Then you must be desperate if you've sought me out now."

"I came to learn what you know about the drowning of the bastard prince," she said. "None of the royal family members have bothered to share information. But the rumor is that the inquisitor thinks Jamison has been murdered."

Marco nodded. "I have heard the same rumors."

"How could anyone tell such a thing from a dead body?"

"They found him in a lake, stripped of his outer clothing and weighted with rocks and branches," Marco said. "If he had fallen in accidentally, surely he would have been dressed. And he wouldn't have had heavy objects stuffed down his underthings."

Elyssa drew a quick breath. "No. I see that. Do they have any idea who might have wanted to kill him?"

"Anyone who ever met him?" Marco asked in a sardonic voice.

She met his gaze steadily. "Did that include you?"

He loosed a crack of laughter. "Oho! That's the real reason you're here this morning, is it? You want to see if I'm tangled up in this mess."

"Well, you're the one who's been threatening to assassinate a prince," she fired back.

"Not *this* one," Marco said. "Not such an insignificant target as the bastard who has three legitimate heirs between him and the throne."

"So you were not involved in his death," she said evenly.

His back was to me, so I couldn't see his expression, but there was a sneer in his voice. "If you really think I killed Jamison, you have boundless courage in meeting me here."

"Yes," she said, still in that level tone. "I have risked a great deal for you."

His voice softened. "Well, it's not me Malachi and his men will be looking for. I have been in Camarria more than two weeks, and apparently they think Jamison has only been dead a few days. I don't think I will get swept up in their net."

I felt Elyssa relax at his words; she had been genuinely worried, I realized. Perhaps she cared for Marco more than she knew. "If not you or your fellow revolutionaries, who might have killed him?" she asked again. "A serious answer this time!"

He shook his head. "I don't know, but it's damned inconvenient timing."

She was amused. "I said exactly the same thing when we first learned of his death! But why is it problematic for *you*?"

"Because Jamison's death makes Malachi suspicious of everyone!" Marco exclaimed. "And causes security at the palace to be doubled, I would expect. It will be nearly impossible to get anywhere near Cormac for the next few months."

Her amusement deepened. "Ah. So then Jamison's untimely death puts the rebels at a standstill."

"Something like that," he said.

"Well, I can't say I'm sorry to hear it."

The sneer was back in his voice. "Oh, so you've grown fond of the prince and his brother, have you?"

She came abruptly to her feet. "I'm not fond of anyone. Don't you remember?"

He was instantly standing beside her. The echo and I were the last to rise, but no one was paying any attention to us. "When can I see you again?" he demanded. "When can you come back here?"

"I don't know," she said. "I have no idea who might be watching me even now."

"A week from today," he pleaded. "Around this time."

She turned toward the entrance and began walking back, her pace slow as if she did not want to go. Marco fell in step beside her, the echo and I behind.

"If I can," she said. "I make no promises."

"You never do," he said. "And yet there you always are."

"I do not entirely favor of this war of yours," she warned. "Do not take me for granted."

He laughed and sketched her a mock bow even as they continued to stroll forward. "My lady," he said, "I would never make that mistake with you."

Elyssa paid a carriage-for-hire to take us back to the palace, seeming to be lost in her thoughts for the whole return journey. But she reverted to her usual liveliness when she led us to the breakfast room, where about half the noble guests were gathered, gossiping. Apparently, all of them had heard the news that Jamison might have been murdered, and they could not stop speculating about who might be involved.

"Of course, the last place anyone saw him alive was in Alberta—at your father's house, wasn't it, Elyssa?" someone asked, clearly intending to be provocative.

"So I understand," Elyssa replied, smiling widely. "But if my father had wanted him dead, I think he could have found any number of places on his own property to bury the body where it would never be discovered. I think we must look for another culprit."

Some of the nobles looked shocked at her answer; a few tried to stifle their laughter. Elyssa merely took a bite of a pastry and asked, "Has anyone planned an outing for this afternoon? It's so dull just to sit around thinking about murder."

In fact, the women from Banchura had organized an excursion to Amanda Plaza, so a large group set out shortly after the meal. More activities unfolded in the next few days, as men headed off to see horse races and women entertained themselves with shopping. I noticed that Lady Marguerite and Lady Vivienne skipped most of the group expeditions, but Elyssa was game for any outing. I didn't think she particularly enjoyed these excursions, she just couldn't bear to be left behind.

I didn't care much for the shopping trip, but I did rather enjoy the excursion on the following morning, when a noble from Sammerly took about ten other guests to the site of a new bridge that was being built in a fashionable part of town.

"Garnet Reach will be the highest bridge in the city when it's done," the Sammerly man explained to those of us who shared his carriage on the ride over. "Taller than any building! They say it's quite the engineering feat."

The new bridge, when we arrived at the construction site, appeared to be about two-thirds of the way to completion. I took advantage of Elyssa's lax control to crane my neck and stare at the marvelous combination of metal and stone. It rose at a steep angle over a pretty little public square built around a central fountain. As with the bridge over the Amanda Plaza, Garnet Reach seemed to have no purpose except to be ornamental, since anyone would have found it simpler to walk across the square than to climb up and over its high arch.

"Do you see that?" the Sammerly lord demanded, shepherding us over to the shadow directly underneath the span. "Here's a grate where people can toss money for the goddess. You know it will be a game with people to stand at the very top and see how many coins they can drop in without having them bounce away."

Lady Cali shaded her eyes and gazed up at the bridge's underside, which from this vantage point was a highly exaggerated curve. "When will it be completed?"

"In a couple of months, I think," he answered vaguely. "Cormac would know."

"Well, I think it's charming," pronounced one of the Banchura triplets, whom someone had just addressed as Leonora. "I don't know that I will ever go to the effort of crossing it, but it's very pretty."

Nobody could muster more admiration than that, so in a few moments we were all bundled back into our carriages and returning to the palace. It was almost lunchtime, and the rest of the day stretched ahead of us with a disquieting emptiness.

"How shall we occupy ourselves tonight?" asked Nigel as a group of us crossed the enormous palace foyer. "Shall we play cards again?"

"No, haven't you heard?" Leonora exclaimed. "We're organizing a musical evening."

"That sounds like fun," Cali said, but Nigel looked wary.

"What—you're bringing in professionals or—"

"No!" another triplet replied. "*We* shall perform—all of us! Or at least, any of us who have musical abilities. We've asked the servants to set up a special room, and anyone who wants to can play and sing. Everyone else can listen."

"How delightfully provincial!" Elyssa drawled.

"Yes, well, no one's asking you to perform," said Leonora. "Or come make fun of the rest of us who do."

"But I wouldn't miss the chance to see everyone's hidden talents on display."

"Talents?" asked a man's voice behind us. "How will they be displayed?"

Almost as one, the six nobles and their echoes swiveled around to greet the new arrival. All of the women looked delighted to see Prince Jordan, but not one of them could have felt her heart bound as wildly as mine did. Elyssa hung back a little, but the Banchura women all surged forward, patting him on the arm and murmuring condolences about his brother. He was dressed in sober black and looked like a raft of driftwood in a sea of compassionate blue.

"Thank you," he said finally, holding up his hand to indicate he was done with expressions of sympathy. "It has not been easy, but we are coping as best we can. But Cormac wants you all to know—*I* want you to know—that we are very much aware that we have guests in the house and we cannot ignore you any longer." He made a point of touching each of the nobles with his gaze, and then he looked straight at me. I stared right back, and I saw him give the briefest nod. "We want you to know that we have not forgotten you," he said, and I knew he was speaking directly to me. "And we hope you realize our thoughts are with you." He emphasized the word *hope* very slightly. I felt the faintest smile curl my lips and then I cast my eyes down, breaking the gaze. Otherwise I was afraid some stupidly giddy expression would cross my face and someone would surely notice.

"That's thoughtful of you," said Leonora. "But we realize what a difficult time this is. If you wish us gone, we would all be willing to pack up and leave in the morning."

"No—that's the last thing my brother or I would want," he said. "Cormac thinks he will be ready to join you again tomorrow night. Perhaps at a simple dinner."

"We would welcome that," said another triplet.

"But what is this activity you are planning for tonight?" Jordan went on. "I know you have been forced to devise your own entertainments."

"A musical evening where anyone who wishes may get up and perform," said the third triplet.

"Does it not sound fabulous?" Elyssa asked. "Does it not make you wish you were not in mourning so that you could attend?"

He glanced her way, briefly looked at me again, and answered seriously, "I do wish I could be there. I find myself enjoying every conversation with our guests, even the most unexpected ones. Alas, I am doubtful that I will be able to leave my father's side tonight. But perhaps tomorrow."

Leonora patted his arm again. "We understand. We're just glad we've had this chance to see you and to tell you how sorry we are."

A few more words along these lines, and then Jordan bowed and continued on his way. The rest of us headed straight for the dining room, where servants were already laying out the noon meal. Afterward, some of the nobles went off to practice their musical selections, others gathered to play cards, and the rest simply retreated to their rooms.

Since Elyssa had absolutely no interest in either cards or music, she had little choice but to head upstairs. Once inside our room, however, she seemed to find it difficult to settle, and she spent at least a half hour pacing. The echoes and I sat motionless behind the screen, trying not to breathe, hoping she had forgotten our existence. It was a relief when she flung herself onto her bed and willed herself to sleep.

The air behind the screen was close and stifling, so I rose from my narrow bed and crept out into the main chamber. It was a risk, of course, but I could feel the drugged drag of Elyssa's dreaming; I didn't think she would wake any time soon.

There was a divan set right before the window, positioned to catch the afternoon sun, but I didn't sit. Instead, I stepped up to the window and rested my forehead against the glass, gazing down at the streets and shops below. All those people hurrying by, bent on their own errands, carrying on their own individual lives. What would it be like to be one of them? To wear a red dress because I wanted to, to cross the street because there was something intriguing on the other side, to drink wine or not drink wine or laugh or weep or merely breathe? Autonomous and unafraid? Would I know what decisions to make? Would I be able to earn money, decide how to spend it, learn how to cook, feed myself, clothe myself, rely on no one but myself to navigate my days? I longed for freedom, but what if it destroyed me? I had never even walked out of a room of my own volition. How could I manage an entire life?

A slight noise behind me made me spin around, sending one fearful look toward the bed. But Elyssa was still deeply asleep, curled in an unhappy knot under the covers, her face drawn into a closed ball of worry. The sound had come from behind the screen—and it came again. A shuffle of feet, an awkward bump against a piece of furniture, another footfall on heavy carpet.

And then the echoes stepped out into the room, the hurt one limping along with the aid of the other one. They had their arms around each other's waists and their gazes trained on the floor as if studying the pattern of the roses worked into the rug. But they were making their way slowly in my direction. Following me to the window.

Following *me*.

CHAPTER FIFTEEN

Somewhat to my surprise, almost all the noble guests attended the "musical interlude" that night, though my guess was that most of them only showed up because no other entertainment was available. However, a few of them genuinely seemed excited about the event, and I myself was rather looking forward to it. It had to be better than pretending to play cards.

Servants had set up one of the larger parlors as a performance venue, with a small stage in the front of the room and rows of chairs lined up to face it. They had managed rather theatrical lighting that kept the stage bright but most of the chairs in shadow. There was some jostling for position as individuals tried to find seats for themselves and their echoes near people they found congenial, and those who intended to perform insisted on sitting by the aisles. Elyssa and Deryk had hung back to whisper together, so by the time they entered the room most of the more desirable chairs were taken. They ended up seating themselves in the second-to-last row. There was room for Deryk's echoes next to him, but I had to sit in the very back row, Elyssa's echo on one side of me and a few empty seats on the other side. Unaccountably, there was a space of about five feet between the last row and the one in front of it, as if a section of seating had been removed for some reason. But as this put me even farther from Elyssa, I didn't mind at all.

Once the performances started, I was impressed by the depth of talent on display. In particular, the Banchura sisters were excellent singers, backed by a chorus of their echoes who merely hummed along in harmony, as they were incapable of producing words. Still, the effect was gorgeous and a little eerie.

I found myself wondering if I could sing. I had never made the attempt—never even considered the notion. I tried humming the last few notes of the song I had just heard, but the faint vibration in my throat felt so foreign that I instantly stopped. If I ever *was* living on my own, I doubted I would take up singing.

The hour was relatively late, and a few audience members had already gone upstairs to seek their beds, when I heard the door behind me open as someone quietly slipped into the room. I didn't look up until the newcomer dropped onto the seat next to me, three echoes settling down beside him. Then, keeping my head bowed, I cut my eyes over—to find Prince Jordan regarding me with a lift of his eyebrows. The room was not so dark that he would miss my start of surprise and the look of pleasure that crossed my face.

"I hope I am not unwelcome?" he asked in a low voice, once again putting the emphasis on the word he had decided should be my name.

"No—decidedly not," I whispered back.

"I enjoyed our last conversation very much," he said. "I have been wishing for a chance to have another."

"And I have been wishing for a chance to tell you how sorry I am about your brother."

He nodded gravely. "It has put the whole family in chaos. There has been no time, these past few days, to do anything but grieve."

"I'm sorry," I said again.

"The blow has been most severe to my father," he said. "His relationship with Jamison was always complicated by guilt as well as love, which is why, I think, he allowed Jamison so much license. He could not bear to punish Jamison for his transgressions because Jamison was the living proof of his own."

"You sound like you are not mourning quite as much as your father."

He made an uncertain gesture. When he rested his hand again on his thigh, his arm pressed slightly against mine. He did not move it away. Through the velvet of his jacket and the silk of my sleeve, I felt the heat rising from his body. "I found Jamison difficult to love," Jordan said. "When we were younger, he was a bully. When we were older, he alternated between being resentful and being cruel. I always thought it was an object with him to see how far he could push my father. Cormac was closer to him than I was, but even Cormac would get fed up from time to time. And now Cormac is wrestling with his own guilt because *he* is the one who insisted Jamison stay behind in Alberta to make amends for some transgression. If not for that, Jamison would be alive today."

"That must be very hard."

"My stepmother, of course, is delighted that he is dead," he went on. "Tabitha is not fond of any of us, but she *hated* Jamison."

I was a little surprised that he was speaking so freely to someone who was a complete stranger—and who was *strange* in many other ways—but then I thought perhaps he had had no one else to talk to these past few days. And, obviously, there was no risk that I could repeat his words to anyone. I was the perfect confidante. "Your stepmother isn't fond of any of you?" I repeated. "Are you including your father on that list?"

Jordan nodded. "She is his second wife, you know. An Empara girl, chosen in a desperate attempt to keep peace with the western provinces more than twenty years ago. She hates my father and he hates her, but he at least attempts to maintain civility. Tabitha only makes an effort in public, and even then it is easy to read past her pretense."

"It does not sound like a comfortable way to live."

He exhaled a laugh. "No, there are days it is unbearably tense. Cormac and my father and I have a tight bond, and that has not changed, but everything else is extremely fraught." Now he sighed. "I had thought at least Cormac might be happy when he married Vivienne, but now even that is to be taken away from him."

"Do you dislike Lady Marguerite?" I asked softly, glancing at her where she sat a couple of rows away.

"On the contrary. From what I've seen of her, she is a gentle lady with a great deal of kindness. I have sometimes thought she was a little sad, but every time I had the thought she would smile and banish the impression."

"What would she have to be sad about?"

He shrugged. "I think perhaps many of us conceal worries and disappointments from the world."

It was a daring question, but in the dimly lit room, with my voice partly obscured by Cali singing, I felt oddly brave. "What makes *you* sad?"

We had been sitting side by side, facing the stage, trying as much as possible to appear as if we were not engaged in conversation at all. But now he looked down at me, deliberately and unwaveringly, and I did indeed read some melancholy in his fine eyes. "I dread the day I am forced to marry Elyssa," he said. "I have always thought she is colder than my stepmother, and just as cruel. To be bound to such a woman for the rest of my life seems like a terrible fate."

I was still feeling brave—and consumed with curiosity. "Is there someone else you would prefer to marry?"

He shook his head. "I have met most of the eligible noblewomen of the realm and found many of them charming and many of them silly and all of them eager to wed into the royal family," he said. "I have formed no *aversion* to any of them—except Elyssa—but no particular attachment, either."

"Not even one of the triplets?" I asked, gently teasing.

He smiled. "I enjoy them," he admitted. "I think they would be easy lifelong companions. Though it is hard to imagine them ever separated. I think they are more likely to find three hapless low nobles and carry them off to their manor in Banchura and keep them there like pets of whom they are exceedingly fond."

I did not know the triplets well, but I could instantly envision that scenario. "I think that would be a happy household," I said.

"Much happier than mine is likely to be," he agreed.

"How certain is it that this marriage to Elyssa will go through?"

He shook his head. "I don't know. I do know my father is constantly negotiating with the rebel factions of the western provinces. Some of his advisors recommend force instead of diplomacy—but that would lead to civil war, and so many lives lost! If bloodshed and violence can be averted because I have agreed to marry a woman I cannot stand…Well, what does my happiness count against the safety of the realm?"

"That's a noble sentiment."

"My father informs me that the life of a royal appears to be one of privilege and indulgence, but, in fact, it is bounded by sacrifice and selflessness." He took a deep breath. "And so, if it is demanded of me, I will marry Elyssa."

"Maybe it won't be as bad as you fear," I said. I was sure it would be worse than he imagined, but I didn't want to say so.

He glanced down at me again, his face very sober. "I don't know how I will bear it," he said quietly. "It was bad enough before. But now—knowing about *you*—it seems impossible. The only advantage might be that if we are in the same household, I will be able to shield you in some fashion. But to carry out the duties of a husband while knowing you are nearby—even in the same room—" He shook his head.

I felt a little faint. Somehow I had not put all those pieces together—that if Elyssa married Jordan, I would be spending the rest of my life just a few feet from him. Unable to talk to him, unable to touch him. A mute and miserable witness to their most intimate moments—

Which was when I remembered the last time Elyssa had shared intimate moments with a man who possessed three echoes. I had successfully fended off Lord Roland's echo, but would I want to submit to Jordan's? Someone who looked so much like the prince but who was completely devoid of his soul? Would I be able to pretend the echo was actually Jordan? Would that make the experience better or worse?

I spoke in a strangled voice. "You might be glad to know that Elyssa probably would prefer to carry out marital relations without the echoes as witnesses. She would no doubt banish us to another room."

He gave me a crooked smile. "I suppose that would make it better, but only a little," he said. "I have my doubts that I will be able to perform at all."

I could not help myself. I laughed, though I was able to smother the sound with a hand across my mouth. "I feel certain this is not a proper conversation for you to be having with *anyone*, let alone the echo of the woman you are supposed to marry," I said.

He looked shocked and guilty. "No! It is not! I apologize most profusely! Normally I am the most decent of fellows and I never say anything remotely inappropriate. I don't know what's gotten into me. It's just that you—" Another glance down at me. "You're different," he ended lamely.

"I'm glad."

"And it *won't* be strange to be married to Elyssa, because you will not be there," he said with renewed energy. "My attention has been taken up with this business with Jamison, but I *will* look into your situation. I promise."

"Has the inquisitor learned anything new about Jamison's death?" I asked.

I felt Jordan's body grow tense beside me, and then he relaxed and made another gesture. This time, when he dropped his hand, it was to the space between our bodies. Right next to my own hand. His knuckles brushed against mine, and my fingers uncurled just a little in response. He bent his own fingers back and intertwined them with mine.

I sat there absolutely motionless, absolutely speechless, in an ecstatic trance.

It was a long moment before Jordan spoke, but he did not disengage his hand. "Malachi has learned something with potentially devastating consequences," he said, staring straight at the stage where the lord from Sammerly and his echoes were setting up stringed instruments. "Jamison most likely was killed by a high noble."

It was difficult to care about Jamison's murderer when Jordan was holding my hand, but I managed to summon a shocked tone as I said, "How dreadful! What makes him think that?"

"Because they found a second body in the lake next to Jamison's. And it appears to be the body of an echo." He glanced at me, then back at the stage, where the lord was tuning his strings. "That information is not generally known yet, but it will be shortly. The thought is that perhaps Jamison argued with a noble and they came to blows. Jamison was knocked into the lake, but brought an echo into the water with him. So whoever is missing an echo is the likeliest suspect."

"But—an echo looks exactly like his or her original! It would seem to be an easy mystery to solve."

"Ah, but there is a strange feature to echoes. As they die, they start to lose their differentiation. If our dead echoes lay side by side, apparently, within a couple of days you would not know which one was mine and which one was yours."

"I do not have an echo," I reminded him. "I *am* one."

Unexpectedly, he lifted my hand to his mouth and kissed the palm. "No," he said. "You are an original."

I could not speak. I could only stare at him and wish he would never relax his grip.

There was a slight noise behind us, and Jordan quickly looked around. Two figures stood in the doorway, quietly talking. I thought one might be the inquisitor but the room was dark enough that I could not be sure. Was it also dark enough to conceal how closely Jordan was sitting to an echo?

I freed my hand and murmured, "You must go."

"I must," he said regretfully. "But I promise you, I am thinking about you every day."

You cannot possibly be thinking about me as much as I am thinking about you. "I am glad to hear it," I said quietly.

He hesitated, as if he would say more, then merely nodded and stood up, his echoes all rising beside him. In a moment, they had filed out of the row, out of the room, out of my life.

But he had kissed my hand.

Kissed my hand.

Oh, if I hadn't felt real before, I certainly did now.

For the next few days, I felt like my skin had taken on an extra layer, a thin sheen of crushed diamond that sparkled with a sensation that was either scalding heat or numbing cold. I couldn't tell. I just knew that I almost gasped every time I touched some new material, whether it was the velvet of a rose petal or the silk of bath soap. All my senses were on high alert; it was like I could hear a low, continuous murmur all around me, all the time, from every argument and whispered conversation of every single soul residing in the palace. I could stand at the window and look down at the street and read the denominations of the coins in the hands of passersby.

I was so *alive*. I could see and feel and hear *everything*.

Every other visitor to the palace was irritable and bored, but I was delighted by every new detail that came my way. I noticed the buttons on the livery of the footmen, the pattern woven into the dinner napkin, the scent of wax on the freshly polished bannister. To me, nothing was dull, nothing was insignificant, nothing was ordinary.

Over those next few days, I watched ceaselessly for Jordan's appearance at every meal, on every excursion. Each time I saw him, my heart started beating with a riotous delight. I had to look away, focus on the floor, so that my eyes did not convince my mouth to break into an ungovernable smile. But I always had to look up again, to be ready to meet his gaze when he glanced my way—and he always glanced my way. Every day. Every time.

There were no more chances to talk at any of those meals, any of those encounters in the hallway. A few days after the musical evening, Cormac arranged for another ball. I almost fainted from the excitement of imagining the possibility of another waltz with Jordan—but I was not the only one who remembered the last time he had solicited Elyssa's hand for a dance. She was determined not to be supplanted again, and the two times he approached us that night, she made sure her echoes were safely behind her. He could do no more than flick swift, rueful glances in my direction while he bowed over Elyssa's hand and I curtseyed to one of his echoes.

But I could still stare up into the face of his echo and dream.

CHAPTER SIXTEEN

The morning after that second ball, Cormac invited his guests to accompany him to the botanical gardens. Even the reclusive Lady Marguerite, who often opted to skip events, joined the others for this outing. Elyssa did not bother to mention that she had been to the gardens only a week ago; she just accepted the invitation with every appearance of enthusiasm.

The day was warmer than usual and many of the nobles seemed to find the stroll through the gardens less enjoyable than they had expected. Before we had even made it to the reflecting pool at the center of the garden, several of the women had settled onto decorative benches and expressed the intention to merely sit and enjoy the sunshine.

Lady Vivienne offered to share her bench with Elyssa, but Elyssa shook her head. "I have been idle for too many days. I will walk for a bit," she said, striding on at such a lively pace that no one else was tempted to keep up with her. After a few bends in the pathway around tall ornamental grasses and fat blossoming bushes, she was out of sight of the rest of her party.

As she wended her way past a small trickling fountain, she was abruptly joined by Marco, falling in step beside her. She must have been expecting him because she didn't start in alarm.

He said, "Did you need to bring a whole entourage with you to protect yourself from my importunities?"

"I didn't invite them, I accompanied them," she retorted. "But I thought, as long as I was here, I would try to separate myself and see if you had any news."

"Some, though you may have already heard it. They've found a second body in the lake. Near Jamison's."

She nodded. "My maid tells me it was the body of an echo. Apparently this has convinced the inquisitor that a noble was involved in Jamison's death."

Marco nodded in turn. "The theory I've heard is that Jamison must have tried to seduce a noblewoman, she resisted, and both Jamison and one of her echoes tumbled into the water."

"It sounds plausible enough," Elyssa said dryly.

"And apparently the echo has rotted so much that they can't determine who her original is," Marco added. "So the king's inquisitor will be interviewing every noblewoman in the Seven Jewels and counting the echoes at her back."

"I'm not worried," she said. "I have my three."

"I only see two," he said.

That made her laugh. "Oh, Marco! My dear! Have you been fretting about me? How impossibly sweet. But I assure you, my third echo is even now moping in my bedroom, nursing a hurt ankle. And if that evil little inquisitor wants to go nosing about in my room to make certain of it, I will hand him the key myself."

Marco watched her a moment, his expression serious. "Would you tell me?" he asked. "If Jamison had tried to harm you and you had pushed him to his death?"

She seemed to debate the point. "Would I tell you I had accidentally killed the king's son? No, I don't believe so. But I'm not surprised to find someone else did it. He was a dreadful man."

"And he was never called to account for his actions," Marco said. "That is one reason we need revolution, so that the powerful are forced to pay for their sins."

"I thought your rebellion was on hold for the moment. Didn't you say security had grown so tight around the palace that you wouldn't be able to get in?"

"I did. But I've learned about a way in that might offer easier access. There are always guards at the front, of course, and so many servants at the back entrances that no one could slip in unobserved. But there's another door on the north side, close to the stables. It's only used by servants getting carriages ready for their masters, so it doesn't see much traffic. And it's never guarded because it's always kept locked from the inside."

She just cast him a sideways glance and shrugged.

He came to a halt, put his hand on her shoulder, and turned her to face him. "But someone could unlock it at a predetermined time to allow a friend inside."

She stared at him. Forgetting to train my vacant gaze on the ground in front of me, I stared at him. The echo beside me, seeming almost as shocked as the rest of us, stared at him, too.

"You want me to unlock this secret door for you?" Elyssa demanded. "For what purpose?"

"I think you know."

Now I felt shock ripple through Elyssa with a force that sent all three of us a step backward. "So you can murder Cormac?"

"It would change the stakes dramatically. It would force Harold to acknowledge how serious we are."

"It would ignite civil war! *And* be the death of a man I have no reason to dislike."

Marco frowned and closed the small space she had opened between them. "You know there will be bloodshed if the western provinces are to obtain their freedom. You know there is a cost to liberation."

"I never said I favored this war of yours! I don't care if Harold sits on the throne. I don't care if Alberta gains its independence or continues to swear fealty to the crown. Do you understand me? I don't *care*. And I'm not about to assist in the murder of the prince. I can't believe you would even ask it of me."

With a flounce, she turned to go, but Marco caught her arm and stopped her before she could take three steps.

"Then do you plan to tell the prince of the plots being hatched against him?" he snarled. "If you won't help me, will you betray me?"

She jerked her arm away and kept moving. "I will not be involved in your scheming one way or the other," she said over her shoulder. "I will not help you—but I will say nothing."

His voice revealed his frustration. "That's how it always is with you! You will not commit to one action or another! You will not say if you are with us or against us."

She walked on faster. "I am for *me*," she said in a hard voice. "I do not care about causes or countries."

He came to an abrupt halt. "Do you care about *me*?" he demanded.

She continued on a few paces, then swung around to face him. "Show me the life I could have with you—show me it could be a *good* life—and I will allow myself to care," she said. "Until then, I will fight only for myself."

She spun around and continued down the pathway so rapidly that the other echo and I almost had to run to keep up. Marco did not come after us, but I fancied I could feel the weight of his despairing gaze following us past the fountains and statues and rustling trees.

Elyssa was making some effort to calm her agitation, but I was nearly beside myself. Marco was still making plans to break into the palace and assassinate Cormac! Elyssa had refused to help him, but that didn't mean he wouldn't find another way in. I knew that, all this time, Marco had been plotting revolution—I had overheard enough of his passionate speeches—but I had never exactly put the pieces together. War. Assassination. Jordan's brother.

Like Elyssa, I hadn't cared.

But that was before I knew Jordan.

That was before I knew I could speak.

Jordan had not accompanied the group to the garden, so there was no chance of bumping against him and whispering a warning in his ear. Maybe tonight at dinner, or during whatever entertainment had been planned for the evening. But if I could not catch his attention, if I could not signal how important it was that I speak to him—and if he could not find some way to separate me from Elyssa—how could I ever let him know what the rebels were plotting?

I fretted all the way through our return journey to the palace. For these group excursions, we always took carriages, though I knew full well the distance to the garden was walkable. On the trip over, we had shared a vehicle with Nigel and his echoes, but for the ride back, Elyssa had managed to snag a smaller carriage that we had all to ourselves. She seemed lost in thought during the entirety of the short ride, staring out the window as if memorizing the layout of the city. I gazed out my own window, but my eyes were as blank and unseeing as any echo's should be, and I didn't notice a single sight or landmark.

When our caravan pulled up at the palace courtyard, I straightened in my seat in anticipation of climbing out, but Elyssa sank against the cushions and shut her eyes. What's more, she suddenly exerted control over the other echo and me, so that I felt compelled to lean back and feign sleep. I couldn't imagine why, but I could neither ask nor disobey.

All around us, we could hear the commotion of the other nobles exiting their carriages and calling back and forth. I kept waiting for one of the footmen to come open our door, but since none of our faces appeared impatiently in the window, they must have thought our vehicle was already empty. Soon enough, the nearby voices faded away and our carriage lurched into motion again with a slow, lumbering turn. I was still held by Elyssa's will, so I couldn't sit up and look out to see where we were going next.

Wherever it was, the trip didn't take long, because a few minutes later we came to another halt. I heard men's voices speaking in heavy country accents, caught the clanking and hammering sounds of people at work. When I inhaled, I breathed in the strong scents of manure and horse. My best guess was that we had arrived at the stables behind the palace.

It might have been ten minutes more that we sat in the carriage, pretending to sleep, while the noises from outside indicated that grooms were unhitching all the horses and leading them away. Our own vehicle rocked a little as the team was released. The motion made Elyssa sit up and place a hand over her mouth as if smothering a yawn. Then she slid across the seat, unlatched the door, and cautiously stepped out of the carriage. The echo and I were right behind her.

I got one quick look around the stable yards—which consisted of a cluster of large wooden buildings, fenced corrals, piled bales of hay, and muddy grounds—before someone noticed us and let out a yelp. Suddenly we were the center of a group of curious men, all dressed in rough workman's clothes and sporting a great deal of facial hair.

"My lady," said one, a big-boned middle-aged fellow who had an air of authority. My guess was that he was the head groom. He offered a deferential nod, but he was frowning. "How do you come to be back here?"

"I must have fallen asleep on the ride home," she said plaintively. She looked around apprehensively. "I don't even know— Where *am* I?"

"At the palace stables, my lady," the head groom answered. Looking over his shoulder, he issued a sharp command to the others who just stood there staring. "You lot get back to work now." Then he addressed Elyssa again, "It's just a short walk around the north wing of the palace there—you see?—and you'll be almost at the front entrance."

We all made a quarter turn to see where he was pointing. The palace reared up behind us, enormous and imposing, its terra-cotta walls looking fire-warm in the afternoon sun. From what I could tell, we would need to follow the long curving wing all the way around to make it to the courtyard in front.

"Oh, I don't think I can walk that far," Elyssa said breathily. "I'm not feeling very well. Isn't there a closer way in?"

He hesitated and then gestured toward an ivy-covered wooden fence that appeared to be a demarcation line between the bustle of the stable yard and the more civilized serenity of the palace grounds. Through an open gate, we could see the back wall of the palace, though the angle of the sun blurred it with dense shadow. I could barely make out a plain, narrow door set into the stonework of the lower story. "See right there? That's the nearest door," the head groom said. "But it's always locked unless someone's on his way out to come to the stables."

My heart tripped and then picked itself up and leapt into a frightened sprint. *This is the door Marco told her about. She said she wouldn't help him, but she's thinking about it.* The only reason I could control my breathing was that Elyssa remained so calm.

"Oh, yes, I see it," she murmured gratefully. "And I see a little bench there, right to the side. Could I just sit there awhile? Maybe someone will come out in a few minutes and I can step in."

"Maybe," he said doubtfully. "Why I don't have one of the boys go tell Lourdes you need assistance? She'll send someone right away."

Elyssa moved off, stepping daintily to avoid the patches of mud and piles of manure dotting her way. The echo and I followed with equal care. "I don't think that's necessary, thank you," she said. "I'll just sit there until I feel well enough to walk around to the front."

I could feel the head groom watching us as we made our way through the gate in the vine-covered fence and onto the palace grounds. Elyssa maintained the drooping posture and slow pace of someone claiming to feel faint, but her eyes darted around with interest, noting places a man might take cover if he was trying to avoid being seen by anyone from the palace or the stables. I could tell, because my eyes were glancing around just as rapidly as hers.

I was not surprised when Elyssa walked all the way to the door and pulled on its brass handle just to be sure it was locked. It was. She regarded the door for a moment in silence, as if wondering how else it might be breached, then made her way to the nearby bench. She sat on one end; the echo and I crowded together on the other end, trying to make sure we didn't accidentally touch her.

I figured Elyssa wouldn't want to stay there long—the day was hot, and she was not a patient person—but I also figured she wouldn't have to. I assumed that the head groom had instantly dispatched one of his underlings to the front of the palace and that

Lourdes herself would soon be sailing through the door. I guessed that Elyssa was counting on the same thing. For this plan to work, she would need to know how to find this door from inside the palace, and I was very sure we had never been to this region of the building before. From the scents drifting around us, I was guessing we were not only near the stables, but also the middens. Only servants would be familiar with these particular passageways.

We had been sitting there for a much briefer time than I had expected when the door did, in fact, swing open. But it wasn't Lourdes who stepped out. It was the stocky, sinister shape of the king's inquisitor.

He looked straight at us—as if he had known we would be there, though the expression he managed to fix on his face showed mild astonishment. He came directly over and offered a slight bow. "Lady Elyssa," he said. I couldn't tell if there was anything in his voice at all—doubt, suspicion, concern, surprise. Anything. "Is something wrong?"

She produced a wan smile. "So stupid. I fell asleep in the carriage on the way back from the gardens and ended up here at the stables. I was just sitting for a few moments until I felt strong enough to walk to the front entrance. It feels so far away!"

"If you will accept my escort, I'll take you in right here through the servants' door. I warn you, the passageways are narrow and you may encounter a few unpleasant odors."

"Oh, would you? But I hate to divert you from your own tasks."

"They can withstand the delay of a few moments," the inquisitor said as he helped her to her feet. Neither of them glanced back to see if the echo or I needed assistance.

"Your hand is cold," he remarked as they paced slowly to the door. "That's not a good sign on such a hot day."

"No, I think I might need to lie quietly in my room for a few hours," she said.

He pulled the door open and we all stepped through, then waited as he turned to reset the locks. These included a dead bolt as well as a heavy chain that made a grim clinking sound when it was put in place. Then he took Elyssa's arm again and we continued down the haphazardly lit corridor. The inquisitor was right; the hallway stank of rotting food and what might be sewage, and it was dark and uneven besides. Elyssa covered her nose with one hand, and the echo and I did the same, but it didn't really help.

"I would apologize," Malachi said, "but I am certain you must have similar reaches in your manor house in Alberta."

"I suppose so, but I have never been to them!" she replied with a faint laugh. "But I am not complaining! I am grateful to learn of the shortcut."

"That's the laundry room," he said as we passed an open door where the much more welcome smells of strong soap and damp air came drifting out. "And most of these rooms are for storage. Linens and furniture, primarily."

"It seems provincial to exclaim, 'How big the palace is!' But its size truly is impressive," she said.

"Yes, it is a remarkable building filled with remarkable people," Malachi replied.

Neither of them made any additional effort at conversation for the rest of the short walk, which eventually took us directly into the great foyer that opened off the main entrance. I supposed every hallway on the ground level at some point led to this space. Elyssa surreptitiously glanced around to note what signposts could lead her back to this specific passageway. There was a tall vase full of dried red flowers and a small brass plaque hanging on the wall. Otherwise, there was very little to distinguish it from a half dozen hallways branching off from the main foyer.

"Thank you so much," she said, sketching the barest hint of a curtsey. "I know my way from here."

"Then I will return to my own pursuits," Malachi said. "I hope you feel better quickly."

Elyssa made her way to the stairwell slowly, as befit someone who felt faint and fragile, and even clung to the bannister as we climbed the stairs. But she crossed the threshold into her bedroom with her usual quick step, throwing off any pretense at being ill.

She didn't seem pleased to find Gretta already in the room, arm in arm with the injured echo, but Gretta was beaming.

"Look who's up and on her feet again!" the maid said as the echo wobbled where she stood. From what I could tell, the creature wasn't favoring her wounded leg and didn't appear to be in any pain. "I think she's healed! You can bring her down to dinner tonight!"

"Splendid," Elyssa said. "It was the only thing missing from my life."

"Did you enjoy your time at the gardens?"

Elyssa laughed shortly. "Not entirely."

"It's very warm," Gretta agreed. "Would you like a cool bath? Or would you like you to lie down for a while?"

"I'm fine," Elyssa said irritably. "Just—put the echoes somewhere I can't see them, and then go away. I can't think with everyone crowding around me."

Elyssa's back was to the maid, so she didn't see the other woman's sour expression, but Gretta just said, "Yes, my lady."

A few moments later, the echoes and I were in our sanctuary behind the screen, perched on our beds, and listening to Elyssa pace. Obviously, the conversation with Marco had upset her—well, it had upset me, too.

She wouldn't help Marco harm the prince, would she? She had told him the truth. She didn't care about this war, she didn't care about anything except herself, and she wouldn't risk her own reputation—her own safety!—by colluding with an assassin. And she knew how closely the inquisitor was watching over the palace grounds. Surely the fact that he had showed up so swiftly this afternoon had served as a reminder of that fact.

So she wouldn't help Marco. Would she? But that didn't mean Marco wouldn't find another way into the palace.

I had to talk to Jordan.

But there was no opportunity to speak to Jordan that night, at dinner or afterward as we all gathered to hear a concert that

Cormac had arranged. Jordan spent most of the evening with Darrily on one arm and a Banchura triplet on the other. He did manage to give me one quick look and a warm smile, but before I could even mouth the words *I need to talk to you,* Darrily claimed his attention again. She was a striking woman, with a face marked by both intelligence and humor; opals glowed against her dark skin like tiny moons against a night sky. But at that moment I hated her even more than I hated Elyssa.

"You've got your third echo back, I see," Deryk said, dropping into the seat next to Elyssa's when there was a short break between musical performances. "That must make you happy."

"Do you think so?" she replied.

He laughed. "Well, it would make *most* people happy. You're just unnatural."

She tilted her head to one side. "Am I? I find it hard to believe I'm the only noblewoman in the history of the Seven Jewels who has found her echoes to be tiresome."

"They tell stories about some ancestor of the king's inquisitor. A high noble who didn't like his echoes, either."

"What did he do about them?"

Deryk shrugged and settled more comfortably in his chair. Beside him, his echoes did the same. "Had them all killed, so they say."

She turned her head to regard him. I was staring at him, too, but my expression was horrified, while hers was suspicious. "Is that really true?"

"*I* don't know. It happened a hundred years ago or more! But it certainly seems like something Malachi would do, so why not one of his relatives?"

"Well. I'll have to remember that," she said.

Lady Cali, sitting in front of them, turned around just then. "Shh. The next musician is supposed to start!"

Elyssa rolled her eyes but obediently fell silent, and we all pretended to listen to the flautist who performed next. But Elyssa was bored, Deryk was idly scanning the crowd, and I was trying to recover from my shock.

Had one of Malachi's forebears really killed off his echoes? Had he been punished for the act, or did no one care? Had he simply gotten rid of the echoes because he considered them inconvenient—or had one of them developed a sentience that the noble found distasteful? Did Jordan know this story?

How could he believe I would ever get free of Elyssa?

CHAPTER SEVENTEEN

There was no opportunity to speak to Jordan the following morning, either, as he did not join the activity that had been organized for the day. A fleet of carriages had been requisitioned to ferry more than half of the visiting guests to a set of ruins on the northern edge of the city.

"I honestly cannot imagine anything more dreary and pointless," Elyssa complained to Deryk and Nigel, who shared our carriage. "Why would anyone want to go see such a thing?"

"Because it's historic?" Nigel said doubtfully. "Letitia and Lavinia said the place is very picturesque."

"They've been there before and they're going *back*?" Elyssa demanded. "I simply don't understand."

"You could have stayed behind in your room," Deryk pointed out.

"Like the delicate Lady Marguerite, who seems to have a headache every other day?" Elyssa said with some malice. "I don't want people thinking of *me* as some die-away invalid."

"That's not fair," Nigel said. "If she doesn't feel well—"

"I like her," Deryk said. "But I agree. She seems sickly."

"So I will trudge around these stupid ruins with *vigor*," Elyssa said with such emphasis that both men started laughing.

The site, when we finally arrived, was indeed picturesque in a dramatic, mournful way. It held a series of crumbled buildings made of weathered gray stone, all enclosed by a tumbled wall of the same material. The site had apparently been a fortified castle at some point, the last outpost on the road that led across the mountains to a host of unfriendly nations. King Edwin had built the place and installed his most trusted vassal to oversee a small army and be the first line of defense against an invasion.

"They say Edwin kept the lord so well-funded that he couldn't possibly spend all his money on upkeep," Cormac said as we followed him across the uneven ground and peered into the fallen shapes of dairy houses and soldiers' barracks. "The story is that there are crates of gold hidden all over the property. People come from every province in the kingdom, searching for treasure. But as far as I know, no one has found more than a coin or two."

"Well, that does add spice to the tour," Elyssa said, picking up her skirts and heading toward the castle itself. A few of its walls showed damage where window or door openings had enlarged to great gaping holes, but for the most part, the building was intact. Indeed, we could hear the laughing voices of a handful of nobles who had already entered and started exploring. Some even appeared at windows two and three stories up, waving to the rest of us. I assumed that meant one or two of the internal staircases were still safe to use.

We spent a couple of hours with the rest of the party, winding our way through the old stone passageways, wondering aloud how people must have lived several hundred years ago, poking around under loose floorboards looking for treasure. A wagon full of servants had accompanied us, and they served a light lunch, spreading it out over dozens of blankets arranged on the unkempt lawn. The weather was cooler than it had been yesterday, and the breeze rolling down off the mountains in the distance made the day altogether delightful. Even I forgot to fret. Even Elyssa seemed to enjoy herself.

Everyone seemed tired but happy on the ride back; no one in our carriage spoke much, but no one seemed to mind. So it was quite a shock, when we all cheerfully disembarked in the palace courtyard, to find some of the inquisitor's men waiting to whisk Cormac away—and to find the rest of the palace guests milling around in disbelief.

What is it? What happened? What's wrong? Did you hear? It can't be true!

We all crowded around Darrily, who had opted not to join the excursion. But all I heard the Pandrean woman say was, "She's been arrested for the murder of Lord Jamison."

Apparently, half the others hadn't caught the news, either, because many of them pressed forward and cried out, "What did you say? Who's been arrested?"

"Lady Marguerite," Darrily said, raising her voice and speaking very plainly. "Arrested for killing Jamison. She says he tried to assault her, and she fought back, and he fell in the lake. She says it's not her fault."

"But then why didn't she tell anyone?"

"She was afraid no one would believe her story."

"Well, I *don't* believe it!" someone exclaimed, but others shushed him.

Another voice rose above the babble to say, "Hold on a moment, though. Wasn't there an echo killed in the struggle, too? But Marguerite's got all three of her echoes with her, doesn't she? I mean, I never counted, but—"

"She has *seemed* to have three echoes," Darrily confirmed. "But one of them has been her maid! Pretending! All this time!"

That announcement provoked a storm of disbelief and another round of questions. I was too dumbfounded to catch everything the others said. A servant? Acting as an echo? For the entire two weeks that we had been here? How could that be possible? Yet, as I knew from my own experience, most people paid almost no attention to echoes. They didn't look closely at echoes' faces, they didn't notice whether or not an echo precisely mimicked the original's actions. If the imposter made no sudden, independent moves that were drastically different from the original's, the deception could probably be successful for a long time.

I squeezed my eyes shut. The card game. The night Deryk had spilled his wine on Marguerite, and his echoes had spilled wine on her echoes—but only one of her echoes had leapt up in response. Had that been the maid, unable to control her instinctive reaction? But moments later, the other two echoes had also come to their feet in a leisurely, uncoordinated manner. Marguerite might have one imposter among her shadows, but the other two were a little independent as well.

"So sweet little Marguerite killed Lord Jamison," Deryk said. "Now what?"

Darrily shook her head. "I don't know."

But all three of the Banchura triplets, and every one of their nine echoes, looked aghast. The one I thought was Leonora spoke with difficulty. "It is—in Camarria—murder is always punishable by death."

"Death? Don't be ridiculous," Cali said sharply.

One of the other triplets spoke up. Lavinia, maybe. "But it's true. It is one of the ways King Harold has been able to maintain such low crime throughout the city. Throughout the whole province of Sammerly, really."

"But he can't simply execute a high noble," someone said.

"There will be a trial, I suppose," Lavinia replied. "But if they have evidence against her— Oh, this is dreadful!" She burst into tears and blundered into the arms of her sisters, who were also weeping.

The others all looked at each other, stunned. "But Marguerite is a *high noble*," Cali repeated, as if such a station was inviolable.

"And Cormac's intended bride," someone else answered.

"I can't believe the king will have her executed."

"Cormac would never agree to it!"

"*Cormac!*" cried a woman in a hysterical voice, and everyone swung around to gape at the speaker. It was Vivienne, who was usually so quiet and withdrawn. "Cormac will never stand up to his father, never gainsay him, no matter what disastrous course Harold embarks on! Oh, that poor woman! I fear there is no hope for her." She pressed a hand to her mouth and turned jerkily away. A moment later she was running in through the wide doors of the palace.

The nobles left behind just stared at each other. Lavinia pulled herself free from her sisters' comforting embrace and wiped her cheeks with a bit of lacy cloth. "I must go see for myself," she declared. "Maybe it isn't true."

A chorus of agreements following this statement, the whole group moved off in one untidy cluster, into the palace and up the stairs toward the women's guest suites. But as soon as we arrived, we knew that at least some of the rumors were accurate. Armed guards were standing at the open door to what I assumed was Marguerite's room, and from inside we could hear the inquisitor's voice raised in a blunt interrogation. Marguerite's replies were so soft we couldn't catch the words, but it scarcely mattered. Malachi sounded very sure he already knew the answer to any question he posed.

We had been standing uneasily in the hallway for only a few moments when a young servant girl came pushing through our ranks. "Let me through— Excuse me, I need to get past— *Let me through!*" she cried, utterly beside herself. I tried to get a good look as she shoved her way past. Was this the maid who had masqueraded as an echo? Did she love her mistress or hate her? What would become of her once this terrible day was over?

She burst into the room, calling out Marguerite's name, but a few moments later she was being dragged out the door by some of the inquisitor's men. She was still howling and protesting, begging them to let her go, swearing that she did not betray her mistress. She looked so desperate and wretched that I had to turn away when the inquisitor's men hauled her off to someplace where she would cause no more trouble.

The inquisitor himself emerged a few moments later, looking grim but triumphant. He cast one indifferent look at the crowd of nobles gathered in stunned silence and turned his head to speak to one of his men. "Clear the hall," he said, and then strode past the spectators as if they did not even exist.

His assistant was more diplomatic. "You should all go to your own rooms now. Very unfortunate things are happening here, but it does no good to stand around watching."

Darrily stood her ground. "*My* room is just down the hall."

"Well, then, perhaps it's time to go sit in the parlor for a while until the whole situation calms down," the guard said. "Come along now. Everyone disperse."

Ultimately, the whole mass of nobles did stream through the corridor and down the stairs to one of the parlors where they frequently gathered. Even the guests who hadn't been on the excursion to the ruins soon found their way to the room. The only ones missing were Cormac and Jordan. And Marguerite.

They were a changed group, though—no longer flighty and restless and full of laughing gossip. Most of them sat in a tight circle in the center of the room, their echoes fanned out behind them, and spoke in low voices or not at all.

"But how can he *do* it?" Cali burst out suddenly. "If Harold executes Marguerite, won't the governor of Orenza rise up in rebellion? Isn't civil war what the king wanted to *prevent?*"

"That's what I was told," Vivienne said wearily. "And now civil war could very well come anyway."

"This is the worst day I've ever spent in Camarria," said Leonora darkly.

Lavinia just looked at her. "The worst *so far.*"

"What happens to her echoes?" someone asked. "Will they be executed, too?"

"Why bother?" someone else replied. "Anytime an original dies, his echo falls dead beside him. No need to waste the arrows."

I stirred on my chair and tried not to let my surprise show. Was that true? If Elyssa's heart stopped beating, would mine stop as well? Would that be the case even now that I had gained some independence from her? I had always known my actions were tied to hers, but I had not realized that my very life was dependent on her continued existence. It was not a pleasant thought.

Deryk spoke up, his voice holding a certain ghoulish pleasure. "Oh, but when a noble is executed for treason, the echoes are always put to death at the same time," he said. "It's symbolic, you know. Echoes were *created* so no one could ever be certain which body contained the real person, which one was just a shell. To make sure a traitor is well and truly dead, the king must cut down the echoes alongside the original."

"That's horrible," Cali said.

Letitia shuddered. "I want to go home. Can we leave tomorrow morning?"

There was a general murmur of agreement until Darrily spoke up. "But should we just abandon Marguerite?" she asked. "Or should we stay to speak our protests to the king? Even if we can't change his mind, we can let him know how strongly we disagree with his actions."

"And what consequences may arise because of them," added Nigel.

"You might be right," Letitia said reluctantly. "And there's something else to consider. If we all leave the city, Marguerite may think we do not care what becomes of her. If we stay, perhaps it gives her the smallest shred of comfort."

"If we stay, and make Harold face us after he has carried out an execution, perhaps we shame the king," Cali said coldly.

Leonora sighed and slumped back into her chair. "Then we stay," she said. "But the goddess knows these will be bitter days."

Dinner was somber, the card games that Deryk arranged afterward were doleful, and all the nobles sought their rooms well before midnight. Gretta was waiting for us, but she took one look at Elyssa's face and elected to stay silent.

I doubted that anyone in the palace slept that night. I know that no one in our room did.

The next two days were just as quiet, just as tense, just as stuffed full with dread and anger and helplessness and disbelief. Things only got worse the afternoon of the second day because that was when the king held his brief trial of Lady Marguerite. Half the visiting nobles gathered outside the throne room, waiting as Marguerite and her two remaining echoes were marched inside by royal guards. The Banchura triplets attempted to follow them inside, no doubt to express their displeasure directly to the king, but the guards barred the way. It wasn't long before the prisoner was escorted out again, and a palace herald shared the verdict with the waiting crowd.

"Marguerite of Orenza has been condemned to death for the crime of murder," he intoned. "She will be executed at eight o'clock tomorrow morning in Amanda Plaza."

The nobles were all whispering furiously together, shocked and outraged even though they could not possibly be surprised. Almost as one, they turned toward the sitting room where they spent so much time.

Elyssa didn't follow them.

She stayed put just outside the throne room as the others moved away, seeming to be lost in thought. But after a minute or two, she gave one quick, decisive nod and began striding down the hall. In a moment, we were in the wide foyer, ignoring Lourdes as she turned in our direction; in another moment, we were out the door and on the streets of Camarria.

Elyssa didn't slacken her pace at all as she set out in an unfamiliar direction. I had to remind myself that she had been to the royal city many times, even if I couldn't remember those visits, and she probably knew exactly where she was going. She walked so swiftly that the third echo had a little trouble keeping up, because her ankle was still bothering her, but I took her arm to help her as best I could. The second echo copied my movements and added her own support, and we managed to keep from falling too far behind.

It wasn't long before we started passing through neighborhoods that were far less desirable than the ones that bordered the botanical gardens and Amanda Plaza. These streets were narrower, seedier, and a little more dangerous; the four of us drew no little attention from the men and women who hurried by.

Abruptly, Elyssa stopped in front of a disreputable-looking building that seemed to be a tavern, judging from the smells of beer and bread drifting out. For the first time, Elyssa seemed uncertain, reaching a hand out as if to open the door, then drawing her arm back as if afraid to go inside.

We stood there for about five minutes as she debated what to do, and then the door swung open and a man stepped out. He had the rough clothes and weathered skin of a laborer, but his face was young and cheerful. He gave Elyssa a bold and appreciative inspection before coming to a halt and saying, "Hello there, pretty lady, anything I can help you with?"

She didn't waste time being coy. "Yes. I need to speak to someone who rents rooms above this building. Can you take a message or ask the manager to come talk to me?"

The man managed what he probably thought was a fancy bow. "I'd be happy to. What's the name of the fellow you're looking for?"

"Marco Ross."

He laughed in disbelief. "Your luck's in. He just strolled through the door and ordered a pint. Do you want me to fetch him?"

She practically gasped with relief. "He's here? Yes—please. Thank you so much."

"Always a pleasure to help a lady," he answered, and sauntered back inside. Elyssa clasped her hands before her so tightly it hurt the bones. I knew because her agitation had strengthened her bond to her echoes, and all three of us were squeezing our own hands together just as painfully.

It was only a moment before Marco came pushing through the door, looking astonished and worried.

"Elyssa!" he exclaimed. "Is something wrong?"

"I'll do it," she said.

He was wholly confused. "Do what?"

"I'll unlock the door for you. I'll let you into the palace."

He gazed down at her, caught completely by surprise. "What happened?" he asked in a quieter voice. "What changed your mind?"

She made one short, sharp, angry gesture. "He has condemned her to death. As if he has a right to do that."

"Ah. The king has pronounced his sentence on Lady Marguerite. As expected." He glanced around as if looking for a place they could talk in private. There weren't many options. The street was noisy and dirty, but my guess was that the ambiance inside was even more vulgar. He settled for drawing her off the main road, into the questionable shelter of the alleyway between the tavern and a cobbler's shop in the adjacent building. The three of us followed.

"*I* didn't expect it," Elyssa said. "I couldn't believe he would have the nerve to execute a high noble."

"She *did* kill his son, if the inquisitor has his facts right. You don't think the king has a right to his vengeance?"

"She was defending herself from the bastard prince!" Elyssa burst out. "It should have been Harold's job to keep his son in check! And then for the king to decide—out of his own rage and grief—that an innocent woman is to *die*? If he will have his vengeance, well then, so will I."

Marco studied her for a moment, then nodded. "Thus do unjust kings make revolutionaries of us all."

"So I will help you," she said. "When do you want me to unlock the door?"

He thought it over. "When is the execution scheduled?"

"For tomorrow morning."

"Will you attend?"

She looked at him as if he was less than human.

"I suppose not," he answered. "Then that will be a good time for you to unlock the door. The inquisitor and most of his men will be out of the palace—half the world will be in Amanda Plaza—I can slip inside and find a place to wait until an opportunity arises."

"I'm sure there will be a guard or two left behind. If you're seen entering through the doorway or creeping through the halls—"

"No one will question me. I'll be wearing the livery of a palace servant."

Even in her agitation, she was surprised by that. "Where did you come by such a thing?"

He grinned. "Never mind that. What time can you be at the door?"

"The—the execution is scheduled for eight. I will aim to be there by half past the hour. I imagine it won't take long before someone notices the lock has been undone."

"I will be there directly afterward."

He had been standing so that his body shielded hers from the view of any passersby, but now she stepped away from the tavern wall and pushed past him. "But if you encounter me in the hallway, don't speak," she said. "Don't even look at me. Don't give anyone any reason to question *me*."

Marco pivoted to watch her. "Not ready to give your life for the cause, then?"

She gave him a swift look. "As if *you* are."

He laughed softly. "But I am. Tomorrow I very probably will."

She froze. "*What?*"

He shrugged. "What are the chances that I will find Cormac alone and unattended, and that I will be able to slit his throat before he calls for help? I may be successful, but my triumph most likely will come at the cost of my life."

She stared at him a moment. "Then I won't do it."

He came close enough to lay his hands on her shoulders and give them a hard squeeze. "Elyssa," he said. "What is more important? To fight against a tyrant or to keep one or two rebels safe?"

"I don't want you to *die*."

He shrugged. He still had not released his hold. "And maybe I won't. I might be lucky. I will certainly be careful."

She shook her head, genuinely upset. "I don't know, I don't know—"

He squeezed her shoulders again. "Elyssa," he said again. "If you don't unlock that door, I will try another passage. One way or the other, I am getting inside that palace and doing away with the prince. I will have my best chance at surviving this adventure if I come in through that back entrance. If you *don't* unlock it, you seal my doom."

"I hate you," she whispered.

"No, you don't," he said, pulling her into his arms and kissing her. His mouth was so demanding on hers, her response so passionate, that my own skin and body reacted; I felt Elyssa's sensations so clearly it was almost as if Marco had echoes. He kissed her even more deeply, backing her up hard against the tavern wall. The echoes and I lined up beside them, our own bodies grinding against the rough brick as if someone was pressing against us from the front.

Elyssa made a sound and wrenched her mouth away, pushing her fists against his chest when he would have resumed the kiss. *"No."*

"No you will not open the door for me, or no you do not want to come inside with me?" he asked, his voice husky with amusement and other emotions. "I have rooms just upstairs."

Now she broke free completely, smoothing down her hair and her skirts as if trying to smooth some of the wildness from her blood. "I will not come upstairs with you," she said.

He cocked his head. "But you'll unlock the door?"

She hesitated. "But I'll unlock the door."

He reached out a hand to touch her cheek. It was an unexpectedly gentle gesture for someone who could be so brutish. "And if I live through the deed? And come seek you out at your father's house? What kind of answer would you give me then?"

She picked up her skirts and walked deliberately around him so she was back on the street. "If you live," she said. "If this revolution really does come. Ask me again then."

"I will."

"All right. Then I'll—I don't know what to say. Perhaps I'll see you later."

He glanced down the street, suddenly frowning. "Where's your carriage?"

"I didn't use one."

"What, you ran all the way here from the palace?"

"I didn't think it would be so far."

"And so dangerous," he said.

She looked impatient. "No one bothered us."

He shook his head. "You were lucky. You'd better hire a vehicle to take you back."

Her laugh was so faint it hardly qualified as one. "I don't have any money with me. I was so upset I simply walked out the palace doors without even bothering to change my shoes."

"Well, then. I can take care of that. Come on. There's a carriage stand a few blocks away and I know the fellow who runs it. He'll take you home."

She fell in step beside him as they strolled out into the street. Elyssa and her echoes still drew considerable interest as we passed through the neighborhood, but the attention was far more circumspect now that Marco escorted us. It was the only time in my life I could imagine being grateful for his company.

"The driver will take me back to the palace," she corrected. "But that's not home."

Five minutes later, we had found the carriage stand and Marco had paid the driver and helped all four of us inside. He stood there for a moment looking up at her while she, her expression as serious as his own, gazed back.

"Tomorrow then," he said.

"Tomorrow."

The carriage ride back felt much shorter than the walk out, though traffic was heavy enough to make the pace almost as slow. Seeming unutterably weary, Elyssa sat motionless on her bench no matter how many bumps and ruts we encountered, but I was so flooded with anxiety that I almost could not force myself to sit still.

Tomorrow morning! She would set an assassin loose in the palace! I must tell Jordan, I *must*! I was tingling with so much nervousness and dread that I felt as if my whole body was a pincushion, and needles had been poked into every square inch of my flesh. But how could I get a message to him? Would he be at the dinner that night? Would he even look in my direction?

And if he didn't—? How could I have this dreadful knowledge and be unable to share it?

It would almost be better to be an insensate block than to be this writhing ball of inexpressible terror.

Jordan wasn't at the dinner table. Neither was Cormac. More than half of the nobles failed to attend, and those who did barely exchanged a dozen words. No one lingered, and no one attempted to socialize afterward. Elyssa went straight up to her room and sat on the bed for two solid hours without moving. Behind the folded screen, I could not bring myself to sit or lie down, but merely stood there, tense and straining, my fists clenched, yearning toward the door.

Even if I could walk through it without Elyssa's knowledge, would I be able to find Jordan and tell him what I knew? Who else might I encounter in the hallway—servants, noble guests, the inquisitor? How would I be able to explain who I was and what I wanted? And what if Elyssa discovered me before I found Jordan? Oh, my life would be completely over.

So because I was a coward, an assassin would slip inside the palace tomorrow, and Cormac would die, and it was all my fault.

I forced my hands to uncurl. I forced myself to turn toward the bed and look at it as if I might someday lie in it again.

Only then did I realize both of the other echoes were standing. Both had turned when I did, both were staring at their beds.

They were copying *me*.

CHAPTER EIGHTEEN

I woke with a start when I heard Elyssa moving about her room. I hadn't expected to sleep at all, but I must have dropped off at some point because I had that sense of drugged disorientation that came from sudden waking. Judging by the uncertain light peeking through the window, it was around seven in the morning.

Lady Marguerite was scheduled for execution at eight.

And Cormac might be dead by midnight.

During the hours of tossing and turning, I had come up with something like a plan. As Elyssa led us down the stairs and across the foyer, heading toward the malodorous back passage, I would be on the lookout for anyone else we might encounter in the hallways. Lourdes, if we were really lucky, but almost anyone would do. And then I would fall to the floor in a simulated faint, which would cause a great deal of consternation. If Lourdes was involved, servants would be called, and possibly even a physician; Elyssa would not be able to simply leave me behind, but would be subject to questions and her own examination from concerned onlookers. No doubt someone would insist on seeing her back to her room, and people would watch her solicitously all day. She would never have a chance to sneak to the back door and unlock it.

Marco might find a way inside on some other day, but I would have done my best to keep Cormac safe at least for a few hours.

Sitting up in bed, I listened closely as Elyssa moved from bed to washstand to armoire. She was getting herself dressed, I realized. Last night, she had told Gretta that she didn't want to be disturbed until ten or eleven, which meant that she didn't want the maid to know that she was planning to be up and about much earlier.

Up and about and letting murderers into the palace.

Suddenly she grew very still, as if she was listening intently. Then she crossed the room and pushed open one of the leaded windows that overlooked the palace courtyard. Instantly, the warm, heavy scents of summer came drifting into the room—and behind them, the muffled, excited chatter of a large crowd. I could hear indistinct sounds of people calling out to each other, or shouting insults, or just talking in loud voices to their friends. And then there was a swelling roar, as if something thrilling had just occurred. That heightened sound continued for another five or ten minutes before slowly receding, as if a large mob had moved off in one direction, leaving the courtyard deserted and eerily silent.

I knew what had happened, of course. Lady Marguerite had been brought out of the palace while a crowd of onlookers gawked and jeered. Now they were all racing to Amanda Plaza so they could get a good seat for the execution. I wondered if all the other nobles, like Elyssa, had stayed in their rooms and watched from their windows, or if any of them had followed the procession to the plaza to bear witness. I could not guess which would be worse for Marguerite—to have none of her friends nearby at her desperate hour, or to have all of them watching, unwilling or unable to offer aid.

I heard the window being closed and latched, and then the sound of Elyssa's footsteps crossing the room. She was leaving! I scrambled to my feet and hastened around the corner of the screen, the other echoes behind me.

Elyssa heard us and spun around, her hand already on the door. She was dressed in her plainest gown and her hair was covered with a lace cap that might actually have been one of Gretta's, left behind some careless night. Someone would have to look very closely to recognize her or even realize that she was a noble. She grimaced when she saw us and shook her head. "No, echoes," she said firmly. "You cannot come with me."

Before I could think what to do, she stepped through the door and pulled it shut. I heard the lock click from the other side.

I stood there gaping for a moment, then flew across the room to try to open the door. The handle turned under my grasp, but the lock didn't respond. We were truly trapped.

Panic swamped me and I felt all my veins run with prickling heat. What could I do, what could I do? Should I beat on the door, lift my voice in a wail, try to draw the attention of a passing servant or noble guest? By the time someone heard me and fetched Lourdes or anyone else who had a master key, by the time the commotion was investigated, Elyssa already would have completed her terrible task. She would return to her room to find it in utter turmoil. How would she explain her absence? How would she explain leaving us behind? And what awful punishment would she visit upon us once we were alone with her again?

Unless I was prepared to throw off all pretense, declare myself conscious and aware, and suffer whatever fate was reserved for echoes who tried to sever themselves from their masters, I could not risk myself by raising the alarm now.

And Cormac would die.

For a moment I stood there, my head bowed, my hands clasped, my heart still pounding so hard my blood felt that it moved through my body at twice its normal speed. I was vaguely aware that, on either side of me, the echoes had adopted my same pose.

Then I took a deep breath, straightened up, and began hammering my hand against the door. If I was going to speak up later, I might as well speak up now, so I began calling out actual words. "Help me! Can someone unlock the door? Help me!" Beside me, the echoes slammed their hands against the walls and raised their voices in indistinguishable cries.

But no one heard us. Or at any rate, no one answered. Every noble with rooms nearby had either followed the cart to Amanda Plaza or gone to the breakfast room to weep. And any servant who crept down the hallway this morning was too afraid to investigate strange sounds coming from a visitor's room.

No one came to the door.

I finally fell silent and slumped against the wood, breathless and quietly crying. I had never felt so bitterly helpless in my life.

I was still standing that way—we all were—when I felt the tug of Elyssa's presence and realized with a spike of fear that she was coming up the stairs. In a few moments, she would be at the room. Probably fifteen minutes had passed since she had left us; she had made efficient work of crossing the palace and returning. I backed away from the door, the echoes pacing alongside me, too stunned and bemused to realize that we should whisk ourselves behind the screen. So we were just standing in a dumb, anxious clump when Elyssa unlocked the door and stepped back inside.

She started slightly when she saw us—and then, to my surprise, she laughed faintly. "Oh, echoes. *Crying* because I was gone for five minutes? Isn't that a little pathetic? But I'm back and, as you can see, I'm fine. Now go lie down. I want to be by myself for a while."

Did you do it? I wanted to demand. *Did you open the door to a murderer? Or did you have a change of heart? Are you truly without conscience or remorse? Or is there a spark of goodness somewhere inside you?*

But, of course, I said nothing. She brushed past us without another word. The echoes and I turned clumsily and shuffled across the room, slinking behind the screen. I felt Elyssa throw herself on her bed, and I could think of nothing better to do myself. I lay on the mattress and stared at the ceiling, my eyes burning so hotly that I thought tears might leave scars across my cheeks.

Gretta came bounding into the room perhaps two hours later. "My lady! I just spoke to Lourdes, and it's the most amazing thing! Oh, I do hope you're awake!"

I heard Elyssa stirring on her bed. "Yes, Gretta, what is it?"

"The queen has invited you to go for a carriage ride! I *think* she wants to take you for a fancy luncheon."

"The queen," Elyssa repeated. I couldn't tell if she was excited or horrified by the prospect of a solitary outing with Tabitha. It didn't matter, of course; she couldn't say no to a royal invitation. "When does she want me to meet her?"

"Lourdes said you should be ready by noon. We'll have to work fast."

I heard the sounds of Elyssa throwing back the covers and getting out of bed. "Then let's get started."

Gretta was always efficient, and within forty-five minutes she had Elyssa ready to face royalty. That didn't leave her much time to dress the echoes, but it scarcely mattered how we looked: For this outing, all eyes would be on Tabitha.

"There!" Gretta said as the four of us lined up at the door. "Think how jealous all the other ladies will be when they see you heading out with the queen!"

"I imagine most of the other ladies have locked themselves in their rooms so they can recover from the events of this morning," Elyssa said in an acid voice. "But if any of them should happen to see me going off with Tabitha, I shall be sure to look as smug as possible."

With that, she sailed out of the room and down the hallway, the three of us following close behind.

There was no one awaiting us in the grand foyer except Lourdes and a few lurking soldiers. I glanced around swiftly, but I didn't see anyone who looked like Marco hiding in the shadows. In fact, the great open space was as empty as I had ever seen it. I assumed most of the noble guests were up in their rooms, trying to determine how quickly they could pack up and head for home.

Lourdes approached with her usual self-important glide. "Her Majesty is already seated in the carriage outside," she announced.

Elyssa nodded and headed out the door. The carriage was a somewhat smaller version of the big, lumbering vehicles we had used when hordes of noble guests set out on some activity. I guessed this meant that only Tabitha and Elyssa—and their six echoes— would be going on the drive this morning. Of course, there was still the driver and an escort of four soldiers, so we weren't a small group, even so.

A footman handed us in and we arranged ourselves in the two backward-facing benches while the queen coolly looked on. I happened to draw the seat next to Elyssa, across from Tabitha, so I knew I must be very careful. I kept my expression slack and my eyes blank as I focused my gaze on the queen's embroidered shoes.

"Thank you for agreeing to drive out with me this morning," the queen said in her dispassionate way as the carriage jerked into motion.

"I am honored by the invitation, Majesty."

"Recent events have made the air at the palace somewhat oppressive," Tabitha continued. "It feels good to step outside."

Elyssa hesitated before answering, as anybody would have. It was hard to know exactly how the queen viewed these "recent events," and so it was impossible to know how to reply. "Certainly, this is not how I expected the visit to unfold," she said at last.

Tabitha fixed her chilly green gaze on Elyssa's face. "Had you made friends with Lady Marguerite?"

"We had spoken a few times. She was a little quiet for my taste."

"Vivienne is even quieter," the queen remarked.

Elyssa allowed herself a flash of humor. "Well, I have not spoken much to Vivienne, either!"

The queen looked out the window. We were passing a row of buildings that I didn't remember seeing before; we must not have come this way often during our weeks at the palace. "My guess is that Cormac will petition his father to be allowed to marry Vivienne, after all," Tabitha said. "I imagine Harold will agree, since Thelleron has always been loyal—and since its citizens do not seem bent on murdering Harold's sons. And during these unsettled times, it would seem valuable to have *something* settled."

Elyssa seemed to be considering her response very carefully. "Do you think such a wedding might anger the western provinces?"

Tabitha gave her a scathing look. "More than killing the most prominent daughter of Orenza? I think we have no hope of placating the rebellious regions after today's events."

Again, Elyssa seemed to choose her words with caution. "These will be difficult times."

"They will indeed."

Elyssa didn't come up with a quick answer to that, and a short silence fell while we all watched the view through the windows. The farther we traveled, the less familiar anything looked to me. We certainly weren't headed toward one of the more popular destinations, such as the temple or the botanical gardens or Amanda Plaza.

Finally the queen stirred and said in a voice that could not disguise her boredom, "So. Tell me about some of the sites you visited while you were here. What did you enjoy most?"

Elyssa obligingly described the shopping districts and the castle ruins and the Garnet Reach Bridge that was under construction. "And, of course, I enjoyed the chance to spend time with Jordan and Cormac and all of their guests," she added politely.

Tabitha surveyed her again, making it obvious that she was conducting a thorough inspection. "Jordan doesn't like you," she observed.

I felt Elyssa stiffen, but she kept her voice calm. "I'm sorry to hear that, Majesty. I have always tried to present myself to him in a favorable light."

"It doesn't matter," Tabitha went on. "He must marry you anyway. There is no other reasonable choice." Elyssa didn't answer, and the queen continued, "Now that Marguerite is dead, you are the only other high noblewoman of marriageable age who lives in the western provinces and has three echoes."

Elyssa made the faintest shrug. "He could marry a high noble with two echoes. They're littered all over the western provinces."

Tabitha greeted that comment with a wintry smile. "He could— but it would be less than ideal for all concerned. If Cormac marries Vivienne for love, then Jordan must marry you for the good of the country." She paused, made an equivocal gesture, and then said, "At least, marriage to you must remain an *option*. Which means you cannot be allowed to imperil your prospects."

Elyssa could not contain her bewilderment. "Your Majesty?"

Tabitha's expression was absolutely glacial. "You have been observed, Elyssa, meeting known revolutionaries in public places. If Harold had known of your indiscretions, you would have been up on that dais with Lady Marguerite, facing the archers' arrows."

There was utter silence in the carriage. Through the windows, I could see we were passing through a more industrial section of the city, filled with wagons and warehouses and workingmen. The sounds that drifted in were of coarse voices shouting orders and large items being shoved and shifted. The smells were of horse and sweat and lumber.

Finally Elyssa said, "Then why am I instead in a carriage with you?"

"Because I am of a practical turn of mind," Tabitha answered. "If you are the best choice for Jordan, I want to make sure your name is unsullied. I will protect you as long as I believe you are worth protecting. But if circumstances change, I will withdraw my favor. It is no more complicated than that."

Elyssa took a hard breath. She was clearly struggling to understand how much the queen knew and how much danger she was in. "And Harold knows nothing about my—activities?"

Tabitha permitted herself that chilly smile again. "There are certain members of the household staff who report to me first and share information with the king only when it is necessary."

"The inquisitor," Elyssa said under her breath. I thought she had not meant to utter the words aloud, for she cast a quick, dismayed glance at the queen.

But Tabitha gave a composed nod. "Indeed. Malachi is an old friend from Empara. We have the same goals for the well-being of the kingdom."

Elyssa lifted her chin with a show of spirit. "What do you intend to happen now? I shall return to the palace, chastened and grateful for your support?"

"You may return to the palace sometime, but it will not be today," Tabitha said. "I am taking you to an inn at the edge of the city, where you shall spend the night. I will return to the palace, where your maid will be informed that you have been called home suddenly. She will join you as soon as possible, with all your belongings, and you will set out for Alberta."

"But—it will seem—how odd it will be for me to disappear so suddenly!" Elyssa exclaimed. "Everyone will wonder and whisper questions—"

"Very likely," Tabitha agreed. "I suggest you come up with some story that seems plausible that you can share with your friends. But the tale I intend to tell is that your father sent for you on urgent matters that he declined to discuss, and that I helped you undertake your journey with all speed."

"You are—this is—I am not happy at this turn of events!" Elyssa said.

"I don't much care if you are happy or not," the queen said. "Who is ever happy? What I care about is that you are not compromised. I do not want you to spend more time in Camarria meeting with rebels and perhaps being observed by servants who are loyal only to Harold. Thus I am removing you from risk."

"But if I—"

The queen turned her head to look out the window. "I have no more to say," she announced.

We traveled for another half hour in silence. Beside me, Elyssa remained a ball of defiant fury, her hands in knots and her teeth clenched to hold back angry words. This was bad, and she had to realize that. If Marco was indeed a "known revolutionary," the fact that Elyssa had spoken to him in the streets even once would be enough to brand her a traitor. I couldn't imagine why Tabitha had decided to hide the truth from the king, but I had to think her motives were wildly suspect. No doubt there were more layers to this story, and probably some dark scheme of Tabitha's at play, but in the end it didn't really matter. The queen knew about Marco, the queen was sending Elyssa home, and Elyssa was absolutely powerless to refuse.

And an assassin was on the loose in the palace, and Cormac could be dead by nightfall—and Marco could be captured and executed before another day had passed, and we would know none of it. *None* of it. The agonizing uncertainty was almost too much to bear.

I shifted on my seat, unable to hold myself as still as Elyssa. Should I tell the queen? Now? Break my silence, destroy my anonymity—and probably suffer dire consequences? If Tabitha knew that Elyssa had conspired in Cormac's assassination, surely she would report Elyssa to the king? And the king would condemn Elyssa to death, as he had condemned Marguerite.

And a noble's echoes were always executed alongside their originals.

If I spoke now, I would surely die.

If I didn't speak, Cormac would die.

I couldn't help myself; I felt my whole body shrink down under a rush of fear. My hands twisted together and I started a gentle rocking. I was so afraid. Only silence would save me—but I could not be silent. I tried to calm myself enough to speak with some hope of coherence.

The queen glanced indifferently in my direction. "Your echo seems oddly agitated."

"All my echoes have some independence when I am in a lax or indulgent mood," Elyssa said.

"So I had heard, but it seems very strange to see one move with such autonomy."

I opened my mouth to speak.

Elyssa snapped her will over me, and suddenly I was slaved to her. My hand lifted as hers did, my head tilted in an ironic nod to the queen. "But as you see, they are still entirely mine. I assure you, she will not cause you any distress or discomfort for the remainder of the journey."

My mouth would not work. My voice would not come. Like Elyssa, I folded my hands in my lap and leaned my head back against the cushions of the seat. "Neither will I," Elyssa added. "We will just complete the rest of our ride in silence."

The carriage came to a halt just past the city limits. After the final few miles of warehouses and industrial establishments, it had been a relief to make it to the green and open spaces of less settled countryside. The air was fresher and the view was more appealing, although the mood inside the carriage was no lighter. So it was also a relief when we finally pulled up in front of a small but elegant inn.

"Here we are," Tabitha said, glancing out the window. "You will find a room reserved for you under the name Devenetta. The proprietors know that is the name I use when I travel, and they will treat you with utmost courtesy." She handed over a slim velvet bag. "I thought you might not have any money with you, so I have brought you enough to pay for a meal and any other expenses you might incur overnight. I have also taken the liberty of putting together an overnight bag with a few necessities."

"It seems you have thought of everything."

"I try to. It makes life less complicated."

The carriage door swung open as a servant from the inn came over to help us out. Tabitha made no move to disembark so, after a slight hesitation, Elyssa took the servant's hand and climbed down. All her echoes, still entirely under her command, swiftly followed. The ground was muddy with recent rain and we were all careful where we set our feet.

"Travel safely," the queen said from the interior. "I will hope to see you again in Camarria in a few weeks or months."

Elyssa apparently couldn't bring herself to reciprocate the sentiments. "Majesty," she replied, offering a deep curtsey. We sank so low to the ground that I thought I might get mud on the waist of my gown.

A moment later, the door was closed, the carriage had been turned around, and Tabitha was on her way back to Camarria.

Elyssa stared after her resentfully, then tossed her hair and strode toward the front door of the inn. The helpful servant picked up a large portmanteau that the coachman had tossed down and followed us inside.

The proprietor was a plump Pandrean woman who seemed eager to please. "Ah—yes—Devenetta! We're happy to have you with us tonight. Your room is ready and I think you'll find it quite comfortable."

"Rooms," Elyssa said sharply.

"I beg your pardon?"

"Rooms. I require a second room for my echoes—and my maid, once she arrives."

"Oh, but the chamber we've reserved for you has beds enough for all."

Elyssa slammed the velvet bag to the counter that held the ledgers and accounts. "Rooms," she repeated. "Whatever it costs."

"Yes, of course, my lady. I'm wondering—right down the hall, two doors away—is that close enough?"

"That's perfect."

We were something of a procession as the proprietor, her servant, Elyssa, the two echoes, and I climbed a narrow stairwell and proceeded down a short hallway. The echoes and I were shown to our room first, so I didn't get a chance to view Elyssa's, but I had to suppose it was rather grand, since ours was spacious and well-appointed. There were six beds, two washstands, a small table and various chairs. Clearly a room designed for nobles traveling with their echoes.

The instant the door shut between us, Elyssa released us—*flung* us from her, to be more accurate, with an emotion that read like loathing. I staggered from the force of that disowning, but I righted myself quickly enough and just stood there, taking a few deep breaths. Elyssa could not have wanted to shove us away any more badly than I had wanted to be shoved, but I still needed a moment to catch my balance. This was the first time since we had arrived at the palace that we had been in separate rooms, and I savored the sensation of freedom.

I put my hand to my heart as if I could press down on it hard enough to slow its rapid gallop. Beside me, the echoes mimicked my motion.

I studied them a moment. Neither one lifted her head to meet my gaze, but it was clear that somehow they were focused on me.

Attuned to me. I put my hands to my cheeks; so did they. I lifted my arms to either side, like the triple goddess in her attitude of justice, and the echoes did the same. I touched my forehand, my heart, my lips, and they copied the ritual benediction.

In odd, isolated moments over the past week or so, I had noticed that the echoes seemed to be moving in concert with me, but I hadn't had time to think about it much. Even now, I couldn't really sort out what it meant. Obviously, Elyssa could gather us up and toss us aside whenever she willed it—but I had never attempted to bind the echoes to me whenever Elyssa released us. It had never occurred to me to try.

What did it mean that they attached themselves to me whenever Elyssa turned them loose? Merely that they could not function on their own, and I was the closest living creature with a form they understood?

Or did it mean I was developing a personality, a power of my own? And that one day I might be strong enough to wrench myself free of Elyssa—and take her echoes with me?

It was hard to fathom. Hard to picture such an impossible future. I only knew that, for the moment, the echoes and I were functioning as our own closed unit, all in accord. I lifted my hands again so I could drape my arms over their shoulders, and they wrapped themselves around me, around each other, as we drew into one tight cluster of community and support. They were part of me and I was part of them. It was inexpressibly comforting.

Gretta did not arrive before twilight, which made it unlikely that she would arrive before mid-morning, since coachmen disliked traveling at night for fear of harming their horses. I could feel Elyssa's anxiety rise as the sun set, and she paced the confines of her room with so much energy that my body swayed every time she made the turn from the door toward the far wall. I could almost hear the thoughts bouncing around in her head. *Is the prince dead? Is Marco captured? I don't know. I don't know. I don't know.*

Some of the same litany was playing out in my own mind, though I was more desperate for news of Cormac and Jordan than I was for information about Marco. I thought I might be just as anxious as Elyssa, though I was trying harder to rein in my emotions. I didn't pace, at any rate. But my hands were knotted in my lap and my thoughts circled with a continuous panicked keening in my brain.

A servant girl brought us dinner, setting it on the table after casting us one doubtful glance. Most likely, she wondered how we might go about eating if our original wasn't there to guide us, and then she decided that was not her concern. As soon as she left, I led the others to the table, where we made a hearty meal. The same girl returned about an hour later to bring us water and collect the dishes. She cast us another dubious look and mumbled something about letting her know if we needed anything. I kept my face blank the whole time she was there and let her form whatever conclusions she would.

Clearly, Elyssa didn't care if we were able to eat or clean up or get ready for bed. She didn't come down the hall to check on us; she didn't resume her control over us to ensure that we ate when she did or washed our faces when she picked up her own damp cloth. So I took care of myself and the echoes, and was just as happy to do it. I even locked the door to make sure no one crept into the room at night while we were sleeping.

Then I stood for a moment with my hand on the lock, wondering what would happen if I refused to unlatch it in the morning.

No doubt the innkeeper had a master key and we would be unceremoniously rousted from the room. And that gesture of defiance would snag Elyssa's attention and result in terrifying punishments.

But what a thought. What a dream. How wonderful it would be if I could lock us in, and no one could make us come out, and Elyssa had to ride back to Alberta without us.

I led the echoes to our beds and we all slid under the covers. Then I lay there a long time, staring at the ceiling and watching the faint play of moonlight across the plaster.

What had happened to Cormac? Had Jordan lost two brothers in less than a month? Would he ever forgive me for not finding a way to tell him what I knew? Would I ever see him again—ever have a chance to speak to him in some contraband whispered conversation? Or would Elyssa be permanently banned from the royal court, and Jordan lost to me forever?

If I ever saw him again, would he even remember me?

What was going to become of me?

Despite the fact that I could not answer a single one of these questions, I was so exhausted that I quickly fell asleep. Around me I heard the gentle breathing of the echoes, each inhalation and release timed exactly to mine.

The next morning, the echoes and I had risen, dressed, and eaten breakfast by the time I caught the welcome sound of a commotion in the innyard. I flew to the window and was vastly relieved to see two carriages pull up and one of them disgorge Gretta. She shouted up at the coachman to hand her a particular piece of luggage, then crossed the yard with a purposeful stride.

She was halfway up the stairwell when Elyssa opened her door and stuck her head out—and the echoes and I did the same. Elyssa was so impatient to talk to the maid that she didn't seem to notice or care that we had synchronized ourselves to her again.

"Gretta! You're finally here! Tell me what's going on at the palace."

"You won't believe it! So much has happened," Gretta puffed as she carried the suitcase into Elyssa's room. The echoes and I followed right behind her as if certain we belonged. But we prudently clustered on the other side of the room so we didn't draw too much of Elyssa's attention.

"Well? Tell me!" Elyssa demanded.

Gretta opened the suitcase and began pulling out hairbrushes and underthings. "A man tried to kill the prince!" she announced. "Isn't that awful?"

"Cormac or Jordan? Is he dead?"

Gretta motioned for Elyssa to sit down so she could begin combing out the tangled curls. "Cormac. And no. He's still alive." I felt a sigh of relief rush through my body, though I tried to make no sound. Gretta went on, "He was hurt, though—a big gash on his left arm, but the surgeon said he'll be fine. It was so funny—they said his echoes all started bleeding, even though the attacker didn't even *touch* them."

"Yes, that's the way it works," Elyssa said impatiently. "So Cormac survived? That's good news! Did they catch the man who assaulted him?"

"He got away, can you believe that? Malachi was so angry!"

"How did he manage that?" Elyssa wanted to know. "The place is filled with soldiers and servants."

"Somebody said he was dressed in palace livery, so no one noticed him. Someone else said, no, he climbed out of a window and waited on the roof until everyone stopped looking for him. And someone else said he hid in the midden under the day's trash. I don't think anybody knows."

"Do they know who he was? And why he wanted to kill Cormac?"

"The footman said that Malachi said he was a revolutionary. But I heard that some of the nobles thought that it might have been Lady Marguerite's father, avenging the execution of his daughter."

"I don't think there's been enough time for Orenza to send in an assassin. Marguerite just died yesterday."

"Well, if I was the governor of Orenza, I'd certainly want to kill the prince," Gretta said.

Elyssa was silent for a moment. "Yes," she said finally. "So would I."

CHAPTER NINETEEN

We were back in Alberta at Lord Bentam's house after a long, tiring week of travel. As with the outbound journey, Elyssa insisted that Gretta and the echoes ride in one carriage while she had the second one to herself, but I didn't think any of us minded. Gretta might find echoes odd and unnerving, but I thought she preferred us to Elyssa.

The day we arrived back at the house, she gave her notice. I was willing to bet we would never see her again.

There was, of course, much consternation when Elyssa showed up, weeks before she was expected, with tales of intrigue and attempted murder. Both Hodia and Bentam were displeased and full of questions—but each one was focused on different issues. Hodia worried that Elyssa had behaved badly and been sent home in disgrace, having forever ruined her prospects for marrying a royal or even a high noble. She subjected Elyssa to dozens of interrogations, demanding to know how often she had interacted with Jordan, if she'd ever spoken to the king, and what other nobles had been invited to the palace. She was convinced that Elyssa was hiding information from her—and of course, she was right—but Elyssa calmly answered her questions and claimed that she had maintained good relations with everyone, even the queen.

Bentam was more angry at the crown than suspicious of Elyssa. "To think that the king believes he has the right to *murder* high noblewomen in the plaza in front of the entire population of the city!" he raged, for news of Marguerite's death had preceded us down the Charamon Road. "The goddess knows he'll pay for that bit of arrogance!"

"Do you think the governor of Orenza will rebel?" she asked.

"I would be shocked if Lord Garvin wasn't even now raising a small army."

"And Alberta? Is it arming itself, too?"

He gave her a cold and mistrustful look. "Why do you suddenly want to know?"

They were having this conversation in his study the night after she arrived. The door was closed and the only witnesses were their echoes, motionless in the shadows.

"I have always wanted to know," she replied sharply. "But you would never share your plans with me. I could have helped you—I could have listened for secrets every time I visited the home of some high noble loyal to the crown—but you would never take me in your confidence."

"I was never sure of you," he shot back. "You love wealth and status more than you love Alberta."

She came to her feet with a graceful, disdainful motion. The echoes and I rose quickly behind her. "More than I love *you*, maybe," she replied. "It's not the same thing."

That elicited a harsh crack of laughter from him. He was probably reviewing all the things in the world he loved more than his daughter.

"And I've never been sure of *you*, either," she went on. "Do you want me to marry the prince and secure special privileges for Alberta? Or do you want me to marry the prince and murder him in his bed? Or do you want me to *pretend* to be planning a wedding to the prince while you secretly raise armies to march into Camarria? I don't know what you're plotting, so I don't know how to prepare."

Now his laugh was a little more genuine. "All those things," he said, waving a hand. "What I want—what we all want—are concessions. And failing concessions, we want change."

She moved toward the door, the three of us silently following. "I have seen enough in Camarria on this visit," she said. "I want change, too." Her hand on the door, she paused to look back at her father. "Include me in your councils and your secret meetings," she said. "I can be an ally to you."

She waited for him to respond, but he said nothing, merely watched her for a long moment. She shrugged and led us from the room.

But after that, Bentam did start inviting Elyssa to join him when some of his less savory friends dropped by at odd hours, usually when the rest of the household was in bed. Mostly she sat quietly on one side of the room and merely listened, but now and then she volunteered information about a particular lord or noble family. *I don't think that house would join an uprising—his daughter is set to marry a noble from Sammerly, and they're all loyal to the crown.* Everyone seemed to find her bits of knowledge valuable.

During these late-night councils, we heard news about shocking acts of violence. The governor of Orenza, Lord Garvin, had indeed assembled a band of reckless fighters, and they began harrying any travelers who had ties to the king or his allies. A small band of royal guards traveling north along the Charamon Road had mysteriously disappeared; a merchant caravan from Banchura had been raided, all the contents of its carts and wagons either confiscated or scattered in the dirt. A wall of guards had gone up around Orenza's capital city of Oberton, and anyone wearing royal livery risked his life if he tried to cross that border.

Things were almost as unsettled in Alberta, where half the nobles were enraged at King Harold's cavalier execution of Marguerite, and half were eager to keep the peace between the province and the crown. Some of Bentam's late-night visitors whispered accounts of bloody skirmishes that had occurred between men recruited by rebel lords and soldiers from the houses of nobles who were loyal to the king. And one messenger wearing palace livery was found murdered outside a tavern in a town not far from Lord Bentam's mansion. No one ever discovered who had brought him down.

Elyssa listened to all the tales with cool dispassion, seeming unalarmed by brutality and unimpressed by bravado. "It does us no good to fight with each other," she said on more than one occasion. "You will never overthrow the king if all the lords don't work together."

"Maybe not," someone snarled once in reply. "But we'll show him we're not afraid to take drastic measures." And the stories and the arguments would go on.

As for myself, I felt sick and powerless as I listened to their plots and their plans. I could understand the rebels' desire to free themselves from the king's influence—after all, I myself was desperate to separate myself from an unfair master—but I didn't understand why such a step required so much violence. I came to dread these midnight sessions—though I dreaded just as much the long days in between clandestine meetings, when no new information came in and I had no idea if anyone in the royal family had been harmed in the interim. So even though I hated waking up in the middle of the night and hastily dressing and hurrying down to Bentam's study, I would have gone even if I had been able to resist Elyssa's compulsion.

She hurried eagerly to each secret meeting, racing down the stairs and through the hallways so quickly she was almost breathless upon her arrival. And then we would enter the room and she would look swiftly around and her excitement would falter and die. It didn't take me long to realize she was hoping, every time she opened the door to her father's study, that Marco Ross would be on the other side. But we had been back from Camarria for two months now, and so far he had not joined any of her father's councils.

I didn't believe he had written to her, and no one had mentioned his name within my hearing. I wondered if she was too proud to ask her father for news, or afraid to let him know how much she cared about the man. Marco was a landless rebel with nothing to recommend him but his passion. If Bentam knew about their affection for each other, he probably would ensure that they never saw each other again.

I would have felt sorry for her, except I hated her. And I hated Marco. And I lived in terror of how one of them might harm Jordan. So I was glad, in a petty and spiteful way, when the weeks passed and there was only silence from Marco.

As that second month came to a close, we did receive news from the palace from an unexpected source. We were at dinner one night when Hodia held up a note she had received that afternoon.

"A low noble from Banchura will be passing through Alberta on his way to Orenza and wonders if he can stop here for the night," she announced. "He says he is an importer with contacts in Ferrenlea, and he is looking to expand his markets in the western provinces. In fact, he brings with him a Ferrenlese man who can talk knowledgeably about the opportunities overseas."

The topic could hardly have interested Elyssa less, so she didn't even lift her eyes from her plate, but a look of speculation crossed Bentam's face. "Ferrenlea," he repeated. "I've often wondered if there might be a market for lavender over there. When did he want to come?"

"In five or six days. It seems he is in Pandrea now, traveling with his nephew and this foreigner." She scanned the letter again. "Apparently someone in his family married above his station, for his nephew has three echoes."

That did cause Elyssa to glance up, malicious amusement on her face. "How did he find a way to work that information into a note, I wonder? 'I'm a low noble, so I'm hardly worth your notice, but my nephew has so many echoes that any lord would be happy to receive me.'"

Hodia laid the paper aside. "He was a little less clumsy than that. He merely noted that, if we agreed to house his party for a night or two, his nephew would require a room with four beds."

"Oh, that is clever. I applaud that," Elyssa said. "Did he mention his nephew's name? Perhaps I met him in Camarria."

"Deryk," Hodia said.

"Deryk!" Elyssa repeated, showing the first signs of real pleasure she had exhibited in weeks. "Oh, *do* let them come! He's one of my favorites."

"I don't see any reason not to allow the visit," Bentam decided. "They might prove to be valuable contacts for me."

"Excellent," Hodia said. "I'll write him in the morning."

Deryk, his uncle Norbert, and a Ferrenlese man showed up five days later, riding in a carriage fine enough to catch Bentam's attention. It was clear Bentam was thinking that if this was what overseas trade could buy for a low noble, a high noble might make a fortune from such commerce.

Hodia and Elyssa had planned a couple of social events for the visit, which was supposed to last two days, but this first night there was no one at dinner but family members and guests. The six of them sat together at a compact table loaded with candles, silver serving dishes, and gleaming white china; their collected ten echoes were arranged in a ring around them, sitting at much plainer tables and making do with the faint illumination that filtered back from the tapers in the center of the room. It was so dark I could barely see Elyssa's echoes on either side of me, and I certainly couldn't see Deryk's across the room.

But I could see Deryk's face, and that was enough. Here in his uncle's company, he comported himself with more restraint than usual, drinking moderately and refraining from scandalous conversation. I thought there was very little family resemblance between them, for Norbert seemed to be a quiet and thoughtful man with a serious turn of mind.

I had an even better view of the Ferrenlese man, and I watched him with some curiosity. He was short and small-boned, with silver hair, shrewd eyes and a ready laugh. He spoke our language flawlessly, but with a heavy accent that lent a delightful flourish to even the most mundane utterances. Norbert and Deryk treated him with some deference, Hodia and Bentam with practiced courtesy. Elyssa smiled at him from time to time, but otherwise made no effort with him whatsoever. He was neither a titled lord nor a passionate revolutionary, so he held no interest for her.

Hodia made sure no one discussed business over the meal, so instead they labored through talk of the weather and the roads. When the meal finally came to a close, the three older men withdrew to talk commerce, while Hodia joined Elyssa and Deryk in one of the parlors. Hodia seemed to be there only for the sake of propriety because she took a chair on one side of the room and picked up a novel, and for the next two hours she never once looked over at Elyssa and Deryk.

The two of them instantly dropped to a small love seat and put their heads together. "Tell me *everything*," Elyssa demanded in a voice barely above a whisper. "We've heard hardly any news out of Camarria, and I can't *stand* it."

"You knew that someone tried to kill Cormac, of course?"

"Yes, *that* much information has found its way even to the backwaters of Alberta! But does anyone know why? Or who? Or—anything?"

Deryk gave her a meaningful glance. "I would think someone from the western provinces might be able to answer those questions better than *I* could," he said.

She affected exaggerated surprise. "Oh! So they think the attacker was part of some rebel plot, and not a lone malcontent who hates the king?"

"I think that in Camarria these days, they believe everyone who hates the king is part of some rebel plot," he corrected her. "But since they've never discovered who the would-be assassin was, they can't be sure."

"Poor Cormac! Is he very afraid? Hiding in the palace?"

"On the contrary, he's been very visible. I'm not his greatest admirer, as you know, but he's appeared quite brave."

"How long did everyone else stay after I left?"

"Only a couple of days. After Marguerite's death—" He gave a dramatic shudder. "Most of the women cleared out the next morning. Darrily even said to Cormac, 'Good luck finding a bride *now*.'"

"Oh, I have to think little Vivienne of Thelleron would be willing to forgive Cormac anything," Elyssa said.

"She did stay," Deryk said. "Or at least, she was still there a day later when I drove off."

"So do you think their engagement is back on?"

"That would be my guess, but there's been no announcement."

Elyssa sank back against the cushions. "Well, good," she said. "It appears I didn't miss too much by leaving so suddenly. I suppose everyone gossiped about me after I was gone."

"There was a little talk," Deryk admitted. "But Tabitha said you had received urgent news from home. And at that point, we were all plotting our own hasty departures, so no one wondered too much about yours."

"Ah. Of course," she said.

He gave her an arch look. "So what *did* happen? Since I would have thought nothing would send you scurrying back home except news of your father's death—and he appears to be very much alive."

She smiled, put a finger to her lips, and shook her head. "I'm not allowed to say. Though I promise you, it was very exciting! But I did regret having to leave so abruptly, and I'm glad to hear that no one thinks too badly of me."

"Not even Jordan," Deryk said. "And I never thought he was that fond of you, to tell you the truth."

Elyssa just looked at him. "You and Jordan were talking about me?" she said finally.

"Oh, nothing like that. But before I left, I had a chance to make a formal goodbye to the whole royal family. Harold asked what my plans were, and I said I would be traveling through the western provinces with my uncle. Tabitha said that if I saw you, I should tell you she sent her best wishes for your father's health. Then Jordan said he hoped you—" Deryk paused and wrinkled his forehead, trying to get the wording just right. "Jordan said he hoped that you remember your interesting conversations and that you will have a chance to dance together again soon. Or something like that." He smoothed his expression and smiled at her. "So I think maybe he likes you better than I thought."

I could sense Elyssa's mixed and chaotic emotions. She considered herself a rebel now, so she wanted to feel disdain at the notion that anyone in the royal family might harbor a fondness for her. Yet there was still a shallow, greedy part of her soul that would always covet the status and prestige of marrying a prince. But her astonishment, gratification, and uncertainty were nothing compared to the turmoil in my own head. My veins ran with silver heat; my hands curled with sudden chill.

Jordan said he hoped that you remember your interesting conversations and that you will have a chance to dance together again soon.

That was surely a message for me, not Elyssa. He had not forgotten me. And he would try to find a way to be with me again.

No other moment during Deryk's visit was as exciting or memorable as that one, as far as I was concerned, although there were a couple of other interesting exchanges. One occurred the following morning, when the Ferrenlese visitor happened to take a seat next to Elyssa at the breakfast table.

He produced his easy smile and said in his charming accent, "You must forgive me, but in all the introductions last night, I could not perfectly catch your name."

"Elyssa," she said, giving him a perfunctory smile.

"Alista?" the man tried.

"No. *Elyssa.*"

"Ah. It sounds very much like a word we have in Ferrenlea," he answered. "Amelista."

"That's pretty."

"Indeed! The prettiest word in the whole language!"

"What does it mean?"

His small hand traced an uncertain gesture in the air. "It is hard to define. It means *I see you and you see me.* We are each of us whole because the other exists. It is a word of profound connection."

I could tell Elyssa had already lost interest. "Indeed. I don't believe any such word can be found here in our kingdom."

"No," he said regretfully. "I have traveled to five other nations and nowhere found a similar concept. It is hard sometimes to do business with people who do not think the same way."

"I generally find no one thinks the way I do, but it doesn't really bother me," Elyssa said sweetly.

The Ferrenlese man looked so taken aback that he couldn't think of a reply. Elyssa gave him a polite nod and turned all her attention to Deryk, who had dropped onto the seat on her other side. As far as I could tell, she didn't speak to the man one more time during breakfast—or the rest of his visit.

That night, a dozen or so local nobles were invited for dinner. Some of the older ones withdrew immediately after the meal to discuss how well their lavender products might sell in Ferrenlea, but the younger visitors instantly began organizing card games and impromptu dancing. Deryk and Elyssa spent much of the time paired up as dance partners, mostly so they could whisper about everyone else in attendance.

"I'm sorry you'll be leaving in the morning," she said, when they had exhausted their store of malice. "And you must be sorry, too! Your travel companions seem very dull."

"I pray nightly that the triple goddess spares me any more contact with people from Ferrenlea," Deryk said, "but my uncle is far more interesting than he might at first appear."

"You *must* tell me what you mean by that."

"He's not simply a merchant trying to set up shipping lines. He's here on behalf of the king, trying to broker peace between provinces. From here we go on to Empara, and then Orenza."

"You'd best be careful for your life then," Elyssa replied. "My father says Lord Garvin will never forgive the king for Marguerite's death. And I am not exaggerating when I say envoys have been murdered outright at the Orenza border."

"My uncle knows. But he's hopeful. His reception here in Alberta has been warmer than he expected, and your father has agreed to talk with some of his other compatriots. No one wants bloodshed, after all. If there is a way to solve problems through commerce, that's a better answer than war."

"Listen to you!" she exclaimed. "My shallow Deryk, talking policy! I never would have believed it."

He swung her in an energetic circle; I was practically lifted off my feet by the enthusiasm of his echo. "But, my dear," he drawled, "people tend to let down their guard when they think you're nothing but a fop and gossip. They're careless about what they say. You would not believe some of the secrets I have learned."

Now she stared up at him in silence, perhaps reviewing any offhand remarks she might have made that could have compromised her father. I myself found it hard to believe that the frivolous Deryk was a spy for the king, but it did make me wonder how many people at the court—how many people in the kingdom—were keeping secrets. Presenting false faces to the world. Living lives entirely contrary to appearances. Most of them, I decided.

Deryk laughed at the expression on her face. "Oh, not you, my sweet!" he said. "You're far too clever to give anything away. Besides, what lies could you possibly be hiding in your cold little heart?"

She smiled back, but I thought it took her some effort. "I am relieved to hear it! And most pleased to hear that the king is negotiating for peace. I'd hate to think of you cut down by Orenza soldiers and bleeding out on the hard ground."

"I'd ruin my waistcoat," he agreed.

She freed one hand to tap his forehead, right above the scar through his eyebrow. "And mar your pretty face."

He recaptured her hand, kissed it briefly, then returned to the proper dancing pose. I could feel the moist imprint of the echo's kiss against my skin. "We are both shallow," he said. "And both so much more than we appear."

CHAPTER TWENTY

L ife was frankly boring once Deryk and his uncle departed, but boring was fine with me. I had had enough excitement for a lifetime. My days were even quieter than before because Elyssa had developed the habit of leaving her echoes behind whenever there was no one in the house but family. Hodia didn't like it, and protested strongly, but Elyssa merely shrugged. She did agree to always have us in her train when anyone else, no matter how insignificant, was visiting the manor, but there were many days when that did not apply.

I reveled in my newfound freedom. Of course, I was confined to Elyssa's suite of rooms, but I could move around at will and think my own thoughts and not be afraid of catching her attention or sparking her anger. In many ways, it was the most carefree stretch of my existence.

Elyssa did bring us with her when the whole family set out on a short expedition a couple of weeks after Deryk's visit. Before we left the house, Trima—who had resumed her role as Elyssa's maid— dressed us all in prim, high-necked frocks and arranged our hair in the simplest of styles.

"Goddess have mercy on my soul, Trima, could I possibly look dowdier?" Elyssa exclaimed, surveying herself in the mirror.

"It's Counting Day, which means you want the goddess to notice you," Trima said firmly. "Do you want her to notice you appearing pious and demure, or looking vain and showy?"

"If I didn't go to the temple, my echoes would disappear tomorrow," Elyssa said.

"And *that's* what you want?"

Elyssa was silent a moment. "Sometimes."

"If I were you, I wouldn't be too eager to do away with my echoes until both the princes were safely married to other women," Trima advised. "After that— Well, drown them in the river, if you like. But I think you'd be sorry."

"I wouldn't," Elyssa said. "I don't like them. They're always watching me. Listening."

Trima motioned for Elyssa to stand up, and we all came to our feet. "Don't be ridiculous," she said. "Now go on downstairs. You're almost late."

Sure enough, Hodia and Bentam were already in the hallway, both dressed soberly enough to be attending a funeral. "Good," Bentam said, heading out the front door without another word.

We followed, catching our breath at the chill of the blustery, overcast day. Bentam and his echoes took possession of a small curricle that he drove himself, while the women piled into a large carriage with multiple benches. Hodia shared a seat with one of her echoes, but Elyssa made sure all three of hers were crowded together on the bench behind her.

The drive was accomplished mostly in silence, but fortunately it was less than an hour to the nearest little town that boasted a temple to the triple goddess. Trying not to be too obvious about it, I leaned forward to gaze out the window as we traveled slowly through the streets. I must have been there many times—if for no other reason than to observe more than twenty Counting Days in the past. Surely that steeple looked familiar, and that small bakery? I must have seen that fountain a dozen or so times. I could almost remember it.

When we finally stopped and disembarked, I studied the front entrance of the temple. It was much smaller and plainer than the one we had visited in Camarria, boasting only a single door set with a triple-paned window. It was far less grand inside as well, with ten or twelve rows of wooden benches set on a plain flagstone floor. In the front of the sanctuary were half-size statues of the goddess in her accustomed poses, and a rough wooden table holding twenty or so lit votives. A few embroidered wall hangings softened the dreary gray of the stone walls, but otherwise it was not a particularly comfortable or welcoming space.

Maybe twenty people were already scattered through the pews, if you counted both echoes and nobles, and two priestesses moved among them offering benedictions. Hodia marched right up to the front of the sanctuary and the others followed, though I was fairly certain both Bentam and Elyssa would have preferred to sit in the back. Hodia, her echoes, Bentam, and Elyssa took seats in the very first row; Bentam's and Elyssa's echoes sat behind them.

I had to tamp down a lively curiosity as I waited for whatever was supposed to happen next. Would the goddess herself manifest, come floating down the aisle in some spectral form, silently chanting the nobles' names and counting the numbers of their echoes? Or did the priestesses keep records that they updated every year, checking off the names of their visitors and comparing their list to some vast national register?

Or was this a pointless ritual, a traditional observance that had no power and made no difference? Did the goddess really know that all of Elyssa's echoes were still alive, still more or less whole, and did she really care?

And if she did know, and if she did care, what did she make of *me*?

Maybe the goddess noticed, maybe she didn't. There was no sign either way. The ten of us sat there in silence for perhaps thirty minutes, though Elyssa shifted impatiently on her bench and Bentam never stopped drumming his fingers against his thighs. When a priestess came over to offer them benedictions, Elyssa was on her feet before either her aunt or her father had reacted. I was sure she didn't care about the ritual so much as the fact that it signaled the end of her vigil. She bowed her head so the priestess could touch her face, her chest, her lips, and she didn't even protest when the woman leaned across the bench to repeat the same gestures on the echoes and me. Within a few moments, Hodia and

Bentam had also been blessed, and we were all back outside in the chilly gray air.

Did you see me? I silently asked the goddess as we climbed into the carriage. *Did you count me? Do you know anything about me at all?*

It was a couple of weeks after Counting Day when Trima came to Elyssa's suite in the middle of the night. I woke up as soon as the outer door opened, and I heard the maid knock on the inner door to Elyssa's bedroom.

"My lady," Trima said through a yawn. "The housekeeper woke me. There's a visitor waiting in your father's study."

It had been a late night, and I heard Elyssa give a low groan before she forced herself out of bed. She had fought too hard to be included in her father's councils to let a little exhaustion hold her back now. "Then help me get ready," she said.

Soon enough, Trima had the four of us brushed and dressed, though we all looked dazed from lack of sleep. We pattered downstairs and through the darkened corridors to Bentam's study, where the lord was already in low-voiced conversation with a single man dressed all in black.

The man looked up and Elyssa fought to hold back a gasp. It was Marco Ross.

"Good, you're finally awake," Bentam greeted her. "Sit down. He has news."

Elyssa recovered quickly and offered Marco a cool nod. His face was so impassive he might never have seen her before in his life—although he had had the advantage of knowing she was about to step into the room. Elyssa had had no warning at all.

"Haven't I met you before?" she asked as she took a seat nearby. The echoes, as always, arrayed themselves in the shadows. "It might have been two years ago, when you were doing some work for my father."

"That's right," Marco replied. "I'm pleased to see you again."

"No need to be talking over old times," Bentam growled. "Listen to what he has to say."

Marco turned to face Bentam, seeming to ignore Elyssa completely. She kept her eyes on his profile and listened without moving. Marco said, "As you know, the king has been negotiating in secret with some of the lords of the western provinces."

Bentam nodded. "Norbert came through here a month ago, on his way to Orenza. I liked what he had to say."

Marco nodded. "A lot of the lords did. Generally speaking, there's been an easing of tensions. No more fighting. At least in Alberta and Empara."

"So Orenza's the sticking point. As always," Bentam said.

"The governor is the sticking point," Marco said deliberately. "The other nobles of Orenza are interested in the king's deal. Harold is offering merchants a chance to use the ports in Banch Harbor without paying taxes for a year. Some of them have suffered heavy losses with recent shipping disasters, and this gives them a chance to recover more quickly than they expected."

"Even those of us who haven't suffered losses are pleased at the chance to make significant gains," Bentam said. "I've argued in favor of the negotiation."

"Will the Orenza nobles be able to persuade the governor?" Elyssa asked.

Marco barely glanced at her. "They have—for now. But I am not convinced Lord Garvin will stay appeased for long."

Bentam leaned back in his chair. "Ah. You think there may be a schism in Orenza. Garvin going rogue and mounting his own forces, despite what the nobles across the western provinces agree to."

Marco nodded. "I wouldn't be surprised."

"And if Orenza stirs up trouble, the whole deal may be scotched—for *all* the western provinces."

"Exactly," Marco said.

Bentam brooded for a moment. "Garvin is proving to be something of a liability," he said at last.

"You're not the first noble to say so," Marco replied.

"And yet he has been a strong ally up to this point. A leader, in fact."

Marco nodded and said nothing. I was straining not to sit up in my chair, aghast. Was I correctly interpreting their roundabout speech? Were some members of this uneasy group of rebels considering eliminating the governor so he could not interfere with negotiations? I had known they were cold-blooded enough to plot the assassination of a prince, but could they be ruthless enough to turn on one of their own? I thought even Elyssa felt a chill run down her spine as she contemplated the plotters.

"Well, it is a situation to watch closely," Bentam said.

"And there's another thing," Marco added.

"Tell me."

"Six weeks ago, there was another attempt on Cormac's life."

Bentam sat up straight and Elyssa almost jumped from her chair. "I have heard nothing of this!" Bentam exclaimed.

Marco nodded. "It has been kept very quiet. In fact, there are some who believe it is only a rumor, but my source is certain."

"Who made the attempt?"

Marco spoke deliberately. "He is believed to be a low noble from Alberta."

At this, both Bentam and Elyssa gasped. "Identify him," Bentam demanded.

"A man named Leffert."

Bentam frowned. "Not someone I know. Are you sure he was an Alberta man?"

"Not sure at all," Marco admitted. "There is some thought that he was using a false name, so he might have been claiming a false heritage as well. You can imagine that the inquisitor is looking into the situation with the utmost care."

"Does anyone know who hired him?" Bentam asked.

Elyssa spoke up. "The governor of Orenza, perhaps?" she suggested. "If he is angry that all the other nobles are negotiating with the king—"

Marco glanced at her briefly. "Some people have suggested that," he agreed, "though Garvin has adamantly denied it."

"Then who?" Bentam said. "Some madman with no agenda who simply hates the king? Or—"

"Or some new player that none of the rest of us know," Marco finished up.

Bentam leaned back in his chair again, frowning heavily. "I dislike factions," he said. "Unless we all act together, we will never wield any power. If we sign a deal with the king, but some lunatic kills Cormac anyway, Harold will instantly negate the contract! We need to present a united front."

"Difficult to do," Marco said, "when there are so many people involved and they want different things."

I wondered if that was Marco's way to subtly remind Elyssa that he was one of the rebels who preferred to cut ties with Camarria completely. *He* would not be enthusiastic about any plan that kept the peace while maintaining the divisions between the lords and the lower classes. A treaty that enriched the nobles brought no benefits to *him*.

"There are enough of us who want enough of the same things," Bentam said gruffly. "We must work together."

Marco bowed his head as if in acquiescence. "Then we will succeed."

Bentam stirred in his chair. "Thank you for the report. Where do you go next?"

"Pandrea."

"I would not have thought we had allies there," Bentam commented.

Marco smiled. "Not allies, precisely. Friends. Sources of information."

Bentam grunted. "Well, I won't keep you. But you're welcome to stay a day or two if you need a break from your travels."

"I would be grateful for the rest."

Bentam looked at Elyssa for almost the first time since this colloquy had begun. "My daughter will see that you are given a room."

Elyssa came to her feet without even glancing at Marco. "The housekeeper is awake and already taking care of it," she said, making a general curtsey to them both. "I'll see you in the morning. Goodnight."

And she left without a look back.

Through a combination of excitement, anger, longing, and something that felt like dread, Elyssa barely slept the rest of that night, so the echoes tossed and turned along with her. She was awake early, but didn't rise from bed until Trima arrived at her usual hour to dress us all for the day.

"You look tired," Trima commented as she added touches of rouge to Elyssa's pale face.

"How kind of you to say so," Elyssa snapped.

Trima shrugged. "If your sleep is more important to you than your relationship with your father, tell him you no longer want to be woken up in the middle of the night."

"My relationship with my father is of practically no value," Elyssa said, still sharply. "But what I learn from these late-night visits—*that* matters to me."

"Then stop complaining."

Unexpectedly, Elyssa laughed. "Well, I'll try."

Trima patted the last curl in place. "And smile more. You're such a pretty girl."

Elyssa stood up. "And a hungry one. Time for breakfast."

Only Hodia was in the dining room when Elyssa arrived there, and they made only the most desultory conversation while Elyssa ate a brief meal.

"I believe there's a guest in the house, but I haven't seen him," Hodia said as Elyssa stood to go.

"Oh?" Elyssa said carelessly. "Do I know him?"

Hodia frowned. "I wouldn't think so. One of your father's less savory connections."

Elyssa laughed. "So I don't have to be nice to him if I encounter him."

"In fact, you should take every precaution to make sure you do *not* encounter him."

"That's what I'll do."

Then Elyssa fetched a cloak and headed out a side door and practically ran to the gazebo on the far edge of the property.

Marco was there waiting, and she flung herself into his arms without the slightest restraint. He crushed her against his body, dropping hungry kisses all over her face. She clung to him, breathless, trying to speak, but all she managed were a few disconnected words. "So afraid…so worried…thought you were *dead*." His low replies were barely more audible, apologies and reassurances and promises to never be so careless again.

The echoes and I simply stood a few yards from the gazebo, dumb and gaping. The minute we had passed out of sight of the back windows of the mansion, Elyssa had released us, and we had only followed her because we were so accustomed to traveling in her wake. But I remembered her last encounter with Marco in this very place, and I knew she was even less likely to want us as witnesses today. The painted white trellises were still heavily covered with vines, but winter had stripped away everything but a few dead leaves, so the meeting spot was not nearly as private as it had been last spring. Surely Elyssa would realize that.

I grabbed the echoes and pulled them to a bench we had passed about twenty yards away. It commanded a view of the gardens and—more important—faced away from the gazebo. Then, moving in a low crouch and taking cover behind bare trees and desiccated shrubs, I snuck back toward the trysting spot. I wasn't keen to watch Elyssa and Marco escalate their passionate embraces, but I wanted to learn whatever Marco knew about the situation at court.

When I was close enough, I lay down in the dead grass and listened intently.

"But I didn't *know*," Elyssa was saying, sounding perilously close to tears.

"But how could I get word to you?" he demanded. "Surely your aunt and your father watch your mail."

"Hodia does, but— You could send a note to Trima. My maid."

"Who is paid by your father and no doubt reporting back to him."

"No, no, she would do anything for me. She is the only one in the whole household I trust."

"Maybe," he said. "If the news is urgent enough."

Elyssa's voice dropped to a caressing murmur. "What will always be urgent is news about you showing up at my father's house."

He laughed. "I didn't realize he would call you down in the middle of the night! My best hope was that I would get a glimpse of you this morning and maybe find a chance to talk in private."

"But you will be gone so soon," she whispered. "It might be months before I see you again. I can't bear it."

"I should be back through Alberta in about ten days," he said. "The governor is having a party to celebrate his daughter Sorrell getting engaged to a lord from Thelleron."

"I thought Lord Vincent was loyal to the crown."

"He is—but some of his guests are not."

Now Elyssa's voice took on a more speculative tone. "There might be some way I can attend this event. Sorrell doesn't like me— because she only has two echoes and I have three—but I think I can make her invite me anyway."

"Well, I will be there," he said. "If you really think you can manage to attend—in a household where no one will be paying much attention to you—"

My guess was that he took this moment to draw her tightly against him, for I felt an increased pressure across my entire body. Suddenly, I found it difficult to breathe. Suddenly, I didn't want to be anywhere near Elyssa, catching the backlash of her emotions and sensations.

I crawled toward the bench to sit with the echoes, focusing my mind on blocking out everything that Elyssa was thinking and feeling. I was only partially successful. For the next thirty minutes, while I doggedly stared at the dreary winter landscape, my body randomly ran with heat or reacted with a sensuous bliss to the touch of a hand or a mouth. This was nothing like the sweaty, undignified coupling Elyssa had engaged in with Lord Roland; this was something I imagined could be quite pleasurable if a person had an interest in participating in vicarious desire.

I did not. In fact, I found the whole situation supremely distasteful. But I could not help wondering what it would be like to experience those emotions, those sensations, firsthand, in the company of a man who cherished me, in the arms of someone I loved.

CHAPTER TWENTY-ONE

It was no surprise to me that Elyssa managed to secure an invitation to the festivities commemorating the engagement of Lady Sorrell of Alberta to Lord Clath of Thelleron. Both her father and her aunt seemed pleased that she was interested in going, and Bentam spent some time with her beforehand, outlining the political leanings of all the families who were likely to attend. Hodia also spent a few hours preparing Elyssa for the event, but she was more concerned with the eligibility of the various young lords who might be present and the advantages of possible alliances. Elyssa gratified both of them by appearing to listen closely, but I was not fooled. All she could think about was that she would have the chance to see Marco again.

We took a single carriage across Alberta for the day-and-a-half-long journey to the city of Wemberton, where Lord Vincent, his wife, and his daughter lived. Weather was cold and sleety for the entirety of the trip, so I didn't get much chance to admire the landscape, which was flat and dull anyway. But the sun managed an invalid's weak appearance the afternoon that we arrived in the city. Wemberton wasn't nearly as big as Camarria, but it appeared prosperous and tidy. Elyssa must have been here many times in the past, but my capricious memory yielded no glimpses of those previous visits. It was all new.

The governor's mansion was larger than Bentam's place but smaller than the king's palace, boasting a checkerboard façade of white stones alternating with black. The pattern continued in the small courtyard spread out before the wide front doors.

"Pretty," Trima commented.

"A little ostentatious," Elyssa replied.

"I suppose Lord Vincent has a right to be showy if he wants."

"He only has one echo. How showy can he be?"

Trima surveyed her. "And yet you always complain about how much you hate your own echoes."

Elyssa hunched one shoulder pettishly. "I *deserve* them. That doesn't mean I like them."

Trima snorted and shook her head.

Soon enough, we had disembarked and were being greeted by our host and hostess, each of them short, richly dressed, and trailed by a single echo.

"We were so happy to learn you were available to join us," said the governor's wife, kissing Elyssa on the cheek. I had to wonder if she was sincere.

"I can't wait to congratulate Sorrell. When will be the wedding be?"

"In six months, we think. We'll be sure to send you an invitation."

"How delightful." I could almost hear the words Elyssa didn't add aloud. *But if Marco won't be present, I have no intention of attending.*

We were shown to a suite that was small, but mercifully included two rooms. One was clearly intended for the maid, as it was perhaps a third of the size of the main room and included only one bed, but Elyssa pointed to it and said, "Echoes. Go sit in there and don't come out." As we filed through the narrow door and perched on the hard mattress, I heard Elyssa say to Trima, "I suppose we can get someone to move one of these beds into the other room."

"Where do you think *I'm* going to sleep?" the maid asked.

"You can be in the main room with me. Unless you snore. Then you're sharing a bed with an echo."

"Sometimes you're the most unpleasant girl."

"I know. But you love me anyway."

"Lucky for you I do."

The first evening at the governor's mansion was very similar to all the evenings at the royal palace in Camarria, except there were fewer people present, many of them were much older than Cormac's guests, and there weren't quite so many echoes. But before dinner, during dinner, and after dinner, people fell into small groups to talk about everything from society gossip to royal politics. The newly engaged couple were introduced with a few toasts and polite applause. They looked comfortable with each other if not madly in love, so I thought their marriage might be arranged but satisfactory to both of them.

Unlike the marriage Prince Jordan might have to make.

He was on my mind, of course, because the situation in Wemberton reminded me so much of the one in Camarria. And because he was usually on my mind. Then someone mentioned his name.

It happened after the meal as Elyssa was standing with a few of the younger lords. She was so bored that she almost looked happy to see Lady Cali approach.

"Well, hello, Elyssa, how unexpected to find you here," Cali said.

"Oh, but I simply *had* to come offer my best wishes to Sorrell!" Elyssa exclaimed. "I had no idea I would have the pleasure of *your* company as well."

Cali offered her usual warm smile in return. I liked that she never seemed to care what Elyssa said and never seemed to lose her general air of good nature, but somehow managed to give as good as she got. "Oh, yes. Sorrell and I have been friends forever. I've spent half my life in the governor's mansion."

"Do you know what kinds of activities have been lined up for the celebration?"

"I believe there is to be a theatrical production tomorrow night—some new play that's all about the triumph of love. Sorrell's very excited."

"A theatrical performance," Elyssa repeated. "It would never have occurred to me to plan something so—unusual."

"No, I've always thought you were quite conventional," Cali replied, still smiling.

Elyssa laughed. "Conventionality," she said. "My most obvious sin."

"Then there's to be a ball the following night, and after that we're all supposed to go home," Cali went on.

"A short visit," said Elyssa, "but I'm sure it will feel long enough."

"Sorrell's disappointed, though," Cali said. "Lord Vincent invited Prince Cormac, but he won't be able to make it."

For a moment, Elyssa went entirely still. I could tell what she was thinking. *Prince Cormac at this event? Is that the real reason Marco planned to be here? But he told me he was no longer planning to assassinate the prince.* Then a slight shake of her head. *What do I care? The king killed poor Marguerite, so it serves him right if someone kills his son in return.* "How exciting that would have been!" Elyssa said. "But I suppose we shall just have to make do with a few high nobles."

"There is some talk that Jordan might come in his brother's place," Cali added. "But it seems unlikely." She paused to give Elyssa a quick inspection. "Or do you know something I don't? Perhaps that's why you're here."

Elyssa laughed again. "To meet up with Jordan? Oh, my dear. You shouldn't listen to gossip. There's no special understanding between the prince and me."

"No?" Cali said with another smile. "How frustrating for you. You must be even more disappointed than Sorrell."

"Not at all," said Elyssa. "I find the world rife with possibilities."

After this edged exchange, I thought both women were relieved when they were joined by Sorrell and Clath. The conversations continued, but I had stopped listening. Jordan might come here? To this very place? Would there be a chance for us to speak, or at least to exchange a glance or two? Would I find it impossibly frustrating, as Cali said, to be so close to him, but still unable to communicate? Or would the joy of seeing his face be enough to sustain me?

I wanted to see him, I decided. Even if I had no contact with him except through the medium of his echo's touch. I wanted just another hour's proof that he was still alive and still remembered me.

As I was not used to getting what I wanted, I assumed this meant he would stay safely in Camarria. And truthfully, if Marco was here, it was probably better if Jordan did not make an appearance.

As the night wore on, that became the central question: Was Marco, in fact, at the governor's mansion? I could tell that, although she tried to be casual about it, Elyssa was watching for him closely. She inspected all the footmen who passed through the rooms, in case Marco had managed to insinuate himself into this household by posing as a servant, but he was not among them. Perhaps he had hired on as a groom or a gardener. Perhaps he was making deliveries to the kitchen door. Perhaps something had detained him on the road and he would not be here after all.

Elyssa had much too much poise to show her bitterness and disappointment in public, but I could feel her unhappiness mounting as the evening wore on. I wondered what kind of temper tantrum we would be subjected to once we returned to her room.

It was therefore with some trepidation that I followed her up the stairs after the dinner party finally concluded. She stalked down the corridor to our suite and barely waited for the last echo to step across the threshold before she slammed the door shut. Trima looked up in surprise from where she sat by the fireplace, sewing a bit of lace.

"What's put *you* in such a mood?" the maid asked. "Didn't you enjoy the dinner?"

"I *hate* Sorrell and Cali and all the rest of them! So smug and insufferable." She picked up a decorative pillow and threw it across the room.

I didn't wait for instructions. I led the echoes into our little room and swung the door so it was almost closed. Not enough for her to notice the sound of the latch engaging. Not enough to prevent me from hearing the rest of her conversation.

"I thought it was your idea to come here!" Trima said.

"I've changed my mind. I want to go home. Can we leave tomorrow morning?"

"That's too rude, even by your standards. And your father will be displeased if you offend Lord Vincent."

I saw another pillow fly across the room, almost knocking a vase to the floor. "I hate my father, too."

"Be that as it may, I don't think you want to make him angry. Now come here. Let me unlace your dress and take down your hair. You'll feel better in a few moments."

"I *won't*," Elyssa said pettishly, but I saw shadows move across the room, and I assumed that she submitted herself to Trima's ministrations. For a little while, there were only the muted sounds of fabric rustling, hairpins dropping to the top of the dresser, jewelry being laid aside.

"Here, let me wipe your face," Trima said. "Oh, I almost forgot. One of the maids delivered a note this evening."

"A *note*? And you didn't tell me? Where is it?" She must have spotted it at that exact moment, for I heard her cry of satisfaction and then the sound of paper ripping open. There was silence while she scanned the contents, and then she laughed softly.

"Well! This changes everything!" she said, in an utterly different voice. Low and throaty and silken and pleased.

Trima's voice, by contrast, was full of disapproval and doubt. "Who's that letter from?"

"Never you mind."

"Some ineligible boy, I suppose. Who is he? How did he learn you were here?"

"You don't need to know any of that." A sudden change of tone, almost threatening. "And don't you tell my father."

"I never tell your father anything. But don't *you* do anything stupid."

"I'm too clever to do stupid things. But I need to think about this—I need to come up with a plan for tomorrow night—"

"What's happening tomorrow night?"

Another laugh, light and delighted. "Among other things, Lady Sorrell is presenting a theatrical performance. Which I will need to figure out—hmm. I have to think about this."

"Elyssa—"

"Don't worry, Trima. I shall be very careful."

Trima answered under her breath. "When people are set on mischief, no one is ever careful enough."

The echoes and I fell into an exhausted sleep, but it seemed that Elyssa had lain awake half the night, plotting, because in the morning she knew exactly what she wanted to do. I could only guess that the note had come from Marco, that he was nearby, and that he wanted her to meet him that evening while the play was being performed. I couldn't imagine how she planned to make it to a rendezvous, but it seemed Elyssa had already planned every detail.

"I'm only taking two echoes down to breakfast," she told Trima when the maid began to dress us for the day.

Trima gave her a long, suspicious look. "Why?"

Elyssa smiled. "Does it matter? Be glad I don't leave them all behind."

Trima pressed her lips together and said nothing more. I made certain that I was one of the echoes who was dressed for the day. I could not be left behind. I *had* to know what Elyssa was plotting.

Most of the guests were already seated around the breakfast table when we arrived and took our places by Cali and her echoes. I was surprised that Elyssa would seek out someone she disliked so much, but then I realized she was counting on Cali to be both observant and spiteful.

"Good morning, Elyssa, I hope you slept well," Cali said, making room for her. "But you look so disheartened—what's wrong? And aren't you missing an echo?"

Elyssa laughed faintly. "I thought maybe no one would notice, but I see I was too optimistic."

"I'm sorry, pretend I didn't say anything." Cali took a sip of juice. "But really. What happened?"

Elyssa sighed. "You might not remember, but when we were in Camarria, one of my echoes injured her ankle."

"Oh, I do remember hearing that. It seemed so odd."

"Well, apparently it's never properly healed, and this morning when she got up, it was all swollen again. She could hardly walk. I left her upstairs with my maid, and I hope she'll be better tonight but—" Elyssa shrugged. "It's so embarrassing."

"Unfortunate, perhaps, instead of embarrassing?" Cali said quizzically. "And painful for the poor echo, I would think!"

"I suppose. But to be at a gathering of high nobles, wanting to present the best appearance—and have an echo missing. I *am* embarrassed."

Cali, as always, was smiling. "And here I thought absolutely nothing damaged your sense of self-worth," she said. "I see I was mistaken."

Fortunately, at that moment servants began bringing the food around, and Elyssa could break off her conversation with Cali and begin talking to the young woman on her other side.

And I could puzzle over how exactly she was planning to turn a missing echo into an opportunity to meet her lover in secret.

The morning's entertainment consisted of a gaggle of local painters setting up easels in a well-lit drawing room and dashing off quick watercolors of any visitors who wanted to sit for portraits. All the women seemed delighted with the idea, though the men were less enthusiastic, with the result that Lord Clath took half of the male guests off on a trek through the city.

After her own session with the artist drew to a close, Elyssa made her way across the room to where Sorrell's mother was standing alone. The woman offered Elyssa a friendly smile and asked, "Was there something you needed?"

Elyssa produced a rueful laugh. "I have a favor to ask you, but please, *please* feel free to tell me no."

The governor's wife raised her eyebrows and said, "I will, but I'm certain you can't ask for anything I would be unwilling to give. What is it?"

"It's my maid. Trima. When she was a little girl, she wanted to run off and join an acting troupe, though her mother made sure she took up a much more respectable profession! But she's always had a fascination with the theater. When she heard there was going to be a performance here tonight, she begged me to find out if she could attend. Of course I said no, but she—"

"But how charming!" Sorrell's mother interrupted. "A servant with a longing for the stage! I certainly don't mind if she wants to sneak in and watch the production."

"I would make sure she sat in the very back row," Elyssa promised. "No one would even notice she was in the room."

"Then I see no problem whatsoever."

"Oh, that's so kind of you!"

The governor's wife smiled. "We are gathered to celebrate a joyous occasion," she said. "How nice if we have opportunities to spread that joy a little further."

I listened to the conversation with growing bewilderment. Only two echoes to follow Elyssa around all day. Trima to join the audience for the night's theatrical performance. I couldn't see how either of these developments would enable Elyssa to slip out of the house to meet Marco. Out of sheer curiosity, I was almost as impatient as Elyssa for the evening's festivities to begin.

For dinner, Elyssa, one of the other echoes, and I were all dressed in dark-purple silk gowns that laced up the front and showed off the Alberta amethysts to perfection. Elyssa put on her favorite gold necklace, the one with the three intertwined circles and the massive jewel set at the center. Of course, everyone at the dinner table wore similar colors and jewels, so the dining room looked like a field of lilacs and violets. It was a rather pretty effect, I thought.

After the meal, the group filed from the dining hall to the ballroom, which had been transformed into a theater, complete with one long, hastily built stage facing many rows of ornate chairs. Elyssa paused at the door to whisper to the governor's wife. "I must go fetch my maid. Thank you so much for this! Make sure no one else sits in the back row."

"I'll shoo everyone else away."

We flew back up to the bedroom, where a deeply unhappy Trima had dressed the third echo in an identical purple gown. "I do not approve of this foolish scheme," the maid said.

"Who cares if you approve or not?" Elyssa replied. Too impatient to wait for Trima's help, she began unlacing the front of her dress.

"If your father ever learns—"

"And who's going to tell him? You? The echoes? No one else will know."

"But if something goes wrong—"

"Nothing will go wrong! Now quickly!"

They must have hatched this scheme at some point when I was too far away to overhear because at first I could not figure out what was happening. But soon enough, Elyssa was out of her fancy clothes and stepping into one of Trima's severe high-necked black dresses. She coiled up her hair, pinned it to the top of her head, and covered it with a plain lace cap. The change in her appearance was drastic. If you looked closely, you could still tell who she was, but without the lush black hair framing her face, without the deep-dyed purple fabric calling attention to her full curves and alabaster skin, Elyssa was wan and unremarkable. If anyone glanced her way, which seemed unlikely, they would think she was a servant.

She took one final glance in the mirror, said "I never realized I could look so drab," and motioned to the echoes. We all rose quickly to our feet.

"You must stay here until I get back, since everyone thinks I'm you," Elyssa said to Trima as she headed toward the door. "It should only be a couple of hours."

"Wait—what about your necklace?"

Elyssa turned back impatiently. It was clear she wanted to go *running* back downstairs to make her assignation with Marco. "What about it?"

"You wore it to dinner. Someone might wonder why you're not wearing it now."

Elyssa heaved an exaggerated sigh but seemed to think Trima had a point. "Fine. Take it off me and put it on one of them," she said, presenting her spine to the maid. "But for love of the goddess, please *hurry.*"

Trima made no answer, just reached under the fabric on the back of Elyssa's dress to undo the clasp and slide the necklace free. Since I was the echo standing nearest to her, I wasn't surprised when she stepped behind me to fasten the chain around my own throat. I felt her warm fingers on the back of my neck, but they were no warmer than the gold of the necklace itself, heated by Elyssa's wild blood.

Elyssa scarcely waited for Trima to complete her task before she reached for the door handle. "Be careful, my lady," Trima spoke up in a sharp voice.

Elyssa's only reply was a laugh.

As the four of us stepped into the hallway, Elyssa pushed me ahead of her. "You first," she said. At the same moment, she asserted her control tightly over the three of us, and I found myself marching down the hallway with my movements precisely tied to hers. We looked like a high noblewoman, her two echoes, and a devoted servant hurrying through the mansion.

When we arrived at the ballroom door, we paused and peered inside. While the stage remained well-lit, the rest of the room was in shadowy darkness, but I could see that most seats were already filled with Sorrell's guests.

The governor's wife hurried over and spoke directly to me, as I was still in the lead. Her voice was barely a whisper. "I made sure the whole last row remained empty for you and your maid."

Under Elyssa's compulsion, my lips shaped a silent *thank you* and I gave the woman a grateful nod. Then the four of us made our way to the seats that had been reserved for us. As it happened, the last *two* rows were both empty, since apparently everyone else wanted to be close enough to the stage to hear all the dialogue. I ended up in the middle of the row, Elyssa on the aisle, the echoes in between us.

I understood her plan now, of course. Everyone believed one of her echoes was injured and confined to her room, so no one would question the fact that Elyssa only appeared to have two echoes now.

She had dressed herself as Trima merely to shepherd us to this venue, getting us settled in a place where no one would be expected to speak to us for more than an hour. And then, I supposed, she would sneak out of the ballroom at some point to meet with Marco. No one would even question why a maid would leave a play in the middle of the performance, whereas if Elyssa herself tried to exit, everyone would expect her echoes to follow. And she was headed to a rendezvous she did not want even her echoes to witness.

If only I'd known, I thought, as I folded my hands in my lap and gazed at the stage, just as Elyssa was doing. *I could have saved you all this trouble. I could have led the echoes down here, taken our seats— even exchanged a few words with the governor's wife!—and no one would have known it wasn't you. I don't care if you ruin yourself with disastrous romances. I'd have been happy to abet you as you made plans to meet with your secret lover.*

It was only one of the many ironies of my present situation.

We had not been in our seats very long when three hard knocks against the wooden dais signaled that the performance was about to begin. The crowd rustled a bit more, then settled down. A single figure entered from the far right, bounded up the stairs, and burst onto the stage. He was dressed in clothing that even I could tell was meant to be old-fashioned, as it was overornamented with gold braid and bright velvet, and he wore a hat that I had never seen any man wear, either in the countryside or the city.

"Gorsey!" he exclaimed in an affected accent. "I never thought that *I* would be a man to meet the king! But I suppose you never know at the start of your life what sorts of miracles it might contain."

I had to agree with the sentiment.

He had been speaking a few minutes, explaining his situation, when a trio of women mounted the stage from the other side. They, too, were dressed in outdated but extravagantly beautiful clothes, and they fell on him with cries of wonder.

"Tell us! Tell us! What did you learn from your expedition to Camarria?"

As he launched into a recitation, I felt Elyssa's head jerk in the direction of the door. All her echoes immediately glanced that way, but I couldn't see past the others to determine what had caught Elyssa's attention. I could guess, though. She dropped her strict control over us, but issued a silent, powerful command that I interpreted as *Stay.* Then she rose to her feet, glided furtively to the door, and disappeared.

I stared after her, thinking impossible thoughts. What if I took this opportunity to try to escape her—left the echoes where they were and simply snuck out of the ballroom, out of the manor, and into the streets of Wemberton? How long would I survive, friendless and penniless, with no history and no skills? Would I find some kind soul to give me shelter and ask few questions, or would I be attacked, humiliated, perhaps killed, before a week was out? Would Elyssa even try to recover me—and if she did, what punishment would she mete out to me then?

With these questions revolving in my head, I completely lost the thread of the story being told onstage. So when there was a sudden stir and murmur in the audience, I looked up in surprise, thinking there must have been an unexpected plot twist in the play. But no. The action on the stage had been momentarily suspended, and all the nobles were rising to their feet. Everyone was gazing toward the door, where a small knot of people engaged in low conversation. The ballroom was still dim, but servants in the hallway were holding enough lamps to show a cluster of fresh arrivals, their hair and outer coats glittering with a dust of snow.

"Please—don't announce me. I hate to be a disruption!" a man said in a soft and pleasant tone.

I held my breath. I knew that voice. I knew that shape at the door, and those repeated shapes, like shadows with weight and substance—

"But, prince, everyone has already seen you! There has already been a disruption!" the governor's wife protested.

"Yes, and I am sorry for it," Jordan replied. "Just let me sit quietly. You can announce me when the play is over."

By this time, I was also on my feet, craning my head to look around the echoes, straining to see through the dimness of the room. Jordan! Here! Had my wandering mind conjured up delicious hallucinations or was it really the prince?

He stepped into the ballroom, accompanied by the lady of the house and a wavering circle of light. Everyone in the audience bowed or curtseyed in one convulsive, rustling wave, and Jordan bowed back in a restrained way, as if still trying to minimize the effects of his presence. I saw his eyes flicking quickly over the crowd, trying through the inadequate lighting to determine who was present and who might be friendly to the crown. His gaze landed on Elyssa's echo, the one nearest the door, and I saw him first start back and then grow eager. I could almost read the thoughts in his head. *Oh, no. Elyssa's here. But wait, does that mean Hope is, too?*

His gaze moved to the second echo and then to me. Praying he could see me even through the shadows, I stared back, holding his eyes with my own. I gave the smallest nod.

Jordan turned to the governor's wife, who was leading him toward the front of the room, and murmured, "I'm just going to take a seat here in the back where I won't bother anybody."

"But, Majesty—"

He marched across the floor, entered the row of seats from the other side, and came to stand right next to me, his echoes lining up beside him.

"Everybody, please sit," he said, and dropped onto this chair.

The whole world sat down.

And I was sitting next to Jordan.

CHAPTER TWENTY-TWO

For a moment, the silence in the makeshift theater was absolute. The actors, frozen in mid-gesture, stared out at the crowd as if waiting for permission to speak. The guests, once again facing the stage, held themselves with tense alertness, as if straining toward the back of the room to detect any word or motion on Jordan's part. If anyone even breathed, they did so without making a sound.

Then the governor's wife made a helpless gesture toward the stage and said, "Please. Resume."

One of the actresses cleared her throat and said. "So—Lord Michael—tell us what other news you heard in the royal city."

The actor playing Michael stumbled over his first few words, but soon he was declaiming with his previous flair and confidence. The noble guests relaxed their stiff poses and pretended a renewed interest in the play, though one or two glanced over their shoulders in Jordan's direction. Jordan sat very straight in his chair, his attention seeming fixed on the stage, but I felt his hand reach tentatively for mine.

I closed my fingers over his with a hold so tight I might very well have bruised the bone.

"Hope?" he whispered so low not even the people two rows in front of us could hear.

"Yes," I answered, just as quietly. "I can't believe you're here."

"I almost didn't come. When Cormac asked me to, I wanted to refuse."

"Elyssa almost didn't come, either. She managed to secure an invitation only a few days ago."

I saw his gaze skip down the line of echoes before coming back to me. "Where is she? How can *you* be here if she is not?"

I managed the ghost of a laugh. "Oh, she went to elaborate lengths to make it happen! Everyone believes that one of her echoes is up in her room, injured, and that Elyssa's maid accompanied her to the performance. But Elyssa was dressed as the maid and she slipped away as soon as she got us settled in our chairs."

"One has to admire her ingenuity," he said, though I could detect no admiration in his voice. "And where did she slip off to?"

I hesitated and he nodded. "An assignation, I suppose," he said. "House parties like these are unendurable unless you've managed a little intrigue on the side."

"You're very lenient."

"I'm very grateful! Because of her machinations, I have a chance to speak to you alone!"

I offered that soundless laugh again. "Alone with fifty other people in a public place."

"It feels like privacy at the moment."

"I was so afraid," I said earnestly. "So afraid I would never see you again."

"You would have," he said with utter certainty. "I would have found a way to make it happen, even if it meant riding all the way to Lord Bentam's house and demanding an audience with you."

"This is better."

He strangled a laugh. "*So* much better. And to think I only came tonight because my father thought it might be a smart move politically. I don't know if you're aware, but there has been so much unrest—"

"Oh, yes. I've heard a great deal about it."

"And I thought, if my presence can be a calming influence— But I didn't think, I didn't even hope—" He stopped short, and then he squeezed my hand. "Hope," he said again. "Every time I say the word, I think of you."

"I got your message," I said. "The one you sent with Deryk."

Even his whisper sounded pleased. "You did? I wasn't sure he would deliver it. I wasn't sure you would know it was meant for you."

"I tell myself you couldn't possibly be thinking of me—"

"Thinking of you all the time," he said.

I lifted my free hand, making a vague gesture at the stage, and the two echoes beside me mimicked my motion. "This reminds me," I said. "Of that night in the palace—"

"Yes! The musical evening—"

"Where we sat in the back of the room—"

"And we talked about everything," he finished up. "Just everything."

"Then we were discussing Jamison's death," I said. "And now we hear that someone has been trying to kill Cormac. I can't imagine how frightening it's been."

"It's terrifying," he said. "There have been two attempts so far, and we have to assume there will be more. And perhaps malcontents will target my father next, or me. We have doubled our security, so that everywhere we go we are followed by a dozen guards, but it is hard to ever feel entirely safe. We know that the first man to make the attempt was an outsider who somehow snuck into the palace—but the second one? My father believes he was brought in by someone who either works at the palace or was an invited guest. Which means we were betrayed by someone we trust."

"Someone you shouldn't trust," I said, my voice as quiet as I could make it, "is Elyssa."

He was silent a moment. "Her father is allied with the revolutionaries. That we know," he said. "But I have never thought Elyssa cared enough for politics—or her father—to agitate against the crown."

"There is a young man named Marco Ross. One of the rebels. She is enamored of him."

"Ah," he said, nodding. "Love will convert anyone to a cause."

I started to speak, but the crowd around us burst into laughter at some exchange onstage. I was glad, as it gave me another moment or two to formulate my next words, which were unexpectedly difficult to say. I wasn't sure why. I hated Elyssa, I hated everything she had ever done, and yet I still felt as if I were being disloyal by exposing her now. "The man who tried to kill Cormac. The first one. It was Marco. Elyssa let him into the palace," I said.

He looked down at me, his amiable face completely cold and set. "You're certain of that?"

I nodded. "I would have thought the inquisitor would have figured that out."

"What do you mean?"

"A couple of days before the assassin came in, Elyssa found a back entrance to the palace. One that you reach through a gate by the stables."

"But that door is always kept locked from the inside."

I nodded again. "We were sitting outside, trying to determine how to get in, when Malachi came out. He offered to escort us through the back hallways to the front entrance. Everyone says he's such a clever man. I would have thought he would have realized that Elyssa was the one who unlocked the door a few days later. He had just *seen* her there."

Jordan frowned, thinking that over. "*I* certainly would have been suspicious if I'd known that," he agreed. "But Malachi…" His voice trailed off. "Malachi," he repeated.

I felt shock tingle through me. "Surely you don't think the inquisitor could be plotting against your family. Hasn't he been at the palace forever?"

"Since my father married Tabitha," Jordan said in an icy voice. "Her family sent him along with her to Camarria, saying she needed someone in the palace to look out for her. He became an inquisitor and eventually the top man. But I would not be surprised to find his loyalty is more to Empara than the crown."

"Would Tabitha have any reason to want Cormac dead?"

"She hates us all, so I would say the answer is yes! But Malachi—" He shook his head. "It makes no sense! It was Malachi who would not rest until he discovered that Lady Marguerite had killed Jamison, and he has searched just as assiduously for Cormac's would-be assassin. If he knew, all this time, that Elyssa was acquainted with the man, why wouldn't he have had her questioned?"

"Maybe he liked having knowledge that he could draw on later if he needed it," I said tentatively. "Something he could use against Elyssa—or Lord Bentam—if the circumstances ever arose. If Cormac had actually died, Malachi might have arrested Elyssa, but since he survived—" I shrugged. "Malachi found the knowledge to be a weapon in his hand."

"That sounds very much like Malachi," Jordan agreed. "But perhaps the reason is even darker. Perhaps Malachi has only been *pretending* to search for the attacker because he has his own schemes in place for harming the crown."

"That would be terrible!" I exclaimed. "You must tell your father."

"I will. The minute I'm back in Camarria." He squeezed my hand again. "How unexpected and fortunate that you were able to give me such news! I wonder what other information you might have that my father would never be able to pick up on his own."

I managed a smile. "I would be happy to spy for you and report back anything happening in Lord Bentam's house."

"You could write me reports every week and send them in secret."

I shook my head sadly. "I can't write. *Or* read."

"I'm sorry—I didn't think—well, we'd find *other* ways to communicate," he said firmly. "I know! I could come visit Bentam's estate every few weeks."

"Oh, wouldn't that be lovely."

"The difficulty would be in getting you alone during every visit. I don't think we can count on Elyssa dashing off to meet paramours when she knows I'm expected in the house."

"No, but I'm starting to feel quite adventurous," I said. "Maybe I could climb out a window at night and meet you in the back gardens."

His shoulders started shaking with helpless merriment. I could feel my own laughter bubbling up, and I put a hand across my mouth to hold it back. "How intrepid of you!" he managed to whisper. "Next you will tell me you've taken up sword fighting and other dashing skills!"

"No, do you think I should?"

"They might come in handy if you're going to be a spy," he said. "You also might—"

A crashing noise from the hallway interrupted him. All the heads in the ballroom jerked in that direction as if pulled by a common cord. There was another crash, even louder, and the sound of shouting voices. Now a few members of the audience, mostly men, were on their feet; the poor actors had again stopped spouting their lines and stood helplessly on the stage, listening like everyone else.

I glanced from the door to Jordan's face. His expression was both grim and apprehensive. "I don't like that," he said.

The shouts grew louder, then suddenly a seething mass of struggling bodies boiled through the ballroom door. Someone screamed; chairs overturned as more people leapt up. I was on my feet, my fists clenched and my body shaking. Because the room was so dim, it was hard to tell what was happening, but I thought I could see men in royal livery battling a group of desperate attackers.

Jordan's men. And rebels bent on killing him.

The nobles in the audience began to shift and murmur in alarm, looking for somewhere safe to go, but fighters blocked the only visible door. In the dimness and the confusion, I almost didn't see three small figures making their way to us from the front of the room, but then I realized Sorrell and her echoes had come to find the prince.

Sorrell touched Jordan's arm and cried in a low voice, "This way! There's a back exit."

With one more glance at the furious battle, Jordan nodded, and Sorrell took off at a run. Her echoes were so close to her they must have been treading on her heels, and Jordan and I were only steps behind. She led us to a concealed door at the back of the ballroom, little more than a smooth seam in the ornate painted wall, and we slipped through in a swift, panting parade. When Sorrell shut the door behind us, we could still hear the sounds of raised voices and clashing weapons as the fight raged on.

"This way," she said again and plunged down the hallway. We were in a narrow corridor, lit only sporadically with a few dim lanterns—a servant's passageway, no doubt. "This leads to the kitchens—and a small parlor that my mother uses—and my father's library, but—"

There was a sudden swell of sound as the door behind us burst back open and bodies tumbled through. Sorrell shrieked and we all began pelting faster down the hall. I tripped once, and Jordan grabbed my arm in an iron grip and hauled me along beside him. Dimly I was aware that two of his echoes were offering their own rough support to the echoes following me.

Behind us were more shouts, the clash of metal against metal, the sounds of bodies hitting the walls and floors. Jordan had said he traveled with a dozen men; how many did the rebels have? No doubt the governor had troops of his own nearby, but how quickly could they arrive? Would Jordan already be dead?

The back passageway abruptly fed into a main hallway, and Sorrell shoved open the first door we came to. As soon as we all rushed through, she slammed it shut. "There's no lock," she said in a breathless voice.

"Furniture," Jordan snapped, spinning around to assess the options. This space was even darker than the ballroom, with faint light coming only from the dying embers of a banked fire and moonlight drifting through narrow windows too small for a man to crawl through. But we could make out the dense black silhouettes of wingback chairs and occasional tables, massive bookshelves lining each wall, even a large credenza in one corner.

Jordan had only taken two steps toward the credenza when the door flew open and more bodies poured in, still locked in noisy combat. Sorrell screamed again and I saw one man pause and throw her out into the corridor; her echoes stumbled after her. Jordan threw his arm around me and swept me across the room, as far from the door as possible. We took shelter behind a grouping of chairs and peered fearfully over the backs, trying to see who was fighting, who was winning, who was here to save us, and who was here to kill us.

Jordan had placed himself behind me and braced his arms against the chair on either side of me, so that any weapon would have to go through him to hurt me. His echoes similarly protected mine as they huddled behind their own chairs. I tried to squirm away, whispering furiously, "No! Protect yourself!" But he merely clenched his arms more tightly and shook his head.

"We will stand here and maybe die here, but I am not sacrificing you," he answered.

The fighting slowed and seemed to stop, though I could hear moaning and gasping from men still on their feet and men fallen to the floor. From what I could make out, there were two people still standing just inside the door and a handful outside. None of them rushed over to make sure Jordan was unscathed, and my heart squeezed down with a painful pressure. These were not royal soldiers, then.

As if to prove it, one of them called out to comrades we couldn't see through the doorway. "All right! What's our situation?" His voice was smoother and more refined than I would have expected.

A voice came back, fainter and hoarser. "The hallway is ours! But we're five men down—and the king's soldiers are at every exit."

"So we're trapped."

"Aye."

The speaker turned his head to survey the room. In the chancy light, he couldn't see much, but I saw him look directly at the arrangement of chairs where Jordan and I crouched in hiding. "But we've got the prince," he said. "So we have a prize to negotiate."

"Or to kill," said the voice in the hallway.

"If he dies, so do we," said the man in the room. "If he lives, we might very well live, too."

I felt Jordan's arms close around me again in a reassuring squeeze. There was a bit of hope after all.

For a moment, everyone was silent while the man in the room seemed to think things over. He appeared to be the leader of this ragtag group and, judging by his voice, he was a noble. Maybe I would even recognize him if I could see his face.

"All right," he said again. "Somebody bring me some light. It's time to talk to the prince."

Jordan straightened and stepped away from the safety of the chair, though I clutched his arm to try to hold him back. "Let me stir up the fire," Jordan said. "And there may be a candle or two in the room. I'll see what I can find."

The noble in the room laughed. "You're a cool one," he said.

"Civilized," Jordan responded. I saw him grope along the hearth to find the shovel and poker, and a moment later his body was illuminated by a burst of light as the coals shifted and flared up. The shapes behind him looked like shadows created by the fire, but I knew they were his echoes. He glanced around quickly, located a branch of candles on a nearby table, and soon had several small flames sending a dancing illumination through the room.

"I'll thank you to put that poker down," the rebel said.

"I'll thank you to sheathe your sword," Jordan replied.

"Not likely."

Jordan shrugged and kept the poker in his hand.

The rebel smiled and came deeper into the room. The man behind him followed closely, which was when I realized he had an echo. Definitely a noble. "So we find ourselves in an interesting position," he said. "Let's see if we can talk our way out of it."

From the hallway came a low, piteous cry and a thumping sound. "How many of *my* men are dead?" Jordan asked. "How many wounded?"

The rebel snorted. "I haven't counted. I don't care."

"Well, I care. Get the wounded out where they can receive attention and then we'll talk."

"You aren't in a position to be dictating terms."

Jordan just shrugged and dropped into a chair on the other side of the fire. My guess was that he was trying to draw attention away from me, in case the attackers hadn't realized that I was also in the room. He laid his poker across his knees and regarded the other man in silence.

The rebel stared back for a long moment, during which we heard more moans and curses from the wounded men. "Fine," he snapped, then he strode to the door. "Drag the injured off to be cared for!" he shouted.

There was a muffled commotion in the hall, and the sounds of bodies changing position and hurt men yelping and boots scraping along the floor. Through it all, Jordan sat patiently, motionlessly, and the rebel shifted restlessly from one foot to the other. When a call of "All clear!" came down the hall, the rebel faced Jordan again and snapped, "Satisfied?"

"Yes. Thank you," Jordan answered, unruffled. "Now perhaps we can talk in peace."

"Peace," the other man sneered. "You're a madman if you think there's peace to be had in the Seven Jewels."

"What is it you want?" Jordan asked.

"What I *wanted* was your death, but it looks like I might have to wait for that."

"No, I meant in the larger sense. What is it you think my death will accomplish? What message are you trying to send to the king?"

The rebel came two steps closer. "That we don't *need* a king. That we can govern ourselves better and more efficiently on our own. Stop trying to control the western provinces and just let us go!"

"I understand that a number of individuals feel as you do," Jordan said, still calmly. "*My* concern is that you are in the minority. Have you put the issue before all the landowners? Have a majority agreed? If that is the case, I assure you, my father will listen. But if it is just a vocal few—"

The rebel clenched his hand on his sword and half raised it, as if it was taking all his willpower not to rush forward and stab it through Jordan's heart. His echo lifted his own hand, but fortunately, it was empty. "It's not just the nobles!" he exclaimed. "The merchants and the common men, they want to be free of the crown just as much as we do."

Still holding the poker in one fist, Jordan spread his hands in a gesture of inclusiveness. "By all means. Put the vote to the entire population. Ask every man, woman, and child of the western provinces if they want to secede. Tally up the answers. If it is more than half the population, my father will listen."

The other man stared at him uncertainly. "It can't be that simple."

"Of course it's not that simple. Make sure they understand that any province not tied to Camarria will pay for its own roads and its own defenses, and its merchant ships will not be guarded by the royal navy. Its goods will not be protected by tariffs. It will have to use money minted by its own treasuries, since we certainly will not act as its banker—"

"It's not about money and roads!" the rebel shouted, suddenly so angry that even in the bad lighting I could see the redness of his face. "It's the way you and your damned father do whatever you want! Take whatever you want! Kill whoever you want! You think you're above the law—you think you *are* the law—" His voice failed him and he turned away to hide his emotions.

That was when I guessed who this must be; perhaps Jordan had known it all along. "Your sister murdered my brother," he said, his voice still utterly composed. "My father was enacting justice by executing your sister."

Marguerite's brother whirled around to face him again. "Then he can enact more justice when I kill you!"

"If you kill me, you will never leave this house alive," Jordan said. "Two more dead, and what will have been solved?"

"The king will have suffered!"

"Believe me when I say he has already suffered more than you could imagine."

"It's not enough. It will never be enough."

"Which one are you?" Jordan asked abruptly. "She has many brothers, does she not? What's your name?"

He hesitated, as if not wanting to answer but unable to find a reason to refuse. "I'm Renner. The youngest."

"And were you close to Marguerite? Were you one that she specially cared for?"

Renner hesitated again, but now I read surprise on his face. "What's that got to do with it?"

"I was only curious. Something she said once made me think—" He paused, as if suddenly realizing he was broaching delicate subjects.

Renner came closer, his face now drawn into a pugnacious frown. "Made you think what?"

"I thought perhaps there was very little love between Marguerite and her siblings."

Renner stared. "This doesn't have anything to do with *love*," he spit out. "You dishonored all of Orenza."

"And how much dishonor do you think you will do to Orenza if you assassinate me tonight?"

There was a short, pregnant pause—and then, before I knew what was happening, Renner had rushed across the room with an inarticulate cry and jammed the tip of his sword against the heavy gold braid of Jordan's jacket, right above his heart. His echo crowded behind him, his arm pointing toward the same spot on one of Jordan's echoes. I thought my own heart would burst from terror, but Jordan merely looked up at him, utterly unmoving.

"Any more talk like that, and I swear I will run you through," the other man hissed.

When Jordan didn't reply, Renner stood there a moment, breathing heavily. Then he dropped his sword arm and strode back toward the door, his echo at his heels. "We'll talk later," he bit out. "I need to see to my men." And he stalked out, slamming the door behind him.

I was left alone with Jordan.

CHAPTER TWENTY-THREE

For a second, Jordan and I stayed frozen where we were, then my whole body loosened with a sobbing gasp, and I fell to my knees behind the chair. I heard Jordan leap up and rush over, and suddenly he was kneeling beside me, pulling me into a reassuring embrace. Around us, the five echoes had also dropped to the floor and were seeking comfort in each other's arms.

"No, no, you can't fall apart now," Jordan said, tilting my head up and planting a kiss on my cheek. "He'll be back soon enough, and we'll have to be prepared to engage again."

"It's just—I was so afraid—and you were so brave —"

He dropped to a sitting position, settled his back against the wall, and drew me against his chest. Never in my life had I felt so cherished and so safe.

Despite the fact that a band of armed rebels clustered thirty feet away, bent on murder.

"I don't feel brave," Jordan admitted. "But I don't think he'll have the nerve to kill me face-to-face. One of his paid men might do it, but Renner himself? I don't think so. Especially not now when he can't hope to escape. If I die, so does he, and he knows it."

"So what do we do now?"

"Wait for him to realize he has no options and come begging for safe passage."

"Will you grant it?"

He nodded. "I meant what I said. I don't see how more deaths will help the situation. We need to figure out how to come to terms, not just keep avenging wrongs." He thought that over, absentmindedly running a hand down the silky length of my hair. I was more pleased by the touch than I ever would have expected.

"It's discouraging, though," he said at last. "My father really thought the western nobles were interested in a new trade deal that he put together. So were they just stalling, waiting for the next chance to strike a blow?"

I lifted my head, even though that made Jordan still his hand. "No, they *are* interested," I said. "Bentam and his friends. And they were angry that the governor of Orenza didn't want to sign the agreement."

Jordan cocked his head. "You mean there's a schism in the rebel ranks?"

"Yes. Bentam and the others are worried that Lord Garvin might go rogue. They've been trying to decide how to make him fall in line."

Jordan leaned his head against the wall. "So this little stunt was all Garvin's doing. Bentam wasn't involved in it."

"I don't think so."

"And Bentam and his cronies will be furious if Renner murders me and ruins all prospects of a deal with the crown."

"As I understand it, yes."

"That's worth knowing. It allows us to plant a little more discord among the rebels and strengthens our own hand—assuming we get out of this alive, which is by no means guaranteed!"

"You have so many people working against you!" I exclaimed. "Bentam and his friends—the governor of Orenza—the inquisitor—"

"Yes, our enemies do seem to be piling up," Jordan agreed. "And since they don't all appear to be working together, it's hard to know where to feel safe and where to put our trust."

"You can trust me," I said timidly.

He laughed and tightened his arm so much I was momentarily crushed against his chest. "You! You're the only person in this entire dreadful night that I have been happy to see with my whole heart! I trust you *and* I like you *and* I marvel at the way you've managed to create this entire—" He lifted his other hand to make a circle in the air. "This *existence* inside an impossibly narrow margin of life."

"That's what it feels like," I said. "A secret life inside of someone else's."

"I'm going to set you free," he said seriously. "I'm going to ride back to Camarria and tell my father about you."

"But what can he—"

He raised his voice to talk over me. "And I'll have him invite Elyssa to the palace. And once you're there, he'll tell her that you have achieved independence and that she must leave you behind."

"She won't agree."

"She'll have to. He's the king. And he'll send her away and you'll stay behind in the palace and then—and then—well, we'll see."

I was breathing a little faster. "*Maybe* she would be willing to do it," I said. "She hates her echoes. She's always saying she wants to get rid of us."

"She *says* that? To your *face*?"

"Well, she thinks we can't understand her, so why wouldn't she say it in our presence? The only reason she doesn't drown us in a river somewhere is that she likes the prestige of having three echoes."

He peered down at me, and by the uneven firelight, I could see the worry in his face. "She wouldn't really do that. Drown you, I mean. Harm you in any way."

I made a scoffing sound. "She harms us all the time. Remember when we were in Camarria and she told everyone that one of her echoes had tripped and hurt its ankle? What happened was that Elyssa stomped on its leg in a fit of rage."

"But she—I mean—has she done that before?"

Reluctantly enough, because I hated to leave his embrace, I pulled myself away from him and loosened the front laces of my bodice. Just enough so I could pull the gown down off my right shoulder and expose the long white expanse of my upper arm.

Decorated with a cascading pattern of reddened scars, straight lines and circles. Slash marks and burns. I wasn't sure if he could see the evidence in the uncertain light, so I lifted his hand and molded it around my arm so he could feel the patches of raised skin carved into the flesh. "Over and over," I said. "It's the first thing I remember. Feeling pain."

Slowly, as if afraid the pressure would hurt me, Jordan tightened his fingers over my mutilated skin. "Hope," he whispered. I could hear the shocked horror in his quiet voice. "My dear." The room was too dark for me to see clearly, but I thought his eyes glinted with unshed tears.

"There's more," I said, pulling the dress back up to my shoulder. "On my stomach. On my back. On my legs. Anywhere I'm likely to be covered by clothes."

"Just you?" he asked. "Or all of the echoes?"

"All of us," I said, "though I have more marks than the others. When she was a girl, she realized that if she—if she hurt me enough—I would show an expression of pain. The other two never reacted, no matter what she did to them, so she didn't bother with them very much. Just me."

"Does she—does she do it still?"

"Not really. She seemed to lose interest when she was eighteen or twenty. When there were balls to go to and men to flirt with and she wasn't so bored. She still hits us when she's in a rage, but these days she mostly tries to keep as far away from us as she can. We've learned to stay out of her way."

"That's why you're so afraid of her," he said. "You think if she learns that you're conscious, she'll harm you in some terrible fashion instead of simply letting you go."

I think she'll kill me. "Yes," was all I said.

"Then we'll have to have you safely in the palace with guards at the door when my father tells her she must leave you behind."

I shook my head. "I'm not sure it will work. She still has power over me. She can draw me to her—make me mimic her every movement. If she doesn't want to leave me behind, she'll just bind me to her and walk out the door, and I'll have to follow. I'll be helpless."

"I'll hold on to you," he promised. "I won't let you be dragged out of the room. My father's guards will escort her so far out of the city that her bond with you will be broken."

"Does that really happen?" I asked wistfully. "Is there a distance at which the connection between an echo and her original is simply snapped?"

"I don't know, but if there is, we'll find it."

"I hope so," I said, my voice very low. "I so much want to be free of her."

"Then maybe we shouldn't wait," he said. "You can come back with me to Camarria tomorrow—assuming we survive the night, of course! I'll tell her that while we were trapped in this room together, I was astonished to learn you could speak—"

I was gripped by ungovernable terror. "No—no—you can't do that," I pleaded. "Not until we're at the palace and *surrounded* by your father's guards. She will find a way to bend me to her will, and I'll have to stay with her, but then she'll *know*, and she'll do something awful—"

He cupped his hand around the back of my head and pressed his lips to my forehead, soothing me with small rocking motions. "Shh, it's all right, I'm sorry. Shh now. Very well, I won't tell her that you've gained consciousness and a voice. I won't do anything until I have you safe in Camarria and she can't stop me from taking you away from her."

"Thank you," I said against his coat.

"I don't like it, though," he added. "I'll be so worried about you."

I lifted my head so I could smile at him. "I wish I could say I'm sorry, but that's something I'm actually glad to know."

He lifted a hand to touch my face. "It's still amazing to me," he said. "That I'm sitting here talking to you. That you even exist."

"It's amazing to *me* that you ever noticed me," I replied.

"There's this lovely word they have in Ferrenlea, and I just learned it," he said. "Amelista."

"I know that word!" I exclaimed. "Lord Bentam entertained a man from Ferrenlea and he was trying to explain it to Elyssa. She wasn't very interested."

"It means *I know you*, or something like that."

I remembered the conversation from a few weeks back. I said, "'I see you and you see me.'"

"Yes. I feel that's true with us. We see each other in ways no one else ever has. We share amelista."

It was a good thing he couldn't see me blushing in the dark. "I am very glad it was you," I said in a low voice, "who first set eyes on me and knew I was there."

It occurred to me that, since my gown was still half undone, he was seeing rather more of me than was strictly proper. I straightened the neckline, then reached for the laces so I could do up the bodice again. But Jordan pushed my fingers aside. I looked up at him inquiringly. He lifted his hands to my shoulders and tugged on the dress, sliding it lower on both sides until my arms were exposed down to my elbows and my back was uncovered down to my waist. His hands moved slowly up my naked arms, his skin so warm and mine so cool, and his fingers paused briefly at every bump and scar.

Then his body lifted; he came to his knees and brought his arms around so he could run his flat palms over the skin on my back. There was one scar that was particularly long and deep, a gash that had bled for days and seemed to heal reluctantly. It started at the bottom edge of my right shoulder blade, crossed my spine at a diagonal, and ended at the lowest point of my left-hand rib cage. Jordan traced its whole ugly path with slow, sensitive fingertips.

Still on his knees, he began moving around until he was directly behind me. I thought he wanted a better look at my scars, so I shifted a little to be closer to the firelight, and I drew my heavy hair over my right shoulder. Hiding nothing, letting him see every sad, marred inch of skin.

He bent forward and pressed his mouth against the scar, first at the shoulder blade where the dagger had entered. Then on the next inch of ripped skin, then the next, then the next, until his lips were on the edge of my rib cage and there was no way he could miss the fact that I was barely breathing.

Before I could speak—before I could think of anything I might say—we heard voices in the hall. Jordan and his echoes jumped to their feet, but he motioned me to remain where I was. "Stay hidden. It might be an advantage to us if the rebels do not realize you are in the room."

I shrank back into the shadows, pulling my dress back up and tightening the laces as Jordan moved to the center of the room, the poker somehow back in his hand. A moment later the door burst open and Renner strode in, his echo at his heels.

"We have talked with your captain," he said. "He says he will allow my men and me to leave unmolested if you will write out instructions to that effect."

"I will, if you bring me paper and ink."

"The governor's wife says both can be found in the desk against the wall."

Jordan picked up the candelabra and raised it to shoulder height so that the thin flames illuminated the whole space. Indeed, a delicate wooden writing desk was situated across the room, a single ladder-back chair beside it. I had the irrelevant thought that both pieces of furniture looked so uncomfortable that no one in this house must spend much time writing.

"Then this should be settled very soon," Jordan said, making his way to the desk and rummaging in its drawers. His echoes followed behind him, pantomiming his every movement. Once he unearthed writing materials, he dropped onto the chair and began scratching out a message. He wrote quickly and confidently, without seeming to worry overmuch about the phrasing.

"No tricks now," Renner warned. "Don't pretend you're guaranteeing safe passage while you're telling him to slaughter the lot of us."

"You may read every word," Jordan said, not even looking up. "And if you don't like what I've written, I'll throw the paper into the fire and let you dictate my letter."

"Well, I just might," Renner said.

Jordan finished with a flourish, then unscrewed one of the candles from its metal base, tilting it so the wax dripped over the paper. As it cooled, he pulled a heavy ring from his right hand and pressed the seal into the wax. Still sitting at the desk, he held the paper up for Renner. "Read it," he said. "Let me know if you approve."

Renner snarled but crossed the room to snatch the note from Jordan's hand, his echo grasping at empty air beside him. My guess was the Orenza man would have no idea how to word a letter begging for his own safety, so he was merely posturing when he demanded to see what Jordan had written.

"It will do," he said when he had skimmed the contents. "Once I deliver it, I will come back to escort you from the room. No matter what your man promises, I don't believe he will allow me to walk freely from the building unless I leave this room with you beside me, a knife at your throat."

"That seems excessively dramatic."

Renner sneered. "It has been a season for drama," he replied. Without another word, he exited the room, once more slamming the door behind him.

As soon as he was gone, Jordan was on his feet and bounding over to me, his echoes in pursuit. "When Renner returns, you stay here," he ordered. "I don't believe he realizes you're in the room, and I don't want to give him another hostage. Once Renner is safely gone, I will find Elyssa and send her to collect you."

"All right," I said. I put a hand to my temple. "What an evening this has been, from first to last! My head is spinning."

"Yes, and we aren't out of danger yet," Jordan said. "Anything could still go wrong—"

There were sudden shouts in the hall, and the sounds of thudding bodies and clashing swords. Jordan whirled for the door. "As I said," he murmured. "Trouble. Stay out of sight."

Almost before he finished the words, the door flew open and Renner flung himself inside, his echo a ghost behind him. "You've betrayed us!" he cried, waving his sword wildly. "Your guards have come bursting in from both sides—they're attacking my men—"

"That is not what I asked for," Jordan said. "If you lead me to my captain, I will tell him—"

"They're being *slaughtered!*" Renner wailed, charging forward. "And you will die for it!"

Jordan darted behind one of the wingback chairs, his echoes practically tripping over each other to fall in line behind him. Still brandishing his weapon, Renner feinted from one side to the other as Jordan kept the furniture between them. The clamor from the hall grew louder, full of angry bellows and howls of pain and the scraping metallic sound of swords engaging.

"You can still ride away from here," Jordan said. "If you harm me, you will die."

"Filthy lying royal bastard," Renner panted. "I am dead anyway. I am taking you with me."

He shoved the chair so hard that it hit Jordan in the stomach, knocking him back into his echoes and sending two of them careening to the floor. Jordan caught his balance, but Renner had already darted around the chair and was slashing at him with a frenzied rage. Through all this, Jordan had retained his grip on the poker, his only weapon, and he wielded it with desperate grace, parrying all of Renner's frantic blows. But Renner managed a lucky thrust or two. I saw blood start up from a cut on Jordan's face, and I was pretty sure his left arm had been seriously wounded.

Unable to sit still and watch, I jumped to my feet and scanned the room for a weapon of my own. Out in the hallway, I heard more screams, more heavy thuds, and then an urgent voice. "My liege! Where are you?"

"In here! Under attack!" Jordan called back.

The byplay seemed to enrage Renner even further, and he fought with the abandon of a man who had nothing left to lose. Grunting and swearing, he hacked at Jordan with his sword, kicked at him with his heavy boots, and succeeded in knocking him to the floor. Jordan flung up one arm to protect his head as Renner brought his sword down in a flashing arc. I saw blood well up as Jordan cried out in pain.

I was already on the move, snatching up the coal shovel that rested against the hearth, and racing across the room with an inarticulate cry. Renner swung around in astonishment, but he was badly positioned to defend himself from the angle of my attack. I swung the shovel hard, first connecting with the wrist of his sword arm and then, when he dropped his hand, smashing him across the cheek. He cursed and stumbled back, his free hand coming up to cover his bleeding face.

"Who—what are you—how—" he stuttered.

Jordan had rolled to his feet, clutching his injured arm to his chest. "End this, Renner," he said grimly. "I swear I will speak on your behalf—"

"You do nothing but *lie!*" Renner howled and sprang forward.

I shrieked, Jordan loosed an oath, and what seemed like a dozen bodies crashed through the open door. Maybe six of the newcomers wore royal livery; three of them sprinted to Jordan's side, while the other three charged toward Renner. But more men poured into the room, and *more*, until there was so much noise and chaos I could barely follow what was happening. Almost whimpering from fear, I scrambled back toward the poor safety of the wingback chair, glancing around madly as I dove for cover. Jordan's guards had pushed him behind them and formed a barrier between him and the fierce action among the fighters. I saw him slumping against the wall, still cradling his arm to his chest; his face was drawn in pain but his eyes keenly watched the combat.

I heard a muted roar from the hallway, then the heavy sound of many booted feet running in unison. A moment later, a fresh cadre of guards shouldered through the door, all of them wearing purple sashes that I assumed marked them as the governor's men. There had to be a dozen of them, and voices in the hallway indicated that another ten or fifteen were on the scene.

Their appearance broke the will of the rebel fighters—all of a sudden, the brawling in the room stopped, and the few remaining insurgents flung their hands in the air. "Yield! Yield!" they cried, one after the other, dropping to their knees and laying aside their swords. The rest of the royal guardsmen slowly backed across the room to join the cluster around Jordan and his echoes—but I noticed that none of *them* surrendered their weapons.

A tall, harsh-featured man strode to the door and called out, "We've secured the library!" An answering voice shouted back, "We've secured the rest of the house. All fighters have surrendered."

The tall man spun back and raked the room with his eyes, quickly focusing on Jordan. "Are you the prince? Are you hurt?"

Jordan shoved himself away from the wall and allowed one of the soldiers to assist him across the room. It was not a simple trek, considering he was wounded, there was very little light, and the floor was littered with bodies. "Yes to both questions," he said, "though I do not think my injuries are severe."

Before the soldier could reply, three more people rushed through the door. I had only met him briefly, but I recognized Lord Vincent, the governor of Alberta. He was shorter than Jordan, powerfully built, with a round face that was meant to be open and smiling. Tonight it was grim and weary. His two echoes looked even more discouraged and tired.

"Prince! You are unharmed?" he demanded, bowing deeply.

"Not quite that, but I survive," Jordan replied.

Vincent turned to give a quick order to the tall man, whom I assumed was the captain of the guard. "Start clearing the room of bodies," he said. "Make sure anyone who is still alive is tended to."

"What of the wounded rebels?" the captain asked. "Tend them as well?"

Vincent hesitated and glanced at Jordan. Who answered sharply, "Of course. We will sort out later who deserves what punishment, but for now, anyone who is alive should be cared for."

Vincent nodded at his captain. "As he says. And make sure a medic is sent to the prince as quickly as possible."

The captain turned away and began issuing orders to his men, who efficiently set to work on their gruesome task. I had been crouching on the floor; now I pushed myself back to settle against the wall in the darkest shadows of the room, where I hoped I would be unobserved. The echoes silently took their places beside me. We all peered around the chair as best we could to watch the drama unfold.

Vincent and Jordan were facing off in the middle of the room, surveying each other with some distrust. I thought Jordan was swaying on his feet, but he made no move to sit down. Instead, he pulled himself up to take advantage of his greater height and spoke sharply.

"What happened here tonight? How did rebel fighters penetrate the house?"

"Renner Andolin presented himself at my door, announcing that he was here for my daughter's party. As he has been here many times before, my staff admitted him. It was only after he was inside that his men came in from two other entrances, and my servants were overwhelmed."

"Surely you had guards within close call."

Vincent's eyes gleamed in the firelight. "Surely *you* did. Yet they were caught as unprepared as my own."

"When my father accepted your invitation on my behalf, he assumed you would make yourself responsible for my safety," Jordan said. I had never heard his kind voice so stern. "And yet I find myself wondering if you had any inkling that revolutionaries might be targeting your house. If, in fact, I was invited here to give them an opportunity to harm me."

Vincent sucked in his breath and tried to maximize his own height, though he couldn't rise to Jordan's level. Behind him, his echoes glared in the prince's direction. "If I had plotted against you so foully, my prince, don't you believe you would be dead?" he answered. He gestured at the royal guards standing a few feet away, their weapons still at the ready. "There are enough men at my disposal to account for all of yours. But we fought with you, not against you. I am not one of the western nobles who wishes you ill."

"I hope that is true," Jordan said. "My father thought we had come close to an agreement with the western provinces. But—"

"You have," Vincent said quickly. "Those of us who are loyal to the king have persuaded the more contentious lords that the deal will be good for all of us. Renner and his father have proved hard to convince, but we are working with them still." He paused and glanced around. "I was told he was here in this room with you. Is he among the wounded?"

Jordan looked over his shoulder at his own men, one of whom took a pace forward and said, "He's dead, liege."

"*Dead?* Renner?" Vincent exclaimed. "Oh, no. Surely not. His men brought out a letter of safe passage, stamped with your own seal! Did you never intend to honor that?"

I saw Jordan's temper begin to fray, though I thought he had done a remarkable job maintaining his calm up till now. "Of course I intended to honor it! But he came at me in a fury— he inflicted these wounds *after* I signed the paper because he had decided that both of us should die after all. My men found him with a sword at my throat and responded the only way they could."

"But he is *dead?*" Vincent repeated. I thought he seemed more upset by this news than anything else that had transpired tonight. "My liege, this is bad. Very bad."

"It is a tragedy for that young man and his family, but entirely brought upon himself by his own actions."

"That is not how his father will view it! Lord Garvin will see that he has now lost *two* of his children to the arrogance of the crown! And the nobles who were undecided about which cause to support will be swayed by this latest execution."

Jordan put a hand to his forehead; when he dropped it, I thought a smear of blood had been left behind. When he spoke, his voice was level but edged with hostility. "I traveled here in good faith. To try to maintain good relations between Alberta and Camarria. Without offering any provocation of my own, I came under the attack of a violent young man who sought to kill me. And because he is now dead, the nobles of the western provinces will rise up in revolution? It makes no sense."

"It may make no sense, but you may take my word for it," Vincent said. "The events of this night have truly ignited civil war."

Before Jordan could answer, there was another flurry of activity at the door, and I craned my neck to try to see who had entered now. One newcomer was a small, nervous older man who headed straight for Jordan with a low exclamation of concern; I guessed him to be a medic. The others were all women—Sorrell and her echoes, I thought.

"Oh, thank the triple goddess! The prince is unhurt!" Sorrell exclaimed.

The medic was urging Jordan and his echoes over to a set of chairs and calling for someone to bring him more light. He didn't look up at Sorrell's words, but he did make an acerbic response. "Hardly unhurt, but he looks very much alive."

Jordan allowed himself to be pushed into a seat, but he did turn his head to smile at Sorrell. "Thanks in no small part to you," he said. "My profoundest gratitude, my lady, for leading me to safety. Vincent, I would not be alive to argue with you now if it were not for your daughter's quick thinking."

"She has always been most resourceful," Vincent said, but I thought he spoke with an effort.

One of Sorrell's echoes pushed forward to stand at Sorrell's side, which I thought was astonishing until I realized who the figure really was. "Oh, please, my lord—my prince—my echoes got lost during the mayhem and I must find them!" came Elyssa's anxious voice. "Sorrell thought perhaps they were following Jordan as she led him to safety—"

Jordan had been looking down at his arm, which the medic was laying bare, but he quickly lifted his head to survey her. I noticed that, before she had come looking for us, Elyssa had had the fore-thought to change from Trima's plain clothing into her own fash-ionable purple gown. "Ah, I was sure you must be missing your echoes," Jordan said. "Yes, they somehow got swept up with my own as we were making our escape and they have been cowering in the corner of the room all night. I have never seen any creatures so helpless in all my life!"

"Then they're here! Oh—! I'm so relieved! Where—" She simultaneously did a slow pivot, trying to see into all the shadows of the room, and issued a silent command that all her echoes had to obey. As if my brain had somehow been snapped off of my body, I felt myself lose control over my own arms and legs, even the expression on my face. Completely without desiring to do it, I clambered to my feet and minced across the room to Elyssa's side, the other echoes at my heels.

Elyssa didn't hug us, of course, or dissolve into tears of emotion. She merely brought her hand to her heart—a gesture that we all copied—and gave a sigh of relief. I wondered if anyone would think it odd, or even notice, that one of her echoes was wearing her signature necklace while Elyssa's own throat was bare.

"Thank you for keeping them safe," she said. "I was so distressed when they were gone."

Vincent turned on her with a frown. "Yes, well, they were hardly *safe* here in this bloody room!" he exclaimed. "Sorrell, take Lady Elyssa back to join the others while the prince and I conclude our business. And tell everyone that I have everything well in hand and will share what details I can in the morning."

"Yes, Father," Sorrell said in a subdued voice. She took Elyssa's arm, and her echoes reached out for Elyssa's echoes, to lead them from the room.

Sorrell had only two echoes to Elyssa's three, so I was left unpaired. I fell in behind the others as they filed out of the room, and with all my will I resisted the imperative to follow. I couldn't just walk away from Jordan like this, I *couldn't*, not without another word, a final goodbye. If war was truly coming, if the western provinces really did secede, would Jordan ever visit Alberta again? Would Elyssa ever return to Camarria?

Would I ever see him again? It was the question I had asked myself almost every day since I met him.

I could not slow my footsteps—I could not gainsay Elyssa's command and refuse to walk out the door. All I could manage was one last, despairing look over my shoulder, one final glimpse of Jordan's face.

But he was watching me, gazing past the body of the doctor who bent over him to bind his arm. Jordan didn't say anything, didn't change his expression in the slightest, but he lifted his free hand and kissed the tips of his fingers. I didn't know if the gesture was a promise or a farewell.

Chapter Twenty-Four

As we set out for home the following morning, the only advantage to sharing a single carriage with Elyssa and Trima was that I was privileged to hear every word of Trima's furious scold.

We, like the rest of the guests, had slept badly for what remained of the night before staggering downstairs for a late breakfast, where we learned that Jordan had already left. I was so disappointed not to have one more chance to look at his face that I felt physically ill. I had to force myself to eat—or appear to eat—as much as Elyssa did. The servants had done a remarkable job of putting the house back in order and erasing all traces of blood, but there was no erasing the air of palpable shock and horror that still reverberated through every room. It was clear that our hosts wanted us gone with all haste—equally clear that every visitor was eager to decamp without delay. No one lingered over the morning meal.

Trima had overseen the packing while we ate, and ours was among the first carriages to pull away into the busy streets of Wemberton. That's when the tirade began.

"Never has anyone been as reckless as you!" Trima raged. "You have risked everything—*everything!*—and it is only by the grace of the goddess herself that Lord Vincent and Prince Jordan did not instantly demand how it was even *possible* that you got separated from your echoes—"

"Jordan didn't even seem to wonder! He merely said they had gotten caught up in the chaos. It sounded perfectly reasonable."

"No doubt he had more to worry about just then, such as how to keep himself alive! But when he gets back to Camarria and begins telling this tale to his father, the king—"

"He will have more to worry about then, too. I heard Lord Vincent say Renner's death will lead to civil war. He won't even remember my echoes were in the room with him."

"You *hope* he won't remember—you *hope* he won't start wondering. And you *hope* the governor's wife doesn't start counting bodies. 'Wait. Didn't Elyssa come downstairs with only two echoes? How did three of them end up in the room with the prince? And why was an echo wearing Elyssa's favorite necklace?'"

"No one will bother with any of that. Jordan was attacked on Alberta soil! And Renner of Orenza is dead! That's all anyone will care about."

"Well, your father will care."

"And I suppose you're going to tell him? Because I certainly won't."

"No one will have to tell him if you suffer the consequences you deserve."

"What's that supposed to mean?"

Trima nodded darkly. "You were off with that boy, weren't you?"

Elyssa actually laughed, a low and taunting sound. "He's hardly a *boy*."

"No, that's right, he's a man. A man with no land, no prospects, no future except to be caught and executed as a traitor to the crown. And yet there you were, running after him—dressed as me and lifting up your skirts like any common merchant's daughter—"

Elyssa yawned and turned her head to look out the window. "So what if I was?"

"So what if you get pregnant?"

There was a long silence in the carriage. "I didn't get pregnant last time," Elyssa said finally.

"You were lucky! Do you think you'll be lucky twice?"

"We were careful."

Trima loosed an exclamation of scorn. "The only way to be careful is to keep your knickers on and your legs shut tight."

"Don't be vulgar."

"*I'm* not the one doing vulgar things."

There was another long stretch of silence while Elyssa continued to look out the window and Trima continued to glare at Elyssa. "If I get pregnant, I'll marry him," she said.

Trima almost screeched. "You will not! A man like that? Who's *nothing*? Your father won't permit it."

"I don't care what my father says."

"He couldn't possibly support you. He couldn't possibly *want* to marry you."

"He loves me."

Trima snorted. "Love doesn't provide food and bedding, does it? Does he even have a place to call home? Or does he expect you to live in some squalid cottage with his mother and his brothers and his sisters and all *their* babies?"

"I love *him*."

Trima leaned forward and spoke each word with venomous precision. "You don't have the faintest idea what love is."

Elyssa turned her head to give the maid the coldest, blackest stare I had ever seen on her lovely face. "Maybe because no one has ever loved me."

We completed the trip in one very long day, continuing on even after the sun had gone down, and we pulled up at Lord Bentam's house a couple of hours past full dark. Elyssa didn't bother waiting for the rest of us to disembark before she stalked into the house, and she didn't bother binding the echoes to her again, either. The three of us climbed slowly from the coach, then stood uncertainly in the courtyard as the servants swarmed around the vehicle, unloading luggage. Should we go upstairs to our room? Or should we follow Elyssa to her father's study, where I was certain she was even now pouring out the story of Renner's attack? What behavior would seem most normal? Which course of action would be less likely to rouse her anger?

Should we just stand here all night, shivering under the light of a high half-moon? Or should we turn back to the road we had just traveled and begin hiking in the general direction of Camarria—

My thoughts were interrupted by the sound of Trima berating the footmen. "Careful with that trunk! You don't want to spill all of Elyssa's underthings into the mud!" She must have turned and caught sight of us, because she spoke again in a completely different tone.

"What are you doing out here like this? Did she— Oh, that wretched girl. I suppose she just left you—Well, come along, then. Inside. I suppose you're so stupid you'd just stand out here all night and freeze to death. Come on."

She herded us into the house and up to our suite, then gave us the hastiest possible cleanup before nudging us toward our beds. I wanted to point out that we hadn't had dinner, and luncheon had been hours ago. But obviously I couldn't say any such thing. And truthfully, I was just as happy to be safe in my own room with the door shut and Elyssa nowhere in sight. The minute Trima left us alone, I sighed with relief.

There was so much to think over. So many fresh memories to treasure, so many new worries to keep at bay. I had held Jordan's hand, he had kissed the scars on my body, he had promised to find a way to free me. But the world had flung itself disastrously closer to civil war, and the whole kingdom might soon flare into violence. Worse, I might never see Jordan again. All my happiness was tinged with apprehension, all my fears made bearable by hope. I fell asleep trying to sort out the tangled swirl of emotions, but they followed me even into my dreams.

The following two weeks were strange, fragmented, and full of an anxious excitement. From what I could tell, messengers were flying all over the province—probably all over the kingdom—carrying the news of the attack in Wemberton and the death of Lord Renner. What conversations I was able to overhear centered on how many troops could be raised, what kinds of provisions could be commandeered here in the dead of winter, and how much funding would be required. The prosaic calculations of war.

But, alarmingly, I had limited opportunities to skulk behind Elyssa and listen to her father's confederates make their plans. She had returned to Lord Bentam's house in a black and sullen mood, and it showed no signs of lifting.

The first day we were back, she didn't get out of bed at all. Maybe she needed the rest after the adventure we had just been on. But she wasn't much livelier the next day, or the next. She slept late, she napped often, and she spent hours locked in her suite, pacing slowly back and forth or simply staring out the windows. I felt her rub the palm of her hand along her flat belly, over and over again; I could almost read the confusing, conflicting thoughts in her head. She was terrified that she might be pregnant, but a small part of her felt a mutinous trace of hope that she might be carrying Marco's child. And mixed with the fear and the hope was a gnawing, ungovernable desire to see him again—and a dread that she would never have the chance.

Naturally, while she stayed within the suite, the echoes and I remained prisoners in our own small room. I was even more restless than Elyssa, less interested in lying abed sulking, and more likely to be pacing the floor. The other echoes took their cues from me, and we spent many an hour walking back and forth between the window and the door, our shoulders touching as we navigated the cramped space, our footfalls absolutely silent.

Other times, we merely sat on our beds and stared at each other. There was nothing else to do. More than once I wanted to throw my head back and scream.

Now and then, Trima brought trays of food up for all of us, but that stopped shortly after the first week. "Your aunt Hodia says that if you can't come down for breakfast, you must not be hungry enough to eat," the maid reported. "So come on. Out of bed with you."

"Well, I'm *not* hungry."

"Get up anyway. Here, you can wear the purple dress. That always cheers you up."

Still protesting, Elyssa finally climbed out of bed and let Trima wash and dress her. In another half hour, she had flounced out of the room, allowing the door to fall shut with something like a slam.

Leaving me and the echoes behind.

We were already on our feet, lurking near the inner door, waiting for Trima to come in and dress us. But Trima vanished when Elyssa did and didn't even return with trays of food. The echoes and I waited a few more moments, staring at the door, but fairly soon it was clear that breakfast was not going to be on our agenda. There was nothing to do but sit back down on our beds and start looking forward to the noon meal.

But no one fetched us for lunch, and Elyssa didn't return until mid-afternoon. I could pick up a renewed sense of energy from her that made me think she had been outside in the fresh air, perhaps strolling through the garden. But the exercise hadn't improved her mood any. She went straight to bed and didn't get up again until Trima returned to dress her for dinner.

Once again, she left the echoes behind.

I was starting to get concerned. We could go a day without food, I supposed, but what if this neglect stretched longer than a day? Elyssa would bring us down for meals whenever there was company in the house, but what if days went by before Bentam entertained any high-ranking visitors? Would Hodia notice how long the echoes had been absent? Would Trima remember that even echoes had to eat?

Had Elyssa finally decided that she was done with echoes forever? Was her plan to get rid of us simply through neglect?

Would she really allow us to starve to death?

At the moment, the most pressing concern was thirst. We had had nothing to drink since the previous night's dinner, and my tongue felt thick and dry inside my mouth. I waited until Elyssa had been downstairs for a good fifteen minutes, then I cautiously opened our door and crept out into the suite, the echoes at my heels.

There was always a pitcher of water by Elyssa's bed and I was relieved to see, as I made my way through the sitting room and into her bedroom, that the pitcher was there tonight. But when I picked it up, I was disappointed to find it less than half full.

Still, better than empty. I filled the glass on the nightstand and drank the contents straight down. Then I filled it again for each of the echoes, who gulped down the water as greedily as I had. I shared the final half-glass of water among the three of us. I was still a little thirsty, but I felt immeasurably better.

We prowled around the room looking for other tidbits. There was a single orange sitting on the windowsill—a remnant of the previous day's breakfast, perhaps—so I peeled it and distributed the slices equally. I couldn't remember the last time anything had tasted so delicious. But we found nothing else lying around the room—no forgotten rolls of bread or boxes of candy. For a few moments, I studied the vase of roses in the sitting room but decided the petals probably had no nutritional value and the water at the bottom would be tainted and moldy. Still, if the pitcher by the bed had been dry, I might have sipped from the flower vase and counted myself lucky.

We were so relieved to be out of our cramped space that we stayed in the sitting room until we could sense that Elyssa was on her way back upstairs. By the time she came through the door, we had retreated to our room and were sitting meekly on our beds. We were still sitting there when Trima arrived a few minutes later.

She did not, as I had been hoping, bring a dinner tray with her. She merely got Elyssa ready for bed and disappeared for the night. Elyssa fell asleep right away, but the echoes and I lay awake for hours, trying not to listen to the sounds of our stomachs rumbling.

The following day was almost exactly the same.

Elyssa left us behind when she went down for her meals, and nobody else remembered that we also needed to be fed. I was beginning to be seriously worried. Shouldn't *someone* in the household care that Elyssa's echoes might be starving to death? Elyssa had always hated us, and if she really believed she might marry Marco, she would have no more use for us, but surely she could not do away with us *before* that wedding took place? Surely Hodia or Bentam still considered us valuable properties in the endless fight for status?

They must not have given any thought to how we were being cared for when we were not at Elyssa's back. They must have believed someone was feeding us even if Elyssa wasn't. I wondered how I could draw attention to our plight without giving myself away. Perhaps the echoes and I could be lying on the sitting room floor, weak and semiconscious, when Trima entered tomorrow morning. *That* might raise the alarm.

On the other hand, Trima had never protected us in the past when Elyssa had bedeviled us. Maybe she wouldn't care if we were wasting away. Maybe more extreme measures were called for. Maybe tomorrow morning the three of us should be lying on the floor of the hallway where passing maids and footmen would discover us. It would be a risky move—but I wasn't sure how many options we had if we wanted to stay alive. I would reconnoiter tonight and pick our best spot.

I waited until Elyssa was sound asleep before I belted on a heavy velvet robe and crept out of my tiny bedroom. The echoes rose to follow me, but I was able to close our bedroom door before they had made it out of the room. They didn't have enough volition to turn the handle on their own, so they stayed on the other side of the door, but I could feel their anxiety. I shut my heart to it. I had to focus on our survival.

Taking a deep breath, I silently opened the outer door to the hallway. I had never stepped across this threshold unless it was at Elyssa's heels, and I hadn't realized how strange it would seem. Yes, I had explored every inch of the bedroom suite under my own power, but that was a confined space, safe and familiar. Past this heavy door, the whole world waited, so big I could not imagine navigating it, filled with hazards at every turn. How easy it would be to get lost! How terrifying to be out in it on my own!

How exhilarating…

I paused for a moment to orient myself. Elyssa's room was down one end of a short corridor that fed off the main stairwell; Hodia and Bentam had rooms on the other end. If the echoes and I wanted to be noticed in the morning, we should be found languishing on the stairwell itself—someplace that saw a fair amount of traffic from the other residents of the house.

I glided forward soundlessly on the smooth wood floors and descended the first three steps, then bent to peer over the carved bannister toward the lower level. Most of the house was in darkness, but lamps were set at widely spaced intervals down every hallway to guide anyone who happened to be up in the middle of the night. I could see a faint flickering from the hall that led to the kitchen and the servants' quarters at the back of the house.

The kitchen...

I tightened my grip on the railing and thought about it. Well, why not? It was late and no one else in the whole mansion seemed to be awake. I could make a swift foray into the kitchen, gather up a few items, and return to my room without anyone being the wiser. *That is probably a terrible idea,* I thought, but I was so hungry that I wasn't sure I would be able to tell good ideas from bad.

I took another deep breath, kept my hand curled around the bannister, and tiptoed down the stairs.

The shadows seemed deeper and more menacing on the bottom story, and I stood for a moment getting my bearings before making my way forward again. Truth to tell, I was only guessing where the kitchen was, as I had never been there before in my memory. But I knew which hallways the footmen used when they brought in platters for meals, so I knew the likeliest direction to try. Though I might make a wrong turn if I wasn't careful.

I picked up one of the lamps as I passed it, holding it at shoulder height to light my way. I never would have thought the house I lived in could look so foreign. Doorways I had walked through a thousand times seemed portals to dangerous realms; chairs and bookshelves took on a crouching, predatory appearance. A half-size gold statue of a young girl—an object I passed almost every day—seemed to leap out at me like a child thief aiming to slit my throat. I had to strangle a scream as I saw her bright face grinning at me from its dark corner.

I finally made it through the common rooms of the house and to the much less cluttered corridors used primarily by the servants. The enticing scents of roasted meat and warm yeast led me directly to the kitchen. I paused to glance around at the long worktables, big sinks, and oversized oven, imagining how busy the place must be when the cook and her helpers were putting together a formal meal. Then I set my lamp on one of the tables and began searching for something to eat.

The first thing I found was a barrel of apples, so I dropped two into the pockets of my robe and ate a third one while I continued looking around. There were three loaves of bread on the center table; a round of cheese sitting next to them with a sharp knife lying conveniently nearby; and a basket of carrots and onions off to the side. I wasn't keen on biting into a raw onion, but everything else made me almost faint with desire.

I cut a wedge of cheese, stuffed most of it into my mouth, and considered the best way to carry part of it upstairs to the echoes. Was there something here I could use to wrap up a few pieces? Tomorrow morning, would the cook remember how much of the round had been left the evening before? Would it be better to simply take the whole thing and let her think one of the servants had made off with it in the night? Or would it be better to appropriate only a single loaf of bread?

I was still debating my options when I heard a jingle and a footfall behind me. I whirled around to see a shadowy shape moving down the hallway, straight for the kitchen door. My purloined lamp was close enough to illuminate me clearly while shedding no light on the newcomer at all.

I couldn't move. I stood frozen in abject terror as the figure grew closer and resolved itself into Hodia.

Frowning at me as if at the vilest creature in the world.

"What are *you* doing up roaming the halls?" she demanded.

I had never spoken in the presence of a noble, and I was not about to answer her now. Maybe she would conclude I had—somehow, unbelievably—sleepwalked through the house, untethered from Elyssa's will but not really acting under my own power. Maybe she would take my shoulder and say, "Poor, silly thing," and guide me upstairs and tell Elyssa in the morning that she needed to keep her echoes under better control. If I kept my eyes averted, my expression blank, she wouldn't realize that I was conscious, that I was awake, that I was here of my own desire—

"Are you hungry? I wouldn't be surprised. You hardly ate a thing at dinner," Hodia went on. "But I didn't think you even knew your way to the kitchens for all the interest you've ever shown in holding together a household."

She thought I was Elyssa.

While I tried to assimilate what that meant, she came deeper into the room and began rummaging in one of the cabinets. She pulled out the ruins of a layer cake, covered with swirls of white icing and curls of roasted coconut, and set it on the table between us. "This was very good," she said, using a fork to take a bite of it without bothering to cut a piece first. "Did you try any? Oh, but you don't like coconut, do you? I always forget."

She thought I was Elyssa. Could I carry out this charade well enough to keep her convinced? There was certainly no one who knew my original better than I did. I shook my hair back and rested my fingers on the table. My palms were sweating so much I thought I might leave handprints behind. "I don't like a lot of things," I said in Elyssa's sullen way.

"Well, that's the truth," Hodia agreed. "A lot of things and a lot of people."

"*You* should talk about disliking people," I scoffed.

Hodia's stern face relaxed into a wintry smile. "Yes, but I know how to pretend to like them," she said. "You never bothered to learn that skill."

"When you're beautiful," I said outrageously, "you don't have to make that kind of effort."

Now Hodia's mouth pressed into a hard line. "Even if you're beautiful, you could profit by displaying intelligence as well," she shot back. "So far, I see you making only stupid choices."

I rolled my eyes. "I'm still young," I said. "Plenty of time left."

"Not that young," Hodia said cuttingly. "Not that much time."

I shrugged. My heart was racing but I was trying to act careless and unconcerned. I reached for the loaf of bread—and then, as if it was an afterthought, for the wheel of cheese. "Well, I don't want to waste my time having pointless conversations in the middle of the night," I said. "I'm hungry. I'll just take this upstairs."

Hodia said nothing as I balanced the bread on top of the cheese and strolled right past her toward the door. I didn't have a hand free to pick up the lamp, so I hoped I would be able to find my way in the dark. "You shouldn't take food up to your bedroom," she said as I was stepping into the hallway. "You'll draw rats."

I turned to look back at her, knowing I was far enough from the lantern that she wouldn't be able to see my face clearly. "I'm used to rats," I said softly. "They're everywhere." Then I turned on my heel and sauntered out. Behind me, Hodia said nothing. I thought I heard her fork clatter slightly against the metal of the cake pan as she took another bite.

I continued walking with confident insolence until I was completely lost to darkness, and then I had to come to a brief stop and compose myself. My hands were shaking so badly I thought I might drop the items I had come so far, risked so much, to secure. Sweat was dripping down my armpits, and I could feel hair matted to the back of my neck.

I had pretended to be Elyssa, and someone had believed me.

Sweet goddess have mercy on my soul.

CHAPTER TWENTY-FIVE

Exhilaration had kept me awake half the night, but when I woke in the morning, it was a different story. My head was pounding and my belly harbored a gnawing pain. Both symptoms were likely the aftereffects of starvation, I thought. The echoes and I had devoured the bread and cheese last night, but it wasn't enough to make up for two full days of missed meals. Though the cramping in my gut didn't feel exactly like hunger—in fact, I entertained the possibility that I might throw up.

Moving carefully to avoid jarring my poor head, I pushed aside my covers and swung myself to a sitting position. That was when I noticed the feel of wetness between my legs, and I glanced down at the nightgown bunched around my thighs.

Blood. A patch of it staining the fabric.

I looked over at the bottom sheet where my body had lain. More blood. Not much, but a bright enough red to scream with alarm and warning.

I slapped a hand over my mouth and forced back a cry of terror. What was happening to me? Had I contracted some terrible disease that was breaking down my body from the inside? Had my activities and exertions of the past few months overburdened this frail echo's body, which hadn't been built to withstand so much independent motion? Or—just as bad—had Elyssa developed some awful illness that was being reflected in her echoes? Would she be subjected to a slow, wasting death that dragged the three of us down alongside her?

Or was it just me?

Once I had recovered my self-possession, I would have to check the echoes' bodies to make sure. They had woken when I did, sat up when I did, but their expressions, as always, were remote and serene. From where I sat, I could not see any bloodstains on their clothing, but I would need to make a closer examination.

Across the suite, divided from me by two doors, I felt Elyssa wake up and stretch contentedly in her bed. There was a moment of startled surprise, and then she began laughing.

I closed my eyes and pushed myself back on the bed so I could lean my aching head against the wall. I was dying and Elyssa was laughing. It seemed entirely congruous with the rest of my life.

I had been sitting there only about five minutes before Trima came bustling into the suite and into Elyssa's room. "Oh, good, you're awake," she said. "I hope you remember we have company arriving today, so you'll have to attempt to seem like a civilized human being."

Elyssa laughed again. "Look, Trima! Do you see? The best news!"

A moment of silence while Trima examined whatever Elyssa had to show her. "Well, then. You get lucky again," was all the maid said. "The triple goddess certainly looks out for you."

"I've never been so happy to see blood in all my life."

My eyes flew open. *Blood.* If Elyssa was also bleeding—

I wasn't dying. I was merely experiencing monthly courses, the same as Elyssa. It had never happened before. In fact, somewhere I had gained the impression that echoes, who were sterile, never produced the bodily fluids that led to reproduction.

If I was bleeding, it wasn't because my expanded activities had overtaxed my body. It was because I was becoming more real with every passing day.

Except for the way it started out, this day was closer to normal than any day we'd had since returning from Wemberton. I did have to exercise some ingenuity to hide my soiled sheets and garments, then bundle them up with Elyssa's laundry when no one was looking. Fortunately, my bleeding stopped almost immediately, so I didn't have to figure out how to manage for the rest of the week. But the same problem would arise in a month—or so I thought—and I had better start working on solutions.

But for the rest of *this* day, the focus was all on food. While Elyssa entertained company over breakfast, the echoes and I ate as much as we could cram into our mouths without drawing attention to ourselves, and we slipped bits of fruit and bread into our pockets. The visitors lingered through lunch, so again we devoured everything in sight. They were gone by dinnertime, but Elyssa hadn't bothered to go upstairs and mope, so we just followed her into the dining hall when the meal was announced. I fell asleep that night feeling sated and happy.

The next two days were hit or miss, with Elyssa bringing us along for only a single meal each day, so the echoes and I made the most of our limited opportunities. Still, I did not like this trend and the precarious existence it portended. I was even more worried the following day, when Elyssa rose late, left us behind, and never returned to the suite until she was ready to crawl into bed. As the hours unfolded, the echoes and I shared the fruits and nuts and hard rolls we'd managed to sneak to our room on previous outings, but we went to bed hungry and nervous.

Morning seemed to come earlier than usual, and it brought Trima barging into the room without her usual courtesy. Through the closed door, I heard her roust an unwilling Elyssa from bed.

"Up. Now. Your father has visitors, and he wants you there."

"Who is it? I don't even care. I'm going back to sleep."

"You're not. It's Marietta and Fannon, and they seem to have dire news. I'm guessing it has something to do with the death of that boy from Orenza."

Elyssa yawned but forced herself upright. In our room, the echoes and I did the same. I wasn't happy about the early hour, but I was ecstatic at the prospect of breakfast. If there were nobles in the house, Elyssa would have to bring us downstairs with her. I could hardly wait.

We were quickly dressed in sober, prim attire that wouldn't have been out of place on Counting Day, and heading downstairs to greet the visitors. Sure enough, Bentam and his guests were already in the breakfast room, and Elyssa and the rest of us filled our plates before sitting down. Elyssa joined the other three at the main table, while I sat with the other echoes—Bentam's two, and the single echoes each of the other nobles had brought along.

"You seem very serious," Elyssa said. "What's so urgent?"

One of the visitors looked over. I had met her before and remembered her name as Marietta. She was a graceful older woman with graying blond hair and faded blue eyes; she had clearly once been a great beauty, the kind of woman who might care only about clothes and fashion. But her hostile expression and pursed lips made her look anything but frivolous. "Orenza is on the move," she said. "There is an army three thousand strong marching south along the Charamon Road."

Elyssa looked impressed and slightly uneasy. "Is this because the prince killed Renner?"

"Maybe," Bentam replied. "But Orenza has been stoked for war ever since Marguerite died. This was just the final fuel."

"Do you join him? Or try to turn him back?" Elyssa asked.

Marietta managed a grim smile. "The very question we were discussing."

"He can hardly hope to take on all the king's troops on his own," Elyssa said. "If Alberta and Empara don't join him, his men will just be massacred."

"That's the news of the day," the other visitor said. He was a large man with a poet's fluidity about him—long flowing hair, loosely draped clothing, restless hands. I would have expected such an affectation to look a little silly on a man who had to be close to sixty, but he had an air of hard certainty that negated the softness of his appearance. I thought Trima had called him Fannon. He went on, "Empara has mounted an army of its own, and it's even bigger."

Bentam rapped an impatient fist against the table. "Empara!" he exclaimed. "All this time, they've been the most reasonable of the lot! Even when the rest of us were clamoring for war, they were preaching the benefits of negotiation. And now they've armed five thousand men and massed them on their own northeast border."

The echoes and I were shoveling our food in, but Elyssa was just toying with the items on her plate. "Why the sudden change?" she asked. "Did they care that much about Renner?"

Fannon snorted in disdain. "*No one* cared about Renner Andolin, even his father. No, this is all about the Devenettas and their desire for vengeance."

I frowned over my toast because I couldn't remember who the Devenettas were, but Elyssa inadvertently came to my rescue. "Queen Tabitha's family? I would have thought they were the last ones to want to go to war!"

Marietta glanced between Elyssa and her father. "You didn't tell her?"

Bentam grunted. "The news came late last night. This is the first I've seen her."

Elyssa laid down her fork. "Tell me what?"

The poet spoke as if he were savoring each word like brandy. "The queen has been arrested for treason."

"For conspiring to kill the crown prince," Marietta added.

"How did she—when—*what?*" Elyssa demanded.

Bentam nodded, as if that was a perfectly reasonable response. "You remember. Marco Ross told us there had been a second attempt on Cormac's life. Apparently, the king hired a Pandrean man to investigate it, and he turned up evidence that Tabitha and the inquisitor had plotted the assassination together."

"The inquisitor?" Elyssa asked faintly. "Malachi?"

"That's his name," Bentam said. "He's from Empara, just as Tabitha is. Apparently, they've been plotting against Harold all this time. Then, two and a half weeks ago, the inquisitor simply disappeared."

Two and a half weeks ago, I thought, *when we were in Wemberton*. I had warned Jordan that Malachi might be a traitor, but even as I had been speaking the words, Malachi was making good his escape from the palace.

"I was in Camarria when he vanished," the blond woman said. "The palace was in an uproar. The king had all the assistant inquisitors combing the streets, looking for him—or looking for his body—or looking for someone who knew what had happened. They found absolutely nothing."

"Then why was Tabitha implicated?" Elyssa said. "I don't understand."

The aging poet took up the tale. "The story I heard was that the king had learned the truth about Malachi and the queen, but he had decided not to accuse her. He was afraid that such a move would rile Empara—"

"As it has," Bentam muttered.

"And bring on a civil war. So he had decided to tell no one except Cormac and Jordan."

"He should have told no one, especially not the princes, if he truly wished to preserve peace in the realm," Marietta said.

Bentam gave her an astonished look. "And keep beside him on the throne a woman who tried to kill his son—and might try again? I understand the value of keeping peace, but no man could be expected to manage such a charade."

"So what happened?" Elyssa demanded.

"Apparently the queen said or did something that Cormac took as a threat to Vivienne," said Fannon. "And Cormac accused the queen of plotting against all of them—and the room was full of witnesses. Two lords from Banchura and Vivienne's parents from Thelleron and a handful of Pandrean nobles. After that, Harold had no choice but to arrest her."

"Well." Elyssa folded her hands on the table, clearly done with the meal, so the echoes and I had to reluctantly stop eating. Truth to tell, I was so engrossed in the story I'd almost lost my appetite, anyway. "How does the situation stand now? Does he plan to execute her in Amanda Plaza?"

"I don't think a sentence has been pronounced yet, but treason is generally punishable by death," Fannon said.

"And that's why the Devenettas are on the move," Marietta finished up. "And they're bringing along all their own allies—all the lords who had stayed out of rebellion out of respect for Tabitha's family."

"So it's finally come," said Bentam gruffly. "War."

"Do we join in? Or do we hang back?" Marietta demanded.

"Either way, we have something to lose," Fannon said.

Bentam slammed his hand down. "Damn it! I wanted concessions! Not battles and dead men in the streets!"

Marietta looked at him coldly. "One way or the other, there will be dead men."

"What would it take," Bentam said, "for Empara and Orenza to turn back? What would Harold have to offer them?"

Marietta kept her blue eyes fixed on Bentam's face. "What would make *you* turn back," she asked him, "if the king had murdered *your* daughter?"

Now Elyssa lifted her gaze and rested it on her father's face; now the poet also surveyed Bentam with a thoughtful expression. I saw Bentam's skin flush and his expression turn mulish.

"I would hope to never have to make that decision," he snarled. "But one life is never worth the lives of a thousand others."

"In other words, he would not avenge me," Elyssa said lightly. "So I'd better not try to assassinate a prince."

You already did try, I thought, *or at least you assisted at an attempt.* Elyssa must have been thinking the same thing—and realizing that, if her role had been discovered, her father would have settled for concessions rather than revenge. I could only imagine how much that added to her bitterness.

Bentam ignored her. "The question before us today," he said, "is what do we do now? Do we raise our own armies and join forces with Empara and Orenza? Or do we throw in our lot with the king?"

"Can we do both?" Marietta asked.

The men looked at her. "What do you mean?" said Bentam.

She shrugged. "Gather our soldiers. Join the others—but make it clear that we are making a final effort to talk peace with the king. And then send a delegation to Camarria to try to negotiate that peace."

"You just said it yourself," Fannon pointed out. "Nothing will turn back the grieving fathers of Empara and Orenza."

The woman made a scoffing noise. "Garvin Andolin never cared any more for *his* daughter than Bentam does for Elyssa."

"I never said that!" Bentam bellowed.

"It's not grief that spurs them on, but pride and greed and rage," Marietta continued. "You can't reason with grief, but you can pay off a proud and greedy and angry man."

Fannon was watching her with a look that was half speculative and half admiring. "I never realized how cynical you are."

"I find it easier to do away with pretense," she said. "So the question is: What will it take to appease the rebel lords?"

"They want independence—we all do," said Fannon. "If the king will grant sovereignty to the three western provinces, then I think we can stop this war."

"That's a start," Marietta agreed. "That'll assuage rage and greed. But to heal their pride, they'll want blood. Something was taken from them, and they'll want to take something from the king in return."

Fannon sneered. "You think Harold will turn over one of his sons to be killed by bloodthirsty revolutionaries?"

"Not to be killed," Marietta said. Her voice held a thread of humor as she added, "Unless you count marriage as a kind of death, as some men do."

Bentam looked thoughtful. "You think a marriage between Jordan and my daughter will pacify the rebels."

"It is the best way for Harold to prove he negotiates in good faith," Marietta replied. "He cannot ignore the voices of the western nobles if his own son is married to one—if his own grandchildren have Alberta blood running through their veins."

"But I don't want to marry Jordan," Elyssa protested.

"And I'm sure the prince would rather not marry you," Marietta replied. "But if we want to stop blood from running in the streets, you will both do what is best for the kingdom."

"But—"

"If we take this offer to the king, we had best make damn sure that Orenza and Empara empower us to negotiate on their behalf," said Bentam.

Fannon began arranging saucers and saltshakers on the table. "According to my best intelligence, Orenza's forces are about here. Empara's here. They should meet at the southernmost point of the Charamon Road within five days, but they are moving slowly. We can intercept them before they turn north. We can tell them that we're sending a delegation to Camarria—but that we're also raising our own armies in case Harold proves recalcitrant."

"That might work," Bentam agreed.

"Our next question is: Who shall undertake what task?" Marietta asked. "One of us must remain behind in Alberta and collect the troops that the nobles have promised in the past. One of us must stay with the rebel forces and make sure Orenza and Empara keep to the bargain. And one of us must ride to Camarria to confront the king."

"I will camp with the rebels," Fannon said. "I have some influence with Garvin Andolin, and I usually get along well with the Devenettas."

Marietta nodded. "Bentam, you have always had the strongest voice among the Alberta lords, so you stay behind and gather our armies. I will travel to Camarria with your daughter."

"If my daughter is to be married off, *I* should be the one heading to Camarria," said Bentam.

She surveyed him coolly. "You will remain in Alberta," she repeated, "because I do not trust you in Camarria. You would negotiate some deal all to your own advantage."

"That's a lie!" Bentam roared, slamming his palms on the table and rearing up from his seat. At the table with me, his echoes did the same.

Fannon spread his hands in a gesture calling for calm. "Easy, now. We cannot afford to fight amongst ourselves. Marietta spoke harshly, but her reasoning is sound. If she and Elyssa are both in Camarria, Marietta can lay out the terms for the provinces, while Elyssa looks out for the interests of your house."

"That's what I meant, of course," Marietta said.

"But I don't *want* to marry Jordan," Elyssa said urgently.

Marietta turned her faded blue eyes Elyssa's way. "Then make sure the marriage is short," she said softly. "But have his child first because that will bind Harold to us more surely than a treaty. After that, I don't care if the prince meets with an unfortunate accident on the hunting field someday."

There was a moment of stunned silence before Fannon began laughing. "Goddess have mercy on my soul, but you're the coldest-hearted woman ever born," he said.

Now she turned those icy eyes on him. "I'm practical," she said flatly. "And I'm tired of these years of plots and posturing. The time is now. We make our last desperate stand, or we unleash a blood-bath. Which do you choose? I vote for peace."

This second silence was longer and more thoughtful. "I vote for peace, by any means possible," Fannon said.

Bentam grunted. "Peace," he said.

"Good," Marietta replied. "The two of you know what you must do. Elyssa and I will leave for Camarria in the morning."

CHAPTER TWENTY-SIX

Back in the coaches again, once more traveling half the length of the kingdom. Back to Camarria. Back to Jordan.

I could not see a way out of this tangle. Marietta might very well persuade Harold that only Jordan's marriage to Elyssa would prevent bloodshed and that the marriage must proceed immediately. Once wed to Elyssa, would Jordan still be able to sue the king for my independence? Or would he drop that notion entirely, not wanting to incur the displeasure of his new bride? If he *did* find a way to separate me from Elyssa, I didn't see that I would be much better off. No doubt I would be sequestered somewhere far away from Elyssa—and far away from her husband, the one person I wanted to be close to.

Meanwhile, Elyssa might very well be plotting to kill him the minute she got him into the marriage bed.

And if he refused to marry her, the country would be rent by war.

There were no easy answers. I couldn't find *any* answers.

We traveled with some difficulty through a dismal ice-covered landscape, arriving in Camarria late on the sixth day. The city had been transformed. The busy streets were no longer crowded with nobles and merchants, servants and clerks, the rich, the poor, the ambitious all mixing together in one energetic swell of humanity. Instead, the public spaces were largely deserted except for a few uneasy souls who scurried about on unavoidable business, keeping their heads down against the sharp wind. But pairs of soldiers could be seen patrolling every avenue, and whole troops were gathered in some of the larger squares and plazas that we passed.

The houses and shops no longer maintained their friendly aspects with doors thrown open and summer blossoms decorating the windowsills. Instead, all the plants were brown with winter, all the doors shut tight, the windows covered with heavy curtains. Our carriages moved noisily through cold, empty, unwelcoming streets, and the only people who marked our passage were the soldiers who clearly assessed us to make sure that we offered no threat.

The reception at the palace wasn't much warmer. Marietta, Elyssa, and their combined four echoes were allowed to step into the cavernous foyer, but there we were stopped by the redoubtable housekeeper, Lourdes.

Marietta supplied their names, speaking with the arrogance of the high noble who believed she was better than any mere servant, no matter how exalted. "I know we are unexpected, but we have come for an audience with the king. Please show us to a parlor where we can wait in privacy until he has time to see us."

But Lourdes was a match for anyone who did not enjoy royal approval. "Certainly, my lady, but first I must check to see if any of our sitting rooms are available. We have had so many visitors at the palace lately. You understand."

"I understand that I will not be left waiting here like any common petitioner!" Marietta exclaimed.

Lourdes shook her head. "It's unfortunate," she said. "I'll be back as quickly as I can."

And despite Marietta's protest, Lourdes disappeared without another word. "How dare she," Marietta fumed. "I'll tell the king of her rudeness!"

Elyssa was contriving to look detached from the whole enterprise, but I was not fooled by her relaxed posture; she was tense and wary and deeply unhappy to be there. "You'll tell him if he consents to see us," she said. "But he may have us escorted from the premises. And then we will face the end of all our plotting."

"He will see us," Marietta promised, "if I have to hunt for him through every room in this wretched building."

It was probably only fifteen minutes before Lourdes returned, although—as we were subjected to stares from every servant and visitor who passed through the foyer—it seemed infinitely longer. "It turns out that the rose parlor on the second floor is unoccupied," the housekeeper said. "Will you follow me upstairs?"

The rose parlor was small but had a lovely view of the city, which I thought was a hopeful sign. I was even more encouraged when Lourdes promised to send refreshments. Surely Harold would not make us wait long to see him.

Would he bring either of his sons to this conference?

Food arrived shortly, and we were all nibbling on sweet cakes and tea when the door opened again. Harold swept in, three shadows at his back. My heart leapt up, and I found myself hoping one of them might be Jordan, but they were just his echoes, almost as dense and whole as the king himself.

We jumped to our feet and made our curtseys, which Harold acknowledged with a brief nod. During my last visit here, I had only caught glimpses of the king, so now I took an opportunity to study him. He looked a great deal like Cormac, with black hair and dramatic cheekbones, though age and care had left him with a grim expression and an air of heaviness that his son lacked. Or maybe he had been a generally cheerful man until he had learned of his wife's traitorous activities.

"Sit," he commanded, slipping behind a small desk. The rest of us disposed ourselves around the room. I took a chair that allowed me to see Elyssa's face as well as the king's. "I suppose I know why you are here," he added.

"If you do, then my mission is more easily accomplished," Marietta said. "I am here to prevent war."

"Rebel troops are already massed along the Charamon Road," Harold replied. "How do you propose we keep them from marching north to the city?"

Marietta leaned forward, fixing those chilly eyes on Harold's face. "Give them up," she said. "The western provinces—let them go. What they want is independence. Allow them to form their own nation."

Harold drummed his fingers on his desk. "And then you have two weak countries instead of one strong one," he replied. "We lose half our negotiating power, half our defenses. Our neighbors to the north might cross the mountains, seeking to annex us—Ferrenlea might send its navies into Banch Harbor, attempting conquest. Is the short-term solution really just a step toward long-term disaster?"

"It doesn't have to go that way," Marietta said. "In a generation, or maybe two, what's left of your kingdom and whatever confederacy arises from our coalition might become powerful allies working toward common goals. We would come to each other's aid, we would stand together against our joint enemies."

"We *should* do that now," Harold pointed out.

"But we don't! Instead we argue and undermine and create so much dissent that any foreign power that tried to invade us would find us easy to subdue."

"I disagree," Harold said. "What's more, I know nobles from Orenza and Empara—and, yes, even Alberta—who are just as set against secession as you are for it. You might solve your own internecine quarrels before you come here with demands."

"If you know there are armies camped a few days south of Sammerly, you know enough of us are in accord to burn this city down," she replied coldly.

Harold eyed her for a moment, and all his echoes stared at her just as fixedly, as if they were actually seeing her and weighing the truth of her words. It was more than a little unnerving. "I think Orenza and Empara hate me for more reasons than my refusal to dissolve the kingdom," he said softly. "Do you actually speak for the leaders of all three provinces?"

I thought a slight flush came to Marietta's face. But she lied without hesitation. "I do. But I am glad you realize peace is not possible unless you make personal reparation to both the Andolins and the Devenettas."

"I suppose you've determined what those reparations would be."

Marietta leaned forward in her chair and her echo copied the pose. "It would not take much to appease the Devenettas," she said. "Release the queen into their custody. No one will deny that she plotted against you, and they will promise to keep her under lock and key for the rest of her life. But if you execute her for treason, no treaty ever signed will stop Empara's march upon this city."

Elyssa turned her head to give Marietta a thoughtful look, and I guessed we were both wondering the same thing. *When exactly had Marietta come up with that plan?* She hadn't mentioned it during her conference with Bentam and Fannon.

Harold actually laughed. "I remember now," he said. "Your mother was an Empara woman, wasn't she? Devenetta's sister, if I've got my bloodlines right. Is this whole farce of a negotiation merely an attempt to get Tabitha her freedom? I admire your nerve, if so."

Marietta reddened even more, but her gaze didn't waver. "I admit, I would be loath to see my kinswoman murdered, but I am fighting for many more lives than hers. I would think you, too, would value the thousands over the one."

Harold inclined his head but did not actually agree. "And Garvin Andolin? With two children whose deaths can be laid at my door? How would you suggest I make reparations to him?"

"One of your children for two of his," Marietta replied.

I thought Harold might explode in rage, but he merely cocked his head to one side. He had probably seen this coming even before he walked into the room. "Since Garvin's daughter killed my son, I believe I have already lost one of my children," he said. "I am not willing to sacrifice another."

Marietta smiled. "I spoke metaphorically."

Harold's glance flicked to Elyssa and back to Marietta. "You would think to wed my son to the daughter of a noble rebel."

"It is a time-honored way to smooth over disagreements."

"*Alberta* is placated if this one marries Jordan," Harold said, indicating Elyssa with a dismissive gesture. "But I do not see how Orenza benefits in any fashion whatsoever."

For the first time since we had entered the room, Elyssa spoke up. "Then marry Jordan to an Orenza girl," she said. "My father and I would support that decision."

Marietta showed her an expression of profound irritation. "There is no Orenza girl worthy of marrying the prince, now that Marguerite is dead."

Elyssa's gaze was limpid. "I'm sure that can't be true."

"None with three echoes!"

Elyssa's mouth twisted. "Let him marry a girl with two echoes, or one, or none! There are so many more measures of value."

Harold made a sound like a suppressed laugh. "I actually agree with you, my lady. But since nobles from Orenza seem to die at my hands, I'm not sure you'd find any family in the province that would permit its daughter to marry my son."

"Another reason why Elyssa is the best choice," Marietta said smoothly.

"Elyssa is the *last* choice," Harold said.

The flat rejoinder clearly caught Marietta by surprise. "Majesty?" she said.

"I have evidence that Lady Elyssa already conspired to kill my son Cormac. I have no faith she would restrain her murderous tendencies if she was married to Jordan."

The silence in the room was so weighty that it crushed out all the air, and no one could move or breathe. I felt Elyssa's start of rage and terror, felt her call on every ounce of her will not to bolt for the door, but she said nothing and showed no expression. Finally, Marietta managed to squeak out a couple of faint syllables. "My liege?"

Harold nodded. "Oh, it's true. You knew, of course, that there have been two attempts on Cormac's life, right here in the palace?" He waited until Marietta assented; he didn't even look at Elyssa. "We never caught the first man, but we rounded up some of his

300

associates. They told us how he was able to get inside the palace, and it's because Elyssa unlocked a service door. I think even your cold heart would shrink at the idea of marrying your brother's would-be killer."

I wondered if it was just me, or if everyone else felt like the room was spinning around them. *Jordan told him,* I thought, still fighting to draw breath. *Jordan repeated what I'd said about Marco. But did Jordan tell him how he knew? Did he tell the king about me?*

"It would—if the story was true," Marietta shot back. "Obviously, someone was trying to stoke your rage against Alberta! I can't believe you would be so foolish as to listen to the lies of your enemies."

"And yet, here I am, listening to you," he retorted. He let that sink in before going on. "You are right to assume I would like to avert war. You are wrong to think I would agree to all your terms. I tell you this—if all three provinces can send me representatives that speak for the majority of the nobles, I will sit down and negotiate. I am adamantly opposed to the dissolution of the kingdom, but we can discuss compromises that give more autonomy to each of the provinces. I will not compel Jordan to marry some rebel's daughter—but I will entertain the possibility of returning my wife to her father's house."

Marietta's head jerked up at that; my guess was that she had considered that concession the least likely to be granted. "That would be generous," she said.

"I have no wish to execute my daughter's mother," he said grimly. "Princess Annery has been wild with grief at the news of her mother's imprisonment and betrayal. I would welcome a solution that spares my daughter any more pain."

"Thank you, my liege," Marietta said, nodding. She came to her feet, and Elyssa and all the echoes followed suit. Harold remained seated, watching her with guarded eyes. "I will take your replies to the leaders of the western provinces, and they will choose representatives to meet with you."

"No, you won't," Harold said calmly. "I will send my own emissaries to issue the invitation. You will stay here as tokens of good faith—and a sort of insurance that the rebel lords will not attack my city."

Marietta smiled thinly. "I think the rebel lords will react with anger rather than caution if they think you are holding us against our will."

Harold's smile was much wider. "Perhaps you're right. But I now have hostages from both Empara and Alberta to strengthen my hand, and I am not ready to give them up." He stood up in a leisurely fashion and surveyed us as we all gaped at him, trying to adjust our minds to how our situation had changed. "My house-keeper is preparing rooms for you. I hope you will be very comfort-able as my guests."

Lourdes herself led us upstairs to a wing of the palace that was familiar from our stay here over the summer, though we ended up in a different hallway. A pair of soldiers followed at a discreet dis-tance, clearly intended to reinforce the notion that we were prison-ers. Marietta was shown to a chamber that, from what I was able to glimpse, looked large and well-appointed; the rest of us continued down the hall.

"All our guest rooms were full when you stayed with us a few months ago," Lourdes said as she paused to open a door. "For some-one like you, with so many echoes, that resulted in rather crowded accommodations."

"A prisoner does not expect her jailor to care about her accom-modations," Elyssa said sweetly.

Lourdes smiled. "But now, when we have so few guests, we can give you more space." She took a few more steps down the hall and opened a second door. "A room for you, and one for your echoes. We find that many of our visitors appreciate such an arrangement."

Elyssa could hardly contain her delight, though she didn't want to give Lourdes the satisfaction of seeing her pleased, so she merely offered a regal nod. "Thank you. I would not have expected such thoughtfulness from the man who is holding me against my will."

Lourdes ignored this. "And, of course, your maid has a room in the servants' quarters. Your luggage has already been brought upstairs."

With a bow that was not nearly as deferential as it should have been, Lourdes turned to go. "Wait," Elyssa said, and Lourdes turned back. "Am I confined to my room?"

"It is not my place to say," Lourdes replied with a certain relish. "However, I assume the guards have been requested in order to make sure you do not leave the palace. Now if you'll excuse me, I have a great many tasks awaiting my attention."

The housekeeper pivoted smartly and headed back toward the stairway. Elyssa stared after her resentfully, then huffed into her room and slammed the door.

I stood in the hallway with an echo on either side of me and tried to control my breathing.

Two rooms. Elyssa might think the gesture had been meant as a courtesy to her, but I knew the arrangement was intended for my benefit. I was more convinced than ever that Jordan had told his father about me. For the first time, I started to hope that the king might be willing to offer me asylum.

I ushered the echoes inside, closed the door, and looked around. The room was almost as large as the one we'd stayed in over the summer, with a single ornate, canopied bed and two smaller ones. Clearly it was intended for a noble and two echoes, not three echoes who were trying to avoid their original. An interior door connected this chamber to Elyssa's, so I assumed this set of rooms was frequently given to noblewomen who were traveling with their daughters, or to married couples who liked to keep a little distance between them while still maintaining easy access.

I slowly walked around, opening dresser drawers and armoire doors, finding all of our clothes tucked neatly in place. I paused at the window, looking out at the half-deserted streets of Camarria, and tried to count how many soldiers I could spot. I lost track after a hundred. I sat on the big bed, more plush and luxurious than any I'd ever sampled, and allowed myself a couple of light bounces. The echoes sat on their own beds and bounced along with me.

I wondered what, exactly, I was supposed to do with myself. I was too bored to sit, too tense to sleep, and utterly without occupation to pass the time. I thought the chances were good that I might lose my mind. In the adjoining chamber, I could feel some of Elyssa's own impatience, dread, and restlessness. When she got up to pace the floors, I could think of nothing better to do, so the echoes and I also came to our feet and began crisscrossing the room.

We might have been walking for a half hour when I heard a soft knock at the door. I froze, and the echoes turned statue-still on either side of me. The knock came a second time. Lourdes, returning with food? One of the other servants, bringing coal or water? Or some more welcome guest?

As quietly as possible, I flew across the room and tugged the door open. And there was Jordan.

"Hope," he breathed.

I put a finger to my lips and pointed at the adjacent wall. He nodded and slipped inside, shutting the door soundlessly behind his last echo. Then he flung out his arms and I walked straight into his embrace. Behind me, I felt my echoes and his come together in one big cluster of affection.

With Jordan's arms around me and my cheek against the velvet of his jacket, I was speechless with amazement. How could it be that Jordan was cradling me against his chest, whispering my name, pressing his lips to my hair? How could this be happening to *me*?

"When I saw you last—in Wemberton—all that chaos, all that blood, and I didn't even get to say goodbye!" he murmured.

I managed a shaky laugh. "We never get to say goodbye," I reminded him in a whisper. "We're always dragged abruptly apart without a chance to make plans or explain."

"Not this time," he said. "You're here, and I'm going to make sure you don't go away. Not with Elyssa, not ever."

I was reluctant to leave my supremely comfortable spot, but I had to know. I pulled back so I could see his face. He dropped his arms but caught hold of my hands, and that was almost as good. "You've told your father about me, haven't you?"

He nodded. "Told him everything. I didn't think he would believe me, but then he said—" He shook his head. "He said he had lately heard another impossible tale about echoes, except it turned out to be true, and he had started to think there was more to them than we had ever realized. He promised that we would find a way to keep you here even once we've sent Elyssa home."

"I can't believe it," I said. "I never thought it could happen."

He set his hands on my shoulders. "But we can't separate you from her, not yet," he said seriously. "Until we have found some way to negotiate peace—or until this damn war actually starts—we need you at her side, acting as a spy for us. The knowledge you could gain is too valuable to give up."

"I know. I agree," I said. "In fact, I need to tell you—"

There was a sudden thump and curse from the other room. All of us jerked our heads in that direction, our bodies coiling in readiness to run. "I think she threw something against the wall," I whispered. "She's *so* angry about being here."

"About being my father's prisoner?"

I shook my head. "About being here at all. It was Marietta's idea to revisit the notion of a wedding between the two of you. Elyssa made it plain she wanted no part of it. Marietta told her that the marriage just had to last long enough for Elyssa to bear a child."

"And then what?" Jordan demanded, his voice somewhere between amusement and horror. "She would murder me in my bed?"

"Or try to," I replied, nodding. "Yes."

"Thanks for the warning! Add it to the list of reasons I never want her as my bride."

"What is your father going to do? How is he going to stop this war?"

Jordan shook his head. "I don't know. I don't know that it *can* be stopped. We have sent emissaries to Pandrea, Thelleron, and Banchura, requisitioning troops for the crown. We should have the numbers to defeat the upstarts, but at what cost? Is it better to allow secession after all?"

"What does your father say?"

"That he knows some of it is his fault. That he should not have executed Marguerite of Orenza. But that's one thing that can't be undone."

"If you—" I started, but then my head whipped back toward the connecting wall. Elyssa had paused in her vexed and aimless pacing, and I felt a certain determination come over her. A second later she was on the move, and I was swamped with terror.

"She's coming!" I hissed, shoving Jordan toward the outer door. "Go! Before she sees you!"

He and his echoes practically tripped over each other as they dashed into the hall. I couldn't breathe, I was so desperate to shut the door behind them before the door between rooms flew open.

But I had misunderstood Elyssa's intent. She wasn't entering our room; she was stepping into the hall. Her door swung open just as mine clicked shut. I could feel her wary surprise at the sight of Jordan and his echoes clustered right outside.

"What are you doing here?" she asked sharply. You didn't have to be her echo to read the turmoil and suspicion in her tone.

Jordan spoke so smoothly you wouldn't have known he was even slightly disconcerted. "Oh, that's your door," he said. "I must have been knocking at an empty room. No wonder no one answered."

"That's where my echoes have been put," she said. "What do you want with me?"

"I just wanted to ask you if it's true."

"Is what true?"

"That you conspired with rebels to murder my brother last summer." Jordan allowed disbelief and pain to color his voice. He was a much better actor than I would have expected.

Elyssa's laugh was short and bitter. "Of course it's not true! I know my father's enemies will say anything to discredit him, but how anyone could come up with a lie like that— But I suppose you hate me so much you're willing to believe the worst things anyone says about me."

"It's not that I hate you," he said. "It's that I love my brother. I would do anything to protect him."

"Then turn your attention to the people who truly mean him harm."

"We are looking for them," Jordan said. "I'm glad to hear you're not one of them."

"Your father doesn't believe me."

"My father has been betrayed by two of the people who were closest to him. I'm not sure he'll ever believe anyone again."

There was a short silence. "Then what becomes of *me*?" Elyssa asked finally. "How long will he keep me here? Am I his prisoner or his guest?"

"I imagine the length of your stay depends on whether negotiations are possible. And I assume you are to be treated like a guest— who is not free to leave."

"I shall go mad."

"I hope not," Jordan said. "But these are trying times for all of us." I heard a rustling sound, as if he and his echoes were bowing. "Now, please forgive me, but I must return to my father's side. I expect I will see you many times in the days ahead."

I felt Elyssa curtsey—felt her resentment and building rage as she watched him stride away from her. She probably only waited until he was out of sight before she hurried down the hall. She didn't command the echoes to join her, so I couldn't be sure where she was going. My best guess was to Marietta's room, so they could commiserate, recriminate, and scheme.

The echoes and I were left behind with nothing whatsoever to do. *I shall go mad,* I thought, *just like Elyssa.*

But I had something she didn't have. Hope for a future that might contain the dearest wish of my heart.

CHAPTER TWENTY-SEVEN

The next three days were the oddest combination of skitter-ing suspense and ponderous boredom. Marietta and Elyssa found themselves constantly in each other's company. They took their meals together and were allowed to walk in the palace gardens together—as long as they were trailed by a guard and a couple of footmen. The two women had never liked each other much to begin with, and they quickly ran out of casual conversation, so most of these interludes passed in silence. Even the promenades through the garden were unsatisfying, as the weather had turned bitterly cold, and the northern wind left both ladies and all their echoes with reddened noses, watering eyes, and chilled fingertips.

Trima was Elyssa's one source of comfort, alleviating her soli-tude and bringing news of the outside world, but they quarreled on the morning of the second day.

"I need you to deliver a note for me," Elyssa said.

"I suppose you think you're going to write to Marco Ross."

"I suppose it's none of your business."

"It is if you expect me to carry a message for you."

"All right, yes, to Marco. And he'll send a message back with you."

"Well, he won't because I'm not doing it."

"But there's nobody else! Please, Trima, I'm begging you."

"You don't think the king's men follow me everywhere I go? You don't think they'll be right behind me, scooping up any letters I happen to leave behind?"

"You just have to be careful—"

"Nobody can be that careful! The king thinks you have *plotted to kill his son!* If you make one mistake now—one!—you'll be the next high noble to be executed in Amanda Plaza. Yes, and I'll be executed right beside you for abetting a traitor."

Elyssa started crying. "I just want Marco to know where I am. I just want him to know what's happened to me."

"Believe me, everyone in the city knows where you are. If he's in Camarria, he's heard the news."

Elyssa kept pleading, but Trima was adamant, with the result that Elyssa cried, "I hate you!" and sent her from the room. But Elyssa had no other allies at the palace, so the following morning she greeted the maid with a subdued welcome, and the fight seemed to be forgotten.

I didn't even have Trima to talk to. Since Elyssa was never out in company, there was no need for the echoes to be washed and dressed, and Trima never bothered stepping through the connecting door to attend to us. Of course, here at the palace with Jordan as our champion, we were not forgotten; servants brought food and water, and someone made sure the fire was stoked and the linens were clean. I could obviously take care of myself, and I dressed the echoes every day as well.

Jordan came by twice in those three days for the briefest of visits, both of us so alert for a possible intrusion from Elyssa that we could barely relax enough to speak. He did tell me that emissaries were on the way to the rebel armies that had gathered south of the city, and that troops from the three loyal provinces were marching toward Camarria. I let him know that Elyssa was desperate to make contact with Marco Ross, but that Trima wouldn't carry a message for her.

"That's too bad. I'd love to get a glimpse of this fellow," Jordan replied. "But I can hardly pull her maid aside and say, 'It's fine. No one will bother you if you run illicit errands.'"

I had to muffle a giggle with my fist. "What you *might* do," I suggested, "is let Elyssa go for a walk in the botanical gardens. She used to meet with him there, usually in the morning. Maybe he still goes there, hoping she'll come by."

"That's a good idea," Jordan approved. "The weather should be a bit warmer tomorrow—we will propose an outing to her. She will be escorted, of course, but she might find a way to communicate with him even so."

"If he's there."

Jordan nodded. "Even if he's not. An outing to the botanical gardens can hardly be considered a waste of time."

Elyssa reacted with such joy to news of an excursion that you would have thought she had been named queen of the Seven Jewels. The following morning, she was up and out of bed only slightly past dawn, and she was so impatient while Trima dressed her that Trima repeatedly had to tell her to stand still. Naturally, the echoes would accompany Elyssa on this outing, so Trima had to spend some time dressing us as well, but we were all scrubbed and ready to go well before the breakfast trays were brought around.

Marietta and her echo joined us in the hallway and we all clattered down to the courtyard, where carriages were awaiting us. So were about eight royal guards, all sporting official red-and-black uniforms. I was delighted to learn that Jordan formed a member of our party, but I was surprised to see that his sister, Annery, and her echoes were with him.

"I suppose you have no fear that the young princess will be corrupted by revolutionaries like us," Marietta said in her forthright way.

Jordan bestowed a chilly smile on her. "Annery has so many demons of her own to fight that she won't even notice the two of you," he replied. "But I hoped she might enjoy a chance to stroll through the gardens."

I thought the young princess looked too sullen and unhappy to enjoy anything, but Jordan's kindness toward her melted my heart. He helped her into the first carriage while servants assisted the rest of us into a second one, and we were on our way.

By the time we had arrived at the gardens and were sauntering along its winding paths, I was almost as giddy as Elyssa. The sun shone so mightily that the air *almost* felt warm, and it was such a relief to be outside of the palace for an hour that I felt as if the entire world had been offered up for me to devour in a single gulp. The garden was not nearly so attractive in the winter, with no flowers in bloom and all the fountains dry, but there was still much to admire. The spiky skeletons of bare trees stenciled dramatic patterns across the cloudless sky; evergreens whispered together in shadowed groves, sharing their memories of summer. Ivy climbed in runners of blazing scarlet across gazebos and sundials and shivering statues.

It was such a fine day that dozens of other visitors had decided to make a pilgrimage to the park. There were couples strolling slowly, hand in hand; harried mothers chasing after rambunctious children; old men wrapped in their long, patched coats, pacing along with their heads together as they traded stories of improbable winters and glorious springs.

Young men lurking behind tall bronze statues, watching the world parade past.

I might not have spotted Marco if I hadn't felt Elyssa's head jerk in his direction and then, almost as abruptly, swing forward again. Her whole body tingled with the alarm and excitement of seeing him there. I could almost feel her blood yearning in his direction. I looked that way and saw him standing stiff and straight behind the imposing metal figure of some past military hero, almost obscured by the soldier's broad shoulders and bristling weaponry. His eyes watched her with a hunger as deep as her own.

It was tricky to draw Jordan's attention while not rousing Elyssa's suspicion. They were walking side by side and I was a few paces behind them, so I couldn't even send him a quick, meaningful look. Instead, I slowed, which caused Marietta's echo to bump into me and stumble into the path of a soldier, who uttered a curse and veered away to avoid trampling her. The commotion was slight, but Jordan heard it and glanced over his shoulder at me. I cut my eyes toward the statue and nodded once. He inclined his head very slightly in return before facing forward again. But a couple of moments later I saw him casually intercept one of his guards and murmur a few words in his ear.

At the very least, it seemed someone would be able to identify Marco. I didn't want to think too much about what might happen to him next.

Once we were twenty or third yards beyond Marco's hiding place, Elyssa suddenly pulled up with an exclamation of annoyance. "Hold on—something's gotten in my shoe." She hobbled over to sit on a nearby bench and shake out an imaginary pebble. The echoes and I sat beside her, copying every action. Our hands moved with hers as she braced her fist on the back edge of the bench, then casually opened her fingers to let something fall soundlessly to the ground. I didn't look to see, but I was sure it was a crumpled ball of paper.

A moment later, we were all on our feet and rejoining the group. I could tell by Elyssa's rising euphoria that she felt hundreds of pounds lighter. Jordan didn't look my way again, so I couldn't direct his attention to the letter, but I supposed it didn't matter. If some of the king's men were following Marco, they would see him pick up the note and decide whether or not to seize it.

Part of me was filled with a grim elation that Elyssa would be made to pay for some of her terrible cruelties. And part of me felt oddly sad for her. The emotion was so fresh and unexpected that I didn't know what to do with it, so I simply shoved it away.

We had been walking for about an hour, and the chilly air was beginning to defeat the valiant sunshine, when we heard urgent footsteps behind us. The nobles, the royals, and their echoes turned swiftly in response, but the soldiers were even faster, instantly raising weapons and falling into a battle formation to protect the prince and princess from danger.

But the man racing in our direction wore palace livery and a look of dread. "Liege," he panted, as the soldiers parted to allow him to address Jordan. "The king wants you back with all speed. There's been a skirmish on the Charamon Road and so many are dead."

Jordan strangled an oath and shot Marietta a look of anger. "So all your talk of negotiating was just a sham?" he demanded.

But Marietta looked just as appalled. "No, I swear it! No one in Alberta wants bloodshed. I thought—*we* thought—"

Jordan turned his back on her. "No point in discussing it now," he said, striding toward the gates. "I will see what my father has to say."

As we all hustled back to the waiting carriages, I didn't see a single soldier stay behind to intercept Marco. I supposed news of war trumped rumors of assassins, but it still made me feel peculiar to think that Marco had slipped through the net so easily. The whole outing had been a waste of time, then—from the king's point of view. From Elyssa's, a success.

I sighed and waited my turn to be handed into the carriage. Closing my eyes, I lifted my face so I could feel one last caress of sunshine across my cheek. I would count the excursion as a success on my part, too, for no other reason than that.

Over the next few days, information came first with frustrating slowness and then with horrifying detail. There was no news at all for the rest of that day, but the following morning, Harold summoned us to the rose parlor where he had entertained us upon our arrival. He was standing, staring out one of the windows, and he did not bother to look at Elyssa or Marietta when they entered and curtseyed.

"Five hundred men dead in two days of fighting," he said, speaking to the windowpane. "An entire battalion of soldiers from Thelleron—handpicked by the governor. They were led by Vivienne's uncle, who is also dead."

Marietta looked like she was having trouble keeping her balance or remembering her bloodlines. "Vivienne—?" she repeated stupidly.

"The affianced bride of my son Cormac. One day to be queen of the Seven Jewels." He was briefly silent before adding, "I certainly will be expected to avenge his death."

"Majesty, I am so, so sorry."

He nodded. "Would you like to hear the names of the Alberta men who have fallen?"

Elyssa caught her breath, but Marietta merely said, "Yes." The king reeled them off, but none of them were people I recognized. Elyssa flinched at one name; Marietta dropped her face in her hands at another.

"The list is incomplete, of course," Harold went on. He still hadn't looked at them. "We are more than a day behind events because of the time it takes for news to travel from the battlefield. Everyone you love could already be dead."

"Majesty—"

Harold silenced Marietta with a wave of his hands. "I'll keep you informed as I learn more."

Ten hours later, another summons, another list of names. This time, the heaviest losses had come from Pandrea and Empara. A nephew of the queen's had been killed. "*There's* an incentive for the rebels to keep fighting," Harold said. "Even if I release Tabitha to them, the Devenettas will never be appeased."

In the morning, more terrible news. The youngest brother of the Banchura triplets, fallen in battle. Three more Alberta lords that both Marietta and Elyssa knew. One of the sons of Lord Garvin of Orenza.

"Three of his children dead," Harold whispered. "All of those deaths laid at my door. You wanted civil war? You have it. Nothing will stop the bloodshed now."

Shortly after the noon meal, when Harold presented the latest list of losses to his hostages, Marietta refused to leave the room quietly. "What are you doing to stop this terrible slaughter?" she demanded, aiming her words at his back, since he delivered the name of every casualty to the wall or to the window. "I thought you had emissaries on the way to attempt to negotiate."

That did make him spin around to face her. "Oh, did I not mention it? They were ambushed and killed before they even made it to the battlefield."

She winced but did not look away. "Then send someone else. And someone else. Or are you content to just watch hundreds and thousands more die?"

"I would send *you*, if I thought every emissary was likely to meet the same fate," he shot back.

She smiled coldly. "And I would go, if it meant I was *trying* to do some good instead of just moping."

His features drew together in an angry snarl. "Careful," he warned. "I have nothing to gain any longer by treating you well."

"And nothing to lose by sitting down with me and trying to devise a plan!" she countered. "There must be some bargain you can make, some truce we can negotiate! If you are afraid to send anyone else to enemy lines, then, yes! I will carry an offer for you. But we must try something."

"You think I have *not* been meeting with advisors, frantically trying to come up with solutions? What a very poor king you think I am. No wonder you are rebelling."

She brushed that aside. "Then bring them in—your sons and your councilors—and let us see if we can hash this out together."

Harold eyed her for a moment with something that might have been hatred tinged with capitulation. "Representatives of the eastern provinces will be here later this afternoon to discuss the situation," he said at last. "You may sit in the room with us if you like. Though you must know I will regard anything you say with suspicion."

"Then maybe your friends will show more sense," she snapped. He hadn't dismissed her yet, but she gathered her skirts and stalked toward the door. "Just let me know when they have arrived."

Three hours later we entered one of the much bigger sitting rooms to join a convocation of angry, worried, thoughtful, desperate nobles. Elyssa had not been invited, but she told Marietta that the king would have to have her forcibly removed from the room if he didn't want her to attend, and so I got to see the whole proceedings.

When we entered, the nobles were grouped around a large, polished wooden table, while their echoes sat in inconspicuous chairs
scattered around the perimeter. Harold, Cormac, and Jordan had
taken their places at the head of the table, so I found a chair that
would allow me to watch their faces. Jordan made a point of glancing at each of Elyssa's echoes until he located me; he couldn't bring
himself to smile, but he did give me the smallest nod.

I didn't recognize any of the other participants, though I
guessed them to be the parents and grandparents of some of the
lords and ladies we had met last summer. The large, powerfully
built man with the fair complexion, gray hair, and full beard might
very well have been the father of the Banchura triplets; his face
showed enough grief that I could believe he had just lost a son in
battle. The dark-skinned woman with opals braided into her hair
might have been Lord Dezmen's mother, and the woman beside her
his aunt. I didn't see anyone who looked particularly like Vivienne,
but I was sure someone at the table would be from Thelleron.

"I believe you all know each other, so let's get started," Harold
said, and there were a few rumbles of assent.

"Is there any news from the front?" asked the Banchura lord.

Harold nodded soberly. "The rebel armies have pushed the
defenders back a few miles, so they are that much closer to the
city." At the murmur of alarm that went through the room, the king
added, "I understand that the retreat was strategic, to place our
own forces in a more defensible position. But the rebels appear to
consider our fallback their victory, and there was much celebrating,
I am told."

"There will be much grieving when we attack with our full
forces," muttered a thin, sleek, crafty-looking man. He was wearing
a large garnet ring, so I guessed he was from Sammerly.

A pale-skinned woman looked up. "You mean, we have *not* been
deploying our entire armies?" she demanded. "Why not?"

"Some of our troops are still in transit," Harold explained.
"They are on their way even now, and we hope they will turn the
tide of battle in our favor."

"Yes, because *more* fighting and *more* death will be sure to make the western provinces decide they love you after all," Marietta spoke up.

At least five people began shouting at her at once, and she raised her voice to shout back, "You have brought this on yourselves! Force is not the way to end decades of hatred and mistrust!"

The Banchura lord addressed Harold but pointed at Marietta. "What is she doing here? If she stays, I'm leaving."

"Nobody leaves!" Harold thundered. "Everyone is quiet, and everyone listens, and we try to solve this instead of making it worse!"

The nobles at the table mostly subsided, though several of them threw poisonous looks Marietta's way. No one had even seemed to notice Elyssa, and I could tell that was fine with her. She was sitting at the end of the table, and I had the impression she was trying to make herself as small as possible. I wondered if she wished she had not joined the council after all.

"If we can bring the rebel leaders to a parlay, what could we offer them?" Harold asked.

"Execution in Amanda Plaza!" one of the nobles called out, but the others shushed him.

"Assuming that option is off the table," Harold added.

"But there must be *some* punishment for the rebels who started the war," insisted the crafty-looking Sammerly man. "Or what's to stop anyone from turning to bloodshed anytime they want a policy change?"

"Oh, I don't know—how about policies that are fair to begin with?" Marietta said.

One of the Pandrean woman leveled a hard, steady gaze in Marietta's direction. "Everyone else at the table abides by the same policies," she said in a steely voice. "And yet the eastern provinces don't find them onerous. So the question is: What must we do to keep the peace?"

"One possibility is to allow secession," Marietta replied.

The gaze of the Pandrean noblewoman didn't falter. "And then you would be a cooperative neighbor instead of an unruly subject? Why do I find that difficult to believe?"

Three of the other nobles shouted an agreement, which caused Marietta to raise her own voice in angry response. For a few moments, I lost the thread of the argument, which I was finding wearisome, repetitive, and ever more acrimonious. Harold was trying to calm everyone down, but Marietta and the Banchura lord were now on their feet, hurling insults, and five other people were speaking at once. When the king pounded his fists on the table, it added to the general noise but didn't seem to make any other impression.

And then, suddenly, the whole room fell silent.

The effect was so abrupt and so unexpected that everyone seemed taken completely off-guard. People looked at each other in amazement, as if trying to understand why they had suddenly cooled their passion. Then they glanced at the king, who seemed just as surprised as they did. Then they looked around the room again.

Soon everyone was staring at a figure who stood just inside the door, as if she had entered while all the nobles were shouting and had merely waited until they noticed her. She was a tall, serene, confident woman wearing a white robe belted in red and accentuated with an embroidered black stole. Someone important from the temple of the triple goddess, I was guessing. The fact that she was wearing each one of the goddess's colors must mean she was embodying all three of her personas at once.

I couldn't tell if she had done or said anything to quiet the room, but it was clear that she carried a certain irresistible power and that all the nobles had responded to it, whether they wanted to or not. She didn't speak for another full minute, and neither did anyone else. They just stared at her, and they waited.

"The blessings of the goddess upon your heads," she finally said in a clear voice that carried easily across the room.

"And upon you, abbess," Harold replied quietly. A few of the nobles also murmured a response, but most of them simply watched her.

She took one step deeper into the room. "I come to inform you that the goddess knows of these dreadful battles unfolding just south of the city, and she is wrought with sorrow and pain."

Harold was the only one with the nerve to reply. "Yes, war is a grievous business."

The abbess continued, "She remembers the days hundreds of years ago, before Edwin was king, when all the nobles fought with each other, and death was a constant visitor at every man's table."

Harold decided not to risk another answer; he merely nodded in confirmation.

"So many lives have been taken already," the abbess said. "The goddess cannot bear that any of these names be lost to her. She is instituting an interim Counting Day so that she can be certain which of her nobles and their precious echoes still live. Please present yourselves to a temple the day after tomorrow."

That did cause a buzz of confusion and dissension to run through the room. *What? Another Counting Day? Suddenly, out of nowhere? Ridiculous! It's been barely two months since the last one!*

"We appreciate the concern of the goddess," Harold said respectfully. "But our councils are too urgent and our time too short for us to stop in the middle of our activities and make our way to a temple."

"Besides, half the high nobles of the kingdom are on a battlefield," the Sammerly man pointed out. "How can they observe a Counting Day in the middle of a war?"

The abbess nodded, as if their objections were reasonable—but she had already come up with the counterarguments. "Even now, priestesses are visiting those battlefields, inviting every noble with an echo to observe the ritual," she answered. "There are sanctuaries in the small towns all along the Charamon Road. Every fighter will be directed to the nearest one."

"But—there's not enough time to send messengers all the way to Orenza and Empara and Alberta!" Marietta exclaimed. "And to get the news to every noble family living on some isolated estate—"

The abbess smiled at her. "The goddess has informed all of us, all at once, every priestess who serves in any temple across the Seven Kingdoms. They have time to spread the word to every noble with an echo. There will be a Counting Day the day after tomorrow."

"But—" came from several mouths at once.

The abbess's expression turned unyielding and her words rang out. "Any nobles who do not bring their echoes to a temple on Counting Day will find their echoes vanished in the morning. As has been the case with every Counting Day since the goddess first required the nobles to make this observance in her name."

Now the nobles raised their voices in a strident chorus of dismay and opposition. A few of them flung their hands in the air and two or three came to their feet to make their points. The abbess listened coolly for a moment, then held her arms out as if balancing heavy spheres in each palm. Once again, the room fell abruptly silent.

"Those are the terms," she said. "Observe the ritual, or forfeit your echoes. If you would rather spend your day plotting more death and destruction, you may certainly do so. Just realize that there is a price." She dropped her arms, placed her hands against her thighs, and offered a low bow. "Majesty." Rising to her full height again, she glanced once more around the room, nodded at the assembled company, and walked out the door.

CHAPTER TWENTY-EIGHT

I couldn't vouch for anyone else, but I was glad to see this impromptu Counting Day suddenly appear on the calendar because I could not wait to get out of the palace again. I hadn't set a foot outside since the excursion to the botanical gardens, and I was ready to fling myself out of my bedroom window just for a change of scenery.

Judging by the expressions of the nobles gathered in the courtyard on the appointed day, I was the only one to feel this way. The visitors from Thelleron, Banchura, and Pandrea seemed irritable and short-tempered; Cormac and Jordan looked weary and stressed; and even Harold, who could generally manage to project an air of stoicism, appeared annoyed. Annery was in tears.

"But what about Mama?" she demanded of her father. "If you don't let her come with us to the temple, all her echoes will *die!* That's not fair!"

The king glanced down at her with an impatience that he visibly tried to control. "I will have her escorted to the temple later today," he promised. "Get in the carriage now. We're wasting enough time on this nonsense as it is."

I saw Jordan glancing around the courtyard, searching all the faces until he came to mine, and then he smiled so briefly I was sure I was the only one who noticed. He started pushing through the throng in Elyssa's direction, as if he would offer to sit in the coach with us, but Cormac caught his arm and he had no choice but to ride with his brother. I sighed silently and climbed into an oversized carriage with Elyssa and Marietta and a woman who might be from Thelleron and who had a single echo.

Even in the cramped quarters, even under a louring gray sky, I enjoyed the short drive across the city and the feel of the cool air on my face. Once our caravan came to a halt, all the nobles disembarked and began streaming across the three wooden benches to the temple on the center island. The hour was early but no one seemed in the mood to waste time. They probably wanted to be back at the conference table with all haste so conversations could resume.

It seemed deliberate that the royals and most of the nobles in our party chose to enter through the portal dedicated to justice. Even Marietta and Elyssa headed boldly for the black-painted door, as if sending a silent signal to the king and his councilors that they weren't asking for mercy. As usual, I saw almost no one choose the red door for joy.

We stepped inside the round, high-ceilinged space and paused to grow accustomed to the dim light. On the dais at the front of the room stood the statue of the goddess with her arms held out to either side; at her feet, dozens of candles burned with an uneven light. I thought this incarnation of the goddess looked much as the abbess had two days ago when she delivered her ultimatum to the king.

The pews were more than half full already, so Marietta and Elyssa hurried forward to take their places in the second-to-last row. Marietta's echo squeezed in next to her; I sat right behind Elyssa, with her two echoes on either side of me. The rest of the pew quickly filled with strangers—nobles from Camarria who were not part of the contentious group that had come from the palace. I could catch a glimpse of Jordan's light brown hair as he sat with his family on the very front bench.

"How long do you suppose we have to linger here?" Elyssa whispered to Marietta. "Not long, surely?"

I found myself wondering if she had toyed with the notion of leaving the three of us behind this morning—or simply not joining the rest of the noble visitors as they set out for the temple. I was fairly certain that this was the last Counting Day I would ever see at Elyssa's side. Either Jordan would rescue me and I would never have to make another appearance before the goddess as Elyssa's echo; or he wouldn't, and Elyssa would bring us all back to Alberta with her. I was pretty sure that, after this trip, Elyssa would be done with echoes forever. If she didn't get rid of us in some more dramatic fashion, she would simply neglect to present us at a temple on the next Counting Day. I couldn't help feeling some apprehension about what would happen then.

But first there was today to get through. Marietta bent her head to murmur a response. "I usually stay about an hour, but I would bet Harold will be on his feet and out the door in fifteen minutes. How long can it take the goddess to count a few echoes, after all?"

"And why she can't do it when we're all comfortably in our own rooms in our own houses, I'll never know," Elyssa said.

Marietta snorted. "Because goddesses are just like kings. They like to prove they have power over the rest of us."

Elyssa smothered a laugh.

A few black-robed priestesses were making their way up and down the pews, nodding to the visitors and offering benedictions to anyone who wanted one. Most of Harold's councilors were too impatient to accept, but a couple of the strangers accepted a priestess's touch on their foreheads, their chests, their lips. I was pleased to see that both Cormac and Jordan nodded and submitted to the ritual. Annery, who was still crying, did not. Neither did Elyssa, which meant I could not receive a benediction, though I thought wistfully that I would like to have a single moment when I thought the goddess was aware of my existence.

One of the priestesses headed to the front of the sanctuary as if she was going to address all the visitors. But instead she turned her back on the pews, folded her hands, and bowed her head, as if praying directly to the statue before her. Her stance was so imploring and so devout that the restless crowd grew quiet simply out of respect, even though the silent prayer seemed to last a very long time.

When the woman lifted her head and dropped her arms, Harold practically leapt up from his bench, and all the nobles in the section immediately did the same. I had my feet under me as I prepared to stand, when I realized that neither of the echoes on either side of me had risen when Elyssa did. No, and neither had Marietta's echo—or the echoes of the strangers nearby—or Harold's echoes, or Jordan's, or Cormac's.

All the originals were standing and all the echoes were sitting, lax and motionless, on their benches.

A soft murmur of uneasiness and displeasure began rippling through the crowd, building in volume and intensity. I maintained my slouched pose and empty expression, but I was cutting my eyes back and forth across the congregation, trying to understand what had just happened. I could feel my breath coming faster and my hands starting to clench, and it took all my will to merely sit in place and wait.

Through the clusters of standing bodies, I could glimpse Harold pivoting from side to side, surveying the crowd of agitated nobles and their lifeless shadows. "What is happening? Why do the echoes not respond?" he demanded in a loud voice that rose over the consternation of the crowd.

The priestess at the front of the sanctuary turned, and I realized it was the abbess. "The goddess has decreed that she will hold the echoes at her side until the rest of you determine how to end your war," she said in friendly, reasonable voice. "They will stay here at the temple while you return to your plots and conferences."

"That's insane!" Harold thundered. "You cannot keep our echoes!"

The abbess permitted herself the smallest shrug. "It is not I who keep them, but the goddess. They are hers, after all—she made them, she bestowed them upon you as gifts, and she can take them back if she thinks you do not value them."

"Of course we value them!" declared the Banchura lord. He was in the front row, next to Harold, and he looked furious. "All of us—we treat our echoes with the same care and attention we give our own bodies."

Maybe some of you do, I thought. Elyssa didn't even bother to turn around and give us an apologetic look.

The abbess's voice was gentle, but no less implacable. "And you hazard them in this pointless war," she said. "Dozens have already died, and the goddess has felt the pain of each loss. No more, she says. Risk yourselves, if you must, but not one more echo will ride into battle."

"But—then—how will we get our echoes back?" a lord from Thelleron demanded.

She glanced his way. "You will not get them back until treaties are signed and armies are dispersed."

"But—that could take weeks. Months!" Harold exclaimed.

"I hope not," the abbess answered.

There was a brief, apprehensive pause, then Cormac spoke up. "Is there a deadline?" he asked. "How long will our echoes survive if they are disconnected from us in this fashion?"

The abbess paused to run her gaze up and down the pews, where all the echoes appeared to be peacefully slumbering. I was careful not to make eye contact. "I'm not certain," she replied. "Two weeks, perhaps. Maybe less."

Almost every voice in the sanctuary seemed to repeat her words back to her. *Two weeks! Only two weeks!*

"But we cannot—nothing will—it has taken us *years* to get to this point!" the Banchura lord sputtered. "We cannot resolve our grievances in a matter of days!"

"Then I suggest you accustom yourself to life without your echoes," the abbess said.

That led to another shocked silence. I remembered some of the conversations I had overheard as lords and ladies described the physical pain they felt when they were separated from their echoes for any reason. There must be other nobles who, like Elyssa, either did not have or completely rejected the bond that existed between them and their copies, but most of them seemed to find their echoes as essential to their well-being as their limbs or their organs.

Harold lifted an arm and pointed grandly at the abbess. "You have no right to threaten such a thing," he said in the darkest, most regal voice. "Return our echoes to us at once."

Again she offered that infinitesimal shrug. "It is out of my hands," she said. "The goddess has made this choice, and she will determine if your echoes will be restored or if she will gather them permanently into her arms."

"Then— What are we supposed to do now?" asked one of the noblewomen from Pandrea. "Just leave them here?"

"You may stay with them as long as you like, but they will remain here at the temple, just as they are, until your war is decided. Or until the goddess grows impatient and harvests them," the abbess responded. "But I imagine you will find your time to be more fruitfully employed if you return to your palace and begin negotiations in earnest."

A few nobles started churning through the pews, stepping over the forms of their sleeping echoes and heading toward the aisles, but Harold stood fast. "So those of us who have waged war," he said in a steady voice. "Are *our* echoes the only ones that will be forfeit if a truce is not signed?"

The abbess shook her head. "All echoes. Throughout the kingdom. No matter if the noble is the gentlest woman in the province or the most bloodthirsty man in the realm. All echoes will return to the hands of the goddess if this war continues."

I heard a tearing sob issue from the front of the temple, and then a small feminine shape flung herself at the abbess's knees. "Please don't take my echoes, please don't take them," Annery sobbed. "I'll die without them, please don't take them—"

The priestess laid a compassionate hand on the girl's auburn hair. "I'm sure you will not die," she said gently. "You will just miss them very much."

Jordan and Cormac had hurried over to their sister's side, and now they lifted her to her feet, though she would not raise her head. She wrapped her arms around Cormac's waist and continued weeping into his jacket.

"She has suffered bitter losses recently," Jordan explained to the abbess. "She might not recover from another tragedy."

"I am sorry to hear it," was her grave reply.

He waited a moment, as if hoping she would offer some reprieve, but she said nothing else. A few of the other nobles had already made their way to the back of the temple and opened the wide door; the sunlight flooding in felt as foreign and out of place as seawater. Jordan motioned to his siblings and headed in that direction, sparing a moment to glance at his own echoes where they dozed in their pew. Annery and Cormac came after him and then—as slow and dazed as a man who had just suffered a blow to the head— Harold fell in behind them. The other lords and ladies stumbled along in their wake.

As Jordan passed the row where I was sitting, he cast me one quick, worried, interrogative glance. I lifted my head just enough to meet his eyes and respond with a brief nod. I thought I saw relief cross his face, chased by another kind of worry. I was fairly certain I knew what he was thinking. *Has Hope maintained her independent self in the face of this new development? Yes—there she is, I see her soul in her eyes. But then— Oh, goddess have mercy! Must she remain behind with all these comatose bodies, all these shells of living creatures?*

I saw him halt and half turn in my direction, his hand lifted as if to draw attention to some flaw in the abbess's argument. I quickly dropped my eyes and turned my head away. Right now, with all the other nobles in the kingdom focused on their own distress, it did not seem like the time for me to jump from my seat and demand special consideration.

And there was something else I was not sure of. How did the goddess regard me? Did she still perceive me as an echo, a gift she had bestowed on Elyssa, a gift she could revoke anytime she saw fit? If so—if the nobles could not stop their fighting and the goddess gathered all the echoes back into her close embrace—would I be harvested along with the others? If I ran from the temple right now, followed Jordan to the palace and begged for the king's mercy, would I simply disappear in a week or two as all the other echoes vanished from the kingdom?

Or did the goddess recognize me for who I was? Did she know my name? Had she counted Elyssa's echoes and decided there were only two?

I didn't know. But I thought I was probably safer—less of an encumbrance, less of a conundrum—if I stayed in the temple with all my sleeping siblings.

But when that door closed and the light instantly dimmed— when the priestesses swept out of the room, talking softly amongst themselves; when I was left alone in that silent room, surrounded by lifeless bodies—oh, then I thought my heart might hammer its way out of my body from the sheer petrifying strangeness of that place.

It took the rest of the day for all of the nobles in Camarria to make their way to the temple and leave their echoes behind.

The ones who came before noon had no idea what was about to unfold. I could hear the priestesses directing them toward the round tower set aside for joy—because that was the room that held the fewest sleeping echoes—and then I could hear their astonishment, rage, and fear when they, too, realized their echoes had been lulled to sleep. Some of them wailed, some threatened, some promised to march directly to the palace and demand that the king intervene, but all of them ultimately left alone, full of anxiety and doubt.

Those who arrived later in the day clearly had already heard the news from their neighbors and friends. These visitors swirled through the doors in a state of belligerence or disbelief or alarm, depending on their own personalities. Some of them argued, some begged, some were sobbing before they even put a foot inside. But all of them came to the temple anyway, so afraid that they would lose their echoes altogether if they did not comply. As much as anything, that obedience made it clear to me how deep the connection was between most nobles and their echoes. They were terrified of the sentence that would be pronounced once they stepped through that temple door—but even more afraid of the consequences that would follow if they stayed home. They would submit to the temporary loss to stave off the permanent one.

I guessed it to be a couple of hours before midnight when the last noblewoman left, covering her face with her hands so no one could see her hysterical tears. I heard the priestesses gather to confer in the small space at the center of the three towers.

"That's all of them, isn't it?"

"Yes—every echo within the city limits."

"I thought some of them might refuse."

"I didn't." I couldn't see their faces, but I was pretty sure this last speaker was the abbess. "For the sake of this war, they are ready to hazard their honor, their land, and their children. But the echoes define them in a way I don't think the rest of us can ever understand."

"We don't need to understand," said another priestess. "We just need to use that connection to our advantage."

"But is it enough?" asked another woman in an urgent voice. "Or will they continue to fight—and lose everything?"

The abbess was silent a moment. "I think we will have to wait a few days to find out."

Someone yawned, and someone else laughed. "What a day!" a priestess exclaimed. "I for one am eager to seek my bed. Do you think anyone needs to stay behind and watch over the echoes? I could sleep downstairs if you want someone in the building all night."

"I think the echoes are under the goddess's care for now, and thus immune from harm," the abbess said. "I believe we can all return to our quarters."

Still murmuring amongst themselves, the priestesses turned for one of the doors and filed out of the building. The door shut with an ominous clang of finality and the sounds of their voices grew too faint for me to hear.

And I was alone in a silent, shadowed, haunted room, the only moving creature in a field of inanimate bodies. If this place had been a mausoleum, filled with the whitened bones of the dead, I could hardly have felt more isolated and unreal.

I bit down a sense of rising panic. Nothing here was unfamiliar; nothing here would offer me harm. There was no reason to fear.

But certainly my situation was very strange.

I waited another ten minutes, in case one of the priestesses suddenly returned, then cautiously pushed myself to my feet. Votives still glittered at the feet of the goddess, so I still had enough light to see. I gazed around. All the echoes were slumped on their pews, some resting against each other, some toppled over to lie full-length on the benches. I crept along my row and peered at some of the faces. They all looked peaceful, untroubled, passive. I placed my fingers against one echo's parted lips, but if she breathed, the exhalations were so faint I could not feel the air. I touched her cheek, which was cool as a rose petal. It was the same with the other three I investigated, including one of my own.

If these echoes lived, it was at the very farthest edge of existence.

Stepping over motionless feet, I exited from the pew and then wasn't sure what to do. I wandered up to the front of the sanctuary and stared for a moment at the smooth face of the goddess for justice. The uneven candlelight made her briefly appear to smile, then frown.

I suppose I should pray for your intercession, I thought, *but I don't know if your notions of justice would match mine.* I turned away without making a plea.

Jordan was watching me from the front row.

I gasped and started back, cramming my hand against my pounding heart. No—not Jordan, of course. I had caught sight of one of his echoes, who always appeared so much more defined and present than most. All three of his were sitting straight up in their row, eyes open and heads tilted to one side, as if listening. The effect was far spookier than the simulation of sleep that had taken hold of the more ordinary creatures. I glanced at the figures closest to his. Cormac's and Harold's echoes also appeared to be more alert than the others, but Annery's slumbered at Cormac's side as if worn out from weeping.

I didn't have the nerve to lay my hands on one of their bodies, checking for a pulse, but I thought I could see the lace tremble at the throats of Cormac's echoes as if they were breathing. I decided that was all the information I needed.

I wasn't entirely sure I wanted to investigate the rest of the temple, but I felt an intense curiosity about what I might find in the other two towers. Picking up a candle to guide me through the dark connecting passage at the center of the sanctuary, I tiptoed first to the room for mercy and then to the one for joy. But each scene was the same. Low, flickering light—wooden benches filled with elegantly dressed bodies in sprawling poses—a single statue gazing out over her insensible congregants. There was no sound except what little noise my feet made as I circled the pews.

The more I explored, the more my confidence grew, and the less uneasy I felt. I stopped expecting one of the echoes to gasp and jerk upright, gazing around in horror as it panted for air. If that *did* happen, I was pretty sure I would shriek in terror and go running into the night. But there was something about the quality of silence in the whole building. Nothing and no one in the temple seemed sentient except for me.

I had been delighted to find, tucked like a closet between two of the towers, a tiny room that held a chamber pot and was clearly designed for the comfort of petitioners who spent all day at the temple. But I hadn't come across anything that resembled a pantry. And I was starving.

Once I had completed my circuit of the three towers, I made my way back to the one marked for justice. Settling down beside my echoes, I began rummaging in the pockets of my cloak. Ever since Elyssa had stopped feeding us when we were still in Alberta, the echoes and I had continued our habit of hiding bits of food at every meal. I had an apple and a handful of nuts in one of my pockets, and I devoured those in a few bites. Then I checked to see what the echoes might have secreted away. One of them had two hard dinner rolls, the other a rather shriveled orange. I ate one of the rolls but reluctantly left the other items untouched. I didn't know how long

I would be in this place; I didn't know when I could expect another meal. If it really took two weeks for the high nobles to lay down their arms...

I remembered something one of the priestesses had said. *I could sleep downstairs if you want someone in the building tonight.* In my tour of the towers, I had noticed no stairwell, but was there an underground level to the temple? If it had amenities like beds, might it also have food and water? How could I find this bounty?

I stood up again and began searching. Except for the ones leading to the outside, there were no doors on the curved perimeter of the three towers. But at the very center of the sanctuary was a carved wooden pillar so thick at least three people would need to hold hands to get their arms around it. Maybe it held a hidden stairwell? I set my candle down so I could begin pulling on various protrusions, looking for a latch or lever. It wasn't particularly well-disguised, and in about five minutes I had located and opened the door.

I picked up my votive again and peered into pooled darkness. A metal staircase spiraled down farther than my candlelight would reach; the air that drifted up carried a cool dampness and the faintest scent of mold. From where I stood, it was impossible to tell how big this underground structure was and how far it reached. My heart quailed at the idea of descending into a place so completely unknown. If I dropped my candle or the flame went out, I would never be able to find my way to the surface.

I stepped back and shut the door. Well. I would see what tomorrow brought. Maybe some desperate noblewoman would bring an offering of bread or cake to the abbess, hoping to win the freedom of her echoes; maybe the king would insist on transferring us all back to the palace. If nothing had changed by tomorrow night— except that I was even hungrier—I would chance the perilous journey into the underground cavern.

But tonight I would stay in a realm that was just as fantastical, but marginally more familiar. I made my way back to the tower for justice. Taking a deep breath to steady my nerves, I shifted the bodies of strangers' echoes to the very end of the back pew, then slid the bodies of my own echoes over next to theirs. That left me just enough room to stretch out full length on the bench beside them. I covered myself with my cloak, shut my eyes, and tried not to think about where, exactly, I was.

You are in the goddess's hands, I reminded myself. I wasn't certain I believed it, but I repeated the reassurance over and over until I finally fell asleep.

CHAPTER TWENTY-NINE

A burst of sound—a door clicking open, a group of women laughing—and I started awake so violently I hit my head against the wall. No, not a wall; something wooden. A chair? The light was strange, strained, as if it had had to sneak in past narrow casements. And my bed was so hard I might have been lying on the floor. Where was I?

I was about to push myself to a seated position when memory came flooding back, and I froze in place with one hand pressed against the back of the pew. There were more voices, snatches of conversation, the sounds of footsteps coming nearer. The priestesses were returning to carry out their duties for the day. Had any of them noticed me moving? I held my breath.

"You see?" someone said. "Nothing amiss. It seems all the echoes passed a peaceful night."

"I wonder if the king and his friends slept so well."

"I hope not! I hope they sighed and fretted all night long, and that they spend the day fretting some more! Maybe if they *think* hard enough, they can end this stupid war."

"When do you expect to hear from them?"

A new voice answered—the abbess, I was certain. "I would expect the king or one of his sons to come by sometime today."

"So soon?"

"Not with news of a treaty. But testing our resolve. Hoping to convince us to release the echoes."

"You won't do that, will you?"

There was a smile in the abbess's voice. "I could not even if I would. I have no power over the echoes. Only the goddess does."

The voices moved on, dispersed; I thought some might have come floating up from the hidden stairwell as a few of the priestesses headed down to the underground level. I was annoyed to find myself in a supine pose for what would probably be the whole day, as I could not risk sitting up if anyone happened to be watching. Well, at least it was not an uncomfortable position, even if it was one that prevented me from seeing anything going on around me.

This day was almost as odd as the one that had preceded it, and full of nearly as much anguish on the part of strangers. Several times each hour, nobles stepped through the doors, singly or in small groups, to visit with their echoes. I heard their feet tap across the stone floor, heard soft murmurs of affection and reassurance— caught the sound of tears more than once—then listened as the visitors reluctantly departed. A few of them did pause to plead with the priestesses, but in a weary, hopeless way, as if they knew before they even spoke that they would lose their arguments.

I was so unfortunately positioned that I couldn't *see* who came to the temple on behalf their echoes, and I couldn't recognize most of them by their voices. But shortly after midday I heard two figures enter and make their way to the very front of my tower. There was a small cry in a young woman's voice, and I was fairly certain Annery had arrived and flung herself down beside her echoes. I tensed on my bench, wondering if Jordan was with her, but when her escort spoke, I knew it was Cormac.

"We can't stay very long," he said, but his tone was kind. "Try to stay calm. I'm sure everything will be all right."

By her answering sobs, I could tell she did not believe him. I spared a moment to admire the brother who had taken time out of what had to be a catastrophically busy day to try to ease his sister's frantic heart. And a second moment to wish it had been her other brother here with her instead.

Indeed, they did not stay long, but Annery seemed slightly comforted when they left. "Can we come back tomorrow?" I heard her ask as they pushed open the heavy door and sunlight briefly flooded in. "And every day?"

"If I can't bring you, someone else will," Cormac promised, and then they were gone.

No one else who visited for the rest of the afternoon was some-one I recognized. The priestesses moved constantly in and out of the room, replacing candles, sweeping up debris, and performing other tasks I couldn't always decipher. After last night's vigil among the corpselike echoes, it was comforting to sense their warm human presence. Of course, it was inconvenient as well, since I could only make minute adjustments to my position when any of them were nearby.

But as the day wore on and the light filtering in through the slatted windows grew fainter and more hazy, I began to dread the coming night. No more soft footfalls on smooth stone floors; no more low-voiced conversations and muffled laughter. Just me. And dozens of still, silent, sightless companions.

If the king didn't resolve this war soon, I would probably go mad before I starved to death. It was hard to know which outcome to prefer.

As they had the night before, the priestesses all left together in a group, leaving behind a few lit candles and a cavernous silence. I waited a few moments before sitting up and stretching out my cramped limbs. My whole body ached, I was so thirsty my tongue seemed swollen, and I was starting to feel faint from hunger. I was less frightened than I had been last night, but my anxiety was starting to rise. I truly did not know how long I could endure this.

I fortified myself with the orange and the bread roll from the echo's pocket and felt some of my courage return. Coming to my feet, I visited the chamber pot again, and then nerved myself for what I had to do next. I didn't see that I had much choice but to explore the underground level. I had had a great deal of time to think about it, and I decided that I would bring *two* candles as I reconnoitered. I would leave one at the top of the stairwell, where I would be able to see it even if I dropped the one I carried. I wouldn't be trapped below.

I carried out this excellent plan, leaving the hidden door open for good measure. The metal staircase was a narrow spiral, so I had to navigate it carefully, holding tightly to the rail with one hand. Once I was downstairs, I looked around with interest only slightly tinged with apprehension. My single candle didn't throw much light, but I seemed to be in a place with several hallways branching off from a central spot. Each corridor was in absolute darkness, so it was hard to know how far any of them ran or what they held. I told myself that only benign things were likely to lurk in the basement of a temple, but it was hard to convince myself when the impenetrable black could cover any kind of secret.

I tried a hallway at random. It appeared to be only fifteen or twenty feet long, with doors on both sides. Two opened onto small cell-like rooms, each one holding a narrow bed and a few other stark amenities. I guessed this was where priestesses slept whenever they had reason to spend the night at the temple. One of the other rooms seemed to be primarily a storage closet, holding racks of robes in black and red and white, as well as stoles and other cloths that might be head coverings. There were also boxes and boxes of candles. So at least I didn't need to worry about running out of light.

The fourth room was the treasure trove. It was larger than the other three and had a circular table in the middle set with six or seven chairs. A meeting room, I supposed—but better than that, a modest dining hall, for there were baskets of fruit, loaves of bread, pitchers of water, and covered metal pans holding the goddess only knew what delights. I couldn't restrain a moan of pleasure as I flew across the room and snatched up a handful of grapes. Nothing had ever tasted so sweet.

After I sated my hunger with a sampling of other food, I wandered around a bit more, but I found this dank underground space even more oppressive and unnerving than the towers above. Since I obviously wouldn't be able to get down here again until tomorrow night, I put a pear and a chunk of bread in my pockets so I had something to nibble on during the day. Then I climbed the metal stairs, retrieved my second candle, and stepped out into the shadowed sanctuary. I carefully shut the door before turning to head back to my own particular bench.

One of Jordan's echoes stood there staring at me.

I shrieked and dropped both candles, which promptly went out. Worse and worse! Now I could barely see at all! I couldn't tell where the reanimated echo was, if he had stepped closer, if he was reaching for me with cold, slow hands— I backed toward the center pillar and tried not to breathe.

"Hope?" he asked.

Goddess have mercy on my soul. Now *Jordan's* echoes could speak. I was utterly silent.

"Hope, it's you, isn't it? When I came in, I could find your two echoes, but you were missing. I started looking—"

My breath caught. *"Jordan?"*

There might have been a laugh in his voice. I heard him take a careful step forward, as if he was having just as much trouble seeing as I was. The only light this far into the sanctuary came from the candles at the feet of the three statues, and those were very far away. "Well, of course it's me! Who else?"

"I thought—one of your echoes had come to life—"

"Not so far. I did check on them, but they were just sitting there, quiet as carvings of men."

I was flooded with so much relief that my whole body started trembling. "Oh, Jordan, it's *you!*" I wailed, and cast myself in the direction of his voice.

He caught me reflexively and pulled me close against his chest, and now I was washed with a whole different set of emotions. To feel a human touch again after this strange and solitary set of days! To feel *Jordan's* touch! I almost whimpered as I burrowed into his coat. His arms tightened around me.

"This must have been a macabre experience," he whispered into my hair. "I'm sorry I couldn't come sooner. It's been—well, you can imagine what it's been like."

I lifted my head. "What's going to happen? Can you guess? Will your father and the rebels be able to strike a deal? And if they can't—" I gestured broadly at the towers. "Will all the echoes just disappear?"

And what will happen to me?

"I know they are feverishly working on a plan," he said. "*Every* noble in the city has stormed the palace, demanding that my father come to some kind of arrangement, and I imagine the rebels are experiencing similar pressure from the high nobles who weren't interested in war to begin with. The question is: Do we have enough time to work things out before the goddess exacts her vengeance? But my father is hopeful."

"I am glad to hear it," I said. "But will—"

He pulled back. "I will answer every question," he promised. "But first, can we leave this place? It is so eerie and strange—I cannot imagine how you have stayed here for even a single day and not lost your mind."

"I was beginning to think I would go mad," I admitted. "But—" I lifted my shoulders. "What other choice is there? All the echoes must remain here until a truce is reached."

Even by the faint illumination that reached us here, I could see a stubborn look cross his face. "You're not an echo."

"But I—"

"And the goddess knows it. Or why else would you be up walking around when all the other echoes are sleeping? So you don't have to stay here while the nobles try to come to terms."

My breath was almost a laugh. "Where would I go? I can hardly return to the palace."

"There's an inn nearby. I booked a room for you before I came here tonight. Even if we decide you should return to the temple to rejoin the other echoes when the deal is done, at least you can spend the next few nights in comfort."

I stared at him in the dark. "Stay in an inn? By myself? For days? But what would I—how would I—I don't know how to buy things or pay for things—"

"I've paid for the room. I could arrange to have food brought to you every day. You wouldn't have to leave if you didn't want to—but you *could*, you could walk freely along the streets of Camarria, and no one would stop you or question you or even wonder why you were there. You could experience life as a free woman and see how amazing it will be."

"But when the treaty is signed, I'll have to go back to Elyssa."

"I don't see why. What an opportunity this is! My father could tell Elyssa and Marietta that the goddess gave him a very good idea, and he will keep their echoes until he is convinced of their good behavior."

I felt a rush of hope, and a stab of fear. "Then—if I never went back—"

"There are a lot of details to work out," Jordan admitted. "But we don't have to finalize everything tonight. For now, can we just leave this place? I keep expecting one of the echoes to spring to its feet and start a mindless screaming."

I bit back a laugh because I could certainly sympathize. "But tomorrow. When the priestesses come back," I said. "They'll notice I'm gone. Won't that cause all kinds of trouble?"

He took my arm and began urging me toward the door. "*They* aren't the ones counting echoes," he said. "I doubt they have any idea how many are collected under this roof. It is the goddess who counts, and the goddess who cares. And she knows you are not an echo."

It was what I believed—at least, what I wanted to believe—but even so, it was terrifying to reach that heavy black door, watch Jordan haul it back, and contemplate stepping outside into the frigid, starlit night. What if I was wrong? What if Jordan was? What if the goddess had assigned me to the *echo* side of the ledger of existence, and she remained unimpressed by all the proof I had accumulated to the contrary? What if I walked out of the temple and simply disintegrated into nothing?

What if I stayed, and fell under Elyssa's command again, and lived the rest of my life as her tortured, despairing, sentient shadow?

I put my right foot on the stone step on the other side of the threshold. I took a deep breath. I brought my left foot outside. I stood there a long moment, balancing uneasily, ready to fling myself back inside the minute I felt a tingle of dissolution at my fingertips or toes.

But there was nothing except the inquisitive touch of the night breeze against my cheeks. Nothing but the sound of the door closing behind me, and the feel of Jordan's warm fingers around my wrist.

"Ready to take the next step?" he asked.

I waited just a moment longer, and then I nodded.

CHAPTER THIRTY

The inn Jordan brought me to was cozy, pleasant, and discreet; a clerk nodded at us when we came in, but asked us no questions once Jordan flashed his key. My room, which was on the second floor, was modestly sized but expensively furnished, with two roomy beds, a collection of upholstered furniture, and a large armoire. Because the armoire door was open, I could see several sets of dresses hanging inside.

"You bought me *clothes?*" I demanded. "How did you even have time?"

"They're your clothes," he confessed. "I waited until everyone else was at dinner, and then I snuck into your room and grabbed a few things. I don't know if I got the right things, or if anything matches, because I was in such a hurry! I didn't want Elyssa's maid—or anyone else!—to show up and demand to know what I was doing."

His words conjured up such a vivid image that I started giggling and almost couldn't stop. "It doesn't matter what you brought," I assured him. "I will be so happy to change out of what I've been wearing for the past two days."

"You must be tired, so I won't stay long," he said. "But I'll plan to come over tomorrow and have dinner with you, shall I? Maybe by then I'll have news."

"That sounds wonderful."

He laid the key on top of a parquet table and stacked a handful of coins beside it. "Someone will bring you breakfast in the morning, and if you stay in, lunch as well," he said. "But if you have the nerve to go outside and walk around the city, I think you should! Are you familiar with coins and their denominations? Do you know how to use them to buy a meal or transportation?"

I shook my head. "No. I mean, I've seen people spend money but I never paid any attention to how it was done."

He divided the coins into silvers and golds, explained how much I might expect to spend on certain items, then said, "It doesn't matter, though. If I come back tomorrow and find you've been cheated out of the whole pile by some unscrupulous vendor, I'll just give you more."

"Eventually I'll have to learn how to manage money on my own," I said. "And earn it. And find a place to live and—and create an entire life."

"Eventually," he said. "I'll help you with all of it."

"Thank you." I hesitated, then said, "So the innkeeper and the staff. Who do they think I am? Why do they think I'm here?"

Jordan looked rueful. "Well, I told them you were a friend visiting from out of town, but whenever a man pays for a woman's hotel room, everyone assumes a—a certain relationship exists between them. And they recognized me, of course."

"So they think I'm your mistress."

"They do," he said apologetically, "but it means you'll be treated very well, since everyone wants to please royalty!"

I supposed I should have been offended, but I found the notion of being Jordan's lover very appealing. "And how do your mistresses generally behave?" I inquired. "Are they haughty or friendly? Are they gracious to the servants, or cold and demanding? Do they lie in bed all day or busy themselves with productive pursuits?"

His face looked grave; I thought he was trying to determine if I was serious or teasing. "There haven't been that many," he said. "And each was different. One was playful and one was wistful and one was overly dramatic. I think the only thing they all had in common was that they were kind. Not just to me, but to the people around them. I think it's the one trait that always catches my attention."

"That's so funny," I said. "That's the first thing I noticed about you."

"When?"

"In Alberta, when you visited seven months ago. You thanked the servants for every service. You danced with the shyest woman in the room. You were even patient with Elyssa, though it was clear you didn't like her. I thought you were the most marvelous man I'd ever seen."

His smile was a little crooked. "But you have seen so many more men since then."

I came a step closer. "None of them has impressed me as much as you."

We were only about a foot apart, and the air between us seemed alive with a heated energy. We stared at each other a long time, unmoving, before Jordan slowly shook his head.

"I don't want to take advantage of you," he said. "There could not be a more helpless creature in the city than an echo rescued from an abusive noble! I cannot guess what the future holds for any of us—except I know, I swear, I will make certain that you will be severed from Elyssa. But I don't know what path your life will take after that. I don't know what my father intends for *me*. I can't make you any promises except freedom."

"They still want you to marry her," I guessed. "Despite the fact that she tried to kill your brother. Despite the fact that she has speculated on how quickly she might kill *you*."

He nodded. "It is one of the conditions that keeps being put forward. If Bentam comes around, the rest of the Alberta lords will follow. And if Tabitha is returned to Empara, then Empara will lay down its arms. Orenza cannot win this battle alone."

"You will be even more miserable with Elyssa than I have been."

He managed a smile. "Oh, I doubt that. I can always walk away from her, which you could not."

"If you are married to her, and I am released from her, I might never see you again," I said.

"I will always find some way to keep track of you, but it will be difficult to stay in touch," he admitted. "It is the absolute worst part of the whole arrangement."

"So we have tonight. And maybe tomorrow night, if a treaty has not been signed by then."

"Tomorrow night even if a treaty *has* been signed," he said. "I will insist on it."

"It's not much time."

"We've never had much time," he said. "Just stolen moments and whispered conversations."

"I want a memory," I said.

"What do you want to remember?" he asked, very low.

"What it feels like to love you."

He didn't repeat, *I don't want to take advantage of you.* He merely said, "I want the same thing."

Still, he stood motionless, waiting for me to move closer, to prove I was certain, to show I was unafraid. I stepped forward again, into his arms, into his kiss. His mouth on mine sparked a pleasurable shock throughout my whole body, and I pressed closer, wanting more of the sensation. His arms tightened around me, melding me to him, allowing me to feel the glorious symmetry of leg against leg, breast against breast. Of their own accord, my hands traveled up the backside of his body, from the curve of the lean buttocks to the flat, wide expanse of his shoulders, stopping at every rib in between. I made a sound of appreciation against his mouth.

He pulled back just enough to laugh down at me. "Better without clothes on," he suggested.

"Then let's make it better."

We quickly stripped down till we were completely naked. I thought I would have felt embarrassed, but instead I was swept with a heady sense of desire and a powerful wave of curiosity. When he had kicked his last sock across the room, Jordan turned and reached for me, but I stepped back.

"I want to look," I said. "I may never see you this way again."

I could see his eyes already busying themselves with the contours of my body, and sadness seeped across his face. "I'd forgotten your scars," he said. "There are so many of them."

"But there will never be any more, if you can keep me away from Elyssa," I said.

"I can. I will."

"Then I don't mind the scars I have."

He came nearer, reaching for me again. "Haven't you looked your fill yet?"

I shook my head. "Not even close."

He took my hands and guided them slowly down the ridges and bulges of his body. "Touch while you look," he suggested.

"Your skin is so warm," I whispered, stroking its smooth, irresistible planes. The tapered waist, the flat stomach, the corded thighs. And back up again, running my fingertips between his legs. "And *this*—"

His laugh was more of a gasp. "Sweet goddess," he whispered, "perhaps I need to pause a moment to explain how all *this* works—"

Still rubbing my hand against him, I came in for another kiss. "I have had some vicarious adventures," I murmured. "I think I understand the basics. But I might need some tutoring in the specifics."

He began rocking against me with deliberate intent, and my hand fell away so there was nothing separating our bodies at all. He was right. It was much better without clothes on. He said, "Then let me be your teacher."

I had learned many things during the months that I had been a sentient creature, but none as gratifying as this.

We lay together on one of the elegant beds, facing each other, legs entangled and hands still resting on each other's bodies. I thought that it didn't matter what else my life held, who else I might share it with—I would never again find a man who knew so much about me, whom I trusted so completely. I could not believe the triple goddess had given me the gift of a night with him. I placed my hand on his cheek, smiled with all my heart, and said, "I love you."

He turned his head just enough to kiss the inside of my palm. "I wanted to be the one to say it first. So you could be sure I meant it."

"I will believe you anyway."

"Then I love you." As I dropped my hand, he lifted his own to smooth my hair behind my ear, then curled his palm around the back of my head. "It's so odd," he murmured.

Indeed, everything about this night was odd—I might have said *impossible* instead—so I wondered what exactly he meant. "What is?"

"Your face," he said. "I have known Elyssa more than half my life and hated her most of that time. Just glimpsing her across a roomful of people could turn my mood absolutely bleak. And yet I look at you—" He stroked my hair again, then traced a finger along one eyebrow, down the curve of my jaw. "You look exactly like her, and yet I have the precise opposite reaction. I see *your* face. I see *you.* Whether I see you across the room or lying on the pillow next to me, I am filled with more gladness than I could have imagined. And yet it's the very same face."

"I'm never sure," I said. "When all the echoes are with her, I'm never convinced you'll be able to tell us apart. That you'll know it's me."

"I always know," he said. "I always will."

"There has to be a way," I said. "Even if you marry her. There has to be a way we can manage—" I didn't know how to express it. "More of *this.*"

"I hope so," he said. "It seems like you will be safer if you are in some other city, as far from her as you can be. But I imagine, if we marry, she and I will lead very separate lives. Surely there will be room for you in mine."

"She'll expect to bear your son or daughter," I said. "So your lives can't be completely separate."

He was silent a moment. "Well, my father sired *one* child with Tabitha," he said. "Though I was never sure how he managed it. I'm not positive I'll be able to do even that much. Looking at her and knowing she's not you—" He shook his head. "I don't think I'll be able to summon desire."

Reprehensibly, I began to giggle. Rolling to his back, he started to laugh, too. "And then," he went on, "there will be echoes in the room as well, and I'll be even more distracted, imagining what it would have been like if you were still with her—"

I pushed myself up on one elbow so I could look down at him. "The echoes won't be in the room," I corrected. "I told you, remember? She sends them away when she wants to be intimate with a man."

"It will still be most awkward," he grumbled.

"What was it like tonight?" I asked. "Without echoes?"

He thought that over. "I would have expected it to seem strange to me," he admitted. "Everything else about these past two days has been strange, not having echoes at my back. I have felt—unwieldy— out of balance. As if the echoes always propped me up or weighted me in place. I haven't been able to navigate stairwells without clutching the bannister. I have felt too dizzy to stand for long." He glanced over at me. "But as soon as I found you in the temple, that all went away. And I have felt right ever since."

"I'm glad," I said. "I would not have expected that."

He sat up, pausing on the way to kiss me. "No," he said. "But then, from beginning to end, I never expected any of this. I never would have predicted you."

He came to his feet and began collecting his clothes. "I wish I didn't have to go," he said as he pulled on his pants, "but I do. The situation at the palace changes hour by hour, and the first courier from the battlefront usually arrives by dawn. I must be there."

"Of course," I replied. "Will you tell your father you have rescued me?"

He tugged his shirt over his head, then sat next to me so he could put on his socks. "Yes. And I will suggest the idea of keeping Elyssa's echoes away from her as a surety for good behavior."

"She won't care. She doesn't like her echoes."

He leaned in for a quick kiss. "The point is not to force her cooperation. The point is to get you away from her. So it doesn't matter if she cares."

I frowned. "But I wish there *was* some way to force her cooperation. If you let her loose in Camarria and she makes contact with Marco again—or have you already arrested him?"

Jordan sighed and began working his feet into his boots. "No, despite the fact that you helpfully pointed him out that day we all went to the garden. One of my men was going to follow him home, but we were all distracted by the news of war and—the upshot was, Marco slipped through our fingers." He stood up and pulled on his jacket. "I don't know if she's found some way to communicate with him."

"Elyssa left him a letter that day in the garden, but I wouldn't think she's had another chance to write to him. Trima refused to carry notes for her—Trima's her maid, you know."

"But my father has long suspected that a few of the servants in the palace are employed by rebels. Any one of them could have agreed to carry notes instead."

"You should fire those servants!" I exclaimed.

He laughed. "Oh, if only we knew which ones they were." He held his hands out to me. "Come, my dear, walk me to the door and lock it behind me. I will see you tomorrow around dinnertime—unless the news is so dire I cannot get free by that hour. Then I will arrive later. But I promise you I will be here at some point tomorrow evening."

I climbed out of bed and escorted him to the door, where we paused a few moments for farewell kisses that slowly grew more intense. "I hadn't realized how difficult it would be to say good-bye to you when you were naked," Jordan murmured as he rested a hand at my waist. I could feel him exerting all his willpower not to stroke his fingers higher. "But I *must* go. I will see you tomorrow."

A final kiss and he was gone. I shut the door and threw the lock and then stood with my ear pressed against the wood, trying to catch the faintest last reverberation of his feet upon the stairs.

Then I put out the lights, crawled back in bed, and wrapped myself around the pillow where Jordan's head had rested. It carried the scent of his body, a scent I would have recognized anywhere, a masculine blend of sweat and leather and something like cloves. I hugged the pillow tighter and inhaled more deeply and couldn't decide if I should weep that he was gone or revel in the fact that he had been there at all.

Or simply marvel at the unbelievable shape my life had taken.

CHAPTER THIRTY-ONE

When I woke, my first coherent thought was, *I need to go to the botanical gardens.*

I had lain awake half the night, unable to settle my mind, thinking back over the last hour with Jordan, thinking ahead to the next days and years and months. Finding this elegant, solitary room an even stranger place to be than the temple with its abandoned echoes.

I had never been alone before. The closest I had come was the midnight foray through Lord Bentam's house when I went searching for food, and even then, Elyssa and the echoes were only a few rooms away. But now there was no one at my back, at my side, reminding me to move and breathe and turn my head, assuring me of the endless replicability of existence. All by myself, I seemed so finite and fragile, as if the smallest mishap could carry me away and no one would remember that I had been in this world at all.

To distract myself from a building sense of spinning, formless terror, I started thinking about Marco and how much of a threat he still posed. I wondered if I could find my way back to that seedy tavern where Elyssa had met him so many months ago. If I could tell Jordan where it was, royal guards could keep watch on the place until they caught Marco coming or going. But we had only been there once and I wasn't sure I could retrace our path. I fell asleep as I mentally tried to reconstruct our route. In my dreams, I found myself hopelessly lost, still searching for the tavern as I endlessly wandered the streets of Camarria.

But I woke up remembering the one place that I might be able to find on my own. And the one place Marco might actually go, looking for Elyssa.

Instead, *I* would go looking for *him*.

I washed up with the water that had been in the room when I arrived, changed gratefully into one of the clean dresses Jordan had brought me, and answered the door when a maid arrived with a generous breakfast tray. I smiled at her because it seemed like something a kind mistress would do; she shyly smiled back.

I had never randomly started a conversation with a stranger, but I had such urgent need of information that I plunged right past my uneasiness. "If I want to go to the botanical gardens," I asked her, "what's the best way to get there?"

"Oh, it's so easy from here," she said, crossing to the window and pointing. "See that street? You follow that until you get to the big redbrick building with all the flags. Then you turn right and it's only a few more blocks to the garden."

I didn't remember the building until she mentioned it, but then I could instantly call it to mind. We had traveled past it often enough. "Thank you so much," I said.

"But it's chilly out," she warned. "You'll want to wear your cloak."

"I will."

As soon as I had devoured my breakfast and bundled up, I gathered my keys and my coins and set out on my adventure. Stepping outside of the inn's front door felt like the bravest, rashest, most foolhardy thing I had ever done, and I stood for a moment right in front of its cheerful painted sign, wondering if I had the courage to walk away.

What if I couldn't find the gardens after all? What if I couldn't find my way back? How long would I roam through the streets of Camarria, begging strangers for help but unable to tell them who I was or where I belonged? I hadn't thought to ask Jordan or the maid the name of the inn, and I couldn't read the words on the sign. I studied the letters a long time, trying to commit them to memory so I could trace them out if some kind soul offered to come to my aid. But what if I remembered them wrong? What if no one I asked was familiar with this small, quiet place?

I took a deep breath. Then I would ask to be taken to the temple and I would throw myself on the mercy of the abbess. She would help me—she would get word to the palace. I would not be lost forever.

I must do this. I must take the first step away from the last place where I could claim a shred of belonging.

I straightened my shoulders, turned my face into the biting wind, and set off in the direction the maid had indicated. The streets were still half-deserted as a consequence of war, but even so I encountered plenty of people striding around on their own business. Some brushed by without speaking, some nodded politely, but no one gave me a second glance or seemed to wonder why I was out on my own without an echo or an original to ease my way. The longer I walked, the more confident I became. No one *would* notice me. No one *would* wonder. I looked like an ordinary woman out for a brisk walk on a cold and overcast day.

I could not let my incredulity distract me from my task.

The redbrick building was easily found, the proper turn made, and the gardens located exactly where they were supposed to be. I had a moment of panic at the gate, when the bored attendant reminded me that I needed to pay an entrance fee. "Oh," I said, digging for the coins in my pocket and accidentally dropping a few of them on the counter. She had told me the price but I wasn't sure which coin would cover it. Fortunately, she plucked the right one out of the pile and waved me inside.

Elated that I had made it this far without a misstep, I hurried into the garden and down the winding path that I had taken with Elyssa. The day was gloomy enough that I practically had the whole place to myself, though I did spot a pair of determined lovers strolling hand in hand without the benefit of gloves. The other three people I saw all appeared to be workers clearing away winter debris.

Soon enough I came to the bench where Elyssa and Marco had always met. He was not there, and this time I didn't spot him loitering behind any statues or bushes. I tried not to feel a crushing sense of disappointment. What had been the odds, really, that he would be here waiting for her? He knew she was the king's prisoner. He must guess that the royal family would be very interested in apprehending him. Even if he thought she could get away from the palace, why would he risk his own safety to meet her here? But I had so much wanted to do something grand and meaningful for Jordan, who had done so much for me—

"Elyssa."

The voice came from behind me and I recognized it instantly. I couldn't help a gasp as I whirled to face him. "Marco. You *are* here!" I exclaimed, keeping my voice low.

His dark eyes watched me with something between desperation and hunger. He was standing a proper distance away, but it was clear he was straining every muscle in his body to keep from lunging forward and wrapping me in a crushing embrace. "Yes, I come here every morning, but I cannot believe *you* have made an appearance," he replied. "How did you get out of the palace unwatched?"

"I am far from certain I *am* unwatched," I said, glancing over my shoulder. It wasn't at all difficult to make my voice nervous and my mannerisms jumpy. "Let's just say I had help escaping, but I don't have much time before I'll be missed."

He came a pace closer and now there were only inches between us. "Don't go back," he said. "Come with me. Right now."

I couldn't help taking a step away from him—he was too close—but I covered my instinctive recoil with indignant words. "Are you mad? Of course I'm going back," I said, trying to summon all of Elyssa's contrariness. "I have a part to play in this complicated drama, and I'm going to see it through."

"'A part to play,'" he repeated, his voice flat with suppressed anger. "So you love me—but you'll still marry the prince."

I gave him a look from flashing eyes. "If that's what's required. I always told you I would."

"I thought—after everything—" He shook his head. "Then why are you even here this morning?"

Now I let my voice falter and my gaze drop. "I just wanted a chance to *see* you. If I could."

"I don't suppose you have any news that would be useful to the rest of us."

I shook my head and let a little anger of my own show. "They keep me penned up in my room away from all their councils. But I know there have been messengers riding furiously between the palace and the battlefront. I think they expect to know something within a couple of days. From what I can overhear, they are committed to negotiating a peace."

Now he spoke in a sneering tone. "And all because the goddess took away their echoes! The poor sniveling lords and ladies can't figure out how to walk through the room without two or three shadows at their backs!"

"It is almost comical," I agreed. "For myself, I have never felt so free, but the rest of them are staggering about as if they have lost a limb."

"I wonder…" he said, his voice trailing off.

I was seized with apprehension, but I kept my voice light. "Oh, I mistrust you when you use that tone! You wonder what?"

"If all that bends the king to reconciliation is the loss of his echoes—would he work so hard for a treaty if his echoes were already destroyed?"

"What are you thinking?" I demanded.

"If the temple burned down, say, with all the echoes in it. Would the king still try to negotiate for peace?"

Elyssa might have worn a different expression, but my own face showed disbelief and horror. "You would do that?"

He shrugged. "Why not? *I* don't want a treaty—none of the fellows like me do! We want to see the king overturned and *all* the rules rewritten, or how will we ever get our share? If the king's echoes are burned to ashes, then he'll take up arms again and the war will go on. I like this notion more and more."

Harold's echoes burned…Jordan's…Annery's. *Mine.* All those exotic, mysterious, helpless, beautiful creatures gone in one murderous blaze. I was so appalled I could hardly continue to play my role. "Well, *I* wouldn't mind losing the whole lot of them," I said in what I hoped was a callous way. "But you'd have to burn every temple in the kingdom to make this work. Because the high nobles whose echoes aren't slumbering in Camarria will still press for an end to the war."

I thought it was a very good argument, but he still seemed intrigued by his disastrous scheme. "Maybe," he said a bit absently. "But if Harold is enraged enough—or wounded enough—it might not matter what the other nobles say. This could be a very good plan."

I wanted to throw up. At this moment, I hated Marco more than I had ever hated Elyssa. But I had to cover my fear and my fury with a little laugh. "We're good for each other," I said. "We give each other ideas."

He quickly focused back on me. "We *are* good for each other," he said. "Do you think you can meet me again tomorrow? Maybe by then you will have gleaned a little more information from your secretive hosts."

I was thinking quickly. Could Jordan lay a trap for Marco? How much time would he need? "Not tomorrow—the day after," I said. "Or perhaps the day after that. I can't be sure when I'll be able to slip out."

"I'll look for you every morning," he promised. "And I will understand that if you don't show up, it's because you couldn't get free."

"I will try to manage it in the next two or three days," I said. "I'll meet you right here by this bench."

But Marco was shaking his head. "I saw two royal soldiers patrolling the garden when I arrived this morning. I almost left, except I thought they might be here to make sure the place was safe for the king to visit, and that you might be among the royal party. We need a new place. Somewhere the guards aren't looking for rebels."

"All right—then—let's see—" I stammered, thinking wildly. The only other places I actually knew in the city were the temple and the palace, and both were ineligible as spots for meeting with anarchists. From nowhere, an image popped into my mind. "I know! What about the new bridge? Is it completed yet?"

"Garnet Reach? That's an excellent thought," he approved. "I believe some of the ornamental work still isn't done, so it hasn't officially opened. There should be hardly anyone else there."

"Perfect. Then I will see you there in two or three days. Around this time. If I can."

I turned to go, but he caught my gloved hands and held me fast. I felt my heart ram against my ribs, trying to force its way out of my body. If he tried to kiss me—

"I can't stand this," he said, his voice low and raw. "Just stealing moments with you, terrified that someone might catch us together. Wondering what's happened to you, who else you're with, what path your life might take that will lead you farther and farther from me. Never having enough of you, and never being able to stop thinking about you. It hurts me in ways I can't describe."

Every word of his speech was something I could have delivered to Jordan. His pain was so unmistakable, and so similar to my own, that for a moment I felt a powerful pulse of sympathy for him. But Elyssa would never have showed such a weak emotion. "Would you rather I didn't see you at all?" I said in the sweet voice she used when she wanted to be particularly unkind. "Would that trouble your heart a little less?"

He shook his head and tightened his grip. "No. It is only these fleeting visits that give me any strength at all," he said. "But I want— I want—all I want is to be able to take you in my arms and kiss you in the sunlight. Can you promise me that might happen someday?"

I deliberately freed my hands and smoothed the leather of my gloves, wrinkled from his rough handling. "I can promise you nothing," I said, picking up my skirts and turning back toward the entrance. "Except that I will do my best. Don't follow me as I leave. I don't want anyone to see us together."

Without another word, I began walking away. I kept expecting him to catch my arm or shoulder, or to come running after me to offer one more argument, but he said nothing. I felt his gaze on my back all the way down that garden path, even after its twists and turns had surely hidden me from his view, even after I had passed through the stone pillars of the entrance and was hurrying down the streets of Camarria, desperate to get back to the one safe place I knew.

I flung the door open upon Jordan's knock and exclaimed, "He's going to set the temple on fire. You have to go, now now *now*, and make sure the echoes are safe."

"Wait, what?" Jordan slipped inside, quickly locked the door, then took my shoulders in a steadying hold. "Calmly. Tell me what's wrong."

I swallowed and started over. "Marco Ross. Elyssa's rebel friend. He thinks if all the echoes die, then your father won't have any reason to negotiate for peace, and the war won't end. He wants to burn down the temple."

"Ah! A smart plan, though I don't think it would work," Jordan said, not sounding nearly as alarmed as he should. "The rest of the nobles throughout the Seven Jewels are already demanding peace. Unless their echoes are all burned up, too, they'll still insist on a treaty."

"That's what I told him! But he's going to do it anyway."

"And when did you see Marco to have this interesting conversation?"

"This morning, but that's not what's *important* now, Jordan! He's going to set the temple on fire! You have to set guards! You have to *stop* him!"

He pulled me into his arms and pressed a kiss on my forehead. "My dear," he said. "We have already considered this. There are guards posted all around the sanctuary—visible ones, to scare off looters, and hidden ones, to intercept anyone with more ambitious plans. I hope your Marco *does* try to burn the place down. We will catch him at last."

"Thank the benevolent goddess," I whispered, and burst into tears.

He swept me up in his arms and carried me to an overlarge armchair, where he sat and comforted me for the next ten minutes. I was so overwrought it took me that long to return to a more rational state. It was now dinnertime; I had spent the last six or seven hours pacing my room, wringing my hands, trying to figure out how to get word to Jordan about the tragedy in the offing. But I couldn't write him a note, I wasn't sure what I could safely put into a message I dictated to the innkeeper, and I could hardly risk walking to the palace to look for him myself. I was certain that dozens of echoes would be lost to a conflagration and it would be my fault.

"All right. Better now?" he asked as I finally lifted my face and scrubbed the backs of my hands over my cheeks. When I nodded, he continued, "So tell me how this conversation with Marco even came about. Surely he didn't track you down here at the inn."

"No—no—I realized that as long as he is still at large, you and Cormac will never be safe. And I thought—Marco and Elyssa used to meet at the garden as often as they could—maybe he would be there, hoping to see her. So I asked the maid how I could find it, and she told me, and I went, and he was there, and—and—"

He drew back to gaze down at me. "All that way by yourself! How brave of you! I'm impressed."

"Well, I was a little nervous," I admitted. "But it wasn't hard and no one paid any attention to me and it was—in a way it was the most exciting thing! Until I saw Marco and he talked about murdering echoes."

"You spoke with him? You pretended to be Elyssa?"

"Yes."

"And he believed you?"

I made a sound halfway between a laugh and a snort. "If anyone knows how Elyssa speaks to men, it's me," I said. "With Marco she's always played this game—let him get close, then push him back. Be sweet, then prickly. Never give him what he wants. So that's what I tried to do. He didn't seem to know the difference."

"I would know the difference."

I looked up at him through my wet lashes. "I would never pretend to be anyone else to you."

He kissed me quickly. "What else did you talk about, besides killing echoes?"

"We planned to meet at the new bridge in a day or two. I thought maybe you could station some soldiers there and they could capture him."

"What a clever plan!" he said. "I see you have a mind for tactics."

"I wasn't sure which day would be best, so I just said I'd get there when I could."

Jordan touched his fingers to his eyes, as if they troubled him. I thought he looked tired; the whole household had probably been feverishly working around the clock, trying to come up with plans. But when he dropped his hand, he was smiling. "The day after tomorrow might be good," he said. "My father left this morning for a summit with the rebel leaders, bringing five nobles from the eastern provinces with him. They believe they have the makings of a deal. If he arrives at the meeting spot tonight or tomorrow, and they all sign a truce, this might be over tomorrow afternoon."

"That's wonderful! How quickly will the echoes wake up?"

"I'm not sure anyone knows. The minute the contract is signed, perhaps? In which case, the temple might suddenly be full of groggy and confused echoes anxiously looking around for their originals. I know a few nobles who plan to essentially camp out at the temple all day, waiting."

"What will happen to Elyssa's echoes? Did your father like the idea of holding them hostage to ensure her good behavior?"

"He thought that might work for a few days. We would never return *you* to her, of course, but the other two—once the treaty is signed and everything is settled—he thinks we will have to give them back."

Something in his voice made me straighten up and study his face. "That's part of it, then," I said quietly. "A promise that you'll marry Elyssa."

He nodded. He looked miserable. "And as quickly as possible. Depending on when Bentam can get here, it might be as soon as next week." He closed his eyes briefly, then opened them and gazed straightforwardly at me. "I'm sorry," he said. "I have to do it."

"I know," I said. "And if you refused, I would try to change your mind. Peace in the realm is more important than our happiness."

"But I won't abandon you," he went on. "And my father won't. We'll find a place for you to live—here, or maybe in Banchura, someplace you'll be safe. We'll hire someone to watch over you—maybe a retired governess who can teach you to read and write. It won't be so bad."

"It will be wonderful," I said. I would be free of Elyssa, I would be an independent, self-sufficient, *real* human being. Lonely and heartbroken, of course, pining away for a man I could never have—but maybe one day I would outlive the pain. I had had so many lessons in surviving other kinds of trauma.

"But you're here now," he said, tucking his hand under my chin and lifting my head. "And I'm not married yet. And if you're interested in another—"

I didn't wait to hear what exactly he might suggest. I just threw my arms around his neck and kissed him with wild abandon. Oh, yes, I was interested. I had so few chances left to be with him, this kind prince, this gentle lover. I was going to cram a lifetime's worth of loving into the span of days, and regret nothing.

CHAPTER THIRTY-TWO

The following day was almost as adventurous, though significantly less terrifying. Jordan had said he would return again at dinnertime, so I had hours to fill. I was staring out the window, trying to decide how brave I felt, when the friendly maid brought in my breakfast.

"Someplace else you'd like to visit today?" she inquired.

I turned to her with a smile. "I've heard so much about Amanda Plaza," I said. "And its beautiful bridge."

"Oh, it's a lovely spot," she agreed. "I always throw money in the grate, too, hoping the goddess will grant my wishes."

"Could you give me directions? It was so easy to find the gardens yesterday."

She wrinkled her nose. I guessed she wasn't more than sixteen or seventeen, but she seemed relaxed and capable. Had probably been working since she was a child. "It's a walk from here," she said, "and a confusing one at that. But maybe—" The look on her face was speculative. I could almost see her working it out. *This woman is a friend of the prince's and it's always smart to do favors for royalty.* "I could ask my pa if he'd give me the time to take you there."

"Your father owns the inn?"

She nodded. "And my grandpa before him."

"If you could do that, I would be so grateful."

She flashed me a smile. "Well, let me ask him. But first I have to finish my morning chores."

I was not at all surprised when, less than an hour later, the girl turned up at my door wearing a thick coat, sturdy shoes, and a cheerful grin. "My pa says I can take the rest of the day and show you anyplace you like," she said. "So come on before he thinks up something else he'd rather have me do."

I grabbed my own cloak and my money and followed her out in the hall. "What's your name?"

"Bevvie. What's yours?"

"Hope."

She looked scandalized. "*Lady* Hope?"

"Just Hope."

"I can't call you that! It's not respectful!"

I had never heard my laugh so loud and carefree. "Oh, if you only knew how funny that was!"

She grinned again, clearly thought about asking me for some of the details of my situation, and then regretfully decided against it. "Well, come on then," she said, leading the way down the stairs. "Let's go look around Camarria."

Bevvie was an excellent guide and an extraordinarily pleasant companion. She not only knew where every famous spot in the city was, and the shortest way to get there, she also knew every bakery and food vendor in Camarria. "But make sure you barter when he tells you what it costs," she whispered as we approached a cart where a man was selling baked apples on skewers. "He'll see you're rich and double the price."

I took out a fistful of coins and dribbled them in her palm. "*You* pay for everything from now on," I said. "See how long you can make that last."

The game delighted her, and she spent the rest of the day haggling with every small merchant we encountered, from the café owner who gave us lunch to the flower seller who parted with some exquisite blossoms for what seemed an uncommonly low price. There were dozens of small carts set up in Amanda Plaza where people were selling everything from spiced wine to glass figurines. Bevvie bargained with a sour-faced old women to buy two pairs of stitched leather gloves for the price of one, and then seemed astonished when I handed one of the pairs to her.

"To thank you for all you've done today," I told her.

"But I—I was just being ordinary—"

"I think your ordinary is extraordinary."

We paused at the three statues of the goddess in the center of the plaza, their arms stretched out or down or up. Each of us silently expressed our heart's desire before tossing a few coins into the grate at the center of the grouping. I had no idea what Bevvie wished for, but my own plea was simple. *Please let Jordan remain in my life.* Surely the goddess could find some way to grant that request?

"I can't remember when I've been so tired," I exclaimed when we turned our backs to the statues and began our return journey. "Walking around all day has worn me out!"

Bevvie laughed. "I was thinking it was the easiest day I've had in years! But we can hire a wagon to take us home."

"Do we have enough money left?"

She opened her fist to show a small gold piece and a few silver ones. She was grinning again. "Oh, I think so."

It took her a little arguing, but she persuaded the driver of a small cart to carry us back to the inn for about half of the remaining money. As we alighted at the front door, she attempted to drop the last coins in my hand, but I smiled and shook my head. "For you," I said. "For all your help."

Her mouth fell open, and I laughed again. "I'll see you at breakfast," I said, and headed up to my room.

I was fumbling with the key in the lock when the door flew open from inside. Jordan stood there, smiling widely. "Look what I have," he said, stepping back and making a broad gesture.

I hurried into the room, and there were the five echoes— Jordan's three and Elyssa's two. All of them standing and alert, though Jordan's looked clear-eyed and confident and on the verge of speech, while Elyssa's seemed nervous and timid and lost. I exclaimed with pleasure and flung out my hands, running across the room toward them, and it was as if they suddenly remembered how to move. They spread their own hands and flew across the room to meet me in the middle. We huddled together, arms around each other's shoulders, foreheads just touching, and took a moment to catch up on our breathing. I could feel their erratic heartbeats calm to the pace of mine.

I hadn't realized how much I'd missed them. How wrong the world felt when they weren't at my side. I took a deep breath and reminded myself that I would miss them for a very long time once they were returned to Elyssa—and I wasn't.

I dropped my arms and turned to face Jordan, an echo on either side of me. "They feel so frail," I said. "Have they eaten?"

I caught a look of surprise on his face, but he just shook his head. "They wouldn't. They've been very ill at ease since I brought them here."

"I think they will now if we bring them food."

"They're attuned to you," he said quietly. "How long has that been the case?"

I lifted my shoulder. "I don't know. A few months. But only when Elyssa's not in the room."

"How strange. I wonder if—" He didn't finish the thought. "I'll go downstairs and order food. And then we can tell each other how we've spent our day."

My day had been splendid, but Jordan's had been productive. He and Cormac had met with high nobles, dealt with messengers sent by their father, and helped finalize treaty negotiations. Then they'd been present at the temple when, like drugged sleepers abruptly slipping free of a narcotic haze, all the echoes dozing on their benches had trembled, gasped, and suddenly sat up. There had been low-level pandemonium as some echoes were frightened and thrashing about, and others were fretful and huddling together on their pews, but soon all the nobles had shown up to reunite with their shadows and the temple emptied out.

"You never saw so many happy lords and ladies in your life," Jordan said over dinner. The seven of us were crammed around a table much too small to hold that number, but no one seemed to mind. All five of the echoes were eating with the gusto of creatures that hadn't had a meal in days. "An old fellow from Banchura who has never bothered to speak a friendly word to me smiled so hard I thought his face might crack. I hope each one remembers how terrible it felt to be without echoes and works passionately to keep the peace from now on."

"I'm so glad they were rescued before Marco could burn the temple down," I said.

Jordan grimaced. "We thought we had him last night," he said. "*Someone* was prowling around the temple grounds, at any rate, looking highly suspicious. The guards gave chase, but he slipped away."

"You can catch him tomorrow," I said. "If that's when I meet him on the bridge. What's it called again?"

"The Garnet Reach," Jordan said. He sipped from his wineglass and nodded. "That seems like the best plan, if you're still willing. I will put soldiers in place, disguised as ordinary men, so Marco is not aware he's being tracked. As soon as you start speaking to him, they'll arrest him."

"Of course I'm still willing. I don't think you'll be safe while he's still roaming the streets of Camarria."

"Once he's in custody, we'll have to assume Elyssa no longer poses a threat to me or Cormac." He took another swallow. "And then we'll have to return her echoes to her and start treating her like a guest instead of a prisoner."

"Treating her as your betrothed," I said quietly.

He nodded. "I'm afraid so." He gave me a long look. "I'm sorry."

I shook my head. "This day was always coming. The days I didn't expect were the ones we've just had. I'll be sad, but I won't be sorry. That's so much more than I could have hoped for."

He reached his hand across the table and I took it. All our echoes joined hands as well, though two of his had to be content with the hands of one of mine. "More than it ever even *occurred* to me to hope for," he said. He shook his head. "Hope," he repeated, as if he might offer some profound observation about the meaning of my name. But he just shook his head again, squeezed my fingers, and said nothing.

✤ ✤ ✤

There was much to do back at the palace, so Jordan didn't linger after the meal. I missed the chance to spend another night in his arms, but I told myself there would be other nights—one or two, at least, before all the details of the treaty were finalized, and Bentam arrived in Camarria, and Jordan and Elyssa were wed. And then ... and then ... well, my life would go on without him. In some fashion. And it would be a good life, no matter how hard it was. It would just be lonely.

For now, it was inexpressibly sweet to be reunited with the echoes. I hummed as I undressed them for the night and tucked them into the second bed. They didn't speak or laugh or show much change of expression, so they weren't companions in the sense that Bevvie had been, and yet simply having them in the room with me gave me a sense of comfort I couldn't describe. I curled up in my own bed and felt relaxed and tranquil as I hadn't for days. I fell asleep almost at once.

And woke at dawn, ready to play my part in another dangerous game.

A crackle pattern of frost across my window warned me how cold it was outside, so I ate heartily and dressed warmly. I debated leaving the echoes behind, but I wasn't sure how agitated they would become if they were left alone in a strange place. So I dressed them warmly as well, pulling the cloaks of their hoods down closely around their faces. As soon as I reached for the door, I felt their movements effortlessly synchronize with mine. I had not intentionally drawn them to me, but even so, they were copying my every move.

I spared a moment to wish I could keep them with me once I was out on my own. Elyssa didn't want them, after all. But it would be hard enough to make my way in the world, fumbling along as I figured it out, without having two more bodies to feed and care for. And surely Jordan would make sure that they were never again starved or abused. It would be better for all of us if they stayed with Elyssa.

I told myself that about five times in the three minutes it took us to descend the stairs and step outside into the bitter chill.

Bevvie had taught me how to spot a vehicle-for-hire, so the minute I saw one clopping down the street, I waved to the driver and asked how much he would charge to carry us to Garnet Reach. I couldn't tell if the price was high, and I didn't care; I just handed over the coins and helped the echoes into the open conveyance. It didn't take long to navigate the half-deserted streets to the quaint square with its great rearing bridge. The construction appeared to be almost complete, with the soaring arch of stone decorated with a fanciful filigree of wrought iron ornamentation. It might be ten feet across at the highest point, which was about the height of a three-story building; directly below it was a crosshatched metal grate where people could toss money to the triple goddess. A few coins glittered on top of the grill, having fallen in such a way that they hadn't rolled through. Nearby, a pretty fountain sat dry and still, its silent stone lovers clearly dreaming about warmer weather.

At this hour, there weren't many people about—a couple of nursemaids pushing buggies, a few young men deep in earnest conversation, a lone woman sitting in contemplation on a bench. I wondered which ones were the guards that Jordan had promised would be waiting in disguise, since none of these visitors looked particularly warlike to me. Maybe a few were lurking in the shadows of nearby buildings.

One solitary figure stood at the very top of the bridge, covered from head to heel in a long, hooded cloak. His back was to me, but I had to assume it was Marco, come to keep his assignation with Elyssa. Had he been there yesterday morning as well? If I hadn't shown up this morning, would he have come back tomorrow? For a moment, my heart misgave me. He must truly love Elyssa to wait so patiently so many days just in the hope of seeing her face. Then I remembered his plots against the crown, and I hardened my heart again.

I took a deep breath and strode with assumed confidence to the foot of the bridge, the echoes a pace behind me. The arch was steep, but that wasn't why my breath was short and my pulse was pounding as we made it to the top. Surely the man standing so quietly at the center of the span had heard our approach, but he hadn't pivoted in our direction. Maybe he didn't want to show himself until he was certain who had arrived.

When we were only about five feet away, I spoke in a low voice. "Marco. I'm here."

The hooded figure turned to greet us, and I found myself looking into my own face.

"I thought it must be you," said Elyssa.

Chapter Thirty-Three

I was stone. I was ice. I was anything cold and immobile and blood-less. How was she here? What did she know? What did she guess? What had gone wrong?

Her careless gray gaze flicked over me, noting my clothing, resting on the echoes at my back, returning to my face. She seemed more curious than angry, but I could feel it there nonetheless, the fury building at the back of her skull.

"So you walk and talk on your own now? Just like an ordinary girl?" she said in a mocking voice. "So many times I thought there must be *someone* inside that fragile shell, but you would never show me more than a flicker or a grimace. I could never coax you out."

I thought about the hot brands, the keen knives, and wondered at her notion of *coaxing*. But I said nothing. I could not think of anything remotely useful to say. She stepped so close I could catch the faint scent of soap clinging to her skin.

"How long?" she said. "How long have you been hiding in there, watching me, pretending to be nothing but a reflection?"

Again, I kept quiet, and her hand shot out and closed cruelly over my arm. This was so familiar—Elyssa inflicting pain—that I bit back a cry and refused to speak. But this time, for the first time in all our dealings, I didn't drop my eyes.

"Answer me," she hissed. "You know I can make you suffer. How did you come to be?"

I found my voice steadier than I expected. "You woke me," I said. "Every time you cut me. Every time you scarred me. The pain brought me closer to the surface, until finally I never dropped back down into darkness. I am what you have made me."

She released me with such force that I staggered back, knocking into the echoes. "And I can unmake you," she said. "And I will. But first you will explain everything to me."

I tried to calm my breathing; I tried to keep my eyes from darting desperately to the onlookers below. Where were Jordan's men? Where were the royal guards? Why hadn't they come rushing up the bridge as soon as they saw me speak to the cloaked figure?

"What sort of game do you think you're playing?" she went on. "How *dare* you contact Marco and pretend you're me!"

When my gaze snapped to her face, she sneered and nodded. "Oh, yes, I found out. He sent me a note promising he would be here today as we had agreed. Of course, I let him know I had made no such plans, but I couldn't imagine who had written to him on my behalf. And it was you. *You.* How did you even learn to write a word?"

In spite of my overwhelming terror, I couldn't keep a note of triumph from my voice. "Oh, I didn't write him. I met him in the gardens and pretended I was you." Now I smiled. "He believed me, too."

I didn't expect the blow, so it cracked across my face so brutally I felt my cheekbone bruise. "You lie," she cried.

I put a hand to my face and stared at her. "You wish I lied."

Her eyes narrowed and she stepped closer again. I backed up, feeling the echoes move uneasily behind me. "To what purpose?" she demanded, her voice low and intense. "Why meet with him? Why try to lure him out?"

I didn't want to answer; let her figure it out for herself. It wouldn't be that hard. But then I felt it, that familiar, awful compulsion settling in my bones, working its way along my resisting muscles. I felt a rogue despair roil through my blood like spilled acid. She could force me to mimic her every action or she could coerce me into speaking aloud. I felt an invisible touch at the base of my throat, and the words came tumbling out.

"He is a traitor to the crown. He tried to murder the prince."

"Why do *you* care? Neither the king nor Cormac is anything to you."

I was silent.

I felt it again, that pressure on my throat, as if a finger was digging into the skin at the hollow. I coughed and I choked and then I managed a single word. "Jordan."

"Jordan? What about him? I've never schemed against him."

I put my hand to my neck, but I couldn't brush away her probing finger. "When you marry him. You'll kill him in his sleep."

She actually laughed. "Oh, that's right, there *was* some discussion of murder in the marriage bed. But again, why do you care? Jordan is nothing to you and you're nothing to him."

I took my tongue between my teeth and told myself I would bite it in two before I would say a single word about my feelings for Jordan. But maybe I didn't have to speak. Her eyes narrowed and her lips pursed together in a sour frown.

"So you have some affection for the prince," she said slowly. "How did that come about, I wonder? Maybe in Wemberton, when poor Renner trapped you in a room together for an hour or two. Did you pour out your heart to him then? Bond over your mutual hatred of me? What a very interesting evening that must have been!"

Even before then, I thought, but I would not say it, not even if she wrung my neck here on the Garnet Reach. I had started to realize that Jordan's soldiers were not coming. Some greater crisis must have kept them at the palace, maybe something terrible, but I could not spare a second to worry about that. I just kept my gaze fastened on Elyssa and continued taking short, shallow breaths. For as long as she allowed that. I knew she was almost done with me. I knew that I would not survive this encounter.

She lifted a gloved hand to touch my cheek. I tried to jerk away, but I couldn't move. "So the poor little echo has tumbled head over heels in love with the dull younger prince," she said. "Is that it? And you fear that evil Elyssa will marry him and destroy him—or simply marry him and make him miserable—and you will have to bear

372

silent witness? How very amusing! It would almost be worth keeping you around just to know how wretched you would be, watching me subject Jordan to every kind of grief."

I managed to speak now, but not the words she was expecting. "I hate you."

Or maybe she was expecting them, because she laughed. "I know," she said. "And it's just delightful."

For a moment we watched each other in silence. I thought of what Jordan had said—how much he despised Elyssa's countenance, how much he loved mine. Could she read it, the difference in our faces? I certainly could.

"What do I do with you now? That's the real question," she went on in a meditative voice. "Keep you or throw you away? I admit that the idea of making you suffer has endless appeal. And I have always appreciated the status conferred by having three echoes. I very much want to kill you now, for your insolence and your very *existence*, but I think perhaps I should put off that pleasure until sometime after my wedding."

I don't know what she saw in my face because I hardly knew what I felt—relief, revulsion, horror, all of it—but suddenly her hand dropped from my cheek to form a vise around my throat. "But that doesn't mean I couldn't *hurt* you now, just a little," she murmured.

Her grip tightened; I could feel my mouth fall open as I struggled for air. But I could not resist or pull away. I could only stand there, meek and powerless, trying not to pant or plead. Behind me, I could hear the soft sounds of the echoes choking.

Then suddenly, below us on the brick of the square, I heard running footfalls from a handful of newcomers. "Hope!" a voice called out. Jordan's voice, which I recognized even through the buzzing in my ears. "Elyssa, no! *Hope!*"

She hadn't reacted when he called my name, but at the sound of her own, she turned in surprise to gaze at the scene below. She loosened her hand just enough so I was able to break free and take in great heaving breaths of the frigid air.

"Who is calling—is that *Jordan?*" she demanded, peering over the ornate railing. He wasn't far now; he and his echoes were racing for the northern leg of the bridge. "How did he know where— And did he call you by *name?*"

As if in answer, Jordan shouted again. "Hope! Hope! Be careful!" I heard his boots clatter on the ascent.

Elyssa was laughing as if at the best joke she had ever heard. "You have given yourself a *name!* And he knows it! Oh, but this is even better! Does he think he cares for you as much as you care for him? What a sad little tragedy! Or a divine farce."

Jordan and his echoes were now on the top curve of the bridge just a few feet away from us. "Hope," he repeated, more quietly. "Are you—"

Elyssa moved to put herself more firmly between Jordan and me, flinging out her arm in an imperious warning. Warily, he came to a halt, but his eyes went past her to search my face. I nodded, and then I shook my head. Meaning both *I'm all right* and *It couldn't be worse.* I don't know how he interpreted the gesture, but his gaze quickly locked onto Elyssa's face. His echoes crowded behind him, likewise staring.

"What are you doing here?" he asked. "How did you get out of the palace?"

She laughed. "I don't think I shall tell you how I got out, but I will certainly tell you why I'm here," she said. "I learned that one of my echoes has been playing at being real, and I decided to stop that nonsense utterly. And you see I have."

She made a quick, fluid gesture, twisting both of her hands palm up, and the echoes and I copied her movements precisely. I would have sobbed aloud if I had had any control of my voice. But that quickly she had reasserted her will over all of us; that suddenly, I was completely her slave.

"You will have to give her up," Jordan said. "She moves and thinks and speaks independently—she will be recognized as an individual in the eyes of the law. She is yours no longer."

Elyssa splayed her fingers and turned her hands palms-down, then dropped her arms to her sides again. Helplessly, the echoes and I mimicked every motion. "I think she *is* mine for as long as I want her," she replied. "And I am not ready to let her go."

Jordan shook his head slowly. "I will fight you on this, Elyssa," he said. "If it takes separating you from your echoes by force. If it takes negating the contract my father has just signed with all the lords of the Seven Kingdoms. If it takes splitting the world in two. I will not let you keep her."

She laughed again, a silver trill of delight. "Oh, I was right! You *do* love her! But how absurd and how delicious! I told her just a minute ago that I wanted to simply kill her, but now I think I shall keep her alive for years and years. I can torture you *and* her, and there's nothing you can do about it."

He took a step forward; now he was close enough to grab her by the throat and strangle her where she stood. I almost wished he would do it. But I knew he wouldn't. Not Jordan.

"I don't believe you've thought this through," he said softly. "Your echo can imitate you so well your own lover doesn't know the difference. You don't think she could fool all the lords and ladies of the Seven Kingdoms? What's to stop me from locking you in some remote tower, hundreds of miles from here, and keeping Hope at my side to play the noble Lady Elyssa? I think everyone would believe that particular charade."

I was stunned to hear him propose such a deception, though I felt a savage exultation at the notion of giving it a try. Even Elyssa believed him, for I felt the fear and fury tumble through her veins. But she snapped, "You can't do that."

"I can and I will," he replied. "If you don't release her."

She stared at a him a long moment, caught in a bitter internal debate. "And if I do?" she said at last. "What will you promise me in return?"

His voice very dry, he replied, "Being married to the king's youngest son is not a reward enough for you?"

"You hate me," she said. "If I'm going to be trapped in a loveless marriage, I need some assurance that I can find—affection—elsewhere."

"I had assumed all along that you would," he said. "Though I regret to inform you it won't be with Marco Ross."

She couldn't control her flinch, and the three of us winced behind her. Now fear lined her veins with ice. "What's happened to him? What did you do to him?"

"Soldiers went to arrest him this morning. Unfortunately, he was not willing to go with them peacefully."

The fear and the ice both intensified. "Then he— What happened?"

"I'm afraid he's dead."

The shock of that left her, for a moment, so hollow that I could not draw a breath or detect my own heartbeat. "No," she finally said.

"I'm sorry," he said. "But it's true."

"No, no, no, *no!*"

This time Jordan didn't answer, merely watched her, with something resembling compassion on his face. A would-be assassin and a highborn traitor—how could anyone feel sorry for either of them? Yet Elyssa's pain was so sharp and so bottomless that even I felt a resonant twinge of sympathy.

"And *that's* the way this goes?" she demanded, her voice riven with grief and edged with hysteria. *"You* are to get everything you want, while I have nothing?" She whirled around and grabbed my arm so swiftly I could not copy the movement and spin around myself. It was a shock to realize she was addressing me, not Jordan. "You are to have love—and status—and the admiration of every noble in the kingdom—and I am to be left heartbroken? Forgotten? *Discarded?*"

"Elyssa—" Jordan said.

She shook her head wildly. Her fingers dug like claws into my flesh. "Oh, no no no no no," she repeated. "If I can have none of it, neither can you."

She flung my arm aside but immediately imposed her will on me again, so that I was once more copying her slightest motion.

With a pivot and a lunge, she dove toward the side of the bridge and wrapped her fingers around a decorative metal curlicue. The echoes and I rushed to the railing beside her, our own hands gripping the metal border, our own muscles bunching in anticipation.

"We will all die together in the shadow of the Garnet Reach," she declared, tightening her grip on the metal. With a single scrambling leap, she brought her feet to the flat edge of the railing and hauled herself upright. The three of us jumped up next to her, our skirts tearing on the metal ornamentations. "If I cannot have Marco, Jordan cannot have you." She released her grip and swayed forward.

"Hope, *no!*" Jordan cried. My own hands were open—there was nothing to hold on to—there was nothing before me but a three-story drop onto unforgiving brick. My body tilted forward and I felt every muscle simply let go—

Then rough arms hauled me back; I was almost torn in two by the ungovernable desire to leap forward and the unyielding iron grip that forced me in the opposite direction. All around me was a confusion of wild motion and straining bodies and shouts both near and far.

And then the pain. The pain. As if all my bones shattered, as if my skull snapped from my spine. My soul fled my body in one fleet, unraveling shot. I dissolved into dust, into liquid, into nothing, and my mind went blank.

I felt Elyssa die.

The world emptied out and there was only white silence.

CHAPTER THIRTY-FOUR

Life slammed back into me with such force that my body spasmed and doubled over. The world swam with color, with sensation; heat poured through my veins like rivulets of lava. My chest heaved as I panted for air. I felt the rich chill of the winter wind against my skin, the close and comforting weight of Jordan's arms around my shoulders. I heard his voice chanting my name over and over, as if he had no other vocabulary, as if there were no other words.

Using almost all of my remaining strength, I pushed myself to an upright position and stared at him. "I'm alive," I whispered.

"Goddess have mercy on my soul," he breathed, crushing me in his arms. "When she leapt—when she leapt—"

"You thought I would fall after her," I finished, the words muffled against his jacket.

His arms tightened briefly, then loosened enough for him to gaze down at me. "No," he said fiercely. "I had you and I knew I wouldn't let you go. But when an original dies…"

"The echo dies with her," I said. "Always?"

"I only know of one instance in recent history when that has not been the case," he said. "Every other time, the noble's death means the echo's death, even if there isn't a mark on the echo's body."

I shook my head. "She's dead. I can tell."

He pressed his mouth against my hair and whispered, "I'm not sorry."

I closed my eyes for a moment. Since my dramatic reprieve from death, I had not looked beyond Jordan's face. I hadn't glanced over the side of the bridge to see the crumpled body below. Crumpled *bodies*, I was assuming, since the two echoes had surely followed Elyssa's heedless plunge.

And yet.

I could feel them. Shadows at the back of my mind. Flickers of motion, comforting weights just behind me, to either side of me. I didn't dare look, I just tilted my head up and said in the quietest possible voice, "My echoes?"

"Safe," he replied.

"How?"

"My own caught hold of yours when I took hold of you."

My bounding relief, my dizzying joy, made me push free of Jordan's embrace and look around. Yes, there they were on either side of me, disentangling themselves from the arms of his echoes, looking just as stunned and unsteady and *whole* and *alive* as I was. I was so glad that it took me a moment to realize something was wrong.

"Jordan—where's your third echo?"

His face crumpled with grief; now he folded me back into his arms. "I grabbed you—it grabbed Elyssa—and neither of us let go," he whispered. "It fell with her to the bottom of the bridge."

I felt my whole body clutch in a paroxysm of pain. "Oh, no no no no," I said, just like Elyssa had when confronted with her own proof of loss. "Jordan—I'm so sorry—I don't know how you will bear it."

His grip tightened, but I could feel his body shaking. "I *will* bear it—I *will* endure it," he said, intense and determined. "I have you. I choose you. I would make that trade every day if I had to."

"But, Jordan—"

"It hurts," he acknowledged. "Hope, my dear, my darling, it hurts."

Now I was the one to tighten my hold; now I was the one to try to offer comfort. When he started crying, I started crying, as if we were as bonded as echo and original. As if we were one person. As if we shared one heart.

❧ ❧ ❧

But we did not have the luxury of time for grieving, not here, not now. I could hear murmuring from the square below us as onlookers clustered around the fallen bodies, checking to see if, improbably, either jumper had survived. Closer to hand, there were urgent footfalls as heavy boots rang on the bridge's curved ascent.

"Your Highness?" asked a voice, respectful but resolute. "Prince Jordan? Are you all right?"

I felt Jordan take a moment to compose himself and assume his usual demeanor, then he lifted his head and let me go. I, too, tried to settle my thoughts and adopt a serene expression. The man who had addressed Jordan was a royal guard; I quickly noted three more at his back and two down below, trying to keep the curious away from Elyssa and the dead echo.

"Yes, thank you, Sergeant, I am well, but there has been a tragedy here today," Jordan said solemnly. "Lady Elyssa received disquieting news and was much overcome. She stumbled against the railing and almost fell, but I was able to catch her before she went over. Unfortunately, one of her echoes, and one of mine, could not be saved."

The soldier gave me a sketchy bow. "My lady," he murmured. From his cool tone, I gathered that he had no favorable opinion of Elyssa. Perhaps he had been assigned to guard her at some point during her current visit.

I was barely able to summon the presence of mind to nod in return. *Lady Elyssa?* Was Jordan seriously going to attempt to pull off this masquerade? It was a good thing that no one seemed to expect me to answer because I found myself bereft of speech.

The sergeant returned his attention to Jordan. "I understand that losing an echo will be a terrible blow to you, Your Highness," he said. "Perhaps it would be best if we got you back to the palace right away."

"Yes—I think you're right," Jordan said a little unsteadily. "Is there a carriage stand nearby? Can one be hired for the two of us and all our echoes?"

The sergeant glanced over his shoulder. I didn't hear him give an order, but one of his men broke free and bounded down toward the plaza. "It'll be here in a moment. It might best if we hired a wagon to bring the bo—bring the echoes back to the palace as well."

"An excellent notion. Thank you," Jordan said. He straightened his shoulders, put his arm around me, and began urging me toward one of the downward ramps.

"Do you want assistance, Your Highness?" the sergeant inquired. "You can lean on me."

"No," Jordan said. "Elyssa is all the support I need."

Truth be told, we were both a little shaky, but we made it safely down the arch and onto the brick of the plaza. We both hesitated, then turned as one to make our way to the bodies and fall to our knees beside them. The other onlookers cleared away in respect for our obvious grief.

Jordan put one hand to his echo's chest, as if feeling for a heartbeat that he already knew would not be there. I could tell he was biting his lip in an effort to stave off another round of tears; this was a wound from which there might never be a complete recovery.

In contrast, I stared at Elyssa's face and felt no sadness whatsoever. But neither did I feel elation. There was horror and disbelief and lingering confusion and even a little pity. But I could not be sorry she was dead.

After a moment, Jordan lifted his hand and rested it on his knee. I saw him glance at Elyssa—then glance again with a slight frown.

"My dear," he said in a slightly artificial tone pitched so that others could overhear. "I will take the ring and pin from my echo's body—you must take the necklace and earrings from yours. They have no need of such adornments now."

I caught my breath. For this clandestine outing to confront a rogue echo, Elyssa had chosen to wear her signature jewels, including the pendant with the interlocking circles and her finest amethyst earrings. Anyone who knew her would recognize those pieces—and would know they did not belong on an echo. "Of course," I murmured. "I will keep them always to remember her by."

It was a slightly gruesome task to lean over Elyssa's body and fumble with the clasp of the necklace, slide the hooks from her ears. The two rings she wore weren't as immediately identifiable, but I confiscated them anyway. Trima would know them, if she happened to see this corpse; there was no point in taking chances. I had just dropped all the pieces into the pocket of my cloak when I heard the clatter of wagon wheels approaching, and the sergeant came over to let us know our conveyance had arrived.

"I've sent a man ahead to the palace," said the soldier, holding out a hand and helping each of us to our feet. "The king will know what's happened before you've made it back. That'll make it easier."

That'll make it more confusing, I thought, but Jordan only thanked the man and assisted me into the carriage, which was just large enough to hold the six of us. The minute the door was closed and the vehicle started moving, Jordan and I fell into each other's arms. On the other seat, all our echoes did the same.

"I came to the inn this morning," he said, his voice ragged, "to tell you Marco was dead. But you had already left."

"I saw her on the bridge," I answered, my voice almost as rough as his. "With her cloak on and her hood up. I thought she was him. And then she turned and—and—"

"I came right here, but I didn't *run*," he went on. "I didn't realize you were in danger. If I had known— But then I got here and I saw you— I saw her—" His arms closed so convulsively that for a moment I couldn't breathe. But it was a much more welcome form of suffocation than when Elyssa had wrapped her hand around my throat.

"It's fine—it's all right," I managed to murmur against his chest. But I was clinging to him so tightly he might not have believed me.

We sat that way another moment, and then Jordan sighed and loosened his hold. "Now, quickly. We don't have much time and we must sketch out our story," he said in quite another tone. His voice remained very low; there was little likelihood the driver could hear us even if we shouted, but I felt the same impulse to stealth.

"You want to pretend that *I'm Elyssa?*" I demanded, my voice almost soundless. "For how long?"

He took my hands in a hard hold and gazed down at me. "Forever," he said. Despite the shock and sorrow marking his face, he looked oddly excited. "Don't you see? If you're Elyssa, I can marry you! The treaty stands—there is peace in the realm—and you and I can be together."

"But I—I—I thought you were just saying those things to make her angry—so she would let me go—"

"I was," he admitted. "But now that she is dead—what an opportunity the goddess has handed us! Unless you don't *want* to marry me."

"It might be the other way around," I said in a low voice. "*You* might find you do not want to be married to *me*."

"I—" he began, but I freed one hand and held it up to silence him.

"You scarcely know me," I went on. "All told, we have spent what probably amounts to less than a day together. You find me fresh and intriguing now—but in a few months? A few years? You may find me so dull and wearisome that you deeply regret this hasty bargain."

He took hold of my raised hand and kissed it. "I suppose it may happen, though I don't think so," he said. "I do believe I have a much greater chance at happiness with *you* than I did with *her*, and I was willing to marry *her* for the good of the kingdom." He couldn't hold back a smile. "If I must marry someone who looks like Elyssa, I would much rather it be you. Now, if there is someone *you* would rather marry—"

I answered that with an emphatic kiss. "I cannot imagine that the world could permit me so much happiness," I said. "But goddess have mercy on my soul! What a deception we are committing ourselves to! I must pretend to be Elyssa—now and forever—"

"No one knows her better than you do," he said. "Her mannerisms, her tone of voice, the way she flirts, the way she mocks. If you could fool Marco, you can fool all the nobles in the kingdom."

"But I don't think I can *do* that," I said honestly. "I don't think I can maintain her—her level of cruelty."

He shook his head. "Then don't. Slowly become a kinder person. Tell anyone who asks that love has given you a change of heart." He laughed and lifted our clasped hands to kiss my knuckles.

I was thinking it over. It might work. Why wouldn't it work? There might be a few people from Elyssa's early life that I wouldn't recognize because she hadn't seen them since I had been conscious, but all the royals? The high and low nobles? The servants in Camarria and Alberta? I knew most of them—and how Elyssa treated them.

"Trima," I said. "Her maid. She's the only person who actually seems to care for Elyssa. She'll know I'm not her."

"I can have her released from your service," Jordan said. "I can tell her it's my decision—that I want my bride to start over with servants who are loyal to the crown. I'll pay her a handsome severance, of course, but I'll make sure she never sees you again, not even today. Unless you think that's too unkind."

I thought that over, too. Trima *had* been genuinely devoted to Elyssa, and I thought a summary dismissal would distress her greatly. But Trima had never shielded me from Elyssa's casual torture, never even made sure I was properly fed or cared for. She was the one person who had had a chance to make my life bearable, and she hadn't bothered to do it. "No," I said in a hard voice. "Let her go."

Jordan gave me a speculative glance but did not follow up with questions. "What about Elyssa's father and her aunt? Should I forbid them the palace and refuse to let you visit them? Anyone would find it believable that the crown doesn't trust them."

I shook my head. "They won't realize that I'm not her. Lord Bentam ignored her until he thought he might get some use out of her, and Hodia only wanted to be sure that Elyssa dressed and acted like a lady. Neither one *knew* her. Neither one cared."

Now his gaze softened to something like pity. "You paint a very sad picture. I always found Elyssa unlovable, but maybe she was just unloved."

"She was both," I said softly. "And it *is* sad." Now I brought his hands up to my mouth and kissed them. "But I find I can't be sorry she is dead. I am only sorry that you have paid such a heavy price for it."

He nodded, his face instantly grave. "The ache is so raw and deep that I cannot even describe it," he said. "I think—when I am alone tonight and finally have time to understand what happened—the pain will bring me to my knees. I have been grievously wounded—but not mortally wounded. I will recover, I am sure, but I will bear the scar forever."

"I'm so sorry."

He squeezed my hand. "It is the price," he said. "The price for you. I would pay it over and over again, until I ran out of echoes." He managed a very small smile. "And perhaps it will turn out to be a fortunate thing."

"In what way?"

"In marriages among nobles, it is thought to be best when the couples have the same number of echoes. When there is symmetry in their lives—and in their bedrooms."

That made me laugh and blush at the same time. "I confess I had not gotten quite that far in my thinking. Now we each have two."

He glanced over at the echoes occupying the other bench. "And you *do* have Elyssa's, do you not? I have seen them follow you, but can you bind them to you absolutely?"

I nodded, and the echoes nodded with me. "Even when I wasn't consciously trying to control them, they would attach themselves to me if Elyssa wasn't nearby. Now—as soon as she died—I felt it. That transfer of allegiance. We might fail in many other aspects of this mad charade, but it won't be the echoes that give us away."

"I would like to tell my father and brother the truth, unless you think that's a bad idea," he said.

"No, I think it's best that they know! Otherwise, they will undoubtedly find some of my behavior very odd."

"And we will have the wedding as soon as it can be arranged."

I shook my head in a wondering way. "Married," I said. "And to you. I still cannot make myself believe it."

He kissed me again, and then he laughed. "The only thing I find distasteful—the *only* thing!—is that I will now have to call you Elyssa," he said. "And because I have despised her so much, I have come to hate the name."

I shifted position so I could snuggle against his shoulder. I had to think we were almost at our destination; we didn't have much time left, and I just wanted to soak up some of his heat and strength before I had to start playing my new part at the palace. "I hate it, too," I answered. "But 'Hope' sounds nothing like 'Elyssa,' so we cannot even pretend it is a pet name you have for me."

"No, we shall have to come up with a word that *sounds* like Elyssa but is something else entirely." He glanced out the window, where the great curving wings of the palace were coming into view; in another minute, we would be pulling to a halt in the courtyard. "Something that both of us— Wait, I have it! *Amelista!*"

I caught my breath. "I see you," I whispered. "And you see me."

He put his fingers under my chin. "That will be my name for you, and I will call you by it so often that soon it will be everybody's name for you," he said softly. "Amelista. Because I truly do know you—and you know me."

"You were the first one," I said. "To look at me and *see* me."

I felt the carriage make a wide, lurching turn in the courtyard before it came to a stop. "Now everyone will see you," Jordan said in a soft voice. "Are you ready?"

I took a deep breath, but before I could answer, the door was flung open by one of the palace footmen, who was already bowing. I thought of all the hazards that lay ahead of me—a lifetime of lies, of pretense, of delicate, perilous conversations where I could betray myself with a single word.

A lifetime of freedom, of choice, of absolute independence, only my own desires determining where I went and what I did.

A lifetime at Jordan's side.

I didn't know how I could be ready for any of it.

"I am," I said.

Jordan and his echoes exited the carriage first, and then he waved aside the footman so he could be the one to help me out. I took his hand in a firm grip, set my feet on the worn brickwork of the courtyard, and stepped forward into my new life.

If you enjoyed the Uncommon Echoes books, try Sharon Shinn's Elemental Blessings series, beginning with *Troubled Waters*.

In a world where everyone is defined by one of five elemental affiliations, Zoe Ardelay is *coru*, a woman of blood and water. She has lived an obscure life since her father was banished from the king's court ten years ago, but now she has returned to the royal city to claim her heritage. As she watches queens and courtiers scheme for power and influence, she finds she can trust only one man—the king's confidante, Darien Serlast, a *hunti* man of stone and wood. Slowly, she learns secret after secret—why her father was banished, what terrible news the king is hiding, and what kind of power she carries in her own veins.

About the Author

Sharon Shinn has been part of the science fiction and fantasy world since 1995, when she published her first novel, *The Shape-Changer's Wife,* which won the Crawford Award. In 2010, the *Romantic Times Magazine* gave Shinn the Career Achievement Award in the Science Fiction/Fantasy category, and in 2012, *Publisher's Weekly* magazine named *The Shape of Desire* one of the best science fiction/fantasy books of the year. Three of her novels have been named to the ALA's lists of Best Books for Young Adults (now Best Fiction for Young Adults). She has had books translated into Polish, German, Spanish, and Japanese. She can be found at sharonshinn.net and facebook.com/sharonshinnbooks.

ABOUT THE PUBLISHER

This book is published on behalf of the author by the Ethan Ellenberg Literary Agency.
https://ethanellenberg.com
Email: agent@ethanellenberg.com